Never Seduce a Scot

MAYA BANKS

BALLANTINE BOOKS • NEW YORK

A Ballantine Books Mass Market Original

Copyright © 2012 by Maya Banks
Excerpt from *In Bed with a Highlander* copyright © 2011 by Maya Banks
Excerpt from *Seduction of a Highland Lass* copyright © 2011 by Maya Banks
Excerpt from *Never Love a Highlander* copyright © 2011 by Maya Banks

Published in the United States by Ballantine Books, an imprint of The Random House Publishing Group, a division of Random House, Inc., New York.

BALLANTINE and colophon are registered trademarks of Random House, Inc.

ISBN 978-0-345-53323-4
eBook ISBN 978-0-345-53603-7

Cover design: Lynn Andreozzi
Cover illustration: Alan Ayers

Printed in the United States of America

www.ballantinebooks.com

9 8 7 6 5 4 3 2

Ballantine Books mass market edition: October 2012

For Welty. Always a good sport
and an even better friend.

PROLOGUE

Peace had come to the highlands. The land whispered softly of its gratitude for a brief respite from violence, rebellion, and bloodshed. Spring had come, bringing with it lush green grass among the rock outcroppings and boulders that were so predominant over the terrain.

The winter snows had fled, chased by the warmth of longer days. All was well. King Alexander II could focus on other matters, but for one thing.

One very big thing.

His two most powerful allies, the two most powerful clans in his kingdom, loathed the very sight of each other.

The Montgomerys and the Armstrongs were at war. This was no simple feud. The king had not the time, nor the desire, to lose such valuable supporters to infighting.

Now that the winter snows had thawed and the long nights had come to an end, battle would resume. Clansmen would be lost.

And so the king devised a plan to force peace between two bitter enemies.

Early one morning, before the sun had fully risen over

the horizon, he sent two messengers on horseback, each to deliver the royal decree to Laird Armstrong and Laird Montgomery.

He only hoped to hell that they didn't kill each other at the wedding.

CHAPTER 1

"'Tis madness!" Bowen Montgomery exclaimed. "He cannot tie you to the wee daft daughter of our most hated foe."

Graeme Montgomery stared grimly back at his brother, unable to formulate a response for the growing rage in his chest. The king's messenger had departed and was even now riding beyond the Montgomery border. Graeme had made sure of it. He felt deeply betrayed by his king and wanted no representative of the crown on his lands for a second longer.

"She's but a child," Bowen said in disgust. "And she's . . . she's . . . well, everyone knows she isn't right. What the hell are you supposed to do with her, Graeme?"

Graeme held up his hand for silence and his fingers trembled, betraying his fury. He turned and stalked away from his brother, needing the distance and solitude to take in the magnitude of what had just been done to him. To his clan.

His king hadn't just made a simple decree of marriage in an effort to halt hostilities between two feuding clans. He'd effectively chosen to end Graeme's chance to pass the mantle of leadership on to his heirs.

Because there wouldn't be any.

It would all end with Graeme.

With no sons to become laird, it would be up to one of his brothers—Bowen or Teague—to assume the role and provide heirs so that the Montgomery name would be carried into the future. His clan might even decide that one of his brothers would be a better choice for laird simply because he would be in a position of having a wife who couldn't assume her role in the clan and he wouldn't be able to sire children.

What a damnable mess the whole thing was.

How could his liege have done this? Surely he understood the future he was consigning Graeme to.

He paced into the small antechamber down the narrow hallway from the great hall. The room was darkened, the furs not yet thrown back from the windows. He chose to leave them covered and instead lit a candle from one of the wall sconces in the hallway.

The glow from the candle did little to illuminate the room, but he found his way to the sturdy table where his da had sat many a night scratching his quill over ledgers. The old laird had been a tightfisted, scrutinizing man who held into account every thing of value owned by the clan.

But he had a heart the size of a mountain and he was fair and equal with his clan. He made sure everyone had what they needed. All were clothed and no one went hungry even if it meant he, himself, went without.

Graeme missed him every single day.

He sank heavily into the gnarled chair and ran his hands over the aged wood, almost as if he could feel the essence of his father in this very room.

Marriage. To an Armstrong. It didn't bear thinking about.

And then there was Bowen with all his babbling about the girl being daft. Graeme hadn't ever paid much heed to the rumors about the lass being touched. It hadn't concerned him. Not until now. It was widely known that something was off about the girl and that the Armstrong clan had closed ranks around her.

She'd even been betrothed before, to the McHugh whelp. The McHugh chieftain coveted an alliance with the Armstrongs, because once allied with them, he became a force to be reckoned with. There was no love lost between the Montgomerys and McHughs. The McHughs were every bit as culpable in the death of Graeme's father, but Graeme knew who'd been directly responsible. And so it was the Armstrongs who were most deserving of his hatred.

He hadn't been sorry that the betrothal had been dissolved and that the two clans weren't formally bound by marriage. The Armstrongs weren't quick to ally themselves with neighboring clans. They didn't need to. They were a powerful enough force that unless many other clans stood against them, they would be assured a victory in battle.

Tavis Armstrong was just as his father was before him. Mistrustful of treaties and promises. He gave no one opportunity to betray him and he trusted his clan's welfare to no one save himself.

If they weren't such bitter enemies, Graeme could almost respect the vigor with which Tavis wielded his power and the fact that he relied on no one for support.

Once the betrothal had been dissolved between the Armstrong daughter and McHugh's son, not much else was said, other than the occasional murmurs that called into question the lass's state of mind. Since the Armstrongs weren't exactly a social clan, and they most definitely held to their own, not much escaped about the only daughter.

No, Graeme wasn't sorry that the marriage hadn't taken place. He knew that McHugh would use his position with Armstrong to feed the fury against the Montgomerys. McHugh wanted more land, more power, and the Montgomery holding was a thorn in his side because they had him boxed in to the north.

But now he was going to be saddled with a woman he knew next to nothing about? It was bad enough she was addled and couldn't perform as a wife, but she was an Armstrong, which meant no matter if she was the most perfect woman in all of the highlands, Graeme wanted nothing to do with her.

When he married, it would be to a lass of his own clan. He'd never marry someone who would bring danger, anger, and dissension to his people. And Eveline Armstrong would certainly do just that.

"Graeme?"

The small whisper came from the doorway, and some of his anger and tension fled as his sister, Rorie, peered in, her expression anxious.

"What is it, sweeting?" he asked, motioning her forward.

Rorie was fifteen winters, but she was behind most other lasses her age. While most had found their womanly shapes and had grown breasts, Rorie was still thin and slight, and were it not for her startling beautiful green eyes and the delicate femininity of her face, she could well pass for a lad.

With three older brothers, one would think she would have grown up able to take on anything, but she was extremely shy, quieter than any lass of his acquaintance. Except around him and his brothers. With them she was bossy, demanding, and impish. She mostly avoided the rest of the clan and preferred to go her own way.

"Is it true what Bowen said?"

She was but a few feet away now, standing in front of the table where he sat, his hands still clenched into fists as they rested on the wooden surface.

"Are you marrying an Armstrong?"

He searched her expression for fear because he'd do anything to soothe her worries. Losing their father had been especially difficult for her because she had been his da's treasure. She more than any of them viewed the Armstrongs as monsters.

But all he saw was a troubled, worried look in her expressive eyes.

"'Tis what the king has decreed."

She frowned. "But why? Why would he do such a thing?"

"It's not your place to question his dictates," he said with no heat. He couldn't reprimand her for such a lack of respect when he himself questioned the very thing.

"They killed Da," she said emphatically. "How can there ever be peace between us? How could the king believe that forcing a marriage between you and one of them would solve anything?"

"Shhh," he said gently. "Enough, Rorie. We've been summoned to the Armstrongs and there we'll go."

Her look of horror was instantaneous. "Go there? To their lands? Where they could kill us all? Why can't they come here? Why are we the ones who must sacrifice everything? Have they done something to gain the king's favor?"

For a moment Graeme smiled, finding amusement in her statement. "It's not likely they feel that handing their daughter over to me in marriage is the result of gaining his favor. I doubt they have any more liking for the matter than we do."

"'Tis said she's touched," Rorie asserted.

Graeme sighed. "I guess we'll find out at the wedding, now won't we?"

Just then, Teague's bellow could be heard down the hallway. "Graeme! God's teeth, where are you?"

Graeme sighed again. Rorie spared a slight smile and

turned just as Teague burst through the door, sweat and blood caked on his body.

"Tell me it isn't true," Teague spat.

"You left training to ask if what Bowen told you was truth?" Graeme asked. "Are you suggesting he would lie to you and that you should leave your duties to question me on such a thing?"

Teague scowled and started to say something, but stopped, only just now realizing Rorie was in attendance. He clamped his lips shut, then glanced down at the blood covering him.

Rorie was . . . well, she was different. To most of the women of their clan, blood, violence, battle . . . It was all a way of life. As normal as eating and sleeping. But Rorie was sensitive to such things. The sight of blood made her go pale, and she hated to hear any sounds of pain or violence.

"Damn it all, Graeme, quit playing the laird for once and just tell me if 'tis true so I can depart from Rorie's presence before I upset her more."

"She's already upset," Graeme pointed out. "Obviously, for the same reason you're stomping down the hallway bellowing my name."

Teague went deathly silent. His body was tense and his jaw bulged. "So 'tis true, then."

"Aye, 'tis true."

Teague bit back an oath before storming out of the room, his footsteps pounding all the way down the hall.

"Well," Rorie breathed. "That went well, didn't it?"

CHAPTER 2

Tavis Armstrong's roar could be heard throughout the keep and well into the courtyard where his men were training. Many dropped their swords while others were quick to raise theirs in defense, wary of what danger had presented itself.

Eveline didn't hear her father, but she felt the vibrations against the stone in the floor and knew that something was amiss in the great hall. Too much movement. Too much force. It was as if a herd of sheep had suddenly run roughshod through the keep.

Her expression unchanging, she peered around the corner just at the stairwell, her curiosity piqued by whatever it was that had the keep in such uproar.

Her father stood, face flushed with rage, a crumpled missive held tightly in his fist. Beside him stood her two brothers, Brodie and Aiden, arms folded over their chests, but even from this distance, Eveline could tell they fair bristled with the same anger demonstrated by her father.

Her gaze drifted to the man standing in front of the laird, a man who looked as though he wanted to be anywhere but here. The evident bearer of whatever ill tidings had been brought by the missive her father held.

She cocked her head to the side as she studied him. He was the king's man. He bore the royal crest and on his right hand, he wore a ruby ring that signified his status as the king's messenger.

It greatly chagrined her that her father was angled so that she couldn't see his lips, but she could readily see the mouth of the messenger—when it finally snapped closed.

When he opened it again to speak, she focused intently, determined to see what it was he would say to her father.

"His Majesty's will be done. He has decreed the wedding take place within the fortnight. You have until then to prepare. 'Tis here that the wedding will take place and the king is sending a representative to see that all is as it should be."

Wedding? Eveline perked up at that. Surely a wedding couldn't be what had her father so upset. And whose wedding? The king was sending a representative? It all sounded terribly important and exciting. Certainly it would provide her new and interesting people to watch.

But then her mother, who'd evidently been eavesdropping, rushed into the room, and Eveline winced at her daring. Her father was always reprimanding her mother about inserting herself into situations where she didn't belong. Not that it did any good and not that her father would every truly remain angry with her mother for long, but this was different. This was the king's representative and an offense to him was an offense to the king.

"Tavis, you can't allow this!"

Eveline could barely make out the words as they passed her mother's lips. Her face was tear-stained. All over a wedding? Eveline frowned. None of this made sense.

Tavis put a restraining hand on his wife's arm and

then turned just enough that Eveline could see him angrily bite out to her brother Aiden, "Take your mother away from here."

Robina Armstrong shook her head fiercely, resisting Aiden's grip. "This is madness. He can't feed her to the wolves that way. 'Tis not right! She's not able to perform her marriage duties. This is a travesty, Tavis. It cannot be allowed to stand."

An uneasy sensation prickled down Eveline's spine. She was starting to have a very bad feeling about just what had her family in such an uproar. Wedding? Her mother in tears? Unable to perform marriage duties? Feeding to the wolves? Who were the wolves?

The king's messenger frowned, obviously not liking the hostile environment he'd landed himself in. "The king has decreed it so. Graeme Montgomery and Eveline Armstrong will marry."

Eveline clamped a hand over her mouth even though she hadn't said a word in well over three years. The reaction was automatic, to quiet the silent cry that billowed up from her very soul.

She whirled around, not wanting to witness any more. She fled the keep, nearly tripping down the stone steps in her haste. Gathering her skirts in tight fists, she ran over the uneven terrain behind the keep and into the grove of trees lining a stream that fed a nearby loch.

Instinctively, she sought out the large boulder that jutted out over the water. There, the stream ran faster, bubbling over larger stones and rocks. She imagined the sound, holding it like a fleeting memory. It had been so long since she'd last heard anything that the memories of sound were fading.

She mourned that loss. Before, she could sit on her rock and remember the gurgling sounds, the rush of the water and the peace it brought her. Over time, those phantom sounds faded into nothing. A blank void she felt herself slipping further into all the time.

Hunching her knees up so she could rest her chin atop them, she closed her eyes, but then quickly opened them. A world without sound *and* sight frightened her.

Married.

Betrothal was what had wrought the deception she'd maintained for the last three years. Tragedy had befallen her, but it had also rescued her from an unwanted marriage—a marriage her father had been determined to make happen.

How was it possible? Panic clawed at her throat at the idea of leaving her sanctuary. She was loved here. Cherished. No one thought ill of her—or at least no one dared to voice such an opinion aloud. Her father would spit the person on his sword who disparaged his only daughter in any way.

But she knew what they said behind her back. Some of the more unkindly ones. Or rather not to her back, but in her sight. Daft. Mad. Touched. Poor lass. Never a use to anyone.

They were wrong, but she wouldn't correct them. It was too dangerous to do so.

She'd been betrothed to Ian McHugh. It was a match highly pursued by Ian's father, the chieftain, and a match that her father finally approved of. Her father was careful with the alliances he made, and Patrick McHugh was one of the few people he seemed to trust. The two men could even be called friends. It was only natural that a marriage be arranged between Tavis's only daughter and McHugh's heir.

Ian, however, was not the charming man he appeared to be. Outwardly, he was perfect. The epitome of a gentleman. He'd won her mother over and had, in fact, gained the blessings of Eveline's overprotective brothers.

But beneath the façade was a man who struck terror

in Eveline's heart. He'd taunted her with promises of what marriage would be like to him and then laughed when she'd vowed to take the matter up with her father. He'd told her that no one would ever believe the aspersions she'd cast on his character. She hadn't believed him until she'd gone to her father to do as she'd threatened.

Her father had not been unkind, but he'd also put her accusations down to maidenly fears. He'd promised her that all would be well and that Ian would make her a good husband. And that furthermore, Ian was a just and honorable man.

Worse, Ian openly courted and wooed her in front of her family. He visited often, making grand gestures of devotion. He played his part to perfection. He had her entire clan eating out of his hand. Only in private did Eveline see into the soul of overwhelming evil.

Eveline sighed and bowed her head to her knees, allowing her skirts to billow over her legs. Secrets. So many secrets. So many lies.

She'd loved to ride horses, but she was never allowed to ride alone—the threat of the Montgomerys was ever present and her father feared what would happen should his daughter fall into the hands of their mortal enemies.

One morning she'd gone to the stables, saddled her own horse, and had taken off riding. Only it was no simple ride she was taking. She had planned to run away. A foolhardy, impetuous decision that haunted her to this day.

She didn't even know if she would have gone through with it, if she would've had the courage to leave the boundaries of Armstrong land. After all, how was a young girl, alone and without the protection of her family, to survive?

That simple act of desperation had cost her more than she could have ever imagined. She had guided her horse on a path they'd trod many times, along a steep ravine where a river carved its way through, making a small canyon. When her horse had stumbled, she was thrown over his back and had plummeted down the ravine.

She had no clear recollection of what happened next, only of being scared and alone, her head aching vilely. And the cold. The bone-numbing cold and the passage of time.

She'd awakened in her chamber to a world of silence. She hadn't understood, hadn't known how to make her ailment known. Her throat was swollen and she suffered a fever for many long days. Even if she'd wanted to speak, the mere effort caused her too much pain and so she'd remained silent, bewildered by the quietness surrounding her.

Later, she would be made to understand that she'd lain close to death for over a fortnight. The healer had noted swelling of her head and had worried her fever was such that it had caused damage to her mind. Perhaps in the beginning, Eveline had believed her.

Then there were times when Eveline thought that losing her ability to hear was punishment for her fateful decision to rebel against her father. It had taken her a long time to adjust, and she was too shamed to tell her parents the truth. They'd looked at her with such disappointment and such devastation in their eyes, and perhaps she *would* have found the courage to tell them all and to explain to them that she could no longer hear, but then the McHughs had come to her father, demanding to know of Eveline's condition.

Unable to gain assurance that Eveline was hale and hearty, Ian was quick to break off the betrothal, and who could blame him? Not even her father could find fault with a man who didn't want a wife whose mental awareness was in question.

She hadn't wanted to admit to having lost her hearing because she'd secretly hoped that it would be miraculously restored. One day she'd awaken and all would be well again.

It was a ridiculous notion, but she'd clung to that hope until it became clear that her apparent daftness was her salvation.

So the lie began. Not one spoken, but of omission. She allowed her family, her clan, to believe her affected by her accident because it protected her from the possibility of marriage to a man she despised and feared.

And it wasn't one she could later rectify, because as long as Ian remained unmarried, were it to be discovered that her only fault was deafness, he could easily petition to have the betrothal reinstated.

It was a deception that grew and took on a life of its own, and the longer it went on, the more helpless she felt to correct it.

Only now it was all for naught because she'd traded one marriage to the devil's son for the devil himself, and this time she was powerless to prevent it from happening.

She shuddered, pressed her forehead once again to her knees, and rocked back and forth.

Graeme Montgomery.

Just the name struck fear in her heart.

The feud between her clan and his clan had existed for five decades. Eveline couldn't even remember what had started the whole bloody disagreement, but bloody it had been. Graeme's father had been killed by her grandfather, a fact that Graeme would never forgive.

The Montgomerys lived to harass, steal from, ambush, or spill the blood of any living Armstrong. Her father and brothers could swear no differently. They'd run a Montgomery through with a sword for no bigger sin than breathing.

None of it made sense to her, but then she was supposed to be a delicate little flower of a woman who had no head for such matters even when she was believed to be in her right mind.

She rubbed absently at her forehead, feeling one of her headaches coming on. They always started at the base of her skull and worked to behind her ears, pressure building until she wanted to scream for the pain.

But she couldn't vocalize anything. She had no way to measure how loudly or softly she spoke. She wanted no one to know of her inability to hear. And so she remained solidly entombed by silence.

She felt rather than heard someone's approach. Since the loss of her hearing, her other senses had heightened. It bewildered her, but she found especially that she could feel things more keenly. Almost as if she picked up the slightest vibrations in the air.

She turned to see Brodie approaching, his expression grim, but it lightened in relief when he saw her sitting on her rock.

Brodie was the one she'd most miss if she was truly to wed the Montgomery chieftain. She could barely breathe for wanting to cry and her throat knotted uncontrollably.

He said something as he approached, but it was lost on her because his mouth was shielded by a limb. When she continued to stare at him, he made a show of letting out a sigh and then sat on the rock beside her, just as he'd done so many times before.

Brodie always knew where to find her. Knew all her secret hiding places. There wasn't anywhere she could go that he didn't already know of.

He reached for her hand, swallowing it up in his much larger one, and he squeezed. His lips started to move again, and she strained forward so she could see what it was he said.

"You're needed in the keep, little chick."

She loved that he called her that and she didn't even

know why. It was an endearment, almost always said
with an indulgent smile. Only today, there was no smile.
Only deep desolation in his eyes and lines of worry
etched into his brow.

Not wanting to cause him any more upset, she put her
other hand in his and waited for him to stand and pull
her up beside him. It was better if she not act as though
she knew. Perhaps she could play dumb about the entire
thing. Surely if the king knew how unsuitable she was
for marriage, he wouldn't sanction such a thing.

That thought cheered her considerably as she walked
beside her brother back toward the keep. Her father had
always said that the king was a fair and just ruler. That
he'd brought peace to the highlands by signing a treaty
with England.

If his representative was to be in attendance for the
event, then surely after seeing her, he would call a halt to
the marriage and report back to the king her unsuitabil-
ity for the role assigned to her.

CHAPTER 3

Eveline tried to remain calm as Brodie led her into the great hall, though it was hard when her heart pounded furiously against her chest.

Her father was pacing before the hearth and her other brother, Aiden, sprawled in a chair at the large wooden table, rage burning in his eyes as his foot tapped a sharp staccato on the floor.

Eveline honed in on her mother and father, wanting desperately to know what it was they said. She pried her hand from Brodie's and moved so she could better see.

"Tavis, you cannot allow this to stand!"

Eveline's father grasped her mother's shoulders, holding them tightly. He stared back at her with tortured, angry eyes.

"The king has decreed it, Robina. I cannot naysay him."

Robina yanked away, turning more toward Eveline, her eyes red and puffy, distress radiating from her in waves. Then her gaze lighted on Eveline and her expression grew even more stricken.

She hurried forward, putting an arm around Eveline's shoulders, squeezed her tightly, and then bore her forward. Eveline could feel her mother trembling against

her, and she worked even harder to keep her own coun-
tenance serene as they approached her father.

Tavis lifted his hand, and it shook noticeably as he put
it gently to Eveline's cheek. Unable to stand the grief in
his eyes, Eveline turned her face into his palm and
rubbed.

"My baby. My most precious gift. Our king has turned
against us."

He dropped his hand down and put it to the back of
his neck, then turned away. Eveline frowned, not wanting to miss any of what he might be saying.

"You must beseech him, Tavis," Robina said, touching her husband's arm to turn him back. "Perhaps he
knows not of Eveline's condition."

Tavis turned back, his brows drawn together, the
blackness of his scowl reminding Eveline of a spring
storm.

"How could he not? He was here just months after Eveline was stricken with illness. He saw that she was . . .
changed. He offered his sympathy that she would never
be able to make an advantageous marriage or have children of her own. And now he's sending her to our worst
enemy as a sacrificial lamb meant to force peace between
us?"

Eveline felt the blood drain from her face and she
hoped her mother didn't notice her flinch at her father's
words.

"Look at her, Robina. She doesn't even understand,"
Tavis said, raising his hand in a slicing motion toward
Eveline.

"You'll not say a word against her," Robina said, her
expression so fierce that Eveline knew she must have
said the words just as fiercely. "She is a sweet and good
girl. She's not daft. She can sew beautifully. She has basic
understanding of things. She's helpful to the clansmen,

and she always has a smile for everyone. That *monster* will crush her."

"I am not disparaging her," Tavis roared. And this time, Eveline knew he had roared because she could feel the vibrations, but also, there were certain sounds—not many—that she could actually hear.

Deep-timbred voices. Nothing high or shrill. Nothing normal or monotone. But every once in a while, she experienced fleeting hearing.

"I love her as much as you, Robina. Do you think I *want* to give my daughter in marriage to my sworn blood enemy?"

Her mother took a step back and put a knotted fist to her mouth. Her father advanced on her, his face purpled with rage.

"I don't have a *choice*. To go against my king is to sign all our death warrants. We'll be branded outlaws, and any mercenary wanting to gain a purse will come after our heads."

"God help us all," Robina said, her face crumpling, her eyes so stricken that it hurt Eveline to look at her.

Her brothers had remained quiet. Perhaps they had no opinion or, more likely, they were loath to step in between their parents when emotions ran so high.

But Eveline couldn't allow them to torment themselves so. If she was meant to be the token sacrifice in an effort to stop the clans from warring, then her fate was sealed, and there was little to be done. She didn't want her family to suffer so much anguish.

She took a step forward, slipped her hand into her father's. He blinked in surprise and made an obvious effort to temper his emotions as he stared down at her solemn face.

And then she smiled and leaned up to kiss his cheek. She patted his shoulder as if to tell him it was all right.

His entire face softened, but the sadness in his eyes

grew. He looked suddenly so much older, his skin grayer and his shoulders slumped in a way she'd never seen her warrior father stand.

He put his hand around the back of her head and drew her toward him to press a kiss against her forehead. She could feel him speaking against her flesh, but didn't want to jerk away so she could see what it was he said.

When he finally did pull away, his lips were moving and she strained to catch up.

". . . sweet lass. You've always been. You're my heart, Eveline, and damn the king for taking my heart away from me."

She turned to her mother, but before she could kiss her cheek as she'd done her father, Robina swept her into her arms, hugging her fiercely.

Her mother was devastated, and Eveline was at a loss as to how to console her. How could she when she was still in shock herself?

It had never occurred to her that she would still marry or be expected to perform as any other normal woman. She'd effectively hidden behind her deafness, using it as a shield. A lie. Deception.

Oh, those were horrible words and they made her feel terribly guilty. She wanted to close her eyes so she could read nothing further from anyone's lips.

The floor jumped beneath Eveline's feet, and she turned before the others did to see who would appear at the doorway of the great hall.

"A message, Laird," Niall said as he strode forward.

His expression was intense, and his body language screamed that this was important. In his hand was a scroll, but Eveline couldn't see the seal to know whom it may be from. Was it another message from the king?

"'Tis from Laird Montgomery." Niall's lips curled in distaste as he spoke the words. "I wouldn't allow his representative in and instead bore his message inside to you."

Aiden rose from his seat, his lips twisted into a snarl as he came to stand beside his father. Brodie stepped closer to his mother and Eveline as if seeking to protect them from whatever would be unveiled in the missive.

Tavis broke the seal, pulled the scroll downward, and scanned the contents, his frown deepening all the more as his gaze drifted lower.

Finally, he lifted his head, his eyes glittering as he carefully rolled the message back up.

"Graeme Montgomery has sent word that he will arrive for his bride according to the king's dictate."

The reaction from her brothers was immediate. Brodie pushed forward and her gaze yanked to him as he spoke.

"This is a farce! The king cannot be serious. Surely he isn't so evil as to send a lamb among lions."

"Montgomerys? On our land?" Aiden asked, his expression clearly aghast. "'Tis something sworn never to happen lest the earth be bathed in blood."

Her neck ached from wrenching back and forth from person to person to keep up with the conversation, but she lost much. Everyone was talking at once. She only understood bits and pieces, most of it exclamations, oaths, and speculation as to why the king would do such a dastardly thing.

She'd never seen Graeme Montgomery. It was God's truth, she'd never seen any Montgomery at all. It was hard not to picture an aging, paunchy man with a bulbous nose and hideous features. She'd never bothered herself with any conversation dealing with the Montgomery clan, because they simply did not interest her. She knew they were her clan's sworn enemies and that her father would die before ever allowing a Montgomery onto his land.

Her father and brothers were warriors who were unmatched by any other in skill and strength. It was boastful of her to think so, but she'd seen nothing to alter her biased opinion of her kin.

So she'd always felt safe from any outside threat because the Armstrongs jealously guarded their borders, allowing no one to pass unless given permission to do so.

Once, long ago, such an encroachment had happened. The Montgomerys had raided and many Armstrongs had paid with their lives. Including Eveline's grandmother. Her grandfather, who was then laird, had grieved mightily and had died avenging his wife's death. He'd killed the Montgomery laird but was struck down by another of the Montgomery warriors.

So many deaths, and Eveline had no idea what had started it all. She'd only heard bits and pieces of the story in passing over the years. She should have listened harder when she had her hearing, but for her, the Montgomerys were monsters of the dark. Almost a fictional beast that bards carried tales of. They certainly had never been a threat in her lifetime.

And now she would be delivered into their fold. Sent away from the safety of her clan and her beloved family. Married. Expected to be wife to a man she considered a myth.

She nearly shivered before catching herself. She didn't want to upset her mother by allowing her fear to show.

Turning away, she left the great hall once more, not even bothering to see if she should stay. She often did things such as that, leaving abruptly and on a whim. No one seemed to even blink over it any longer, and if it was thought odd once, now it was accepted behavior.

She simply needed to sort through this upheaval to her life. How could she face someone not of her own clan? Her clan loved her even if some were wary of her affliction. There were some she'd caught murmuring prayers when she crossed their paths. Were they worried that her daftness was easily passed to others? That if they touched her, they too would be afflicted?

The mischievous part of her wanted to reach out and touch them, just to see if they'd react as if being burned. Or if they'd run screaming in the opposite direction to seek out the priest.

But then she promptly felt terrible because they were still her clan, and it wasn't their fault that she was different. They didn't know any better, and Eveline hadn't done anything to change their opinion. And most were very kind to her. Many went out of their way to do things for her they thought would make her happy.

And she *was* happy here. It had taken her a long while to sort through the confusion of her accident and subsequent illness. She hadn't understood why her hearing had been taken, but she'd been taught not to question God's will.

Now, she had a place. She'd learned to understand much of what people said by watching their mouths. She wished she had the courage to speak, but with no way to know how she sounded—or if she could even form the words after not speaking for so long—she remained silent, locked in her quiet world with only the memory of certain sounds to echo softly in her head.

But no longer would she have that place here. In her clan. Among her kin and the people who loved and accepted her.

Instead she would be sent off to an enemy clan.

A shiver stole down her spine. What would they think of her? Would they be cruel? Would they hate her simply because she was an Armstrong? Would they despise her because of her defect?

Would they taunt her and call her mad and daft?

Would they go even further and cause her harm, thinking that she carried evil spirits within her?

She twined her fingers together in front of her as she hurried back to her rock. No matter that Brodie would know precisely where to find her. It was the only place she could think to go when she needed comfort and peace.

As she stared over the rushing water, she realized that she'd no longer have this sanctuary. She'd no longer be able to come and go as she pleased and sit on her rock for hours absorbing the serenity of her surroundings.

Nay, she'd marry into the Montgomery clan. Become the very thing she'd been taught to hate. And while her father let her do as she liked, her husband might not be as understanding.

CHAPTER 4

The keep had been in a constant flurry of activity for days. On the eighth day after the delivery of the king's message, the Earl of Dunbar arrived as the king's representative to witness the marriage that would force peace between the two warring clans.

Tavis greeted the earl in the courtyard, and once the earl's horse was taken away, the two men entered the keep and strode to where food and ale were laid out on the high table at the end of the great hall.

"Alexander extends his regrets that he will be unable to be present for the marriage," the earl said after he'd sipped from one of the jeweled cups.

There was a gleam in the earl's eye that told Tavis the king had never had any intention of making an appearance for the wedding he'd demanded. And with his absence, there was no one for Tavis to petition to put a stop to the whole mess.

Dunbar had great favor with Alexander and, in fact, was the highest-ranking earl under the king's rule. He and Alexander were staunch allies and friends, and the fact that the king had sent his most powerful earl to attend the wedding told Tavis of its importance to their monarch.

"He knows not what he does," Tavis ground out.

Dunbar lifted one eyebrow, threw back a long swallow of the ale, and then eyed Tavis intently as he leaned back to sprawl in the chair. He looked indolent and arrogant, staring Tavis down as if trying to intimidate him. Tavis hadn't survived as chief of one of Scotland's largest strongholds by backing down from a challenge.

He met the earl's gaze unflinchingly.

The earl sighed and set his goblet down with a sharp bang. "If 'tis any consolation, Tavis, I told Alexander he was mad. I'm well aware of what happened to your daughter, and you and she have my sympathies. She's not suited for marriage, but unfortunately, you've only one daughter and Alexander has it in his head that the only way to force peace between two of his strongest clans is by giving your daughter to your enemy. He feels that if she's wed to the Montgomery laird, you'll never raise a sword against them."

"And what guarantee do I have that they won't come after my clan?" Tavis demanded. "Of course I wouldn't raise a sword against the man who holds the life of my daughter in his hands. But what do I have of his to hold in return?"

The earl rubbed his chin thoughtfully. "'Tis a good question and one I wonder if Alexander considered. Perhaps he thought the marriage enough to forge an alliance, no matter how wary it may be. He wants peace. Now that we've signed a treaty with England, Alexander must focus on internal problems with rebellious chieftains. He needs allies, and the Armstrongs and Montgomerys have always been loyal to the crown, even as they despise each other."

"I would be willing to sign a treaty with the Montgomerys," Tavis said stiffly. It was the hardest thing he'd ever said in his life. Swallowing his pride was painful, but for his daughter, he would do anything, even hum-

ble himself before his enemy. "They can't want this marriage any more than we do. 'Tis as you said. Eveline is
not suited for marriage to any man. 'Tis why the betrothal to Ian McHugh was broken. Graeme Montgomery would . . . crush her, and I cannot bear the thought
of that."

The earl shook his head. "I am not here to bargain
with you, Tavis. 'Tis too late for talk of treaties and
peace. The war between you has gone on for too long.
Alexander is impatient to bring peace to the highlands,
and this blood feud between your clans is a threat to the
stability Alexander wants. I may not agree with his
methods, but he has my full support. He sent me to bear
witness to the marriage and give official report upon my
return. I'm to give his order and blessing upon the ceremony and bear with me the letter having his royal seal
and the official declaration of the union."

"She is doomed," Tavis whispered.

"I believe Graeme Montgomery to be a fair and just
man," the earl said carefully. "I do not think he would
be cruel to your daughter for vengeance's sake."

In all his years, Tavis had never felt so helpless. As he
lifted his gaze, he saw his wife standing across the great
hall, her grief a living, breathing thing in the room.

But she hid it well as she crisply walked forward.
She'd dressed her best in deference to the earl's visit and
only Tavis's keen eye could detect the turmoil that simmered just beneath the surface of her careful composure.

He and the earl both rose as Robina drew nigh.

"My lady," the earl said smoothly, lifting her hand to
press a kiss to its back. "'Tis been many years since we
last met and I vow you've grown more beautiful than
you were even then."

Robina smiled graciously, but it didn't reach to her
eyes. "You're too kind, my lord. You do us an honor by
attending the wedding of our daughter. I do hope you'll

find your accommodations to your liking. If there's anything you require, please make me aware of it and it will be provided at once."

Tavis hadn't realized he'd been holding his breath until his chest began to burn in protest. He hadn't been certain that Robina wouldn't have planted a dagger in the earl's heart if she thought it would save her daughter.

Robina was outspoken, strong willed, and he loved her with every part of his warrior's heart. If she'd been a man, she would be the fiercest in all of Scotland.

Many a man wouldn't tolerate her quickness to speak her mind or that she matched his strength with her own. They'd want to subjugate her. Make her weak and stamp out the very thing that made her so very special.

Robina was no meek lass and for that Tavis gave thanks on a daily basis. She was his and he'd offer no apology on her behalf. He loved her just the way she was.

But then he began to worry. Because Robina was being too nice and too accommodating. Her smile made him nervous. Was she plotting to poison the earl's drink? Or perhaps she'd slip a dirk between his ribs when she escorted him to his chamber. Either was possible, for Robina was ferocious when it came to her children.

"I'll show the earl to his chambers," Tavis said, before Robina could extend the offer. "Have food and drink delivered to him so that he may rest from his journey."

Before he could guide the earl toward the stairwell, one of the tower guards burst into the great hall. He came up short when he saw the earl standing next to Tavis, and then he inclined his head in a respectful bow.

"Laird, a Montgomery messenger has arrived bearing news that the chieftain and his accompanying men will arrive by nightfall."

Robina's lips tightened, but to her credit, she remained

silent even as her hands were fisted into knots at her side.

The earl lifted one eyebrow and regarded Tavis in amusement. "One might gain the idea that Graeme Montgomery is eager to claim his bride."

Tavis's gut rolled into a knot, disgusted by the mere thought of his daughter in the hands of the Montgomerys. He exchanged a look of sorrow with his wife because it was becoming increasingly clear that there was nothing short of declaring war and betraying their king that they could do, and to do so would mean the deaths of their entire clan.

Their beloved daughter or the lives of every single kinsman who depended on them for protection.

It was a choice no man should ever have to make.

CHAPTER 5

Eveline sat atop the rise that overlooked the front of the keep and watched as the impressive line of Montgomery soldiers proceeded on horseback toward the drawbridge.

She wondered if her father would give them all admittance or make the majority of the warriors remain outside the walls of the keep. But then Graeme Montgomery might well never agree to place himself in the vulnerable position of entering his enemy's lair with only a few of his men for protection.

She searched the front of the line with her gaze, straining to see the man who would be her husband. They all looked massive to her and were interchangeable in their armor, holding shields, some with swords drawn.

It didn't look like a wedding party. It looked like a prelude to war.

She shivered and hugged herself tightly, hunching down farther, hoping she wouldn't be seen. Her mother would be looking for her. As would her brothers. She'd purposely not gone to her usual haunt because Brodie would have already been sent to fetch her. Instead she'd chosen this spot because it afforded her a view . . . of her future.

There were three men who separated themselves from

the line of horses, riding forward, and one tilted his head up as if he were bellowing to the watchman. Eveline wished she could hear. It must be an impressive sound coming from a man so large in stature. It likely scared the wits out of anyone in hearing distance.

A few of the horses behind the man shied and had to be quickly calmed by their riders.

She leaned her chin on her knees and continued to stare as the drawbridge was slowly lowered.

Her husband.

He was here to take her away from everything she knew and loved. This was the one place she felt safe and protected. Cherished by her family, indulged by her clan.

But hadn't she once longed for a normal life? A new adventure? To see something outside the walls of her keep? She hadn't ventured beyond the Armstrong borders in her entire lifetime.

There had been a time she'd welcomed her betrothal to Ian McHugh. She'd been flushed with excitement and filled with dreams of a husband, children, her own keep to run. Oh, she'd planned it all. Visits back to her family. They would travel to her husband's holding for the birth of her first child. There would be much rejoicing and happiness.

But that fantasy had quickly evaporated the moment Ian had made known his intentions toward her. Her dreams had been replaced by a nightmare she'd feared never escaping.

She hated hiding here, behind her father and mother and even her brothers. Allowing others to think she was less than she was. But what she most hated was having to give up that dream. And now? It seemed regardless of all she'd done to ensure that she'd always remain safely hidden away on her father's land, the day had arrived when she'd be forced to venture beyond their borders to a new life.

This certainly wouldn't have been the way she envisioned ever broadening her horizons, but she didn't have a choice. Shouldn't she try to make the best of a bad situation?

Her mother was distraught. Her father was grim and worried and in a mood so foul, no one dared disturb him unless it was of utmost importance. Even her brothers were short-tempered. It was as if a black cloud had descended on the keep, and ever since the message had been received that the Montgomerys would arrive before nightfall, the keep had been in a flurry of activity.

Eveline had escaped unnoticed, but they would be looking for her even now. Perhaps to hide her. Perhaps to present her to the man who would be her husband.

She'd watched enough lips to know that with the earl in residence, any act of disobedience regarding the royal decree would be considered an act of war against the king.

Finished with her perusal of the Montgomery clan, she reclined on the ground, closing her eyes briefly against the wash of sunshine. When she reopened them, she focused on the blue of the sky and the softly drifting clouds.

Here she could escape for just a little while, silence surrounding her, but in the deep recesses of her mind, she could conjure the memory of what music sounded like, and as she stared at the yawning blue canvas above her, she could swear that music danced through her ears.

"Look up the hill, to your right," Teague said sharply.

Graeme yanked his head up and then focused in the distance where Teague directed as the drawbridge slowly began to grind its way down.

He almost missed the slight figure and then when his

gaze swept back over it again, he frowned and turned back to his brother, wondering why on earth Teague would have called his attention to it.

"Is that a person?" Teague demanded. "What's he doing up there alone on the hill?"

"Afraid she's going to come down here and knock you off your horse?" Bowen drawled.

"She?" Teague said in disbelief.

"'Tis a lass," Bowen said, nodding his head in the direction of the distant yellowish blob.

Graeme strained forward again. "How can you tell at this distance?"

Bowen gave them both mocking glances and then shook his head in dismay. "Think you any men run around in yellow dresses?"

Teague lifted his eyebrow. "Well, 'tis the Armstrongs, so I suppose anything could be possible."

The men around them laughed, and then the drawbridge hit the ground with a thump, stirring up dust around the horses. When Graeme glanced up the hill again, he could no longer see the girl. How had she disappeared so quickly?

He urged his horse ahead, focusing his attention forward, ready for the impending confrontation. It was the truth he'd rather face battle outnumbered three to one than have to go meekly into the Armstrong keep and join himself to this clan in marriage.

It appalled him on every level. His da would be turning over in his grave. It was a dark day for Montgomerys everywhere and it would be a day long remembered in their history. If he had his way, the entire event would be stricken from any oral or written accounts henceforth.

But of course he couldn't very well do something so permanent with a wife. As tempting as it may be.

He rode into the courtyard to see Tavis Armstrong

standing beside the Earl of Dunbar. Graeme wasn't startled to see the king's man there, though he'd honestly expected the king himself to attend since this was of such importance to him.

Graeme reined in and sat astride his horse, staring down at the chieftain of the Armstrong clan. Tavis stared back, and then beside him appeared his two sons, though Graeme didn't know which was which. The last time he'd encountered the Armstrong whelps, he'd sent them packing after a brief skirmish in the dead zone— the small plot of land that lay between the Montgomery and Armstrong borders. It belonged to the McAlpins, but they'd long since abandoned it due to the proximity to the warring clans. It was a tiny sliver of land, a mere fingerling of their holding, and it was no big thing to keep to the south and away from the feud.

Tavis flinched first, a fact that brought Graeme satisfaction. He'd take a victory no matter how insignificant. He might have been forced to venture meekly onto Armstrong land, but he damn sure wouldn't allow any Armstrong to intimidate him.

Tavis took a step forward, cleared his throat, and said, "Welcome to our keep, Laird Montgomery. You and your brothers are welcome inside. Your men will find accommodations in the outer perimeter where tents have been erected for their use. Food and drink will be provided for all."

For a moment, Graeme didn't speak. Then he glanced to his brothers and gave the signal to dismount. Graeme swung himself over his horse and dropped down.

Tavis motioned several of his men to take the horses and lead them to shelter in the stables.

And there they stood. Montgomery warriors face-to-face with Armstrong warriors. They bristled with dislike. The Armstrongs looked as though they'd just welcomed the devil into their sanctuary and well, maybe they had.

Such a thing had never been accomplished in the history of their clans. Never had they stood so close without swords drawn and much blood shed. Graeme's hand itched for wanting to grip his sword, and his throat ached from wanting to bellow a war cry.

"I do not like this," Tavis said quietly, his voice steady with a thread of steel. "As God is my witness, there is no part of me that agrees to this madness."

Graeme nodded, appreciating the older man's candor. When he spoke, he was just as blunt. "I don't like it any more than you."

"You sacrifice nothing," Tavis bit out. "There is nothing for you to dislike. You walk away with my daughter and you give up nothing in return."

Graeme lifted an eyebrow as anger crept up his nape, seizing the back of his skull. He had to work to keep from losing his temper. It took all he had not to lunge for the other man. All he could see was his da's face and stare at the man whose father was responsible for murdering his da.

"Think you I do not? I am saddled with a defective wife, one who will never bear me heirs. I give up much. I give up *everything*."

"She's not defective!" one of the Armstrong sons roared as he leapt forward.

Teague and Bowen drew their swords in a split second and stepped in front of Graeme to ward off attack. Their arms shook, and Graeme knew what it cost them not to just run the Armstrongs through on the spot.

The entire situation had the potential to explode at a moment's notice. The two sides were too eager to have any excuse to shed the other's blood.

"That's enough," the Earl of Dunbar barked. "The king would be most displeased. He wants peace and it's peace he shall have. When this wedding is done, an oath will be sworn between the two clans and a treaty will be signed in blood. Any breach of the treaty will be viewed as an act of treason against the crown. Your lands will be forfeit and you'll be branded outlaws and hunted as such."

"Brodie, stand down," Tavis said to the son who'd roared in anger. "Aiden, put your sword away."

Brodie glared at Graeme as if he wanted nothing more than to spit Graeme on his sword right here and now. Graeme gave him a slow smirk that clearly said, "Try it."

"She's worth ten of you," Brodie bit out as he backed away.

He and Teague slowly resheathed their swords, but both kept their hands on the hilts.

Tavis held up his hand, and he looked suddenly weary, lines of age creasing his forehead. He looked like a man who'd waged war with the very devil. Graeme couldn't feel any sympathy. Not when the man's father had murdered Graeme's own father. Not when his clan had lost so much over the years to the Armstrongs.

"Come inside," Tavis said in a tone that conveyed just how much he loathed having to issue the invitation. "My lady wife will have drink and refreshment after your journey."

"Indeed, and I should like to meet my prospective bride," Graeme said in a mocking voice.

Brodie's lips turned into a snarl again, but Tavis silenced him with a quick look. He motioned to Graeme and his brothers, and they walked inside the keep, the earl standing between the two groups as they filed into the great hall.

A petite woman rose from her chair by the hearth and laid aside her sewing. It was obvious that she must be

Tavis's wife, though she didn't look to be a woman of any significant age.

Fear engulfed her face even though she tried valiantly to hide it, and it left Graeme disgusted, for he'd never raise arms against a woman. No matter that she was the wife of his enemy, she should be accorded the respect and courtesy due her station.

He walked forward, hoping she didn't turn and run screaming from the room, but she held her ground and returned his stare without flinching.

"My lady," he said, making a deep bow.

When he lifted his head, he reached for her hand and she allowed him to take it. He raised the back to his lips and brushed them barely over the top in a gesture of respect.

"You are Graeme Montgomery," she said in a strained voice.

"I am," he said solemnly. "And you are Lady Armstrong."

"Robina," she amended. "After all we are to be . . . f-family," she stammered out and looked ill for saying the words.

To be honest, they made him just as ill. Family? Never.

"Robina, then."

He turned to his brothers. "These are my brothers, Bowen and Teague."

"You have a sister as well, do you not?" Robina questioned.

Graeme's expression hardened. "I would never bring her here. She is home and well guarded. She is young yet, and I would not have her exposed to a potentially . . . hostile . . . situation."

"And yet I am forced to send my daughter into the bosom of our enemy," Robina said in a near whisper.

"My lady, I do not wage war against women. Your daughter will not die by my hand nor the hand of any of my clansmen. As the wife of the laird, she will be afforded every courtesy due her position."

Robina didn't look heartened by his vow. She looked like she wanted to weep.

Graeme turned, surveying the nearly empty hall. It was as if every Armstrong had vacated in anticipation of the Montgomerys' arrival. Only he and his brothers, the earl and Tavis, and the laird's wife and sons were present.

He then focused on Tavis because he truly didn't want to upset the laird's wife more than she already was. She bore no blame for the sins of her husband and his kin.

"I would like to see the woman I'm supposed to marry. I would make her acquaintance before we are wed."

"Laird Montgomery," Robina interjected, turning his attention back to her. Her expression was pleading. "Please, may I speak to you plainly of my daughter before you seek to have her in your presence?"

"Speak your mind, my lady. I will take no offense if none is intended."

"Has no one told you of her?"

"He called her defective," Brodie snarled from across the room.

Robina whitened, though Graeme couldn't tell if it was in anger or upset.

"I have heard she is . . . unwell," Graeme said in an effort to be kind.

"Speak the truth," Teague snapped. " 'Tis widely known the lass is daft and cannot bear you heirs. 'Tis madness for this marriage to take place. It can solve nothing."

In that moment, Graeme truly believed that if Robina had been armed, she would have tried to kill his younger brother. He stepped automatically into the pathway between her and Teague to ward off any confrontation.

Brodie began to argue loudly while Tavis turned on

Teague. The hall erupted in a fury of yelling, and insults flew. Only the presence of the earl prevented bloodshed.

"Enough!" the earl roared. "Clear the hall!" He pointed at Armstrong's sons and then Graeme's own brothers. "Out. Leave them to discuss the matter before them."

"I'll not leave my brother to be murdered in this viper's nest," Bowen snarled.

Graeme held up his hand. "I am well protected, Bowen. Take your leave. Go check on the men and make sure all is as it should be. The sooner this is done with, the sooner we can be back on our own lands."

Reluctantly, his brothers and the Armstrong whelps took their leave. Then Graeme turned back to Robina. "Now, my lady, speak your mind. I grow impatient."

Tavis came to stand beside his wife, almost as if daring Graeme to show her any disrespect in speech or look.

"Eveline is . . . different. She's not daft. 'Tis God's truth, I do not fully understand the depth of what has afflicted her. When she was younger, three years past, she took a fall from her horse into a ravine and remained there three days before we were able to find her."

Graeme frowned. "Are you saying she wasn't born this way? That whatever affliction she has was because of an injury?"

"Aye. Well, nay. She wasn't born this way. There has never been a sweeter child. Intelligent. Sharp witted. Full of life and laughter. She would have made any man a wife he'd fight for. But she was ill for a length of time after her fall. And she was never the same afterward. She doesn't speak. Hasn't spoken since she awakened from a deep slumber of over a fortnight."

"'Tis all? She doesn't speak?" Some husbands would be grateful for such a gift.

Robina shook her head. "I'm trying to tell you that she won't make you a fit wife. You can't treat her as you would another woman. Please, if you have any mercy at all, you'll treat her kindly and leave her alone. She does not deserve to be punished for what has been wrought by her kin."

Anger was starting to prickle over his flesh and up his nape until his jaw was tight.

"I don't make war against women and the innocent," he growled. "I won't repeat myself again."

"By all that is holy, Montgomery, if any harm comes to my daughter when she is in your care, there is no rock you will be able to hide under," Tavis bit out. "I will come for you with the full force of me and mine and all that ally with me."

"I would think less of you than I already do if you did not do so," Graeme snapped. "Now enough with the endless prattle. I have no more desire to wed a child who isn't in full control of her faculties than you have to see your daughter wedded to me. But neither of us has a choice. 'Tis better to have it done with before things are said and done that cannot be retracted."

"In that we are agreed," the earl said from a few feet away. "You've stated your position, Tavis. There is naught else to be said. Fetch your daughter so that Graeme may meet his bride."

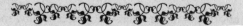

CHAPTER 6

Eveline felt the earth tremble below her and she automatically picked up her head, wondering who had gone riding on the hill where she was sprawled. She saw Brodie astride his horse, his head turning to survey the terrain. When his gaze fell on her, she saw the instant relief in his eyes.

He slid from his horse, dropped the reins to allow the horse to graze, and strode in her direction. As he grew near, she could see what it was he said.

". . . everywhere for you, Eveline. You had me—us—worried. Mother is distraught for thinking you ran away in fear."

She frowned, because where she may have once done something so selfish and cowardly, it was not something she'd ever do again. She might be terrified of her impending marriage, but she would face her future head-on and not give her family any hint of her inner turmoil. She owed them that much.

Brodie reached for her hand to pull her to her feet, and then to her surprise he hugged her fiercely, holding her against his chest for the longest time.

She allowed it, enjoying the show of affection. It wasn't that Brodie wasn't affectionate with her. Of all her relatives, he was the most demonstrative. He also treated her less like a half person than the rest. To him she was his baby sister and that was all.

But this felt different. Almost as if it were he who needed comforting and not her. She wrapped her arms around his waist and hugged him back with all her strength. Which, considering she couldn't even circle his muscled girth and make her hands touch on the other side, wasn't much.

She knew he was talking to her because she could feel the vibrations rumbling from his chest, but she didn't want to give up the hug to push away so she could see what it was he said.

When he finally pulled away, he took her hand and started to tug her toward the keep. She stopped and frowned, then looked back at his horse.

"I'll send someone back for it. I'd thought to have to go much farther to find you. You know I wouldn't make you ride with me."

For a moment, her gaze left her brother once more to find the horse who was grazing contentedly a few feet away. She didn't hate horses. They'd once been something she loved more than anything else. She hated that when she got close, when she could smell them, could feel their power, that she broke into a cold sweat and terror gripped her.

She hadn't ridden since her accident. She missed it. Missed the freedom of riding across open land, hair flying behind her, not a care in the world. Now the mere idea of being astride something so strong paralyzed her. She weighed nothing in comparison. It was so easy for a horse to unseat her.

Brodie tugged again, and this time he led her away more forcefully. She had a thousand questions she wanted to put to her brother, but she had no idea how to formulate them. No way to make him understand that she craved information.

What was the Montgomery chieftain like? Was he grotesque? Was he menacing?

She halted again, withdrew her hand from Brodie's, then touched his arm and tilted her head toward the keep. Then she lifted her eyebrows in clear question.

Brodie pursed his lips and blew out air, his cheeks puffing slightly. He glanced away, ran a hand through his hair and then finally directed his gaze back to her. There was deep sorrow in his eyes. Worry. Love. Concern.

"Graeme Montgomery is here. He wants to meet you. He doesn't want to stay any longer than necessary, and the earl of Dunbar will grant that request because he fears what will happen if the Montgomerys and Armstrongs are forced to remain in each others' presence for too long."

She put a finger to his lips and then shook her head in a negative motion. Then she smiled because she wanted him not to look so sad. If there was ever a time she wished she had the courage to try to speak, it was now. She opened her mouth, willing to try, not even knowing what would come out, but before she could issue those guttural sounds that she hoped formed words, her brother turned sharply and then held up a fist in the air.

He bellowed something she couldn't discern, but felt the vibration from his body. When she looked in the direction he was staring, she saw that Aiden was in the distance, motioning them toward the keep.

Brodie put a hand to the middle of her back and nudged her forward. She was sure he spoke, but she was too focused on the keep as they drew near to try to discern what it was he said. It was at these times that she knew others thought her daft because she simply didn't respond, didn't react. He could be saying anything at all and she'd never know.

When they approached Aiden, he was frowning, and she knew a reprimand was forthcoming so she purposely didn't look at him, because if she didn't see what he was saying, then it didn't really happen.

Perfectly logical in her mind.

Not that Aiden was ever mean. He was just less patient than Brodie. And he worried for her. If he had his way, she'd stay in the keep and never wander far. She'd never forget that it was he who'd found her in the ravine and that he'd feared the worst. That she had died.

She walked into the keep, flanked by her brothers, and she had to admit, it bolstered her courage because being between them, she knew she'd never come to harm.

As soon as she entered the hall, she came to an abrupt halt, her gaze automatically finding the man who commanded the most authority. It was obvious—at least to her—who the chieftain of the Montgomery clan was.

Power clung to him. It was an almost visible aura surrounding him.

She swallowed nervously and her palms grew damp. He was big. Really big. Taller than even her brothers. He was broad-shouldered, with an equally broad chest, more narrow at the waist, and his legs were solid masses of muscle, as big around as she was. Maybe her first impression was a wee bit exaggerated, but he looked like a mountain to her.

His medium brown hair was unruly. It hung to just below the base of his neck and curled at the ends, flipping this way and that. It was obvious he hadn't a care when he had it shorn. Unlike his brothers—or at least she assumed the two men with him were his brothers— he wore his hair shorter.

One of the men with him was beautiful. It seemed odd to describe a man with such a feminine term—and there was nothing remotely feminine about him. But he hadn't a single flaw that Eveline could see. His hair was as dark as a raven's wing and his eyes were a vivid blue. It was a certainty that Eveline had never seen his equal when it came to fairness of face. It was hard to look away from him.

The man who stood on Graeme's other side was nearly as large as his two brothers, and he had a lot of similarities to the really handsome brother. In fact, of the three, Graeme was probably the least blessed with a face that women would fawn over or that poets and bards would compose lyrics about, but still she was drawn over and over to Graeme's features. The lines of his face. The strength in his deceptively casual pose.

Nay, he wasn't beautiful like his brothers, but there was something even more arresting about his appearance. Something that intrigued her and drew her to look at him again and again.

To the unguarded eye he seemed relaxed, but to her he seemed tense and ready to strike at a moment's notice

And then the most amazing thing happened. As she stood there gaping, nearly hidden behind her brothers, an odd vibration echoed through her ears.

It was faint—so faint that she thought perhaps she'd imagined it. But no, there it was again. A deep timbre—a voice! Low-pitched like some of the other rare sounds she was able to hear, though until now she'd never been certain that they were real. She'd thought they were only memories of sounds she'd heard before her world had gone silent.

She pushed around her brothers so she could more squarely see the room, and she searched for the source of that sound. That beautiful sound.

As soon as she made her presence known, the others looked her way, and it was then she saw that Graeme's lips were moving. It was him she was hearing!

Uncaring of how forward or discourteous she might appear, she rushed forward, eager to be closer, wanting more of this delicious sensation in her ears.

But his lips stopped moving the moment she halted in front of him. They turned down into a frown as he stared back at her, almost as if he found her lacking.

Color suffused her cheeks and she lowered her gaze, suddenly shamed. Of course he'd find her lacking. He would have heard the stories and here she came boldly rushing forward, not even refreshed or appropriately dressed to greet her prospective husband. He must think her extremely disrespectful.

She took a step back, her hands shaking at her sides, and then she chanced another glance up at him, hoping that he would speak again, even if it was to voice his displeasure. She craved that sensation in her ears, something to break the endless, suffocating silence she lived in.

Graeme stared down at the tiny slip of a lass in front of him, taking in her heightened color and the sudden shame that had crept into her eyes.

Christ's bones, but the lass was beautiful. Breathtakingly beautiful. He hadn't imagined—how could he have?—that his intended bride would be such a bonnie lass.

She was tiny, almost fragile in appearance. He could likely break her bones with a simple squeeze. Her hair was like a wash of sunshine, only a little paler. Honey blond with the bluest eyes he'd ever seen on a woman. They reminded him a lot of Bowen's eyes, eyes he'd inherited from their mother. And they were fringed by dark lashes, long, making her eyes seem even larger against her small face.

He'd expected a . . . child. Perhaps even someone who resembled a child. This was no girl barely on the cusp of womanhood. She was a woman full grown with gently curved hips and a bosom that, although not overly large, was well beyond the initial budding of a girl in her youth.

He had to remind himself that she wasn't . . . normal. Or at least she was not as a normal woman should be. He still wasn't sure the extent or even the nature of her condition. There was much he needed to know.

He hated the bleakness in her expression. There was something in it that did funny things to his chest. Was she worried that he would deny her? That he would reject her in front of her family and his?

No matter his distaste for the union and the circumstances forced upon him by his king, the idea of hurting such a sweet-looking lass made him ill. Whatever was wrong with her was not of her making, and she was an innocent pawn in a calculated move by the crown.

"I assume you must be Eveline," he said in a gentle voice.

Her chin notched upward, and to his surprise, she smiled back at him, her eyes lighting up—her entire face lighting up—so much so that it made him catch his breath and stare back in awe at her beauty.

"I am Graeme Montgomery. I am to be your husband."

She sobered a bit at that last, so it was evident she had basic understanding of the situation. Her brow wrinkled up, and then she cocked her head to the side as she studied him with those startling blue eyes.

He found himself fidgeting under her regard, which made him scowl. Her eyes widened as she took a hasty step back toward her father.

Hell, he hadn't meant to frighten her. He glanced over to the Earl of Dunbar, allowing his displeasure to show. The earl, however, looked amused, another thing that Graeme didn't find pleasing.

Then, to Graeme's utter shock, Eveline stepped forward and slipped her small hand into his much larger, much rougher one and curled her fingers trustingly around his.

When he turned from the earl to stare back at her, she smiled, flashing straight, white teeth.

Laird Armstrong's groan could be heard throughout the hall. Robina Armstrong put a hand to her mouth and Eveline's brothers just looked really, really angry.

Whatever reservations the Armstrongs had about the marriage, it was evident that their daughter had no such misgivings.

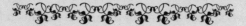

CHAPTER 7

Looking back, Eveline wasn't at all sure what had changed her mind about Graeme Montgomery. It was an impulsive gesture on her part and one that she might well regret. But then there wasn't anything to be done about her marriage. She'd watched enough mouths to know that. Her fate was inevitable, so why not embrace it?

Graeme fascinated her. It wasn't so much that she heard his words, but his voice was like a low hum in her ears. Pleasant. A shaft of sunlight into her dark world of silence. There were other sounds that she'd thought she'd imagined, but now she wondered if she truly did hear a limited number of things. And if so, why?

Her brow was furrowed in concentration, and she wasn't paying the least bit of attention to what her mother was saying to her. It was deeper sounds. She was positive of that. She couldn't remember hearing a woman's voice since the accident. Certainly no screaming. High pitches. And music, which she missed the most, was something completely lost to her.

But deeper sounds. At times she swore she could hear slight noises when Brodie was angry and was surely raising his voice. Once when her father had been angry with her for wandering too far from the keep, she'd been almost certain she'd heard or at least felt a vibration in her ear from his yelling.

It was all a very mystifying puzzle that fascinated her. It made her want to go seek out her husband-to-be again, just so she could make him talk to her. Anything was better than the yawning silence that held her captive. Any sound, no matter how insignificant was welcome.

Her mother appeared in front of her, grasped her shoulders, and shook her gently. "Eveline! Are you listening to me?"

Eveline blinked and stared back at her mother. They were standing in her mother's chamber while Eveline was being fitted for a gown to wear to her wedding.

Robina had the entire keep in an uproar with wedding preparations, and she had no fewer than six women attending Eveline to make sure the dress was sewn quickly enough for the ceremony.

"What were you doing down there?" Robina asked.

There was gentle concern in her mother's eyes. Worry for Eveline and genuine curiosity as well.

"You must learn to temper your responses," Robina chided. "Graeme Montgomery isn't a man to be trifled with. I fear what he'd do if you were to have such a breech in propriety in his keep. I don't know the manner of man he is. He swears he's no abuser of women, but one never knows the full character of a man right off, and you must realize this."

Eveline frowned at that. Graeme hadn't seemed quite so frightening after she'd had time to study him close. His features were set in stone. Some might even say he looked as though he would snap a man in half if the man so much as looked at Graeme wrong. But Eveline had sensed something else entirely and she couldn't even be sure what. What she did know was that he'd been exceedingly kind and patient with her.

He hadn't berated her for her rude intrusion. He hadn't demanded that she back away. He hadn't struck her for her forwardness. He'd spoken kind words to her. Hardly the words spoken by a true monster of a man who planned ill for his new wife.

Surely she wasn't wrong about that much.

But then she wasn't a judge of character. It was a fact she avoided most people simply because she didn't want to be faced with derision, fear, or mockery. She didn't have much experience with people at all outside her parents and her brothers.

She hadn't been wrong about Ian McHugh, though, and she'd keep reminding herself of that fact. Ian had fooled even her own father, not to mention her brothers.

She reached for her mother's hands, pulled them up to her heart. Robina looked startled, her brow wrinkling in confusion. Eveline squeezed her mother's hands and then leaned over to kiss her cheek.

When Eveline pulled away, her mother looked dazed. Her eyes burned with sudden understanding and shock.

"You want this. You want to marry Graeme Montgomery."

Eveline squeezed her mother's hands again and then slowly nodded.

Robina backed away and then slumped into the chair by the small table near the window. "I never expected this. I've been so afraid. I don't want you to leave our care and protection. You're our baby, Eveline."

She looked so distraught that Eveline's heart clutched and her lips twisted unhappily.

"I should have known. I should have realized that you'd want what all normal girls want. A husband. Children. A life of your own. I just hadn't imagined you were capable of it—of understanding your duties. Do you even understand, Eveline?"

Her mother looked anxiously up at her, her gaze seeking information from Eveline's expression or her eyes or perhaps from something else entirely.

There was a lot Eveline didn't understand. She understood well enough the day-to-day things, but there were certainly some matters that hadn't been explained to her. But she wasn't about to upset her mother even further by shaking her head.

Surely the business of marriage wasn't that difficult, was it? She'd watched her mother and father her entire life. Her mother was quite adept at running a household and capable of running her husband as well when it suited her.

Eveline might not have practiced what knowledge she'd gained, but it didn't make her any less capable.

She looked at her mother and simply nodded and let her mother make of that what she would.

Robina sighed and rubbed wearily at her forehead. "I want you to be happy, Eveline, and I hate to think you've not been happy here. We've only sought to protect you. I hope you know that."

Eveline smiled, allowing all the love she felt for her mother to show on her face. Robina's reaction was swift. She rose and then hurried forward, enfolding Eveline in a fierce hug.

Eveline knew no more of what her mother was saying, but it didn't matter because Eveline understood. Everything she needed to know was right here in her mother's hug.

"We need to have words, Armstrong," Graeme said as he faced Eveline's father.

Tavis stared back at him with weary eyes, and for the first time, Graeme felt a twinge of sympathy for the older man, but he quickly squashed it. The Armstrongs didn't deserve his sympathy. They'd given no mercy to his clan and he'd give none in return.

"Come, let's sit and have some ale. Then we'll speak of what's on your mind."

Graeme motioned for his brothers to remain back as he followed the laird to the high table on the dais at the opposite end of the great hall. He was surprised Armstrong bothered to show him the courtesy of placing him where honored guests would be seated when in attendance.

A serving woman appeared with a tankard of ale and two goblets. After filling them, she slipped away, leaving the two men alone at the table.

The earl had retired, evidently convinced that there would be no overt hostilities. Bowen and Teague stood across the room staring belligerently at Eveline's two brothers. Graeme gave them a sharp look and then dipped his head in the direction of one of the lesser tables to indicate they should sit down.

Then he turned his attention fully on the Armstrong laird.

" 'Tis clear that neither of us wants this union."

Tavis's lips tightened and he started to speak, but Graeme's expression stopped him.

"But I'll treat your daughter well. I'll treat her with more respect than you and yours ever afforded my clan."

Anger glittered in Tavis's eyes, but he continued to stare at Graeme in stony silence.

"I was truthful with your lady wife. I do not wage war against the innocent, and your daughter is perhaps more innocent than most. She's clearly different. Do not fear my treatment of her, for she will be well provided for. However, do not expect our marriage to be an open invitation for you to step foot on my lands."

"You'd have me send my daughter off, never to see her again?" Tavis demanded. "How will I know if you've upheld your word if I never see the proof of your claim?"

"I will allow her to visit upon occasion only if it's convenient and I can be assured of no foul play, but no Armstrong, save she, will ever set foot over our borders. 'Tis a blood vow I swear and a blood vow it is, because if it should ever happen, blood *will* be shed."

"Know then that no Montgomery, save one who is escorting my daughter, will ever be allowed back on our lands. Consider this an aberration and one afforded to you only by order of our king," Tavis said through his teeth.

"Good enough," Graeme said. "We'll sign the treaty, give the king what he wants, but we have an understanding."

"Aye, we do."

"Now tell me more about Eveline. Does she always act so oddly?"

Tavis started to scowl, but Graeme held up his hand. "I mean no insult. You saw that she came to me and was not afraid. You and her kin acted as though this was unusual behavior for her."

Tavis nodded grimly. "Aye, it is. I've never seen her act thusly. She is usually quite shy and content to be left alone, and moreover, 'tis something I prefer. Not all in our clan are as accepting as others when it comes to her affliction. I would not have her ridiculed or mocked or even potentially harmed by those who view her as a devil's instrument."

Graeme's eyebrow raised. "Devil's instrument?"

"You know well what people think when faced with someone like Eveline. You're a fool if you think it won't happen in your clan. My daughter has two things against her going in. One, she's an Armstrong and will be reviled for nothing more than her parentage. Two, she'll be considered daft, touched, addled, and many other less kind words will be attributed to her. 'Tis a dangerous situation that you will have to monitor closely. If the wrong people have it in their head that she's Satan's instrument, they could well kill her."

"Is she all of those things? Daft? Touched?" Graeme asked in an even voice.

"I do not know," Tavis said wearily. "There are days when I think she understands perfectly what goes on around her. She'll respond when we talk to her. She seems to grasp certain situations. And then other days, it's as if the rest of us don't exist and she's in her own realm."

"And she never speaks?"

Tavis shook his head. "Not since the accident and resulting fever. I know not why. I don't know if she had fever of the brain and it damaged her in some way. Or if she was so deeply affected by the event that she cannot even speak of it."

He leaned forward, his expression serious. "She cannot sit a horse. It's important you not make her try."

Graeme frowned. "Cannot sit a horse? Why has she been neglected so? I don't have a litter to carry her back to my keep and I'm damn sure not going to make her walk."

"It's not that she's been neglected. Indeed, she was an expert horseman. Never saw anything quite like it. From an early age, she just commanded the attention of horses. They gravitated toward her. Liked her. She could make them do anything. And ride like the wind.

"She used to scare me spitless. She'd swing up on a horse bareback in her bare feet, her hair going in all directions, and she'd ride hell-bent for leather across the meadow, back and forth. I was always convinced she was going to kill herself, but she enjoyed it so much that I couldn't bear to make her stop."

Tavis sighed and rubbed a hand over his face. "And

then it happened. Just as I feared. She took a bad fall. Horse was spooked, pitched her right off his back and she fell into a deep ravine. It was three days before we found her, and by then she was gravely ill. She had an injury to her head and a fever that lasted an entire fortnight. After that she was never the same and she's deathly afraid of horses. You needed to know so that you never try to make her mount."

"How the hell am I supposed to get her back to my keep?" Graeme demanded.

"I'll provide a cart for her to ride in," Tavis said.

Graeme let out a disgruntled push of air. His bride was becoming more of a pain in his arse all the time. It was a marriage to prevent further bloodshed, but to him it felt like a death sentence.

"I don't know that she can ever make you a proper wife," Tavis said in a low voice that sounded precariously close to pleading. "Don't force the issue. I wouldn't have her hurt or ill-treated for anything in the world. She is dear to all of us. You are receiving a gift, Laird. Whether you choose to believe so or not, you are receiving something more precious than gold."

CHAPTER 8

Graeme climbed the steps to the chamber he'd been assigned. As the apparent guest of honor, he'd been afforded a room in the upper wing while his brothers had been consigned to the common sleeping hall where many of the warriors slept on cots lining the walls.

Since his room was next to the Earl of Dunbar's, he wondered if the earl had been the one to insist this respect be given Graeme. Armstrong would have likely wanted them all to camp outside the walls of the keep with the rest of his men. Or better yet, never have set foot on Armstrong land to begin with.

Graeme pushed open his door, only wanting to bed down for the night. Tomorrow he'd wed and then leave for home to face the inevitability of his future. Or lack thereof. He wasn't one to focus on the negative, but for the first time he felt a certain bleakness, because any dream he had of heirs and passing his legacy on to his own bloodline was gone. As was any thought of revenge against the clan who'd murdered his da.

When he stepped inside, he was surprised to see candles already burning and a fire laid in the hearth. But he was even more surprised to see Eveline perched on the edge of his bed, her expression guarded as she stared up at him.

She wore the same dress she'd had on earlier in the day. While Lady Armstrong had dressed for the occasion to greet her guests—albeit unwanted ones—Eveline had first greeted him in a simple frock that was similar to a work dress worn by the other women in the clan. And perhaps because it was so simple, it had only drawn a more stark comparison between Eveline's beauty and the plainness of her apparel.

But then Graeme wasn't certain there was a single item she could wear that would diminish what was clearly a beautiful lass.

Eveline looked to be worried that he would be angry over the intrusion. And he should be. It was a breech of his privacy, but it was also improper for her to be alone with him in his chamber on the eve of their wedding. Her family would be outraged if they knew of her whereabouts, and it could call into question his own honor that he so jealously guarded.

And yet he couldn't bring himself to show any temper toward the lass.

Unsure of what he should do, he continued into the room, closing the door behind him. After a moment he turned to look at her, and he could see a hint of color rise in her cheeks, reflected in the soft candlelight.

She looked angelic. Impossibly beautiful. He'd never seen anything her equal. It wasn't that she was the most beautifully fashioned woman he'd ever seen, but she was easily the most . . .

He frowned. The most what?

There was something quite irresistible about her and he couldn't even put his finger on it. She lacked the practiced graces of older, more mature women. But neither did she look like a maiden too young for a man to even look at.

She was . . . just right.

God's teeth, was he lusting over his bride? Self-loathing filled him. He should be treating her gently and kindly. It was obvious there was something off about the lass, even if he didn't know the extent, and here he was looking at her as a prospective wife with all the benefits entailed.

No matter that she was an Armstrong. It was clear she couldn't be punished for or defined by the actions of her family when it was likely she was unaware of most things around her.

As much as he didn't want to label any Armstrong a victim, he had enough intelligence to know she didn't deserve this union any more than he deserved to be forced into it.

She would be taken from her home—the only safe haven she had. From everyone who protected and loved her—and it was obvious she was well loved by her family. She would be thrust into a hostile environment. Could any Armstrong ever find a place in the Montgomery clan? It was going to be a difficult matter, no matter how it was handled, and it was she who stood to lose the most, while all he gained was an unwanted wife and grudging truce with the Armstrongs.

As if she had grown impatient with him just standing and staring at her, she stood with a slight frown and then crossed the room to stand just before him. She reached for his face and his automatic reaction was to flinch away.

Hurt shadowed her eyes and she snatched her hand back, a frown turning her lips down.

Aggrieved that he'd somehow hurt her, he carefully reached down, took her hand and then raised it back to his chin where she'd nearly touched him before. He had no idea of her intention, but he would see how it played out.

She smiled and again he was struck by how such a smile transformed her entire face into a ray of sunshine. Her fingers slid delicately over his rough jaw and to his lips. His eyes widened when she touched his mouth and then pushed up and down at his lips.

When he didn't immediately react, she frowned and pushed more forcefully. Then she removed her fingers and pressed her finger and thumb into his cheeks, squeezing so his lips puckered outward.

Frowning harder, she stared up at him as if to say, *Do you not understand?* It seemed clear the lass wanted him to speak.

He nearly laughed. Everyone treated her as somewhat of a simpleton, but here she was acting as if he were the dolt with no sense.

She wanted him to speak. Of what, he had no idea, but it was clear she wanted him to say something.

"You shouldn't be here, Eveline," he said kindly. "It's not proper and if your father should find out, he'd almost certainly declare war, which would most assuredly displease our king."

Her brow furrowed deeper and she gave him a fierce glare. Then she shook her head and raised her hands as if to say, *Who is to know?*

She put her finger back to his lips, but by now he knew what it was she wanted. With a sigh, he led her to a chair by the fire and motioned for her to sit. He dragged the bench by the window across the floor so he could sit near her.

They were side by side and before he could think of anything further to say, she stood and turned her chair, positioning it so she was facing him. Then she settled back down and leaned forward, her eyes focused intently on him.

He'd never felt so unsettled. His tongue felt tied and he had no idea what to say to the lass. It would be so much easier if she spoke, because then she could ask questions. Aye, he could answer questions easily enough, but to just come up with a topic?

He wasn't someone who spoke overly much and was never one for casual conversations. He was more to the point. His brothers often teasingly said that dragging more than a few words from him was like trying to push a rope through the eye of a needle.

So . . . he'd talk about marriage. Since the wedding would take place tomorrow, he could only assume that was why she was here in his chamber. Perhaps to allay her fears? Find out if he was some horrible abuser of women? Who knew?

He cleared his throat, hating how unsure of this entire situation he was. Give him a sword and someone to kill. He could handle that nicely. But a woman sitting in front of him, staring avidly while waiting for him to speak? Not exactly the subject of any training he and his men had ever endured.

"You understand that tomorrow we will wed," he began gruffly.

She smiled and nodded.

Smiling was good. At least she hadn't run from his chamber like the hounds of hell were nipping at her heals. But that still didn't tell him she fully understood the ramifications of their marriage.

"Do you also understand that as soon as the ceremony has been completed, we will leave your . . . this keep . . . and travel back to Montgomery lands?"

Her expression sobered, but she nodded again.

"'Tis the truth I have no idea what to do with you, Eveline Armstrong," he admitted. "I had no plans for a wife yet. And when I did, I would of course have chosen a lass from my own clan. Someone who was well accustomed to life as a Montgomery and someone well versed in the running of a keep. My men . . ."

He broke off for a moment because she was cocking her head back and forth all the while her gaze was riveted . . . on his mouth. But there was such an expression of—pleasure?—on her face that it took him aback.

He cleared his throat again to continue, choosing to ignore her odd behavior. "My men and I train daily. I have other matters to attend to as chieftain. My clansmen come to me to settle disputes, to air grievances, to ask for guidance."

Her look turned to one of impatience and she shook her head. She made a motion, a wide circling motion as if to encompass the entire keep and then gave him another impatient look as if to remind him that she was a chieftain's daughter and well knew the duties of the laird.

Graeme sighed. So she didn't want a rundown of his duties as laird. Not that he blamed her. It wasn't scintillating conversation at best, but then he didn't *like* lengthy conversations.

"What would *you* like to discuss, Eveline?"

Which sounded ridiculous, given that she couldn't speak, but it was obvious she had no liking for the topics he'd broached.

Her smile returned and she leaned forward and directed one finger at him and then pressed it into his shoulder.

"Me?" he asked incredulously. "You want to talk about *me*?"

He couldn't quite keep the horror from his tone or expression. What was he supposed to say? He felt as though he were on trial. Set before the king and court and a bevy of accusers, forced to give an accounting of himself before God.

How could she make him feel so bloody insecure?

She smiled hugely then, her entire face lighting up, and she nodded vigorously.

God's teeth, he needed to have the lass gone from his bedchamber. This was madness. All of it.

But he couldn't look at the sparkle in her eyes or her imploring gaze and keep the hardness that usually surrounded his heart and mind. What man in all of Scotland could sit before this beguiling beauty and possibly tell her no?

"What do you want to know?" he asked gruffly. Then realizing how stupid it was to question a woman who had no way of responding, he shook his head. "Never mind that. It was senseless on my part."

Still, she stared at him expectantly, waiting for what he'd volunteer. And he had no idea what to tell her about himself. He didn't sit around evaluating himself, his choices or his life. He just . . . was. He was chieftain to his people and with that came great responsibility. He didn't have time to immerse himself in his thoughts or to ponder what manner of man he was.

Perhaps all she needed was reassuring. It occurred to Graeme that he'd assured her father and even her mother that his intentions toward Eveline were not dishonorable, but Eveline herself hadn't been made aware of those same vows.

Aye, that was probably what she wanted to hear and it was something he could comfortably discuss.

"Eveline," he began carefully, wanting to make sure he had her full attention. But he needn't have worried because she was still staring avidly at his face. Indeed, her gaze had never left him. He'd never felt so scrutinized. "I want you to know that I do not hold you accountable for the sins of your family."

She frowned—nay, she *scowled*—her face drawing into a ferocious expression that amused him for its cuteness.

"I understand you are innocent of wrongdoing and that you are a victim in this. I will treat you kindly and with the respect due your position as a chieftain's daughter and now a chieftain's wife. I'll not ever punish the daughter for the sins of the father."

She pushed up from the chair, and to his utter shock, she balled her fist and punched him right in the nose.

He reeled back, his hand going automatically to the place she'd struck. Not that she'd hit him hard enough to do any damage or cause any real pain. He was more flabbergasted by her reaction than anything.

She stomped past him, her feet making light sounds despite the exaggerated fashion in which she was trying to display her anger.

She threw open his door and he was on his feet immediately, knowing that if she succeeded in slamming it—which she seemed very intent on doing—that it would wake the others in adjacent chambers and then everyone would be in the hall to see her stomping out of his room.

And then? All hell would break loose.

He caught it just as she released it and swept into the hall. Then he stood there a long moment, breathing heavy breaths as he watched her disappear down the dimly lit corridor.

Daft or off she may be, but she clearly didn't like for her family to be disparaged in any manner. He smiled ruefully. He admired loyalty. He demanded it. He could hardly respect the lass if she'd sat there stoically and accepted anything ill he said of her clan.

He quietly closed the door and then turned to start undressing for bed. Then he laughed.

The lass had been a complete and utter surprise and he still had no idea what on earth to make of her.

The only thing he could be assured of was that quite possibly he'd never be sure of her or what each day would bring from this day forward.

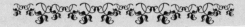

CHAPTER 9

Graeme's first glimpse of his bride was confusing for him. It was as if the woman he'd spent a brief period of time with the night before was someone completely different than this woman standing in the hall where they were to be married.

He paused at the doorway, watching the goings-on, but his concentration was focused on Eveline.

She was adorned in a gown finer than anything he'd seen even at court. Rich blue, intricately embroidered, and the material fell in precise layers from her waist. The top, while modest, drew attention to the lushness of her feminine curves—curves that he still felt guilt for even noticing.

Her blond hair, a beautiful splash of sunshine on a spring day in the highlands, was partially upswept, gathered in a mass atop her head, but the rest fell down to her waist in silken waves. She was beautiful, but there was something missing.

Her spark. The one he'd witnessed the night before.

She looked . . . like she was anywhere but where she was. She had a distant, vacant expression on her face, and nothing that went on around her seemed to register.

She looked tired and defeated and . . . scared.

That part he hated. It angered him and he didn't even know why. The very last thing he wanted was for her to be afraid. It riled protective instincts that he damn sure shouldn't have for anyone named Armstrong. But there it was. He was ready to stomp over and lay siege to whatever was causing her current mood.

He stood a little longer, watching as the activity increased in preparation for the wedding. Eveline stood quietly next to her mother, her hands gripped in front of her. As he studied her further, he realized that it wasn't fear that had seized her. She was just . . . unaware.

That brought a frown to his face. Was she bespelled by good and bad days? Did she gain and lose lucidity in random pattern? Was she afflicted by an illness of the mind that caused drastic changes in behavior?

It could certainly explain the oddness of her behavior with him yesterday.

Unease settled over him as once more it was brought home that this match was in essence a death sentence. Instead of being a husband, he'd be assigned the role of a caretaker. He would protect her and make sure she was taken care of, but she would never be a wife to him.

No one would ever fault him for finding ease with another woman when he was married to someone such as Eveline. No one would even think twice, given that Eveline was certainly not capable of fulfilling her duties in that regard.

But it didn't set well with him. It was dishonorable and it was no fault of Eveline's that she was the way she was. He couldn't bring himself to betray her that way. Or to dishonor them both in such a fashion.

He would be faithful to a woman he would never be intimate with, and it was one hell of a grim future to look forward to.

His gaze swept over the hall once more, and then it came back to Eveline, who still stood in the same place she'd been. So still and serene as if she were someplace else entirely.

But then her gaze shifted, met his, and her entire demeanor changed. She smiled. Light entered her eyes. Her face became alive with color and vibrancy. In just that second, she was here. In the hall. Staring back at him, her look of vacancy completely gone.

Thinking to ward off another encounter where she'd rush forward and start squashing his lips together in an effort to make him talk, he strode forward.

Eveline's mother looked up, her eyes flaring in alarm. Her arm went immediately around Eveline, but Eveline shook her off and took a step forward, beaming at Graeme all the while.

Graeme gave a courtly bow to Lady Armstrong and then turned to Eveline just as she reached out to touch him. On the arm this time.

Just a simple touch, but in that small gesture there was so much more. She left her fingers there on his bare arm, a signal of . . . trust. She tilted her chin so she could look up at him, and she smiled even more, her blue eyes sparkling with what looked to be clear happiness.

Wanting to please her, he spoke, for no other reason than he didn't want her to have to implore him to talk to her.

"You look lovely, Eveline. Surely there's never been a more beautiful bride."

She beamed. Positively beamed back at him.

Her mother looked stunned. Not at the compliment that Graeme had given Eveline. She was staring at her daughter, her lips parted in clear shock. Then she glanced to Graeme, confusion reflected in her gaze.

"What is between you and my daughter, Laird?" she asked in a quiet voice.

Graeme frowned and when he did, Eveline immediately turned to her mother, a frown now replacing her smile.

"My lady, I assure you that what is between your daughter and myself is marriage. Isn't that what we're all gathered in your great hall for? It surely isn't to exchange pleasantries or for the Montgomerys to enjoy a visit to a neighboring clan."

"She reacted to you," Robina said, her lips trembling. She completely ignored the tinge of anger in Graeme's words and the reproach as well.

Graeme's brow wrinkled in confusion. "I don't follow, my lady."

Robina shook her head and brought her hand up to her temple to rub it. It was then that Graeme really saw the exhaustion in her face and eyes. As if she hadn't slept in many days. He found himself pitying her when it was the very last thing he wanted to feel. Sympathy for the enemy. It went against his very soul.

Robina's other hand went up and fluttered as if she were at a loss as to how to explain. "Eveline isn't aware most times. She's happy enough. She's sweet. She's good. But she rarely pays any attention to what goes on around her. I'm not even sure she has any understanding most of the time. But she responded to your compliment. Just as any normal woman would."

"And this isn't normal behavior for her?" Graeme asked.

He knew damn well that Eveline understood what he said when he conversed with her. There was no mistaking that, and it was why he wanted to be careful now. Her mother didn't seem to worry overmuch about discussing her daughter's condition freely in front of Eveline. Graeme didn't want her hurt by the conversation. Was this the way her entire family treated her? Like a mindless idiot?

"Come away with me for a moment, my lady," Graeme said, offering his arm to Robina in a courtly gesture.

Eveline frowned even harder and glanced up at Graeme, hurt in her eyes.

"I'll return in a moment, Eveline," Graeme said. "I would like a moment with your mother to assure her that you are in good hands. It will ease her mind on your wedding day."

Eveline's expression softened and she glanced at her mother, clear love in her eyes.

"Come," Graeme said again, before Robina could speak again in her daughter's presence.

Robina went away almost blindly, her mouth still drawn in shock. When they were at a distance where Graeme thought they could talk without hurting Eveline, he stopped and stared down at Robina.

"I admit to some confusion, my lady. Eveline has responded to me. I would even go as far as to say we've had discourse, though of course she doesn't speak to me. But that certainly hasn't prevented her from letting me know in no uncertain terms what it is she wants and moreover what kind of information she wants."

Robina openly gaped at him, her reaction too raw to possibly be feigned.

"You act as though this isn't normal," Graeme said with a frown.

"Not normal? Laird, what is normal for Eveline is to be the sweet, gentle soul she is. She does respond, yes, but to *family*. Never to strangers. I know not if there are simply times when she does not understand or if she's just more oblivious on some occasions than at others. Most of the time she does what she likes and we've been quite content to allow it because we want her to be happy."

The fierceness in Robina's voice registered with Graeme. How much this woman loved her daughter and how much it hurt her that Eveline wasn't a normal girl looking forward to a normal future.

Again he found himself softening. Toward an Armstrong. If he didn't leave the cursed Armstrong holding soon, he'd be sympathizing with the lot of them.

"All I can tell you," he said carefully, "is that while we haven't conversed in a normal fashion, we have most certainly communicated. Moreover, she is absolutely aware of what's taking place today and she's unafraid."

"How do you know this?" Robina demanded. "She doesn't speak. How could you possibly know what she is thinking?"

Graeme shrugged. "We communicated. You're asking me to explain something I do not understand myself, my lady. But I feel that the more time I spend with Eveline, the more I will come to understand her vision of the world around her and just how much and what she comprehends."

Robina glanced to her daughter and then back to Graeme, clear uncertainty in her eyes. "Be kind to her. She seems taken with you, Laird."

Then without a by-your-leave or even a hasty pardon, she left Graeme's side and hurried over to her daughter.

Robina spoke in earnest and a moment later, Eveline's gaze shifted over her mother's shoulder and found Graeme. And she smiled. It was all she did, but what an extraordinary smile that lit up the entire room. It took his breath away and made his chest tighten to the point of discomfort.

Then her mother drew her into a tight hug and Eveline disappeared from view. Just as well, because at that moment, a hand slapped down on his shoulder and he turned to see Bowen and Teague standing just behind him.

"How much longer do we have to stand this?" Teague demanded. "The men are getting restless. We won't be able to keep the peace much longer. It's like asking a starving wolf to sit and watch you skin a stag without attacking and devouring it whole."

"As soon as her father and the earl make their appearance, the ceremony will take place, and then we'll take our leave," Graeme said.

Bowen frowned. "What make you of this whole thing with the earl, Graeme? I do not like how much time Armstrong has spent with Dunbar. It makes me uneasy. Dunbar has the ear of the king. He's Alexander's favored earl. And let's face it, the Montgomerys are getting the worst of it in this so-called truce."

Graeme frowned. "Nay, 'tis not so. We're giving nothing up while the Armstrongs are giving their daughter to their sworn enemy. It could be said that we have more favor with the king."

Teague's jaw dropped open. "Not giving up anything? Graeme, you won't have heirs. You won't have . . . anything. The lass is useless."

Graeme turned, his expression fierce as he faced down his brother. "She's not useless. Do not say such again in my presence. Or anywhere else."

Teague's eyebrows shot upward, but he fell into silence.

"He could have ordered the marriage of Rorie to one of them," Graeme pointed out in a softer voice. "It would have been logical. Daughter for daughter. Armstrong has two sons of marriageable age and neither are spoken for."

"Over my dead body," Bowen snarled. "Rorie is but a child."

Graeme fixed him with his stare. "And Eveline is less of a child? In a lot of ways, Rorie would be a more competent wife than Eveline herself. Rorie's young, but she's hale and hearty and she'll bear a man children. She's of marriageable age. You and I know she's not ready for a husband. But the king doesn't. He could have very well taken her from us and there would have been naught to do unless we wanted to wage war against the crown."

Teague swallowed, his jaw drawn into a hard line. He was infuriated by the mere idea.

"Now imagine how they are feeling," Graeme said in a low voice. "Imagine how we would feel if we were even now preparing to watch Rorie wed an Armstrong."

"You're becoming soft," Teague hissed. "You cannot sympathize with these bastards. They are not deserving of our regard or sympathy."

Graeme nodded his agreement. "Aye, I know it. I don't expect you to like them. I'm merely asking you to imagine if the situation was reversed and Rorie had been ordered to marry an Armstrong."

"'Tis unthinkable," Bowen said. "I cannot imagine how Eveline's family hasn't rebelled against the crown."

"Because Armstrong knows it would be signing a death warrant for his entire clan," Graeme said. "We may hate the man, but he's not stupid. A daughter for his entire clan? He doesn't like it, but he also knows he has no choice as much as it pains him. Just as if Rorie had been ordered to marry an Armstrong, we would not have a choice either."

"Marry the lass so we can take our leave at once," Teague muttered. "I want to return to our lands before anyone decides that we've not given in return what we are being given. I still say the Armstrongs have favor with the king or the earl. In the king's mind, he's ridded them of a burden and saddled you with a wife who cannot provide you heirs. What are they truly giving up, Graeme? Because the way I see it, the king has done you a great injustice. You are the chieftain. 'Tis your bloodline that should carry on. He's now made it impossible for you to do so."

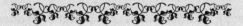

CHAPTER 10

Eveline stood with Graeme in front of the priest as she waited for the ceremony to commence. She supposed it would be proper if she were to have her hand on Graeme's arm or if he were to have her hand tucked underneath. But her hands were locked in front of her, buried in the folds of her exquisite gown so that no one would see how badly they shook.

She'd gathered enough information from rapidly scanning lips in the conversation that took place prior to the ceremony to know that her father would be responding in her stead.

She wasn't sure how she felt about that. She'd give anything to make her own promises, but she was afraid to try. Afraid to attempt to form those words and then have no idea if they came out a whisper or if they came out a bellow.

Perhaps once she reached the Montgomery holding she could . . . she could start anew. Maybe she could even try with Graeme, but not until she was certain that it was the right thing to do.

She was fascinated by the man she would soon be wed to, but he was still a Montgomery, and no Armstrong had any reason to believe the Montgomerys were anything but bloodthirsty savages. Even if everything she'd seen so far of Graeme contradicted that idea.

But she also had to remember that with the earl present and a dictate rendered by the king himself, the Montgomerys would be on their very best behavior.

Eveline would know more about the character of her husband once they reached his lands and he was no longer restrained in his actions and words.

So lost in her thoughts was she, that she hadn't realized that the ceremony not only had begun but that now Graeme was facing her. He reached down for her hand and for a moment she thought he would kiss her.

What a breathless thought. She hadn't imagined such a thing until now, and it made her precariously light-headed.

But all he did was hold up her hand, turn to the others, and then he made an announcement, one she couldn't see since she wasn't facing him.

Whatever he said, she could only assume he'd announced that they were man and wife. Or perhaps that she was now a Montgomery. Or perhaps he'd even said he was taking his leave now. But whatever it was he'd proclaimed, it was met with reserve on both sides.

Somber. It was the word to describe the expressions of everyone gathered. There was no joy. No festive spirit. There would be no wedding feast with music and food well into the night.

Nay, her wedding day was as a dark cloud marring a perfect spring day. And now she would face saying good-bye to the only life she'd ever known. To a family who was fiercely protective of her, even as they didn't fully understand her. A family who loved her without reservation or condition.

They cared not if she was daft as a stone or if she was cursed by the devil himself. She was an Armstrong. The only Armstrong daughter. And she was loved.

Graeme tugged on her hand, pulling her toward the door. Panic raced through Eveline as she realized they were indeed departing the moment they were wed and she was his wife.

For a moment she resisted and she expected anger or perhaps impatience. But he merely stood there, their arms outstretched because she hadn't budged from her spot when he'd begun to walk away.

He stared at her, no anger or judgment. He merely waited. And then he said, "We must go now, Eveline. My men await."

It was enough to stutter her forward, her steps shaky and uneven as she followed him out of the hall and to the steps leading down into the courtyard. There she was greeted by the sight of a wooden cart attached to a horse. It was the one her father had fashioned for her when she refused to ever sit a horse again after her accident.

Behind the cart were three horses, two loaded with her dowry. Supplies, spices, jewels. Things that were precious and of great value. And then another cart, loaded with trunks containing all that belonged to her.

It was so final. Every part of her would be erased from her home. As if she never existed. Had never lived here.

Tears clouded her eyes.

Even as she looked forward to the possibility of being a wife and of having the things she'd always thought she'd be denied, she was overcome with grief because she knew she'd rarely if ever see her family again.

Graeme touched her cheek, and it was then she realized he was wiping away a tear that had slid over her skin. She turned to look at him and saw the words forming on his lips.

"Go and bid your family farewell, Eveline. We must be on our way."

Stiffly she walked away, to where her mother and father and her two brothers lined the path from the steps to where the horses waited.

She hugged Aiden, and he returned her embrace with a quick, fierce hold. He said something, but it was lost as she went to Brodie next. He gathered her gently in his arms and hugged her, holding her there for a long moment.

When he released her, his lips were in a firm line and he was staring coldly in the direction of her new husband.

Her mother and father both gathered her close, the three forming a tight circle as they held her in their arms. Her father kissed her temple. Her mother pressed her cheek to Eveline's, and Eveline could feel the dampness of her mother's tears.

Eveline's own throat was clogged with such sorrow that she could barely swallow. What had seemed a grand adventure before was now startlingly real. It was no fantasy. She was truly leaving the bosom of her family and on her way to an uncertain future with a clan who hated her and everything she stood for.

It was all she could do not to throw herself at her father and put him between her and Graeme.

It was time for her to be strong. She'd spent the last years hiding. If she balked, if she showed any distress or any sign that she refused to leave, it could be disastrous.

Her entire clan would suffer. Lives would be lost. All because she was afraid to face the outside world and her fears.

She purposely turned away, her heart aching with every breath. She took a step toward her husband and then another. Her back hurt from holding herself so rigidly erect. She forced calm onto her face even if within she was a seething sea at the height of a storm.

She would bring no dishonor to her father or her clan. She would make her mother proud. She would not worry her brothers. She would leave this place by her choice and she'd accept her husband because it was her choice, not because it was mandated by her king.

When she was but a step away from Graeme, she stopped and tilted her chin up, pride holding her stiff. She met his gaze and then squared her shoulders, her message clear.

She was ready to depart.

CHAPTER 11

The journey from the Armstrong border to the Montgomery border was merely half a day in good weather, and the weather was spectacular. Spring, mostly warm with just a hint of chill when the wind blew this way or that. The sun shone high overhead and the land was awash with a splash of gold.

It was a day when a younger Eveline would have ridden for the sheer joy of sitting astride a horse. She would have turned up her face to the sun and closed her eyes as she thundered across the terrain.

But that was before a senseless accident. She didn't blame the horse, but neither could she go beyond the overwhelming terror that struck her at the mere thought of climbing back on one.

Even the smell of horseflesh was enough to bring back the horror of that day and the memory of pain and fear and then waking to a silent world.

It was little wonder her clan had thought she'd gone mad. It was likely true. In those first months, Eveline *had* been mad. She hadn't known how to cope with what had happened. She didn't understand it and she feared what others would do with the knowledge that she was defective.

Years later, it seemed silly, but how could she possibly have gone to her parents now, after so long, and tried to make them understand what was truly wrong? How could she even explain it?

She cocked her head to the side as a soft echo drifted through her ears. She looked around rapidly, trying to discern the source. She wanted more.

What she saw was each warrior in turn, down the line, throw up a fist and it looked as they were bellowing something loudly. Her ears tingled with the vibration, and she imagined she was hearing their cries. It was an almost, like reaching for something unreachable. Like touching a fingertip when trying to grasp a hand.

And then it died as quickly as it had caught her attention.

She bit her lips in frustration, wanting it to happen again. She lived for those moments when she could almost reach out and grasp sound. She didn't want to forget what it was like, and with each passing day, she feared it would slip away completely, never to return.

The cart bearing her picked up speed. The man astride the horse pulling her urged his mount onward. When they topped the rise, Eveline was able to see into the valley below and it took her breath away.

Armstrong Keep sat atop a rise and it overlooked sloping terrain on all sides. It was built into the side of a large hill, stone and earth put together seemingly and the keep jutting upward from the rise.

But the Montgomery stronghold was nestled between two mountains. A river ran alongside and looped around to meander through the back of their lands only to disappear in the distance, no doubt emptying into a loch.

The earth was green and lush, bursting with spring. Flowers dotted the hillsides. A herd of sheep grazed in the distance. Horses were also out to graze on the opposite side. Three rows of cottages were perched at the base of a steep incline outside the walls of the keep. They staggered upward, eight in each row.

As her gaze scanned the massive holding, she saw more cottages, a few alongside the river where it paralleled the keep. Beyond that and up the opposing hill were more cottages, more haphazardly arranged and not as ordered as the first ones she'd viewed.

The keep itself was well built. She could see no flaws, no sign of disrepair. A stone wall surrounded the keep with a gate in front that boasted two guard towers. The gate was made of immense logs, and Eveline imagined it took the efforts of several men for it to swing open and shut.

Beyond the gate, the keep shot upward, almost a perfect square, but tall. Eveline calculated it would take at least four flights of stairs to reach the top.

It was a holding built with defense in mind. It would take a massive army to infiltrate and beat down Montgomery forces to gain entry into the keep. The only force of such strength, aside from the king's own, was her own clan.

And now they'd been forced to sign a truce neither wanted, and Eveline wondered, feeling guilty for her disloyalty, if either side would honor the agreement in the long term.

The cart rattled its way down the incline, and as they drew near to the keep, the great wooden gate slowly began to open.

Graeme rode ahead, followed closely by his brothers. The cart bearing her was next, and then the Montgomery warriors fell in behind her as they rode into the spacious courtyard.

The cart ground to a halt. Ahead of her, Graeme dismounted, and then he came to help her down. She stumbled slightly as she tried to gain her footing. After sitting in the cart for so long, her legs were as shaky as a newborn colt's.

Gradually, she became aware of all the stares directed at her. Everywhere she turned, there was someone, lots of someones, avidly gazing at her.

Most weren't friendly looks. Indeed, the majority of them were openly hostile. Lips curled. Eyes flashed. Grimaces. Expressions of distaste.

She paused on one person long enough to see the words "Armstrong bitch" on her lips. Eveline's gaze narrowed and she quickly committed the woman's face to memory. She would not forget such a slight.

Graeme was talking to the assembled group of Montgomery clansmen. He had his arm loosely over her shoulders. She'd realized too late that he was addressing his clan and turned too late to know what it was he said.

Whatever it was, it didn't sit well with most, because the expressions grew even more disgruntled, and she caught several more disparaging remarks as they formed on the lips of the people gathered.

She'd never felt so alone and terrified in her life. This wasn't just a hostile welcome. It was no welcome at all. Her skin prickled under such close scrutiny. She felt picked apart, judged and deemed unworthy.

Automatically her chin went up in silent rebellion. She wouldn't allow these people to make her feel inferior nor would they frighten her. She was a laird's daughter. One of the mightiest in the whole of Scotland. She would be cowed by no Montgomery. She wouldn't shame the Armstrongs by appearing weak before this clan.

Graeme led her toward the entrance to the keep. They walked by several of the women of the clan, and not one of them offered so much as a smile in Eveline's direction.

Eveline kept her gaze trained forward, not wanting to see what it was they had to say. She'd already seen quite enough to know her presence was reviled.

The hall was bigger than the Armstrong's great hall. The room was sprawling, with two great stone fireplaces, one on either end. There was a raised dais with a table that could easily seat a dozen people. Scattered over the rest of the room were several other tables, signaling that many ate within the keep.

In front of the other fireplace was more of a sitting area. There were several chairs and a few rests for propping up one's feet. It was clearly a place of leisure.

This was where Graeme led her. He plunked her down into one of the softer chairs that was to the side of the burning fire. She studied him closely, fearful of losing any directive he may give her.

"Would you like food and drink?"

She was hungry, but the idea of putting anything into her stomach was enough to make her insides twist in protest. She was too nervous to eat.

"If you'll wait here but a moment, I'll return and show you to your chambers. I'll arrange to have all your belongings brought up and unpacked for you."

She didn't even have time to nod her understanding before he turned away and disappeared from the hall.

She sat, unmoving, afraid to breathe lest she call more attention to herself. Montgomerys filtered in and out of the hall, obviously with the intent of seeing the new addition to the clan.

Not one friendly face did she find. Nothing to reassure her or offer her comfort. The sorrow of leaving her home and clan was never more keenly felt than in this moment.

She was truly alone and locked in a silent world where people thought her nothing more than the mad daughter of their most hated foe.

A moment later, Graeme returned, and he came to where she sat and offered his hand down to her. Puzzled, she slid her fingers into his and allowed him to assist her to her feet.

He was saying something, but he turned away and

started guiding her across the room. It frustrated her to not be able to see what it was he said.

She tried to quicken her step so she could move ahead of him just enough that she could glance back, but she wasn't able to keep pace with him.

He held out his arm when they reached the stairs, gesturing for her to go ahead of him. Reluctantly, she climbed the steps, and when they reached the landing of the next level, he guided her out instead of having her continue up the stairs.

There were several chambers down the hallway. Toward the end, he stopped, opened a door, and gestured her in.

It was a small chamber, but not tiny. There were two windows, which told her that it was a corner room because there was one on either side. Heavy furs were pulled away from one while they covered the other, secured by leather ties to prevent the wind from flapping the ends.

Sunlight poured into the room, illuminating it without need for the candles that lit the hallway. There was a bed against the far wall, a washbasin, and a chair by the small fireplace. Other than that, the room wasn't furnished at all. It was apparent no one stayed here, except perhaps in the capacity of a guest.

She turned to Graeme, confused as to why he would show her into this chamber. He gestured around and then said, "I'll have your trunks brought up and provide someone to help you unpack and settle in. Perhaps it's best if you rest before this evening's meal."

She stared back in surprise, then glanced once more at the room where they stood. This was to be her room? She frowned, not knowing what to make of this. Graeme was her husband. He should share his chamber with her. It was the way of things. Her father and mother had shared a chamber as far back as Eveline could remember. Indeed, her father would object most strongly to his wife sleeping anywhere else.

Was she to be relegated to a position of guest? An unwanted guest, from the appearance of things.

Graeme backed from the room, leaving her alone to frown as she pondered the situation. Nay, this would not do. It would not do at all.

A wife's place was with her husband. Not shoved into a guest room along with all her belongings. There must be a way to remedy this situation at once.

CHAPTER 12

Graeme went in search of Rorie. He hadn't seen her in the courtyard, and it wasn't like her not to greet him and their brothers after an absence.

He found her, predictably, in the antechamber he used as his accounting room. Where he kept correspondences, returned them, kept ledgers and records of clan business as well as the births and deaths of all Montgomerys under his care.

His da had been meticulous about such things and had insisted that Graeme learn to read and write at a young age. At a time when most boys were being fostered and were learning the art of war, Graeme had been putting in long hours by candlelight memorizing the alphabet and reading accounts kept by his father.

Robert Montgomery had insisted that the mind first had to be shaped and molded in order to be a good warrior and adept physically and that an intelligent warrior would win out over an ignorant one every time.

Graeme wasn't certain he agreed, but then he hadn't any choice in the matter.

Rorie, on the other hand, was determined to learn to read and write and pored over every piece of writing she could lay hands to in an effort to teach herself.

She'd always been an odd little thing, but she was pure Montgomery, and Graeme loved her dearly.

"Still determined to take over as laird one day?" Graeme drawled from the door.

Rorie jerked her head up guiltily and hastily covered the scroll she'd been staring at with such concentration.

"Why weren't you out to greet us?" he asked in a quieter voice.

She sighed. "There seemed little point. You brought home the wee daft Armstrong girl. It's hardly a reason to celebrate, is it?"

Graeme frowned. "When did you become so uncharitable, Rorie? It isn't like you to cast judgment before you've even met someone."

Rorie gave him a look that suggested he was an idiot. "She's an Armstrong, Graeme. What else is there to know? And before you lecture me on being judgmental, do I need to remind you that since birth we've been taught to hate the Armstrong name and anyone who bears it?"

He gave a long-suffering sigh. "She isn't just any Armstrong, Rorie. She's my wife and she's now a Montgomery. I expect you to accord her respect. I'd like . . . I'd like you to seek her out and be nice to her. She's up in her chamber now, likely frightened and alone. Her reception was not kindly. I don't know how much she understood, but even a complete simpleton would realize how hostile the clan was toward her. I need you for this."

Rorie's expression became thoughtful. "How daft is she, Graeme? Really. Were the rumors exaggerated?"

He ran a hand through his hair and blew out his breath. "I don't know. I have much to learn of her. At times she seems . . . distant. Unaware. But I was able to communicate with her. She has a fascination with me talking to her. Which is apparently uncommon, because her mother was flabbergasted over Eveline's response to me. I have to think that all is not as it seems, but as of yet, I've not had time to determine the whole of it."

Rorie crossed her arms over her chest and then sent Graeme a look he'd long ago associated with absolute scheming. She may not like blood or violence, but she had a mind worthy of any bloodthirsty warrior. She always went for the kill, even if it was figurative. "How much is my niceness worth to you?"

Graeme had to clear his throat to keep from outright laughing. The lass had audacity and yet he'd never been able to bring himself to chasten her. She'd been allowed to run wild, no doubt about it.

Raised without a mother figure, Rorie likely spent most of her childhood believing she was a lad.

"What do you want, you little chit," Graeme said in amusement.

"I want a tutor. A real one, Graeme. I want to learn to read and write."

Her chin came up a notch, and she boldly stared him down.

"And where do you propose for me to find this tutor?"

"Father Drummond."

"Rorie, he's a man of God, and he has duties to more than one clan. I can't appropriate him for your own personal gain."

"It seems to me that as you aren't entirely certain of the faculties of your new wife, it would behoove you to have a man of God bless your union and furthermore convince your clan that your bride isn't marked by the devil. In his free time, of course, he could instruct me."

Graeme had to laugh then. The little schemer. What galled him was that she had a very solid point and having the father's blessing on the marriage as well as calming his clan's fears and superstitions could go a long way in ensuring Eveline's well-being and happiness.

"All right, Rorie. I'll send word to the father. You, however, I want to show Eveline every kindness. She's a sweet lass and I think you'll like her. She's just . . . different."

"I've never known you to be so diplomatic," she said dryly.

He pointed out the door. "Just go, you little imp. Before I put my boot to your arse."

She grinned and hurried past him, her hand covering her behind as she fled.

Rorie hesitated outside of Eveline's closed door. As much as she was loath to admit it, she was nervous about the impending meeting with her sister by marriage.

On the one hand, having a sister was an interesting thought. Having a crazed sister was not, however, appealing.

She rested her palm against the wood for a long moment, then sucked in her breath and knocked. She waited, growing more nervous by the moment. When she received no response, she knocked again. Only to wait several long seconds.

She stuck her ear to the door, frowning. There were odd sounds emanating from within. Scraping? As if something was being dragged across the floor. And the sound was growing louder until suddenly the door flew open and Rorie found herself face-to-face with a blond-haired woman barely larger than herself.

Eveline jumped, obviously startled by Rorie's presence. Her face was red with exertion and her hair was in disarray. As Rorie glanced down, she saw that Eveline had dragged one of her trunks toward the door and indeed, it appeared as though she was planning to shove it out of the room all together.

"I'm Rorie," she said, unsure of what she was supposed to do. "I'm Graeme's sister."

Eveline stared at Rorie, studying her intently until Rorie squirmed. There was something intelligent and discerning about her gaze, almost as if she were judging Rorie, and it made her distinctly uncomfortable.

Eveline was the intruder here, not Rorie. Rorie belonged and Eveline was the outsider. The enemy.

Then, to her further bewilderment, Eveline reached out and grabbed Rorie's hand and pulled her downward, motioning toward the trunk.

"Uhhh, Eveline? What do you intend to do with the trunk?" Rorie asked.

Eveline paused and frowned. Then she stood to her full height—not that it was much—and peered out of the chamber and down the hall.

Her expression grew more perplexed, and then she abruptly left Rorie and walked across the hall and opened Bowen's door.

"Hey! You can't just barge into my brother's room like that," Rorie protested.

Eveline stuck her head in, then withdrew and turned to Rorie, her brows drawn together in a deep furrow. She licked her lips almost as if she wanted to speak, but Rorie knew that was impossible. Graeme had said she was mute and had been ever since her accident.

Then she pointed to the open chamber door and raised her palms in question.

Rorie shook her head, confused.

Eveline pointed to Rorie and then back at the chamber and then once again raised her palms.

Understanding finally, Rorie shook her head. "Nay, it's not my chamber. 'Tis Bowen's."

Once more, Eveline grabbed Rorie's hand and fairly dragged her down the hallway to the next chamber. She slapped her palm against the door and then turned to Rorie, that same question in her eyes.

By now, Rorie understood what it was she wanted.

" 'Tis my chamber," Rorie said.

Eveline frowned in displeasure and once more, Rorie found herself dragged to the next chamber. By now she had figured out the point of all this and she was tired of being hauled around by a woman only slightly larger than herself, so she extricated her hand from Eveline's hold and then took Eveline's hand herself so she could direct the movement.

She took Eveline down the hall, pointing at each of the chambers and saying whose it was or what purpose it served. Eveline seemed to grow more frustrated with each one.

Understanding smacked Rorie in the face. "You're looking for Graeme's chamber, aren't you?"

Eveline smiled and nodded vigorously. For a moment, Rorie was spellbound by the change the smile brought to the young woman's face. She was quite beautiful and not all daft looking. No crazed look in her eyes, even if her behavior bordered on unusual. Or maybe a lot unusual . . .

Then Rorie's eyes narrowed. "Why?"

Eveline's smile turned into a quick frown, and then Rorie found herself hauled right back down the hall to Eveline's chamber. There, Eveline pointed at the trunk and then made an away motion as if she were pushing the trunk down the hall.

Then she jutted out her chin, pointed inward to her chamber and shook her head mutinously as she crossed her arms over her chest.

Rorie burst out laughing. Her sister-in-law wasn't happy over her accommodations and she wanted to move into Graeme's chamber. She should be loyal and sternly inform her brother's new bride that if Graeme had wanted her in his chamber, he would have put her there. But the devil on her shoulder told her it could be quite fun to aid Eveline in her endeavor and give Graeme a shock when he retired later.

"All right, I'll help you," Rorie said, still smiling.

Eveline beamed back at her and then bent to grasp the handle of the trunk. Rorie bent down as well, and they slid it out of the doorway and into the hall.

Rorie pointed toward the end. "Graeme's chamber is all the way down. We'll need to hurry if we're to move all your belongings before someone finds us."

CHAPTER 13

Graeme paused outside of Eveline's door, indecision wreaking havoc with his mind. Guilt plagued him because after dumping her in her chamber, he hadn't come back for her. Hadn't checked to see if she'd settled in. He hadn't even assigned a lady's maid to aid her in unpacking her trunks.

The truth was, he wasn't at all sure who he could trust with the task because everywhere he turned, he was treated to overt hostility over an Armstrong taking up residence at Montgomery Keep.

It was time for her to come down for dinner. He wasn't at all certain he should set her among her new clan so soon, but waiting would only prolong the agony. Better to have done with it quickly and then set to work on making her fit in with his kin.

How he was going to accomplish that, he had no idea.

He knocked softly and waited, not wanting to intrude on her privacy even though he had every right as her husband to do as he wished. It wasn't his intention to set her against him or to make her fear him. In fact, the thought was repugnant to him.

After a moment, he frowned when she didn't respond to the summons. He pushed open the door only to find the room completely dark. He took one of the candles from the wall sconce and walked into Eveline's room and to his further surprise, the room was bare.

No trunks. None of her things. It was as pristine as it had been before he'd delivered her to the chamber just hours before.

For a moment he wondered if he'd given her the wrong room, but even he wasn't that absentminded. He retreated quickly and then strode down the hall, throwing open doors left and right.

When he got to his own, he nearly didn't go in, but then thought better of it and opened his door. If he was to find her, he needed to cover every inch of the keep. He certainly would have known if she'd made an appearance below stairs.

This wasn't what he had in mind for his first day of wedded bliss. A missing wife who may or may not be in full control of her faculties.

He almost missed her when he pushed inside his chamber and hastily scanned the room. But he certainly didn't miss the fact that his chamber now housed all the trunks that had accompanied her to Montgomery Keep. They were also unpacked and her things covered most of the available surfaces in his chamber.

Most notably, she was curled into a small ball on the far side of his bed, the side closest to the wall, and from all appearances she was fast asleep.

He blew out his breath, raised his hands and then let them fall to his sides in exasperation. She was everywhere in his chamber. Her belongings. Even her smell. Trunks. Clothing. And then there was the fact that she was in his bed. Where he had to sleep.

She hadn't even eaten, and she had to be starving. He'd yanked her from her home the moment the vows were recited, and she hadn't eaten when they'd arrived here. The lass was slight enough as it was. She certainly didn't need to be missing any meals.

And yet he didn't want to disturb her sleep. She hadn't so much as stirred, and he hadn't been quiet when he'd come into the chamber. The day had likely exhausted her.

Still he crept closer to the bed and leaned over to peer down at her. It was ridiculous that he was tiptoeing around his own chamber out of deference to a wife who'd taken it upon herself to move herself into his private quarters.

She looked angelic in sleep, dark lashes resting against pale cheeks. Her blond hair was tousled and in disarray and spread out. Over his pillow. He frowned. She'd even stolen his pillow.

She was dressed in a white linen plain shift that modestly covered all the necessary parts. All that he could see was her face and one bare arm that rested down her side. The other was tucked beneath her as she faced the wall.

If he woke her, she'd have to dress to come below stairs and by the time she made an appearance, the meal would be over with anyway. He'd just make certain that there would be food available to her as soon as she woke in the morning.

He lingered for another long moment, staring down at the soft rise and fall of her chest. And then he glanced around once more at all the things that now occupied his chamber. Or rather *their* chamber, since it appeared she'd laid claim to his.

He turned away, gripping his nape and rubbing it as he quietly retreated. He had no idea what to do in this matter. He couldn't very well pursue a normal marriage with her. Their marriage couldn't even be consummated.

And yet there she was in his bed, on his pillow, sound asleep as if she fully expected she should be there.

He walked down the stairs and into the hall where the serving women were busy putting food out on the tables. He took a seat at the end where he always sat, Teague on his left and Bowen on his right. Rorie sat on Bowen's other side, and suspiciously, she wouldn't look up to greet him as he sat.

"Know you anything about how Eveline was able to move all her trunks into my chamber?" he asked mildly as he stared down at Rorie. "Or for that matter, how she knew which chamber was mine?"

Rorie's face colored and she stared down, suddenly very fascinated with her food.

"What do you speak of?" Bowen demanded. "The lass moved into your chamber?"

Teague's eyebrows went up. "What's her intention?"

"As she was asleep when I went up, I could hardly ask her," Graeme said dryly. "I'm more interested in how she wound up there."

Rorie huffed. "I helped her."

Graeme's eyes narrowed. "Was it her idea or yours? Is this some trick you're playing?"

"You asked me to be nice to her," she said pointedly. "I went up to her chamber and was met at the door by her pulling—or rather *trying* to pull—her trunks into the hall. She then dragged me down the hall, wanting to know which room was yours."

Graeme held up his hand. "Wait a minute. She asked you this? How do you know this is what she wanted?"

"Of course not. She doesn't speak. You told me as much, and she never uttered a single word. But she certainly has a way of making her point understood."

Graeme couldn't deny that.

"So she just dragged you down the hallway and you surmised that she wanted to know the way to Graeme's chamber?" Teague asked incredulously.

Rorie glared at her brother. "I don't expect you to understand, but trust me, if you'd been there, you would have known what she wanted. And the moment I showed her which chamber was Graeme's, she dragged me back down the hall to her chamber and wanted my help in moving all of her belongings."

Graeme let out a deep sigh. "Who knows what was going on in the lass's head."

"She didn't seem happy with your choice of rooms," Rorie said, her lips twitching as she glanced up at Graeme. "In fact, I think she took insult that you didn't install her in your chamber from the beginning."

Bowen shook his head. "The poor lass is . . ." He broke off and tapped his temple with his finger several times to signify his thoughts of her mental capacity.

Graeme scowled in his direction. "I have yet to determine just how off she is. I have a suspicion that all is not as it seems. Regardless of how touched she is or isn't, I expect you all to treat her with respect and kindness. She is no threat to us. She cannot help her parentage. None of us wanted this alliance, but here we are anyway. We should make the best of a bad situation."

Teague's lip curled. "Blood agreement or not, I do not consider any Armstrong an alliance. 'Tis just words on parchment that have no meaning. Saying I will not attack is not the same as saying they are a trusted ally."

"Agreed," Graeme said through his teeth. "I don't think anyone has suggested such. What I need and want from the three of you is understanding and patience. It won't cause you great harm to be kind to the lass. She doesn't deserve to be treated as a leper by our clan."

"You cannot control what the clan thinks," Bowen said.

Graeme's patience was thinning. "Nay, I can't, but you can lead by example. Our clan's acceptance of her won't happen overnight, but you can aid me by not treating her with the same disdain as the rest of our kin.

In time, perhaps she can make a place for herself here. Think of how she must feel. She's been taken from the sanctuary of her home where she's surrounded by people who love and protect her, and she's been thrust into a hostile world where she likely fears for her life, especially given how she is viewed by others."

He swept his gaze from Bowen to Teague and then back to Bowen. "Imagine if it was Rorie taken from us, as I tried to make you see when we were at the Armstrong Keep. Would you not want her to be treated decently and kindly when we were not there to see to her protection?"

"I won't be taken away, will I?" Rorie asked sharply.

Graeme cursed under his breath at the sudden fear in her eyes.

"Damn it, Graeme," Teague snarled. "'Twas a stupid thing for you to say."

"Nay, sweeting," Graeme said. "'Twas just an example. Your place is here with us and that won't change."

"But it could," Rorie persisted. "I'm sure Eveline's family told her the exact same things you're telling me. They likely offered her the same reassurances, but who's to say that our king won't be offering me up on the sacrificial plate?"

"If he was going to do so, he would have already done it," Bowen said in a soothing voice. "The king has already asked us for too much. Even he won't press us this far."

Graeme wasn't as certain, and he didn't think Bowen and Teague were either, but they wouldn't say anything otherwise in front of Rorie.

"I'd prefer to discuss your attitudes toward Eveline," Graeme said, directing the conversation back to the matter at hand. "I want your promise that you'll ease her transition and show her a friendly face among many hostile ones."

"Very well," Teague said grudgingly.

"I like her," Rorie piped up.

All three of her brothers turned to her in surprise. She'd said nothing until now about her judgment of Eveline. She'd only given an account as to what had happened earlier.

Rorie shrugged. "There's just something about her. She seems . . . determined. I expected to find her cowering in a corner or facedown on her bed in tears. Instead, I found her dragging trunks into the hall and demanding I tell her where Graeme's chamber was. I found it all rather amusing."

Then she turned her gaze on Graeme. "I know not whether she's afflicted or daft or whatever it is that's said about her. I only know that she's courageous. And whether she speaks or doesn't has little to do with the fact that she can communicate because she made it very clear what she wanted—nay, demanded—from me."

"And if she's not daft, then what the hell is she?" Graeme murmured.

CHAPTER 14

Graeme awoke to a female body snuggled up tight against his side. Eveline's arm was draped over his chest and she was tucked securely underneath his shoulder.

For a moment he didn't even breathe. God's teeth, but this was awkward. The night before, he'd eased onto his bed after warring with himself about whether to even sleep in his own chamber. He'd positioned himself on the very edge so there was plenty of space between him and Eveline, who at the time was scooted all the way over against the wall.

But now? She'd gravitated across the bed and was flush against him. Perhaps she'd grown cold during the night and sought out his heat.

He ground his teeth when his morning erection went more rigid than was normal. Guilt plagued him, no matter that it was a normal male response to having a woman's body pressed against his. He had no business thinking of her in that way. Surely it was a sin.

The dilemma that presented itself was how was he to extricate himself from her hold without waking her and causing even more awkwardness? The last thing he wanted was for her to come to sudden awareness and be terrified.

After pondering the matter for another long moment, he slowly inched his way toward the edge of the bed, lifting her arm just enough that he could move away.

He held his breath when she stirred, but then she rolled to her other side. Sighing in relief, he rose and dressed hurriedly so she wouldn't awaken while he was still here.

Just as he was about to leave, he turned suddenly, staring at the bare hearth. She'd moved against him during the night, likely because she was cold. There was a distinct chill to the morning and she'd awaken to chattering teeth.

He maneuvered his way across the chamber, shoving aside one of her trunks and being mindful not to knock her things from where they were draped across his chair and one of the benches. Gathering wood from the floor where it was stacked next to the hearth, he laid a fire and used one of the half burned candles to put flame to wood.

Soon a healthy fire licked over the logs and warmth began emanating from the hearth. At least she could dress by the fire without turning blue.

Satisfied that he'd done his duty, he left the chamber to go in search of Rorie. He checked her chamber first, but knew she was likely already below stairs either breaking her fast or in their father's accounting room trying to teach herself to read.

He shook his head. Not a pursuit he'd normally encourage, but it seemed to mean a lot to her, though he wasn't certain why. He didn't see the harm in having Father Drummond instruct her if it was what would make her truly happy. And he wasn't above using it as a measure to keep her agreeable to his demands when it came to Eveline.

As it was, she was at the table bickering with Teague—a normal event on any day.

Graeme took his seat and rolled his eyes when his siblings didn't even pause long enough in their argument to acknowledge his presence. He cleared his throat and when that got no response, he banged his fist down on the table.

Teague and Rorie jerked their heads in Graeme's direction.

"Where is Bowen?" he asked calmly.

Rorie shrugged. "He's already broken his fast. He said he'd be out with the men."

Graeme held silent while he was given his trencher of food, and when the serving woman moved away, he directed his gaze back on Rorie.

"I'd like for you to go up after Eveline. Make sure she has something to eat. She didn't eat for most of yesterday, so she'll likely be hungry. I'd also like for you to keep her company and perhaps offer your assistance in putting away her belongings."

Rorie wrinkled her nose. "So you're allowing her to stay in your chamber?"

Graeme frowned. " 'Tis none of your affair. However, I see no reason to toss her right back out, at least until she's more settled and comfortable in her surroundings. Who knows what odd ideas she may have formed or why she refused to remain in her own chamber. For now, I want her to be at ease, and if remaining in my chamber accomplishes that, then I can survive a few days."

Rorie turned and gave Teague an impish smile. "I believe I won our wager."

Teague scowled and then shot Graeme a disgusted look.

"And what was this wager?" Graeme demanded.

"Teague wagered that you'd toss Eveline from your chamber come morn. I knew you wouldn't," she said smugly.

He sent them both dark looks. "I'm so happy to have provided you both with entertainment."

"'Tis your bed to lie in now that you've made it," Teague said.

"'Tis none of your concern," Graeme said in an icy voice.

Teague rose, irritation etched on his face. "I'll be in the courtyard sparring if you decide to find your missing cods and come join us."

Graeme decided on the spot that his first session would be with Teague and he'd teach his younger brother a lesson about respect.

Eveline woke and for a moment had no recollection of where she was. She wasn't in her own chamber in her own bed. None of the smells were familiar. It took her a moment to clear the cobwebs from her mind and remember that she was married and was lying in her new husband's bed in his chamber—a room she'd invaded without gaining his permission.

But he hadn't awakened her to throw her out, so perhaps he wasn't angry over it.

The fact of the matter was, she'd felt desperately alone and isolated in the chamber he'd given her. And while he might be her clan's enemy, he'd been kind to her—the only Montgomery who'd been remotely gentle with her.

She frowned. That wasn't entirely true. Rorie had been helpful, though Eveline wasn't certain what Graeme's sister's motives had been. There'd been mischief in her eyes when she'd agreed to help Eveline move her belongings.

As she shoved the covers aside, a cool draft fell over her and she shivered. But as she turned, warmth greeted her and she realized that a fire had been started in the hearth.

Judging by the height and blaze of the flames, the fire

hadn't been started very long ago. Graeme must have had someone light it for her so she wouldn't be cold when she rose.

A man who'd show that kind of consideration to his enemy's daughter couldn't be all bad, could he?

Nothing she'd seen thus far told her that she was in any danger with Graeme Montgomery. He wasn't happy about the arrangement—who could blame him? But he hadn't misused her or shown her ill treatment. Not yet.

Never before would she have considered that a Montgomery could be noble and just, but Graeme seemed destined to change her opinion on that matter.

She wandered closer to the hearth and stuck out her hands to warm her cold fingertips. Once sufficiently baked, she turned to find suitable clothing for the day.

At home, she wouldn't have given the matter much thought. Here, she was suddenly fretting over whether she should leave her hair down or braid it and whether she should wear her plain, simple dress or one prettier. What would Graeme expect of his wife?

She frowned when she realized she had no idea what his expectations were. He didn't seem to have any, other than to put her away and perhaps go on with his normal activities. Perhaps that was why he'd arranged for her to have a separate chamber.

She opted for something plain. The last thing she wanted was for the Montgomery clansmen to think she was uppity and putting on airs. She'd noted the dress of the other women of the keep, and most wore very basic work apparel.

After dressing, she began brushing her hair. It was a chore because the long ride to the Montgomery holding had resulted in having windblown hair and she hadn't brushed it before going to sleep the night before.

She worked the knots from the strands and then began to braid it by pulling it over her shoulder. She perched on the bench closest to the fire as she worked on her hair, but a moment later, she felt the presence of someone else.

Her skin prickled in awareness and she hastily glanced up to see Rorie in the doorway. She smiled, not knowing if Rorie had already said anything to her. Then she motioned her forward.

In that moment, she was intensely glad to see the other lass. The isolation of Graeme's chamber was overwhelming and yet she lacked the courage to go below stairs on her own. The looks from Graeme's kin were still fresh in her mind.

"Good morn, Eveline," Rorie said.

She smiled hesitantly at Eveline as she spoke, and Eveline smiled back, wanting to encourage any conversation Rorie might strike up.

"So, are you planning to stay above stairs all day?" Rorie asked.

Eveline frowned, uncertain of the point of the question.

"Graeme thought you might be hungry. You had little to eat yesterday."

Eveline gave a slight nod.

Rorie's eyes gleamed as she seated herself in the chair opposite the bench Eveline was perched on.

"The women are wagering whether or not you'll be brave enough to show your face outside of your chamber."

Eveline blinked in surprise, and then her brows came together as she stared back at Rorie. What was Rorie's purpose? Was she trying to anger Eveline? Upset her? Remind her of her tenuous position in her new clan?

"I'm sure they wouldn't expect you to boldly march down and demand something to eat," Rorie continued on, seemingly unbothered by Eveline's reaction. "It might be amusing to see the expressions of their faces were you to do so."

Eveline's lips twitched, and then they rose upward in a smile. Rorie was obviously a mischievous sort. It was likely why she'd aided Eveline yesterday in moving her belongings to Graeme's chamber.

Then she simply nodded once.

Rorie grinned. "Then come on. No sense hiding away up here when there's mischief to be had below."

Eveline hastily tied the end of her braid with a leather strip and rose to follow Rorie from the room.

When they entered the hall, the women were clearing away the remnants of the morning meal. Two were sweeping the floors while others pushed away the furs over the windows to allow the light and warmth from the sun inside.

Everything came to an abrupt halt the moment Eveline was spotted. Rorie continued forward and Eveline followed. Rorie said something that the women had no liking for. One scowled openly at Eveline and said, "If she's wanting to eat, then she should be about when the rest of the keep is."

Eveline stared back, refusing to be cowed by this unpleasant woman.

Rorie motioned the woman away and then turned back to Eveline. "Come and sit so you can eat."

Eveline glanced at the tables and then up to the high table on the dais, much like the one back home. Her eyes narrowed, and then she marched forward. She was the chieftain's wife and she would sit at the high table.

She made sure she sat on the side where she could face the rest of the room. She wanted to be able to see what was being said. Rorie settled across from her, a wide grin on her face.

"I like your spirit. Bold move. But a good idea. Show them early on that they can't bully you. The women of our clan can be quite headstrong. They're loyal, mind you, but they're rather fierce in their opinions. 'Tis often said that Graeme is laird, but the women run the keep."

Eveline's eyebrows arched upward. Surely Rorie was jesting.

"Not that Graeme would ever admit such a thing," Rorie added, still grinning. "But they're an intimidating lot. Some like me, and some don't."

Eveline studied Rorie for a long moment. Here, too, was a lass who was likely underestimated. She had a frail, almost boyish appearance and yet she was impudent and struck Eveline as someone who was extremely quick-witted and intelligent.

Then she glanced over Rorie's shoulder because she could see the women conversing. One holding a broom was only making a pretense of sweeping as she spoke with one of the women who'd been clearing a table.

It was hard for Eveline to follow, but she caught enough of the words to know she was the topic of conversation. The usual words were thrown about. Daft. Addled. Touched. She winced when she saw "stupid," "arrogant," and "Armstrong trash" added to the mix.

Anger tightened her jaw. Her first instinct was to defend herself, which was absurd given the fact that she'd spent the last three years allowing people to think of her what they liked, and she'd done nothing at all to correct their assumptions. Beliefs that she'd purposely fed.

But it hurt more coming from these people. They didn't know her. They judged her solely on the fact that she was an Armstrong. Her clan was worth ten of them and the women of her keep weren't as lazy.

The woman who'd sniped at Eveline about eating sooner stalked toward the table and rudely plunked down Eveline's serving of bread and cheese. She shot Eveline a disgruntled look and then turned and walked away. The woman hadn't brought anything for Eveline to drink, and Eveline wasn't going to risk a confrontation over it. She could make do without.

Eveline nibbled at the bread. It was quite good and someone had taken the effort to warm it a bit or perhaps it had been stored close to a heat source in the kitchen. At any rate, it was soft and tasted wonderful.

"Would you like a tour of the keep after you've eaten?" Rorie asked.

Eveline pursed her lips in thought, suddenly nervous about taking that direct an approach. It had consumed most of her courage just to come down to the hall to eat.

"Not scared, are you?" Rorie said with that gleam in her eye.

Eveline frowned and curled her lip, letting Rorie know what she thought of her baiting. But it had the effect Rorie obviously wanted because there was no way Eveline would refuse now. She wasn't going to let a bunch of Montgomerys back her down and force her into hiding.

She was a chieftain's daughter and now a chieftain's wife. That counted for something, didn't it? She may not be a mighty warrior, but one thing she'd learned after observing her mother, was that if anything could fell a warrior, it was a determined woman.

Rorie sent her a satisfied smile and then sat back to wait as Eveline finished eating.

When Eveline was done she sent a pointed glance at Rorie and then rose, taking the initiative and stepping around the table, past Rorie, so she was in the lead and not cowering behind her sister-in-law.

Chin up, she walked down the middle of the hall, boldly meeting the stares of the other women as she passed. At the end, a dark-haired woman stepped into her path, and Eveline had to pull up short to keep from plowing into her.

The woman was pretty enough. Younger perhaps than

the other women who'd been working in the hall. Her green eyes would be pretty if they weren't full of cold malice. She eyed Eveline with open hostility, her nostrils flaring almost as if she were challenging Eveline.

"Armstrong bitch."

The words were formed on the woman's lips with such clarity that there was no possibility of Eveline mistaking them. The woman's daring took Eveline aback and she stared agape.

Rorie pushed in front of Eveline before Eveline could react. She was turned just enough that Eveline could see what she said.

"The only bitch here is you, Kierstan," Rorie said, her features drawn tight with anger. "Back off or I'll tell Graeme that you're maligning his wife."

Kierstan's face twisted in disgust, but she turned and walked away, leaving Rorie and Eveline standing there. Rorie turned to Eveline and smiled.

"There now. That's out of the way. Shall we proceed with the tour?"

CHAPTER 15

Graeme was aware that Rorie was taking Eveline around the keep because he'd been told by no fewer than a dozen clansmen. They acted as though he should lock Eveline in his chamber and keep her there at all times.

He understood their hatred for the Armstrongs because it was a hatred he shared. But he didn't understand their willingness to extend that hatred to an innocent woman. He couldn't say he was surprised by it, but he didn't understand it.

By the time the next person happened along to inform Graeme that his Armstrong wife was walking around Montgomery land as if she belonged, Graeme's patience was wearing thin.

"She does belong," he roared, startling the older man with the force of his bellow.

He turned in a half circle so that everyone within hearing would know of his displeasure.

"'Tis enough! The king has decreed this marriage and there is naught to be done about it. Stop acting as sulky children and cease making an innocent woman suffer for something she has no knowledge of. You should all be shamed by your actions."

Bowen frowned from a short distance away where he was instructing a group of young lads in the use of bows and arrows. He shoved the fistful of arrows at one of the boys and then turned to walk in Graeme's direction.

"You can't ignore what this does to them," Bowen clipped out as he drew near. "You expect them to just accept it and forget all that has happened in the past, as you have done. You expect too much, Graeme."

Graeme faced his brother down, anger crawling up his neck. "You dare tell me that I've forgotten the past? You dare speak to me of what I should expect?"

With each word, his fury grew until he was a seething cauldron of rage. He took a step toward Bowen and met his brother's gaze unflinchingly.

"If you disagree with my handling of the situation, then perhaps you should challenge me for the title of chieftain."

Bowen's eyes widened. "'Tis not what I'm saying or doing at all!"

"You are either loyal to me and support me or you challenge me. 'Tis your choice," Graeme bit out.

"You know I support you," Bowen said in a quieter voice.

"Nay, I do not know. If you supported me, you would cede to my wishes regarding Eveline. You would not sit idly by while your clansmen disparage her. What would Da think, Bowen? Think you that he would condone the treatment of an innocent this way? He was a fair and just man. He'd never allow a Montgomery to be discourteous to Eveline regardless of her parentage."

Bowen had the grace to look abashed. "Aye, you're right, Graeme. I'm sorry. Da would have taken her under his wing and spit in the eye of anyone who had a single cross word for her."

He turned away and then gripped the back of his neck

with his hand. When he looked again at Graeme, there was clear frustration in his eyes.

"I'm just angry. We all are. We've no desire for peace with the Armstrongs. It would be just as well if we could rid the earth of their presence entirely. The king has turned us into women, effectively tying our hands, and he's saddled us with a constant reminder of all that we hate and all that we cannot do now."

Graeme let go of the tight irritation that bound his chest. "I know it well, Bowen. Think you I have any more liking for the situation than you do? Than any other member of my clan? The king has robbed me of vengeance for my father's death. 'Tis not something I let go of lightly. But I cannot bring myself to make a wee lass suffer when none of this was her doing. I must be fair and just because it's my duty as chieftain to be fair and just. How can I expect to be a leader to my clan when I mete out injustice on the innocent?"

"'Tis why you are the laird and I am not, nor do I ever wish to challenge your right to be laird," Bowen said in a somber voice. "You're much like Da. He would be proud. I don't have your sense of justice, because all that runs through my veins is hatred for those who brought suffering to our clan. And to me."

Before Graeme could respond, Bowen turned and walked away. He went past the group of lads who were awaiting instruction and continued until he was out of sight. He'd go riding as he was often wont to do. Of all the Montgomery sons, Bowen had been the closest to their father.

Graeme's relationship with Robert Montgomery had always been different. It had to be. He was Robert's heir and he had to learn his duties to his clan at a very young age. With Bowen, however, his father relaxed more. He was more patient with Bowen and they both loved horses. Graeme didn't resent their relationship. He accepted it as he accepted all else in his life. It simply was.

Bowen was more passionate. About everything. Every emotion was keenly felt. He'd been grief-stricken when their father had been killed, and it had taken Graeme and Teague forcibly restraining him to prevent him from attacking the Armstrongs on his own.

He'd vowed vengeance, and now that it had been taken from him, his instinct was to lash out. Unfortunately, Eveline was an easy target. She was an Armstrong. She stood for everything that Bowen most hated.

Graeme sighed and rubbed his forehead. What a complete mess the situation had become. The king's solution was no solution at all. It was a paltry bandage on a wound that needed sealing with a hot knife.

He ran his hand over his hair and down the back of his neck, turning sideways as he did. To his surprise, Eveline stood a short distance away, worry darkening her eyes. Had she heard the exchange? He glanced after his brother, cursing the fact that their disagreement had been aired so publicly.

Rorie appeared a moment later, lifting an eyebrow in Graeme's direction. "You and Bowen have a spat?"

Graeme was in no mood for Rorie's needling. "How much did you overhear? How much did *she* overhear?"

Rorie shook her head. "We only just arrived in time to see Bowen stalk away to go sulk."

"Enough with your insults," Graeme snapped.

Eveline frowned fiercely at him and then stepped in front of Rorie. She folded her arms over her chest and then glared harder at him.

Behind her Rorie laughed. "I do believe she's protecting me from you, Graeme."

"As if you bloody well need protecting," Graeme muttered. "'Tis I who need protection from your machinations."

Rorie stepped around Eveline and then took her hand, tugging her back toward the keep. "Come along, Eveline. We'll leave the laird to his brooding."

Graeme watched as Eveline followed behind Rorie and he was struck again by how lovely the lass was. Even when she was glaring him down, she was a sight to behold. All that blond hair shining in the sunlight, her eyes so blue that he could drown in them.

She was so lovely to look at that it hurt. She made his teeth ache over the waste. So young and beautiful and a tragedy had taken so much away from her. If after three years she wasn't yet normal, the chances were she'd never be normal again.

Running the gauntlet of women inside the keep again was the very last thing Eveline wanted to do. She'd already had to go through them twice since Rorie had begun showing her around the keep, and each time she'd read taunts on their lips. Cruel and insensitive remarks. And Kierstan was there at every turn, staring holes through Eveline, the word "bitch" on her lips as if that were the only word the woman knew how to speak.

It was enough to make Eveline want to bloody that mouth.

In her own home, she'd been content to let people think of her what they may. It was essential to her deception. But here? She had no reason to allow such a thing to go on. It wouldn't change her circumstances. It certainly hadn't protected her from marriage to Graeme. And it wasn't as if she'd ever be forced into marriage with Ian McHugh now that she was wed.

Any man would have been better than Ian. She'd marry the devil rather than to give herself to a man who'd made it clear how she would be treated under his "protection."

But . . . There always seemed to be a "but." It was the

problem with creating a web of lies and deceit. It spi-
raled out of control until it took on a life of its own, and
she was helpless to correct it. In too deep. She'd been
trapped by her own solution.

What if Graeme was furious that she wasn't daft? Not
so much that he would be angry she wasn't addled—
he'd likely be relieved over that—but he'd been kind and
gentle with her. If he didn't believe her to be "off,"
would he still afford her that same respect and understanding? Or would he allow himself to hate her because of who she was? And would he be furious over her
deception?

She braced herself as they stepped into the hall. Not as
many women were within as had been before. There
was no sign of Kierstan, to Eveline's relief. But the few
who were present halted their activities to turn and
stare.

This time Eveline made no effort to see what they
would say. She forced her gaze on Rorie's back and followed her into the narrow hallway on the other side of
the room. They ducked into a small chamber that was
filled with a musty odor.

Ledgers were stacked on a desk and only a small beam
of light shone through the furs covering the window.
Rorie pushed away the covering, allowing a wash of
sunlight in to illuminate the room.

Then she plunked herself in the chair and glanced up
at Eveline, looking quite pleased with herself.

Eveline cocked an eyebrow in question and then let
her gaze wander around the room. It was tiny, more a
cubbyhole than a true room. There was barely room to
fit the desk and all the stacks of scrolls and ledgers made
the room seem even smaller than it already was.

When she looked back at Rorie, Rorie was talking a
steady stream. Eveline frowned and tried to focus so she
could follow what the other girl was saying.

"... Da's room. But I intend it to be mine. Graeme has promised to send for Father Drummond so he can teach me to read and write. Then I can do the accounting for Graeme and he won't need to worry over the task himself."

Eveline's brow furrowed even more. It seemed an odd thing for a woman to want to do, but then she thought of what being able to read and write would mean for *her*. It would mean a way to communicate, provided the person she wanted to converse with could also read and write. Would such a thing be possible for her to learn, given her inability to hear?

She took another step toward the desk, her stance eager as she stared back at Rorie. Then she pointed to herself and then at the ledgers and scrolls. She cocked her head in clear question.

Rorie frowned a moment as she studied Eveline. Eveline repeated the motion this time, including Rorie so she'd understand what Eveline was asking.

"You want to learn to read and write as well?" Rorie looked astounded by the thought.

Eveline nodded vigorously.

Rorie's eyes narrowed suspiciously and she rose, planting her palms down on the aged wood. She leaned forward, her features drawn into a near scowl. Her eyes met Eveline's.

"Just how *daft* are you, Eveline Armstrong?"

CHAPTER 16

Eveline's lips tightened into a firm line. She wanted to look away, pretend she didn't understand, but if she did that, she risked Rorie seeing more than she already had.

And hadn't she decided that there was no more need for deception? Perhaps she could ease her way into this new life. Take a step at a time.

Eveline swallowed and then slowly shook her head.

"What? No, you aren't daft? No, you aren't normal? What are you shaking your head for?" Rorie demanded.

Eveline squared her shoulders, thrust her chin upward, and then stared boldly back at Rorie. She folded her arms over her chest and then firmly shook her head once more.

"You aren't daft."

Eveline shook her head again.

"Do you even know what I'm asking?"

Eveline nodded.

Rorie blew out her breath and then sank back into the chair, staring at Eveline with clear incredulity.

"Then why on God's green earth do you go around allowing people to think you're touched?"

Eveline held her hands wide apart and then spread them even farther.

Rorie arched up her eyebrows. "Long story?"

Eveline nodded vigorously.

"It's certainly one I'd like to hear."

Eveline frowned unhappily and folded her hands over her arms, leaving them crossed protectively over her chest.

"You're scared," Rorie said.

Eveline hesitated a moment and then gave one quick nod. She hated to admit to such a weakness, but how could she not be frightened? Everyone hated her here.

Rorie still studied her intently as if trying to reach into Eveline's mind and pluck out her thoughts, or at least see how sound it was.

"Not just here, though. At your home as well. You were afraid."

For a long moment Eveline stood there, not wanting to admit that yes, she'd been afraid in the one place she should have felt safest in.

"Eveline?" Rorie prompted.

Her gaze dropped momentarily, but she nodded one more time.

"Tell me this much," Rorie said as she leaned forward. "Have you pretended all this time? Ever since your accident? Wasn't it some years ago?"

Eveline shrugged. Who was to say. In those early days, she truly may have been mad. She didn't remember much. Her world had been in chaos as she'd tried to come to terms with all that had happened. She could understand why her clan had reached the assumption they had. She'd certainly acted like someone not in her right mind.

Rorie's eyes widened as if something had just occurred to her. "Can you speak?"

Eveline shook her head. It wasn't a lie. She had no way of knowing if she could any longer. She had no way to judge the sounds. No way to monitor how loud or soft she spoke. Her lips twitched in memory of how to form the words but she didn't give in to the urge.

"So you pretended to be daft because something frightened you and it was your way of hiding." Rorie rubbed her chin in a thoughtful manner and then cocked her head sideways at Eveline. "I don't know whether that makes you as daft as you're accused of being or if it makes you bloody brilliant. Whatever it was, must have really frightened you to make you go to such lengths."

Eveline's mouth trembled and she gripped her arms until her fingertips went white.

"I didn't mean to upset you," Rorie said. "I can see that whatever it was still frightens the very devil from you. Graeme should know of this, Eveline. He would protect you. He's an honorable man."

Eveline swallowed and then shook her head. She put her hand over her chest and then made a patting motion. Then she put her fingers to her mouth and back again to her chest.

"And how, pray tell, will you tell him?" Rorie asked.

Eveline held out her hand, palm up in Rorie's direction and stared pointedly.

"I'll concede that point. You did manage to tell me, although let me say this is the most one-sided conversation I've ever had in my life. I'm quite worn out now."

Eveline smiled.

"I was prepared to dislike you."

Eveline flinched. Dislike was nothing new to her and yet it still managed to make her feel inferior.

"But I find that for whatever reason I'm unable to. You have a certain charm, I suppose. And now since I like you, it means I'm going to have to protect you from the rest of the clan, which also means they aren't going to be happy with me."

Rorie shrugged as she made the statement.

"They don't much like me either, just so you know.

The women think I'm hopeless and the men think I'm too focused on matters that shouldn't concern a lass my age. They mostly ignore me, but if my brother weren't the laird, I would be treated with higher disdain."

Eveline scowled at that. She knotted her fingers into a fist and Rorie laughed. "As I sit here speaking of protecting you, somehow I think it will be the other way around, won't it?"

Catching Rorie's eye, Eveline put a finger to her lips and kept it there so Rorie couldn't misunderstand Eveline's request.

Rorie sighed. "Of course I won't share your secret, provided it doesn't go on for too much longer and that it doesn't hurt anyone or you. However, I won't allow you to hide up in that chamber. You'll eat in the hall tonight. You can sit by me. I know it hurts you to hear what members of my clan throw at you, but it will only grow worse if you back down and hide."

Eveline knew she was right and furthermore, she had no wish to maintain a solitary existence. At home with her family, she'd been surrounded by people who loved her and yet she'd been utterly alone. Here, surrounded by strangers and enemies, she'd found someone who made her feel not quite so isolated. Rorie knew her secret. It was a start. In time, she'd find a way to tell Graeme of the things she'd hidden and hope that he responded well.

Rorie suddenly grimaced. "Ah, there's Graeme bellowing for us. I can only assume he's been searching to no avail. 'Tis close to time for the evening meal. Come, let's go before he finds us."

Graeme had just come down the stairs from the upper level when he saw Rorie and Eveline enter the great hall.

"Where have you been?" Graeme demanded as he strode toward the two women.

Rorie frowned. "You knew I was taking her around the keep. 'Tis important she be familiar with her new home."

Graeme made a sound of impatience. "Where were you? You went inside the keep long ago and yet I wasn't able to find you and no one's seen you."

"I took her to Da's room."

Graeme glanced between the two women and then gave Rorie a searching look. "Why on earth would you take her there?"

Rorie shrugged. "'Tis one of my favorite places."

Graeme moved his stare to Eveline. "Are you hungry? 'Tis time to be seated for the evening meal, or would you prefer to eat above stairs in your chamber?"

A frown drew Eveline's features tight, but before she could respond, Rorie was quick to answer.

"She's sitting with me at tonight's meal."

Even as Rorie spoke, Eveline moved closer to her until they were side by side. Rorie reached down to take Eveline's hand.

So Rorie had done as he'd asked and reached out to Eveline. Indeed, she appeared to have done far more. For the most part, Rorie was a lass who kept to herself and was usually happy to do so. Here, though, she seemed quite happy to be in Eveline's company. It was something that should content Graeme and lift a burden from his shoulders. He no longer had to worry about what to do with Eveline if she struck up a friendship with his sister.

But then why was Graeme left with an unsettling suspicion that he wasn't privy to all the facts?

"Come, let's eat," Graeme said.

The serving women were already going to the tables and many of his clansmen were already seated, awaiting their portions.

He walked ahead of Rorie and Eveline, leaving them

to follow him to the dais. He took the step up and then reached courteously back to aid Eveline.

Her eyes widened, but she slipped her hand into his before stepping up to the table.

Her touch was a shock to his system. Thunder and lightning all at once. Her fingers were smooth, soft, pleasurable against his much rougher ones. He shouldn't even be holding her hand for as long as he was. Such roughness had no place against such delicateness.

When he positioned her on his right, Rorie frowned and started to protest.

"Sit on her other side," Graeme said. "Bowen can sit next to you tonight."

"He won't like it," Rorie muttered. "It would be better if you were to put Eveline on my other side so she is away from Teague and Bowen. They do not like her."

Graeme sighed. "Think you I'll let them abuse her while I'm sitting here?"

"Nay, but she'll know. She can see the way they look at her."

"I appreciate that you seek to protect her, Rorie, but do not assume that I cannot also give her protection from those who wish her ill. 'Tis my duty as her husband and one I do not take lightly. Now sit. The both of you."

Eveline eased onto the bench and Rorie climbed over to sit on her other side. Graeme took his position at the head of the table. More members of the clan filtered in and then his brothers appeared.

Teague's expression became annoyed when he saw Eveline occupying Bowen's place. Bowen didn't see it until he was nearly there and to his credit, he managed to control whatever reaction he had.

"You'll sit next to Rorie this eve, Bowen."

Bowen was silent as he went to take his place on the

other side of Rorie. Teague settled across from Eveline and sent a frown in her direction.

To Graeme's surprise, she met Teague's frown with a ferocious one of her own. And she didn't back down. Teague, seeing it as a challenge, stared right back and the two were locked in a silent battle of wills.

With each passing second, Eveline's scowl deepened and her mouth was set into a mutinous line.

Surprisingly, Teague was the first one to flinch. He glanced away and then quickly back at Graeme as if expecting a reprimand. The reprimand was in the look Graeme sent his brother. Teague's cheeks colored slightly, but he didn't glance Eveline's way again.

"Now, if we may all eat," Graeme said calmly.

The table was uncharacteristically silent as they dipped into the lamb stew. Usually an accounting of the day's events would be brought forth and the brothers would discuss training strategies or what the next day's plans would bring.

Instead, Bowen turned to their most senior men-at-arms, men who dined at Graeme's table each day, and conversed about the day's training sessions. After a time, they turned the conversation to the amusing tale of the boys whom Bowen had instructed on the use of bows and arrows and how many Montgomery soldiers were still digging arrows from their arses after the practice session.

Determined not to let the meal grow overly awkward, Graeme turned to Eveline.

"What think you of the keep?"

She ignored him, concentrating on her stew. She chewed a piece of bread she'd torn from the round and then reached for her goblet of ale. It was then she glanced at him and blinked.

Her face grew flush and pink tinged her cheeks. She

cocked her head to the side and viewed him in obvious question.

"I asked you what you thought of the keep."

Eveline nodded and then held up her arms and outstretched them so she nearly smacked Rorie's nose.

"'Tis no larger than your own family's holding," he said.

She shook her head in disagreement and then pursed her lips together. After glancing around the room, she then pointed, making a wide sweeping motion and then punched her finger into the table. Then once more she spaced her hands apart to indicate size.

Graeme nodded. "Aye, our hall is larger than yours, but then we house more people, I believe."

Eveline nodded her agreement.

He was about to pose another question when Eveline went tense. Her entire body language was wary and she paused, setting her spoon back into her stew.

'Twas nothing but the serving woman, Kierstan. She carried a tankard of ale and went to Teague first to refill his goblet. Next she came to Graeme, but she went on his other side so that she was between him and Eveline.

"Would you like more, Eveline?" Graeme asked, fully intending to have Kierstan serve her before himself.

But then Kierstan turned and stumbled, emptying the tankard in Eveline's lap. The ale splattered over her chest and arms, soaking her dress. It dripped off her chin and ruined the bowl of stew Eveline had been eating.

Graeme was so stunned that at first he simply stared, aghast at the woman's error. Eveline's eyes flashed with hurt, but then she seemed to steel herself and quietly rose.

"I'm so sorry," Kierstan babbled out. "'Twas an accident, Laird."

"'Tis your lady you should be apologizing to," Graeme bit out.

But Kierstan didn't turn to Eveline. She hastily began pushing the liquid that pooled on the table away from Graeme, but sent it in Eveline's direction.

Eveline was still standing, humiliation tight on her face, her eyes dull.

"Go fetch something to help clean her up," Graeme snapped at Kierstan. "'Tis not me you should be tending."

Then he rose to reach for Eveline's hand. But she brushed by him, ale still dripping from her clothing. She never even looked his way as she walked quietly from the hall.

Rorie was on her feet, spitting like an angry kitten. "Bitch!"

"Rorie!" Bowen said, shock evident in his voice. "'Tis no way for you to speak, even to a serving woman."

"She did it apurpose," Rorie snapped. "She's tormented Eveline all day and she well knows it. She's wasted no opportunity to call Eveline a bitch. I'm merely returning the favor."

"Is this true?" Graeme demanded, turning to Kierstan.

"Nay! 'Twas an accident. I swear it."

"And the other accusations? Did you call your lady a bitch? Did you malign her in any way?"

Kierstan's expression turned sullen and defiance sparked in her eyes. "'Tis not my lady I maligned. She isn't my lady."

"Leave my presence," Graeme thundered. "And keep from my sight. You'll not serve in the great hall again."

Kierstan paled. She started to speak again, but Graeme silenced her with a single look.

"Begone," he ordered.

She turned and fled.

Rorie was still furious, her face red and her fists clenched tight at her sides. "Her punishment is too light, Graeme."

"'Tis over, Rorie. You'll not pursue it further. The clan must be given time to adjust to Eveline's presence."

"And so you'll allow such disrespect until such time as they've adjusted?" she asked incredulously.

His eyes narrowed. "Do you question me? Kierstan won't go unpunished. But neither will I tear down the walls of the keep and raise the ire of the clan when emotions are running high already. You take my desire to mediate as a sign that I'm allowing Eveline to be abused. You should know me better than that."

He turned and strode from the table. Rorie called after him, "Where do you go?"

Only at the doorway did he pause and turn back. "I'm going to see to my wife."

Rorie looked strangely pleased as she retook her seat.

CHAPTER 17

Graeme realized he was completely uncertain of himself halfway up the stairs. He even paused some distance from his chamber, because he wasn't sure what to do with Eveline when he found her.

If Rorie was right and Kierstan had spilled ale on Eveline apurpose, then Kierstan would have to be banned from the keep and sent into the grain fields to work.

He was caught in a difficult position because he didn't want it to appear to his clan that he sided with an Armstrong against them, but neither did he want to abandon his wife—no matter who she was—to the ill treatment of others.

When he finally reached the chamber door, he pushed it open and went inside, only to be greeted by the sight of Eveline standing in the nude, her back to him.

For a moment he was transfixed. Her hair was unbraided and lay in waves down her bare back, just reaching the top of her rounded bottom. There it hung enticingly, brushing the tops of her cheeks.

She was a well-formed lass. Luscious, curvy bottom, slim waist, hips that flared appealingly.

Then he felt immediate guilt for standing here lusting

over her—a woman who likely had no idea of such matters or understanding of them.

He turned away, determined to give her privacy to complete her dress. No matter how tempted he was not only to look, but to wait for her to turn so he could gain a full view.

He heard water from the washbasin being sloshed about and nearly groaned at the idea that she was completing her wash right there a few feet away. All he had to do was turn. It was a sight he'd receive much pleasure from. Watching his wife as she bathed. He could well imagine the path of the washing cloth as it glided over her body.

He should be lying on the bed, enjoying the delectable sight, not standing here rigidly, his back to her because he feared scaring her. His attraction was inappropriate, but his body didn't seem to care what his mind objected to. His body found her pleasing and there wasn't a damn thing he could do about that.

Then he heard a gasp and he realized she must have finally seen him standing there. Slowly he turned, keeping his gaze averted. When he chanced looking up, he saw her clutching the linen from the bed to her naked body and staring at him with wide eyes.

But he read no fear in those eyes and that relieved him immensely. The last thing he needed was a hysterical female in his chamber.

"I wanted to see how you fared," Graeme said.

Eveline nodded, still clutching the linen close to her breast.

"Perhaps I should return when you're fully dressed."

She hesitated a moment before offering a slow nod. He wondered at that hesitation and what she'd been thinking as she stared back at him, those eyes so serious and contemplating.

"Right, then," Graeme muttered. He turned around

and hurried from the chamber, closing the door behind him.

He felt ten kinds of a fool standing outside his bedchamber while his wife made herself decent within. She was his. She belonged to him. There was no part of her that he should be denied. But no amount of telling himself that or rationalizing the desire that simmered and boiled in his veins could convince his mind that he wasn't the filthiest loch slime for thinking of her in that way.

He was still standing there in the hall, hoping no one came above stairs to see him, when his chamber door opened and Eveline poked her head out. She smiled broadly when she saw him and she motioned him back inside.

She was fully clothed now, a fresh, clean dress with a pretty embroidered neckline.

He inched inside the chamber and found her perched on the edge of the bed—his bed—and she smiled when he found her gaze again.

"I'm sorry for what happened below," he said in a low voice. "Kierstan will serve in the hall no more."

Eveline's expression grew somber, and sadness clouded her brilliant eyes.

Graeme sat on the bench in front of the fire, not trusting himself to sit on the bed beside her.

"Do you feel it was intentional, Eveline? Has Kierstan made you unwelcome thus far?"

Her expression became unreadable. She appeared to give the matter some thought, and then her eyes narrowed. She shrugged, but Graeme didn't believe for a moment she didn't have an opinion on the matter, but he respected the fact that she wasn't slinging accusations, even if they were well merited.

He'd worried over Eveline's ability to understand the situation, how she'd fit in, what kind of problems her presence would cause. But so far, her actions had been beyond reproach and it shamed him that his own clan was behaving so childishly, even if he could understand the motivation behind it.

"I want you to feel welcome here, Eveline. 'Tis important for you to be happy."

She smiled again, her eyes shining in the glow of the candlelight of the chamber. Then she cocked her head and pointed at the bed and then to him.

His brow wrinkled a moment, and then he realized she was asking him if he intended to go to bed.

In truth, he never retired this early, but now that he was here, it would be awkward to tell her nay and return below stairs.

So he nodded.

She smiled, seemingly delighted that he wasn't leaving the chamber again. Then she rose and went to the stack of wood for the fire. He glanced over his shoulder to see her shyly skitter past him to add more wood to the fire. He turned quickly, catching her wrist.

She glanced up in alarm, and he purposely made his grasp gentle, but he shook his head.

"You're not to act the serving wench with me, Eveline. I'll be happy to add the wood to the fire. Are you chilled?"

She blushed, shook her head, and pointed to him. Something went soft inside him when he realized that she was tending to his needs. She thought since he was retiring that he'd like the chamber to be warm.

"'Twas thoughtful of you," he said, offering her a smile. "'Tis not necessary, though."

He took the wood from her arms and then tossed it into the fire so the flames roared high once more.

When he moved from the hearth, he saw that she'd perched on the edge of the bed and was staring intently at him. She seemed to want to ask him something. He wasn't sure how he knew it, but there was a hesitant air about her, almost as if she wanted to communicate with him, but feared doing so.

He settled back onto the bench so he faced her. He was determined not to crowd her, to give her plenty of space, and he wanted to appear as nonthreatening as possible.

"Eveline, is there something you want to discuss?"

She twisted her hands in her lap and then glanced toward the pillows on the bed. Then she looked back to Graeme and pointed at the pillow she'd slept on the night before.

She pointed back to herself, then gestured at his pillow and pointed to him.

He frowned, uncertain of what she was asking. She frowned as well and her expression became pensive. Then she pulled back the furs on the bed and crawled beneath them, taking her place on the far side, her head resting on her pillow. She gazed over at him and then patted the space beside her.

His eyes widened as he finally understood her intent. She wanted him to come to bed with her.

Blowing out his breath, he rose, uncertain as to what he should say or do. He didn't know what her expectations were, and he damn sure didn't want to frighten her.

She rolled over, tugging the furs up over her shoulder, and she faced the wall, giving him the same privacy he'd offered to her earlier by turning his back. He smiled, amused by the idea that she'd think him modest enough to worry over undressing in front of her.

Still, it was sweet of her to consider his desires on the matter.

Though he wasn't sure if this was the right thing to do, he decided it couldn't hurt to sleep with her once more. Somehow, he thought that if he were to refuse, that she'd not take the rejection well. She was a sweet lass, and he wanted to spare her feelings at all cost.

Deciding it would be better to simply wear his clothing to bed, he carefully pulled back the furs and slid into the bed beside her.

He could feel her warmth even across the empty space between them, and her scent whispered intoxicatingly through his nostrils. Her soap was delicately scented. A flower in spring.

He reached for the candle at his bedside and blew out the flame, dousing the room in semidarkness. Only the light from the fire in the hearth illuminated the room.

Beside him, Eveline rolled back over and before he could wonder what her intentions were, she snuggled up to his side, laying her head over his shoulder.

He lay there completely still as she melted against him, going limp as she relaxed more and more. She emitted a sleepy sounding sigh and burrowed her head deeper into the crook of his arm. In a moment, her soft, even breathing filled his ears, and he realized that she was already asleep.

As content as a kitten on a fur, she was wedged tightly against him, her legs flush against the side of his.

Sleep was a long time coming.

CHAPTER 18

When Eveline rose the next morning, she went to the window and rolled up one corner of the furs and tied them back with a leather strip. Then she tested the chill in the air, allowing the breeze to blow over her face. Already the sun was high enough to bathe the earth in a warm glow and chase away the morning crispness.

In the distance, the river beckoned. There was a spot in the bend, where the water snaked in its path around one side of the keep. Several trees and a natural boundary of rock outcroppings provided privacy, and it would be hard for someone not well above ground level to see her if she was bathing.

The light clean up she'd done the night before hadn't been enough. She could still feel residual stickiness from the ale. Some had splashed into her hair and it would need a good washing. But she didn't want to visit the bathhouse, where she'd be forced into the company of other Montgomery women.

If Rorie could be found, perhaps she could be persuaded to accompany Eveline and at least stand guard so that no one else would venture down to that particular spot in the river.

Satisfied with her plan and looking forward to a good

swim, she collected a change of clothing, chose one of the warm blankets to dry on, and then dug out the sweet-smelling soaps she'd used to wash up with the night before.

Arms full, she left the chamber. She passed Rorie's open door in the hall, and then she realized that since Rorie had already left her chamber that Eveline had no idea where to find her. Dread filled her stomach and she paused at the top of the stairs. Then anger tightened her lips. She wasn't going to allow the Montgomery women the satisfaction of making her so afraid that she feared leaving her chamber.

She marched down the stairs and entered the great hall, head held high like she owned the place. She never paused even though many, as they'd done the day before, stopped in their duties to stare at her.

She donned her haughtiest look, put her nose in the air, and continued through the doorway that led to the small accounting room where Rorie had taken her yesterday.

When she pushed open the door, to her relief, Rorie was sitting at the desk, quill in hand as she studied one of the scrolls.

Rorie looked up, blinking in surprise as Eveline stood there, arms loaded down with clothing and the blanket.

"Are you moving chambers again, Eveline?"

Eveline grinned and shook her head. She put the armload down on the desk, and then she pointed to Rorie and then gestured out the window.

"You want me to jump out the window?"

Eveline's smile broadened and her shoulders shook in silent laughter. She pointed to herself, then pointed out the window and then put both arms together and extended them, making a swimming motion.

After that, she wrinkled her nose in distaste and gestured toward her skin and hair, pinching her fingers over her nose to get her point across.

"You want to go swimming . . . so you can bathe?" Rorie asked. "Do you even know how to swim?"

Eveline nodded vigorously.

"Eveline, 'tis chilly, not so much out in the sunlight, but the water will be frigid."

Eveline shrugged. It wasn't as if she was unused to such things. The water was just as cold at Armstrong Keep as it was here.

"Graeme won't like this."

Eveline frowned fiercely at Rorie and then shook her head. Then she pointed back to Rorie and then back at herself.

Rorie laughed. "Oh, you want me to go with you so Graeme doesn't find out."

Eveline shook her head. Then she put her hands on the desk so Rorie could see. She pointed to herself and then placed that finger on the desk and made circling motions as if it were her swimming. Then she pointed to Rorie and then put her on the desk a goodly distance away from Eveline. Once she was sure Rorie understood where she would be positioned, she picked up her hands, pointed to Rorie and then crossed her arms over her chest and put on a forbidding face and puffed up like a warrior.

Rorie threw her head back and laughed harder. "Oh my," she said when she finally stopped shaking. "You want me to stand guard. That's amusing. You and I are likely the two smallest lasses in this clan, save those much younger than us, and you want me to frighten away anyone who would come close to where you're bathing."

Eveline nodded.

"Very well, then. This might be the most fun I have all day."

The two women went through the hall and Eveline ignored the suspicious looks cast her way. She didn't make eye contact so she wouldn't know of whatever they said to her, and she made certain she took a wide berth around any of the women who stood in her path.

Once outside, Eveline breathed deeply of the fresh air and turned her face upward into the sun so it could warm her skin. Rorie moved ahead of her and led the way to the gate with the watchmen's towers.

Eveline hadn't considered that others would have to know of their whereabouts and was mortified over what Rorie would tell them.

She was even further appalled when two men on horseback appeared with the obvious intent of escorting them beyond the gate to the river. She stared in horror at Rorie when the lass returned from her conversation with the guard.

Rorie held her hands up in apology. "'Tis nothing to be done for it, Eveline. Graeme has strict instructions regarding such matters. He would never allow two women to leave our gates unescorted. I've told the men they must remain at a respectable distance. They won't see you. But 'tis not possible for us to go down to the river alone."

Eveline glanced warily up at the two warriors, but they didn't scowl at her. There was no judgment in their eyes. Nor did they seem to begrudge their duty to escort the wife and sister of the chieftain to the river.

"They want to know if we'd like to ride with them instead of walking," Rorie said.

Eveline hastily shook her head and took a quick step backward. Panic knotted her throat as she stared up at the gigantic beasts the men sat astride.

Rorie held her hand up. "'Tis all right. I'll tell them to follow behind. Come, let's go. They're opening the gate for us."

* * *

"This whole thing is driving *me* daft," Graeme muttered.

Bowen rubbed his horse's neck and then patted it affectionately as they slowed to a steady plod.

Graeme had gone out riding with Bowen an hour before. He'd needed to take himself from the keep and clear his head for a while. The situation with Eveline was keeping him awake at night. *She* was keeping him awake at night.

She acted as though it was the most natural thing in the world to sleep in his bed, to curl into his side, to touch him as a wife would touch her husband.

Not that she'd become *too* intimate, but it was clear she was curious and moreover, she didn't appear to be frightened of him at all. He had no idea if she had any idea of the reaction she was inciting in him. He couldn't think she was cognizant of the normal course of happenings between a wife and a husband. Was she?

At any rate, being so near to her at night, smelling her, touching her . . . It was more than a man should be asked to bear. If he were another man, he'd have already gone to another woman to find ease. He would have taken a leman. But even before his marriage to Eveline, he'd been mostly celibate, because casually flipping up a woman's skirts for a quick tumble always left him feeling . . . cheated.

His brothers jested and called him Father Montgomery. They teased and said that most monks likely had more experience with women than he did, and maybe it was so.

While Graeme wasn't ignorant of female flesh, he could hardly be considered the expert his brothers apparently were. He knew well what to do with a woman. The problem was, he was having the most perverse fantasies involving a woman he had no business fantasizing about.

"Why are you letting the lass addle you so?" Bowen asked. "If you don't want her in your chamber, 'tis simple enough to banish her to her own."

Graeme sighed. "'Tis not what I want to do. She seems content to be in my—our—chamber. I think it would hurt her feelings were I to make her go. She has an expectation that we should be . . . together."

"Then perhaps you should consummate your marriage," Bowen said bluntly.

Graeme blew out his breath. He didn't want to have this conversation with his brother. He didn't want to have it with anyone. But he needed something. Some advice. Words of wisdom, something to tell him what he was supposed to do without feeling like a complete bastard.

"You've seen her, Bowen. Could you bed her if you were the one wed to her?"

Bowen frowned. "'Tis a hard question to answer since I'm not married to her. You are."

"You aren't a debaucher of innocents. This much I know of you. You've a fair face, a man women like to look at, and aye, you have your share only too willing to bed with you, but I cannot see you taking to your bed a woman whom you weren't completely sure knew precisely what it was that was taking place."

"Many men would not think twice, Graeme. She is your wife. Your property. 'Tis entirely possible she'd bear you heirs with no problem. She seems a healthy enough lass and she seems sturdy. Whatever is wrong with her was not the result of birth but of an accident much later, so you wouldn't have to concern yourself with a defect that would be passed on to your children. I think perhaps you worry overmuch."

"Don't think I haven't been tempted," Graeme said in

a grim voice. "And I think 'tis what bothers me the most. I should not be having such thoughts. I should not even be discussing or weighing my options or my guilt with you because I shouldn't even be entertaining what occupies my mind of late."

Bowen pulled his horse to a complete stop and let out a chuckle. "Well, now, I cannot say I blame you for the thoughts you're having. Indeed, I can well see why you are."

Graeme frowned and looked in the direction of Bowen's gaze only to nearly swallow his tongue. His mouth flopped open and he shook his head, unable to believe what he was seeing.

Across the river, on the side of the keep, Eveline stood waist deep in the water, and she was putting soap to her hair.

"She looks completely normal to me, brother. And very appealing as well. She has the look of a woman grown, and God's teeth, I've not seen such a finely formed woman in many a year. I think your guilt is misplaced and that you weigh heavy over something you should not."

The amusement in Bowen's voice yanked Graeme from his reverie.

"Be gone!" Graeme demanded. "Look not upon her again."

Bowen laughed, but turned his horse and began to ride in the opposite direction. "Think on what I said, Graeme. The lass is certainly not a child, nor even a girl too young. She's a woman full grown and the proof's right in front of you."

His chuckles carried back to Graeme as he rode farther away. Graeme's attention snapped back to Eveline just in time to see her rinse her hands in the water. He sat forward on his saddle and bellowed her name across the river, full intending to tell her to leave the water and put her damn clothes on. Whatever was she thinking to take a bath in the middle of the day where anyone could happen upon her?

But she either didn't hear him or she ignored him. She never even looked up but continued to wade into the water.

Unease gripped Graeme. The river was deep here and the current moved swiftly. Just downstream the water shallowed, but was still deep enough to carry a body swiftly and rocks jutted upward from the bed creating a harder rapid. If she lost her footing or went too deep, she could easily be carried away and dashed upon the rocks.

For a moment she closed her eyes and cocked her head back as if seeking the warmth of the sun. The movement jutted her breasts forward and Graeme groaned. She was, indeed, very beautiful. And perhaps her unawareness or lack of pretension over her looks added to her beauty. He wasn't sure what made her so appealing to him. Which was why he felt so damn guilty over lusting over her. He knew without a doubt that if she were any other woman who'd suffered what she'd suffered and her mental capacity was in question, he'd only feel pity for her. He certainly wouldn't be thinking about bedding her.

Compassion was what she deserved. It was what she needed, but she found it in neither the members of his clan nor him.

Just as suddenly as she tilted her head back, she suddenly leaned forward and dove beneath the surface of the water. He urged his horse forward, his gaze rapidly scanning the surface as he waited for her to come back up.

He was at full gallop, his heart thumping when she remained under. He slid from his saddle while the horse was still moving and stumbled forward as he hurried toward the bank.

She still hadn't surfaced.

He didn't even try to remove his boots or any part of his clothing. He slid down the bank and dove headlong into the water.

The cold nearly made him gasp, but he managed to prevent himself from inhaling a mouthful of water as he powered downward, his arms flailing outward in an effort to feel her. But if she'd been caught in the current, she could already be well downstream by now.

He was about to come up for air and call for help, when he felt a hand in his hair pulling upward. When his head popped above the surface, he found himself face-to-face with Eveline, who looked concerned. For him.

She cocked her head, put her palm to his cheek, and frowned, her eyes clearly questioning his well-being. He had the sudden urge to strangle her.

"What in the world are you doing, woman?" he bellowed. "Have you any idea what I thought? I thought you were drowning, or that you didn't know how to swim, or that you'd been swept downstream and would be killed on the rocks."

She blinked as if none of those thoughts had ever occurred to her. He swore and frowned all the more fiercely at her. He was freezing his arse off and she was treading water next to him, staring at him as if he'd lost *his* mind.

She raised one arm, wiped her fingers along it, then wrinkled her nose in distaste. Then she put her fingers to her nose and pinched her nostrils.

"A bath," he grumbled. "You wanted a bath. God's teeth, and you think you stink?"

She nodded solemnly. Then she held up the wet ends of her hair as if to tell him she'd merely been rinsing it. He shook his head.

But he went completely still when she touched his

chin. It was just a simple touch, but it was if he'd been pressed by a hot brand. Warmth traveled down his body, alleviating the cold numb that had begun to set in.

Her lips worked up and down almost as if she were trying to say something, but then she clamped them shut and instead gave him a sad look that could only be interpreted as an apology.

Then to his utter shock, she wrapped her arms around his neck to give herself leverage, and she lifted herself out of the water just enough that she could press her lips to his.

Several things happened at once.

Her full breasts pressed against his chest. Her nipples were hard and puckered from the cold, and he could feel the imprint on his skin. Her lips melted over his, warm and soft, and he was suddenly as heated as a man who'd been baked in the sun on the hottest summer day.

Ah but the lass was sweet. The sweetest mouth he'd ever tasted.

He gave in to the sinful urge to possess that delectable mouth and he returned her kiss in full measure. His tongue stroked over her lips, coaxing and enticing her to let him in.

She gave a breathy sigh and parted her mouth, allowing his tongue to push inside.

He liked kissing. Many a man didn't have much patience for it. His men jested about kissing being a waste of time and was only for wooing the unwilling lasses. But if a lass was willing, they'd much rather move to the more rudimentary elements of coupling.

But to Graeme, kissing was almost as intimate as the act of lovemaking itself. It wasn't something to be hurried or to be offered as a token to woo a reluctant lass. It was an expression of regard.

Eveline tentatively stroked her tongue over his. One quick brush against the tip of his and then she retreated, but as he deepened the kiss, she came back and soon she was exploring his mouth in the same manner he was exploring hers.

When she finally broke away, she was panting. Her cheeks were colored and her eyes glowed. She had the look of someone who'd drunk a little too much ale. And she looked up at him with such an expression that his entire body raged with arousal and sharp lust. So much so that he wanted to take her onto the riverbank and possess her with the sun warming the both of them.

She touched his lip and then touched hers, her finger lingering over her bottom one that was swollen from the force and longevity of their kiss. Then she smiled and something melted inside him.

"You're going to freeze," he muttered, taking note of the chill bumps that danced across her shoulders and arms.

He hauled her into his arms and carried her to the opposite bank, away from his mount. He turned and whistled and the horse obediently forded the stream.

He saw that Eveline's clothing was folded neatly and on a nearby rock, but she also had a blanket, which was good because now that they were out of the water, she was shivering.

He put her down long enough to reach for the blanket, and then he wrapped it around her, covering her from head to toe. He even made certain her head was covered.

She stared up at him, her eyes gleaming in amusement as she tried to move. He'd swaddled her in the blanket so she couldn't even move her arms, much less walk back to the keep.

He glanced at his horse, knowing it was the easiest way to return, but he saw her follow his gaze and noted the panic in her eyes. Her father hadn't lied. The idea of mounting a horse terrified her.

He cupped her cheek, and she looked back up at him.

"I'll not make you do something that frightens you, Eveline."

She relaxed and then leaned her cheek against his palm. To his surprise, she turned just enough to kiss the inside of his hand. It was such a simple thing and yet he felt it all the way to his soul.

He reached down and lifted her into his arms. The walk to the keep wasn't long and he'd need to put on dry clothing himself. And he liked her in his arms. It felt natural for him to be holding her thus.

As if agreeing completely, she snuggled into his embrace, turning her face into his neck.

Whistling for his horse, he set off for the keep. As he cleared the row of trees that shielded the particular spot where Eveline had chosen to take her swim, he saw Rorie sitting on the ground a short distance away. Her head was down, and as he approached, he realized she was napping. Behind her in the distance were two of his warriors on horseback conversing.

He almost laughed. Clearly Rorie was supposed to have been Eveline's guard and she'd fallen asleep while on duty. At least his men had kept watch, though Eveline could have drowned and they never would have known. But neither did he want them looking on while she swam in the nude.

"Rorie," he called out.

Rorie jerked upward, her eyes wide as she stared around. When her gaze finally locked on her brother and the fact that Eveline was in his arms, she scrambled to her feet.

"What happened? What's wrong?" she demanded.

"Nothing is the matter," Graeme said calmly. "Run ahead and prepare a fire in my chamber. Put out something for her to wear and perhaps place one of the furs from the bed by the hearth so the flames will warm it. Then instruct one of the men to return for Eveline's clothing."

Rorie's brow wrinkled and she looked as though she'd argue, but Graeme sent her a dark look that suggested she wouldn't like the consequences.

"Go," he said again, and she took off across the meadow toward the guard's tower.

CHAPTER 19

Eveline sighed in utter contentment as Graeme carried her through the courtyard and into the keep. She kept her eyes closed, because she was determined that nothing would ruin this moment. No stares from her clansmen. No cutting remarks. No insults.

He carried her into the keep and then up the stairs, and only then did she open her eyes as he bore her down the hall to his chamber.

Rorie was adding wood to the fire when Graeme entered the room. She scrambled up and then gestured toward the bed.

"I put a dress out for her to wear and there's a fur warming by the fire as you requested."

Eveline didn't rear back so she could see Graeme's response, but it rumbled out of his chest. She could feel the vibration, not only in her ears, but against her skin.

She loved the sound and the feel of his voice. It made her long to be able to hear, so she could do nothing but listen to him speak. He had to have the most wonderful voice in the world. Why else would it feel so delicious in her ears?

Rorie gave Eveline a small wave and a look that said, "You're on your own" before she departed the chamber.

Not that Eveline minded at all. She loved having her husband to herself when he would speak directly to her and there were no others to intrude or do things like pour ale all over Eveline.

She was quite liking the idea of Graeme as her husband, if only they could progress beyond the awkwardness wrought by her own past deceptions. She knew she must at some point, reveal herself fully to him, but when? And would it ruin any tenderness he felt toward her? Or did he in fact only feel tenderness because she was an object of pity?

It made her gut knot, because it could all go really wonderfully, but it could also go very, very wrong, and any protection she currently enjoyed because she was viewed as deficient could evaporate if the truth were known.

Graeme set her down in front of the fire, and then he held up the fur that Rorie had set out to warm. She glanced quickly up, not wanting to miss a single thing that Graeme said.

"I'll hold up the fur and you can unwrap the blanket from you and then wrap yourself in this until you're dry and warm enough to dress."

She could see the discomfort in his face and it made her curious. Did he not view her as a woman? That couldn't be the issue at all. He'd kissed her. He'd responded to her as a man does a woman. She'd seen her parents kiss. She'd seen others in her clan exchange passionate embraces. What she and Graeme had shared had certainly rocked her to her bones.

Perhaps he didn't *want* to see her as a woman. Perhaps he didn't even want her as a wife. There was no perhaps there. It was obvious he hadn't wanted a wife and he likely hadn't changed his mind on that account.

But neither of them had been given a choice in the matter and in Eveline's mind it was better to make the best of a bad situation. She liked Graeme. The more time she spent in his presence, the more she grew to like and even respect the man he was.

He'd been kind to her and he'd shown her understanding. Any man who could do that with the daughter of his most hated enemy was not an evil man.

Slowly she let the blanket fall away and Graeme hastily pressed the fur to her. She smiled and tucked it underneath her arms and then held it around her as she sat back down on the bench. Then she patted the place beside her, hoping that he, too, would take a seat and dry in front of the fire.

"I need to take off these wet clothes," he said.

She nodded and turned, because it was obvious he was uncomfortable undressing in her presence. But she couldn't help keeping enough of an angle so she could see him in her periphery.

She was extremely curious about her husband's body and she wanted to see him. She'd never seen a man fully naked before.

She held her breath when he quickly stripped out of his tunic and his leggings. He turned sideways as he reached for dry clothing from the trunk at the foot of his bed.

He was . . . She wasn't sure she had the words to adequately convey her awe or admiration. He had a warrior's body, but it was . . . beautiful.

Thick legs, heavily muscled, as were his arms and broad shoulders. At the juncture of his legs was a dark whorl of hair and his manhood . . . She swallowed nervously, not wanting to be caught out staring, but she was fascinated by that particular portion of his anatomy.

She knew enough of the whole mating process to know what went where, but she couldn't wrap her mind around *how*. It looked way too large to ever fit inside her, and as much as she wanted to be a true wife and consummate their marriage, she couldn't imagine that it could be done without considerable pain and effort on her part.

Still, such a step was important if she was to be a true wife to Graeme and she wanted that. Wanted his acceptance and eventually his clan's acceptance, if they could ever reach that point. She didn't want to forever be the wife that Graeme Montgomery was saddled with, nothing more than a penance he had to pay for forced peace with her father's clan.

She quickly forced her gaze forward when Graeme finished dressing, and a moment later, he settled onto the seat beside her before the fire.

She glanced up at him, not wanting to miss anything he would say, but he remained silent, his gaze focused on the flames.

Perhaps she should kiss him again. She certainly wanted to, but was nervous about how receptive he'd be now that she no longer had the element of surprise.

She licked her lips in anticipation and continued to stare up at him.

As if feeling the force of her gaze, he turned in her direction. His brown eyes glowed from the light of the fire and he seemed to study her, almost as if weighing his thoughts and words.

"I do not know what to do with you, Eveline Armstrong."

She could feel the resignation in the way he held his body and the expression on his face. She frowned, not liking the implications of such a statement.

"I know not if what I am feeling is right and I do not like the guilt that plagues me for enjoying our kiss as I did."

She smiled then, her heart suddenly lighter than it had been just moments before. She felt suddenly shy and would have averted her gaze, but knew it was too important to be able to see whatever he would say next.

Then she reached up to touch his chin, slowly moving her fingers over his lips. He closed his eyes, seeming to find pleasure in her touch. Before he could reopen them, she rose up to press her mouth against his.

The fur fell partially away from her body, but she paid it no heed as her lips covered the firm line of his mouth. She wanted to taste him again, to take his tongue inside again and feel it against her own.

His breath vibrated against her lips as he let out a sigh. Of resignation? Of surrender? She knew not, only that his mouth parted and his tongue stroked warmly over hers, returning her kiss in full measure.

There seemed to be no reluctance, no sign that he was fighting this strengthening emotion between them.

It was the sweetest pleasure Eveline had ever experienced. She wanted the moment to last forever, but Graeme was the first to pull away, his eyes half-lidded as he stared down at her.

Gently, he set her away from him. It felt more symbolic than a simple separation, almost as if he were erecting a visible barrier between them or that perhaps he needed the distance.

"I have matters to attend to," he said.

Without looking at her again, he rose and walked to the doorway of their chamber. She didn't look over her shoulder, as tempted as she was to do so. She was both elated and disheartened by the kiss and resulting reactions.

She stared down at her hands for a long moment, gathering her wildly scattered emotions. She had no experience in matters of the heart. Her one exposure to a potential husband had been disastrous and she'd vowed never to allow herself into a situation such as the one she would have found herself in with Ian McHugh. And the truth of the matter was, she hadn't had a choice with Graeme, and it could have turned out as bad as or worse than any marriage to Ian. She'd merely been fortunate that Graeme didn't seem intent on ill-using her and that he showed her kindness instead of vengeance.

Taking a deep breath, she stood, allowing the fur to fall away, and then she walked to the bed where Rorie had laid out a dress for her to change into. She wouldn't allow anything to spoil today. Not spiteful clan members. Not her own doubts and misgivings or her fears over revealing the truth to Graeme.

She'd enjoyed her first kiss, her first taste of passion, and the stirrings of a desire she wanted to pursue.

Knowing that Rorie would likely be curious as to what prompted Graeme carrying her back to the keep and that she might even be concerned, Eveline headed down the stairs, determined to brave the gauntlet.

She was Graeme's wife, whether his clan wanted to accept it or not. She'd accepted it, and if she had her way, Graeme would accept it soon as well. In time, his clan would follow suit. She had to believe that.

When she reached the bottom of the stairs, she sucked in a deep breath and rounded the doorway leading into the hall. She hurried toward the far end where the exit into the short corridor that housed the tiny room where Rorie liked to spend so much time was.

But the room was dark, furs drawn over the window, and Rorie was nowhere in sight. With a frown, Eveline returned to the hall, deciding to venture out of the keep where she'd hopefully discover Rorie's whereabouts.

Where before the hall had been mostly empty save for a few women going back and forth from the kitchen, Eveline came face-to-face with a veritable crowd, or at least it seemed so with so many blocking her pathway to the courtyard.

At the forefront of the group of women—five women

Eveline counted—was Kierstan, whose surly expression could only mean that this wasn't going to be a friendly encounter.

Kierstan's lip curled. "Whore."

Eveline blinked in surprise. For one, it wasn't her usual method of insult. Eveline had truly thought the lass limited in her vocabulary to a single insult.

The other women nodded, their expressions as fierce as Kierstan's own.

"You'll not take our laird in with your seductive wiles," Kierstan continued. "He's a man, and men can be swayed by a pretty face and a willing body. But you won't be fooling us. We won't let him forget who and what you are. You will never be welcome here, Armstrong bitch."

Fury nearly blinded Eveline. The other women were chiming in with insults no doubt. All agreeing with Kierstan and supporting her statements. But Eveline couldn't keep up with their mouths. The assembled women blurred in her vision as she was gripped by rage.

Eveline turned to the huge fireplace in the center of the hall. A fireplace where two swords hung over the mantle. They were within reach and she doubted they were battle worthy. They looked to be more ornamental. But at the moment she cared not. One would certainly aid in her cause.

If they wanted madness, she'd give it to them.

She rushed to the fireplace, rose up on tiptoe, and yanked at the sword, praying it would come free and then praying that it didn't weigh so much that she couldn't even lift it.

The grip was old and worn and the blade not as thick or as large as the ones her kin carried or even those she'd seen the Montgomery warriors carry.

The sword came away without protest, and anger fueled her strength as she wobbled under the weight. She turned back to the women who now stared at her with unease.

She charged forward, holding the blade high, and bellowed, without worry over how loudly her words came forth. She cared not if the rafters rang with it. The word—the one word—that she was able to articulate billowed from her chest and squeezed out her throat with all the force she could muster.

"O-O-OUT!!"

CHAPTER 20

"Laird, come quickly! She's gone completely mad! You must stop her before she kills someone!"

Sparring ceased all over the courtyard as the woman ran shrieking toward Graeme. Bowen stood down and Graeme lowered his sword. He held his hand out to stop the panicked babbling so he could understand what on God's earth she was hollering about.

Murmurs rose from the warriors as in the background, emanating from the keep came an unholy sounding, "OOOUUUTTT!" More shrieks ensued and the woman in front of Graeme started her shrill exclamations all over again.

"Silence!" Graeme roared. "I cannot hear what is about!"

He advanced on the woman before him—Mary?— and tried to keep his voice calm and measured.

"What is amiss? Who are you talking about going mad and killing someone?"

"'Tis your wife, Laird! She's taken a sword to the other women in the hall. You have to come quickly!"

Graeme dropped his sword and ran.

As he rounded the corner, the scene before him made him stop in his tracks.

"Jesu," Bowen breathed out. "'Tis true. She has gone mad!"

Graeme turned briefly to see that his brothers and most of the men who'd been assembled in the courtyard had followed. Then he jerked his attention back to Eveline who stood in the doorway to the keep, sword outstretched toward the women she was holding at bay, and a scowl etched on her lovely face.

In front of her, a group of women were steadily backing away from the door. Only one seemed to challenge Eveline. Kierstan, the same lass who'd dropped the ale on Eveline the night before.

Graeme could hear her shouting insults to Eveline, and Eveline bellowed loud enough for the entire keep to hear.

"OUT!"

God's teeth, it had been *she* he'd heard. She'd spoken!

He ran the last of the way and pushed in front of Kierstan, inserting himself between her and Eveline. Kierstan immediately dissolved into tears and threw herself at Graeme.

"Oh thank God you're here, Laird. 'Tis horrible. She's threatened to kill us all. She's mad, I tell you. She chased us from the hall. I don't know what happened. She just yanked the sword from above the fireplace and came after us."

Graeme glanced up at Eveline and at first, all he saw was the fury on her face and the tight scowl she wore. But then he saw into her eyes and saw fear and clear distress. As he studied her closer, he saw that her hands shook and she was doing all she could just to hold on to the sword.

"Eveline, put down the sword," he said in a calm voice.

She shook her head, her chin coming up a notch. Then

she pointed to the group of women and bellowed again. "Out!"

Rorie pushed to the front of the ever-growing crowd. She gave Kierstan a look of pure disgust and then turned on Graeme.

"'Tis not her fault, Graeme. They've been horrible to her at every turn. They've hurled insult after insult and missed no opportunity to mock or demean her."

"I don't believe I made any such claim," Graeme said mildly. "What I'd like her to do, however, is to put down the sword before she hurts *herself*."

Graeme took a step forward, his gaze focused solely on his wife. "Eveline," he said gently. "Please give me the sword. No one will hurt you. I swear it."

She turned her gaze to the women still standing several feet away and her lips turned into a mutinous line. "Out," she said again. Then her lips quivered and the firm line dropped. Deep sadness entered her eyes and they filled with tears. When she looked at Graeme again, there was clear defeat in her gaze.

It broke his heart.

Anger gripped him. At the moment, he cared not what his clan's feelings were or whether they had the right to be angry over his marriage to an Armstrong. All he knew was that an innocent was being harmed by their words and actions, and he would stand it no longer.

He whipped around and stared at Kierstan and the other women gathered around her.

"Be gone," he hissed. "All of you. You'll not return to the keep. You'll tend the fields or help in the cottages, but you'll not serve in my keep any longer."

Kierstan paled. The women around her gasped. One wrung her hands. Another burst into sobs. But all he could think of was his own wife, who was so near to tears because she'd been abused by his clan.

"Begging your pardon, Laird, but the keep needs the

lasses for serving duties and also for the cleaning duties they hold," said Nora, the senior woman charged with overseeing the women's duties in the clan.

"Find other women," Graeme snarled. "These will not set foot in the keep again, nor will they address my wife directly. If they disobey me, they will be cast out of the clan."

Gasps and sounds of disbelief echoed through the crowd. Murmurs arose. Accusations flew. Their laird was siding with the Armstrong lass.

Even as he heard the statements, he turned to his brothers to gauge their reaction.

"You know you have my support, Graeme," Teague said in a low voice. " 'Tis obvious they've not made it easy for her. I'll not go against your edict; moreover, I support it."

Bowen took longer answering. He studied the group of women and then he turned his attention to Eveline and stared intently at her.

"She can speak," Bowen said.

It wasn't what Graeme had anticipated and for a moment Bowen's statement took him aback.

Bowen turned his gaze to Graeme. " 'Tis said the lass hasn't spoken a word since her accident, and yet today she bellowed loudly enough to be heard over the entire keep. Whatever it was that forced her to break that silence must have been rather momentous, wouldn't you say?"

"Aye," Graeme said in a grim voice. "I'd say she suffered extreme upset to have broken her silence."

Bowen stared thoughtfully at Eveline once more. "Perhaps then, her madness has also been exaggerated."

Relief was crushing in Graeme's chest. Both his brothers were siding with Eveline against his clan. He knew that if they wanted, it would be easy to turn his clan against him. One of them could even make a play for power, gain the approval and support of the clan, and take over as laird.

But they stood with him. With Eveline.

Graeme went to Eveline, close enough to reach out and cup her cheek. His arm was merely inches above the sword. Were she to make any sudden movement, she could take his arm off. She was wary of it, too. Her gaze tracked downward, and even as he touched her, she lowered the sword, letting it slide toward the ground.

"Give me the sword," he said gently. "I do not want harm to come to you, Eveline. I won't allow them back in the keep. They will not harm you further. They will not serve me again."

Her eyes widened in surprise, and it made him ill that she'd be so shocked and seemingly in awe that he'd side with her over members of his clan. But then what other logical conclusion could she have drawn?

With shaking hands, she extended the sword. He took it from her and without looking down, held it back for his brother to take.

"Come inside," he said, taking her hand.

She glanced at the assembled crowd with stricken eyes, and then she looked up at Graeme, sorrow so deep that he was swamped with it.

"S-sorry."

The word came out raspy and rough sounding, but the fact that she was communicating with him sent excitement up his spine.

"'Tis no matter," he said as he touched her cheek. "Let's go up to our chamber. We'll discuss things there, in private."

She nodded, relief lightening her eyes. She turned and rushed ahead of him, as if she couldn't wait to be away from the others.

When they reached his chamber, she opened the door, hurried in, and then held the door while he entered. As soon as he was inside, she closed the door and slid the sturdy piece of wood through the loop so that no others could enter. As if they would. He didn't tell her that no one would dare enter his chamber without permission. It seemed to make her feel more secure after she'd barred the door, so he left it alone.

She went and sat by the hearth, though only a few glowing embers were left. She was clearly upset over the day's events, but he also sensed that she was nervous and unsure. He wanted to ease her worries and fears.

He had many questions and now it was evident that she did possess at least some ability to speak. The real question was, if she could communicate, why had she chosen not to?

"Eveline, can you tell me what happened inside the keep that upset you so?"

Silence fell. She didn't respond. Didn't turn around to acknowledge him. She acted as though he hadn't spoken at all.

He frowned. "Eveline?"

Still no response.

"Eveline, turn around so that we may speak on the matter at hand."

The order was imperious, purposely said in a biting tone because he suspected . . . He wasn't sure what he suspected, but he'd spoken in a manner that would have most certainly have upset her. She would not have sat there, unmoving, ignoring his dictate.

His mind was a whirl of confusion and gradual understanding. If he was correct . . . Jesu, could he be? Could it be as simple as that?

He strode forward and straddled the bench she sat on. As soon as she sensed his presence, she turned, her gaze immediately going to his face, or rather, his *mouth*. His mind was struggling for answers to the questions that plagued him. There was something very important here. Just within reach.

The nagging suspicion became stronger. It wasn't possible. It sounded preposterous. And yet he found himself mouthing his next words, not giving voice to them.

"Can you tell me what happened, Eveline?"

Slowly she nodded, but then she shook her head and shrugged as if to say she wasn't sure what she could tell him.

His pulse thumped rapidly. He found it difficult to remain calm. One more time, he did the same, still not believing the proof in front of his eyes.

"Can you understand me, Eveline? Do you understand what I'm saying to you?"

She frowned and then nodded, as if she found the question ridiculous.

His discovery floored him. All he could do was stare at her in utter amazement.

"Dear God," he whispered. "You can't hear, can you?"

CHAPTER 21

Eveline's eyes turned nearly black as her pupils grew large. Only a thin band of blue surrounded the darkness and her fear was something he could not only see but he could feel.

She hastily rose, backing away from him, her expression panicked. She ran into one of her trunks, fell backward and then tried to scramble up as she continued her track toward the door.

Graeme shot up and went to her, determined that she wouldn't fear him. He couldn't bear it if he frightened her.

"Eveline. Eveline!" He turned her face so that she was looking directly at him. "Eveline, please. You have nothing to fear. I only want to understand. Please believe that."

He touched her cheek, caressing softly as he tried to soothe away her panic.

Gradually her breathing slowed and some of the terror left her eyes.

"That's it," he said. "Deep breaths. You've nothing to fear. I just want to talk to you. I'd like to understand you, Eveline. I think you have been very misunderstood for a long time now."

He helped her up and then took her hands, leading her to the bed so she could be comfortable. The hard bench in front of a no longer burning fire didn't qualify and he didn't want to take the time to start it burning again. There was too much he needed to know about the woman he'd married.

He settled her down and then sat across from her, bending one leg up on the mattress so they faced each other. He took her hands in his, holding them firmly.

"I'm right, aren't I? You can't hear."

She briefly closed her eyes and issued a short nod. He waited until she reopened them before he continued.

"And yet, somehow you're able to tell what people are saying by watching their mouths?"

Even as he said it, he knew how incredible it sounded and yet it had to be so. It explained so much. Why she seemed to sometimes be aware and why other times she seemed to drift and have no awareness of what went on around her.

Again she nodded.

He was astounded. He wouldn't have believed such a thing possible. There were so many questions crowding into his head that he had to control the urge to blurt them out in succession. He didn't want to overwhelm her.

He leaned in closer, gazing into her eyes. "Eveline, out there, you spoke. You said two words. Have you been unable to speak or have you just been *unwilling* to speak all this time?"

She swallowed hard and then again. She opened her mouth, but paused almost as if she were afraid to even try.

"Try," he coaxed gently. "I won't judge you. Try to say the words."

He held his breath in anticipation, only now realizing just how important it was that she be able to communicate verbally with him. He'd never felt an eagerness like this. His pulse was about to beat right out of his head.

Her hand went to her throat, and then she opened her mouth again. The words when spoken were a little garbled and barely a whisper.

"I w-was a-afraid."

His chest tightened at such simple words, but they conveyed a heavy wealth of emotion.

He nudged her chin upward so she'd see his own words. It was important she understand what he would say. If she knew nothing else, he would have her understand his vow. "You don't have to be afraid here, Eveline. You never have to be afraid with me."

Her eyes brimmed with tears. "Th-they haate mee."

This time the words were rather singsong and they came out in varying degrees of loudness. She started soft, became much louder in the middle before fading away to nearly nothing. It was almost as if she were testing, trying to see what was normal.

And how would she know?

So much was falling into place for Graeme. The pieces were rapidly coming together, almost too fast for him to keep up. He had to force himself to remain calm and not leap ahead of himself in his haste to discover all her secrets.

"Let's start from the beginning, Eveline. I need to know what happened. Was it your accident that caused you to lose your hearing?"

She nodded.

"You were ill for quite a long time."

She nodded again.

"Why didn't you tell your family? Do you not think they would have understood? God's teeth, they thought you were daft. I thought you were daft. You're probably more intelligent than the lot of us."

"I w-was afraid," she said again in a thready voice.

"What were you afraid of, Eveline?"

The color rose in her cheeks. She fidgeted with her hands and then looked down as she pulled with her fingers.

Impatient to find a question she could more easily answer, he once more directed her attention to him and then asked, "Everyone thinks you're daft. But you're merely deaf and you've not spoken since your accident."

She flushed guiltily, but nodded.

Graeme was elated. God's teeth, but he'd felt like the worst sort of abuser lusting over a woman who didn't fully understand the world she was in half the time. But none of that was true. She was normal. Or at least she was perfectly in control of her faculties.

"Why wouldn't you speak?" he asked, touching her cheek again, tracing a line over the silky smoothness.

"I hhad no waay of knowing howww loudly I spoke. At ffirst I was ffrightened. I didn't understand . . ."

Her voice drifted lower and lower until he was no longer able to hear her. He touched her lips. "Louder, Eveline. A little louder."

She cleared her throat, swallowed, and then continued, her cheeks reddening once more. "I didn't undeeerstand what had happened to me or whhyy. It took me a while to comprehend. When I did, I decided to keep it s-secret and l-let those around me think I was addled. Brain fever. Touched. Whatevver they chose to tthhink."

The more she spoke, the more she seemed to gain confidence. It seemed to pour out of her after a very rusty start. Some of her words warbled and some of the sounds weren't quite right, but Graeme had never heard such a beautiful sound in his life.

His wife could communicate with him. Not only could she speak, but she was highly intelligent and could read the words of others from their lips. Daft? If anything, it was her family who was addled for not realizing her deafness in three long years. Perhaps she was the only smart Armstrong of the lot.

She hesitated, and then she peeked up at him, uncertainty written all over her face. "You aren't . . . You aren't angry?"

His breath left him in a rush. "Angry?"

She nodded solemnly, and he knew in that moment that he still hadn't gained the whole story from her. There was still something she held back, whatever it was that had made her afraid when she lived in the bosom of her family.

He cupped her face in his hands so that she wouldn't miss a single word that came from his mouth.

"I'm not angry, Eveline. Far from it. 'Tis a *joyous* moment."

She smiled tentatively and some of the warmth returned to her eyes.

He rubbed his thumbs over her cheekbones and stared down at her, hoping she would see his sincerity.

"What made you afraid, Eveline? What frightened you so badly that you would not admit to your family what was really wrong with you?"

Her face fell and once again she shut her eyes tightly, as if warding off the pain of the past. He didn't press and instead continued to hold her gently, his thumbs feathering over her face.

When she looked back at him again, tears swam in her eyes, making them deep, blue pools. "I was to marry Ian McHugh."

"Just a little louder," he encouraged.

"I was to marry Ian McHugh," she said again.

He nodded. "Yes, I know. The betrothal was broken after your accident. I assume he cried off because of your . . . condition."

She nodded solemnly. "It was mere weeks after the accident had occurred and I was still confused and afraid. But when I realized that I wasn't going to have to marry Ian because my own family thought I was daft, I knew that if I told them differently, I would likely have to honor the agreement."

Graeme stared at her in surprise. "You allowed your family to believe you were mad for three years because you didn't want to marry Ian McHugh?"

"He was evil," she whispered hoarsely. "I was so afraid of him. I tried to tell my father, but he put my concerns down as maidenly fears. He refused to believe me and it hurt, because I love my father dearly. I thought that he'd side with me. Not Ian."

Graeme's brows drew together. He was starting to gain a clearer idea of the whole thing and it was giving him a very bad feeling. He didn't think that he'd like whatever it was she'd have to say to his next question.

"Why do you say he's evil? What did he do to you, Eveline?"

Her breathing sped up. As his hands slid down her neck, her pulse jumped and accelerated rapidly. He could feel her panic. Could feel her fear.

A tear slid down her face and collided with his hand where it rested against her neck.

"He liked to corner me. He'd seek me out when no one was around. He pursued me relentlessly. He even came to my bedchamber one night. He liked to . . . touch me. He'd whisper threats in my ear as he touched me. He'd tell me how my life with him would be. What being his wife would be like and what I could expect when we married. He said terrible, horrifying things. He suggested things I can't bear to repeat. I had no idea such evil *existed* and I don't understand *why*. I never gave him insult. I never did anything to anger him and yet he seemed to hate me and he seemed determined to punish me the moment I became his wife."

Graeme trembled with rage. He had to let go of her

face for fear of hurting her. He dropped his hands, his nostrils flaring at the image of Eveline at another man's mercy. Young, terrified, and vulnerable.

"Did he hurt you? Physically? Did he ever do more than touch you?"

"N-no. He seemed to enjoy taunting me with what was to come."

"I'll kill him," Graeme said starkly.

Eveline paled. "N-nooo. You c-can't. Please. I don't want anyone to know."

"*I* know," he bit out. "No one else has to. But I know and I won't let his sins go unpunished."

Sorrow and shame crowded into her eyes and he could contain himself no longer. He pulled her into his arms and cradled her against his chest.

He had his arms full of a sweet, soft lass. His own. His wife. One he no longer had to feel guilty over desiring. She was as capable of understanding her marriage as he was. They could have a proper marriage if she so desired. He knew he did.

He kissed the top of her head and remained silent, for she wouldn't hear what it was he had to say.

She burrowed trustingly into his embrace and he inhaled her scent, letting it linger in his nostrils as she cuddled against him. They still had much to discuss, but he was loath to end the sweetness of the embrace just yet.

For several long moments, he remained as he was, holding her tightly against him. He wanted her to trust him and the fact that she'd admitted everything to him was a huge step in the right direction. She'd told him something she hadn't even related to her family.

When he finally pulled away from her, he remembered their very first meeting and his brow furrowed in confusion.

"Eveline, the first time we met, you stared at me and I remember having the sense that you were intensely focused on me. Even across the room when you couldn't have seen what it was I said because I was turned sideways. But I saw you from the corner of my eye and I had the sense that you could . . . hear me or at least understand what it was I was saying."

She licked her lips nervously. "'Tis hard to explain. I hear certain . . . sounds. Not like you do or I used to. There are tones that I feel in my ears, sort of a vibration, more of a sensation than anything. I feel that when you speak. It's like a warm hum in my ears, and it was enjoyable. I was shocked and then . . . happy . . . that I could hear certain tones of your voice. It was why I later went to your chamber. I wanted to hear more."

"That's interesting," he said. "It would seem you don't have a complete hearing loss."

She shrugged. "Mostly. I don't hear actual words. I've forgotten so many sounds. I used to remember them. I was able to close my eyes and play the sound in my head. Now it's not so easy. The sounds are gone."

She sounded so sad that it made Graeme's chest tighten. He couldn't imagine being without his hearing, and yet Eveline had made the best out of a terrible situation. She'd taught herself a valuable tool in surviving her situation. If she could read words from people's mouths, then she could effectively eavesdrop on conversations that were well away from her. The possibilities were staggering. No wonder she'd had such a miserable time in his clan. Even if his clansmen were discreet enough to make their remarks far enough out of Eveline's hearing, if they were in viewing distance or even if they whispered, she'd know what it was they said.

She twisted her hands nervously in her lap and then looked back up at him. "I wanted to tell you. I wanted a new . . . start. I thought that here I could start over. That I would be away from the fear that I would be forced to marry Ian. I knew nothing of you, but resolved that you couldn't possibly be worse than him."

"I'm uncertain over whether to take that as a compliment," Graeme said dryly.

She flushed. "'Tis only the truth I speak. I intended to tell you, but when I arrived, I was made to feel so unwelcome. I feared if people knew the truth, they might be even more daring and I also feared . . ."

She bit her lip and turned away, but he turned her back, his expression fierce. "What did you fear?"

"That if you knew I wasn't daft, that any tenderness you had shown me would disappear and that you would treat me like your enemy's daughter. Hated. Loathed. It was a terrible position to be in. Afraid to tell the truth. Wanting to have a . . . normal . . . marriage. Afraid if you knew, you would be angry at my deception."

Graeme sighed. "You've worried yourself into knots, Eveline. 'Tis not a very comfortable position, is it?"

She shook her head ruefully. "Nay, it isn't."

"We have much more to speak on, but I need you to know this. Your place in my clan is assured. I will do anything necessary to protect you and to afford you the respect due your position as my wife. I'll allow no one to offer insult or to harm you in any way, physically or emotionally."

Her shoulders sagged in relief. Then she glanced up at him, her eyes wide and hopeful.

"And will our marriage be real, Graeme? Will I be a real wife to you or do we merely play roles made necessary by a king's decree?"

A low growl sounded in his throat, a noise he knew she couldn't hear, but he damn well hoped she could feel the vibration rumble from his chest.

He tilted her chin upward and then slid his mouth over hers in a long, leisurely kiss.

When he pulled away, she was breathless and her lips were swollen.

"You'll be my wife, Eveline. Make no mistake about that. Our marriage will most certainly be consummated."

CHAPTER 22

Eveline's heart was about to hammer out of her chest. She was nervous, excited, *elated*. So many things all balled up into one huge knot. She felt near to exploding. She wanted to ask when? And where? And how? Or what about *now*? But none of those things were proper or very ladylike. The very last thing she wanted to do was appall her husband.

Wanting to keep the connection to him, to be able to still touch him, she slid her hands over his palms, twining her fingers with his.

"I do not regret having to marry you," she said gravely.

It was very odd to find herself speaking again, to know she was talking, but not be able to hear the words coming from her mouth. The vibrations tickled her throat, and already it was sore from the sudden explosion of words.

Her tongue was dry and she slipped one of her hands from his to rub at her throat.

"Would you like water?" Graeme asked. "Your throat must ache. You aren't used to using your voice."

She nodded, and he rose and went to the small table by the window where a jug of water was kept.

He poured a goblet full and returned to the bed, retaking his position just in front of her, and held the cup out to her.

She took it and sipped, grateful for the cool water against the rawness of her throat. When she'd yelled earlier, it had hurt. Now she would pay for her temper.

He touched her arm to gain her attention and she looked up to see him staring intently at her.

"I do not regret our marriage either, Eveline."

Her eyes widened. She hadn't expected such an admission. She'd made her confession for no other reason than that she'd wanted him to know. She hadn't done it so he would reciprocate. But she couldn't help the intense relief or the warm glow that arose from within her at his statement. Maybe . . . maybe they *could* have a marriage more like her parents'.

"I don't anticipate that our marriage will be easy. 'Tis obvious our families are in opposition. My views on your kin are unchanged and I do not say so to hurt you. I say it because I won't lie to you."

She swallowed, but held his gaze so she'd catch every word even if they did hurt.

"But I do not regret the union that was forced upon us."

He touched her cheek in a gentle caress.

"I'll protect you, Eveline. I'll not let my kin do harm to you, nor will I allow them to disparage you in any way. We must decide now what we tell them. There is no reason for you to live in secrecy, hiding in the shadows any longer. Ian McHugh cannot hurt you here."

The hand holding the goblet shook, and he carefully pried it from her hand, setting it on the floor beside the bed. Then he took both her hands in his and squeezed gently as if to offer her support.

"They'll likely still think me daft," she blurted. "'Tis true I do have a defect."

Graeme scowled. "'Tis not of your doing. You suffered an accident and subsequent illness. You can speak and make known your thoughts, your needs. You can understand what others say to you. You can do everything a normal lass can do. The only difference is that you cannot hear. That does not make you daft or any less intelligent, and anyone who says differently will have me to answer to."

Her heart lightened and warmth traveled through her chest until she was smiling. Relief was overwhelming. After living so long with the fear of discovery, with guilt over her deception, she was seeing an end to it all.

He was offering her freedom of the sweetest kind. Freedom from the stigma of being less than a person, even though she'd brought it on herself. Freedom to have a normal life, one devoid of fear. Never would she have to worry over Ian McHugh again.

"If you wish to tell your clan the truth, I'll not argue the point," she said. "Perhaps then they'll know that when I do not respond, it's not because I'm slighting them. It's because I have not heard their address."

The cadence of Eveline's speech was oddly mesmerizing. It was certainly different. But to Graeme it was pleasing. Others would still likely disparage her when she spoke just because she sounded different. She still struggled over some words and she hadn't learned to monitor the loudness of her tone—how could she have when she hadn't practiced?

It was a task he'd set Rorie to immediately. His sister had developed an affinity for Eveline from the first day. Rorie was a solid ally for Eveline, and Graeme didn't have to worry that Rorie would be disloyal to her. Rorie could help her find the right volume so Eveline would better know how loudly she was speaking by the way the words felt coming out of her throat.

"I think it best they know the truth," Graeme said. "I don't want to give them any reason to continue with their insults and disrespect. Not that you wouldn't be due that respect if you were 'touched.' There's no reason for others to levy such hatred toward that which they do not understand. But this way they'll know what a capable, intelligent young lass you are, even more so because you have no hearing and yet you've managed to teach yourself the very difficult task of reading words from people's mouths."

Eveline's eyes sparkled as she stared up at him in wonder. " 'Tis no small thing for you to think this way. Many would have no such kindness to those weaker or less intelligent than themselves. Even in my own clan, there were many who thought the laird should rid himself of his daft daughter. Many would not only condone or sanction such ridicule but they would participate themselves."

Graeme frowned, not liking the idea that anyone in her own clan would have acted so harshly toward her. "It does not make me more of a man to belittle those under me."

She smiled. "I quite like you, husband."

He blinked in surprise at her pronouncement. Then he laughed. "I like you, too, Eveline."

Then he realized the one word she hadn't said and he was suddenly filled with impatience, wanting to hear it from her lips.

"Say my name," he said huskily. "Graeme. I want to hear you say my name."

"Graaame," she said slowly and with great care.

"A little louder," he encouraged. "You spoke it so softly, I almost did not hear."

"Graeme," she said louder and with more confidence.

The sound delighted him. It sent an uncontrolled shiver up his spine. The ache in his gut intensified. He stared back at her, so close and yet with too much space between them.

It didn't matter that he no longer had to fear taking advantage of a woman who wasn't aware of the kind of intimate relationship that took place between a man and a woman. She was still innocent and he would have to take great care with her. He would have to advance slowly so as not to overwhelm or frighten her.

But his need was savage. Clawing relentlessly at him, growing more with every moment he spent in her presence. He'd experienced lust. He was well acquainted with matters of passion. But this was . . . different.

It transcended simple attraction, a need for a woman—any woman—to assuage his desires. She called to him on a completely different level. She spoke to the very heart of him. Inspired feelings of protectiveness and fierce possessiveness that he wasn't even sure he liked.

Feeling this . . . strongly . . . for a woman was dangerous. It clouded a man's judgment. Made him forget his duty. Made him forget everything else save . . . her.

"I like my name on your lips," he murmured, his voice catching. He was suddenly grateful she couldn't hear him, couldn't tell the difference in his tone. It told too much. It told of his weakness when it came to her.

She smiled beautifully, her eyes lighting up, sparkling with pleasure. "I like my name on your lips as well," she said shyly. "Even though I cannot hear it. I imagine what it would sound like. I feel the vibration in my ear and it's . . . comforting."

His expression sobered. "It must have been very difficult to adjust to hearing nothing, to wake up to a silent world."

"It was," she whispered. "I thought so many things. That it was my punishment for daring to defy my father and even Ian to a degree. But I couldn't imagine God wanting me to marry a monster. He wouldn't be that unmerciful, would he?"

"Nay," Graeme said, touching her cheek. "Perhaps

God gave you to me to protect so that you'd never have to worry about Ian McHugh again."

Her eyes widened. "I had not considered that."

He smiled. "Then consider it now. Perhaps the king's dictate was not such a terrible thing after all. I find the matter of our marriage not nearly as distasteful as I did in the beginning."

Her cheeks blossomed with color, but he could see the warm delight in her eyes. She truly was a beautiful lass and he was falling more under her spell by the minute.

"I'll pull my brothers to the side and gain their assistance in telling the members of our clan of your situation. I'll not make a public announcement. I don't want to discomfit you in any way."

She nodded. "Thank you."

He tipped his finger underneath her chin and then leaned in to kiss her one more time. It was brief—it had to be lest he allow things to go too far this very moment— but it was no less sweet.

"I meant what I said earlier," he said as he pulled away. "Kierstan and those who participated in the abuse you experienced will not work in the keep again. Furthermore, if you have any further issue with them, or anyone else, you're to let me know the moment it happens. They will be dealt with harshly."

Eveline swallowed, but nodded her agreement.

He reluctantly rose from the bed, putting more distance between them. Then he turned so she'd see his mouth as he spoke.

"I go now to speak with my brothers. It will be time to sup soon. Perhaps you should rest a moment and then join me in the hall."

CHAPTER 23

"A word, please," Graeme said to Bowen and Teague as he approached them in the courtyard.

Bowen lowered his sword and backed away from Teague before sheathing it in the leather scabbard that hung from his side. Teague waved his hand to dismiss the group of men they'd been training with, and then the two brothers closed around Graeme.

"The clan is unhappy with your dictate," Teague murmured. "Few are sympathetic to the 'Armstrong bitch.'"

Graeme's nostrils flared and he would have gone for his brother, but Bowen stepped in between them, putting his hands on Graeme's chest.

"He did not call her such, Graeme. He was only repeating what many have said after you dismissed the women from the keep."

"She is not to be spoken of in such a manner regardless of whether you're repeating the words of others," Graeme snapped.

Teague held up his hands. "I'm merely telling you that there is much discontent. They feel you're being disloyal to your own kin by siding with the Armstrong lass."

"She has a name," Graeme growled. "And it is no longer Armstrong. She is a Montgomery."

Bowen sighed. "Aye, we know it. We're on your side. But you cannot ignore what's being said around you because it offends you. You can't make the clan accept Eveline, no matter how much you may wish it. You can tell them how they must act. You can tell them what they must say. But you can't force them to accept your wife, because you can't change what's in their hearts. And what's in their hearts is hatred."

Graeme sighed. He knew what his brother said to be true, and it frustrated him.

"If I can accept her, then why can they not? Her kin is responsible for the death of my father. They are responsible for the loss of our clansmen's lives, and yet I know that I cannot hold a lass responsible for the sins of her father any more than the Armstrongs could hold Rorie responsible for the Armstrong lives that have been forfeit to us."

"Aye, but you're assuming that they would afford the same courtesy to Rorie," Teague said in a grim voice. "Everyone is not you, Graeme. Not everyone has your logic. You can look at the situation and say the lass is not to blame and we should not make her pay for the sins of her kin. But everyone else just sees the enemy and their thoughts turn to vengeance."

"She's not daft," Graeme said, frustrated with the course of the conversation.

Bowen lifted his eyebrow. "Nay? I had my doubts. Why then does everyone in her clan assume so and why has she never corrected their opinions?"

"She's deaf."

Teague's gaze sharpened. "Deaf? She cannot hear? How then does she know what it is we're saying? She understood enough of the insults the women were slinging to go into a sword-wielding rage."

Bowen grinned. "A fierce wee kitten swinging a sword. Now that was a sight to behold."

"She reads the words that are formed on our lips," Graeme explained. "'Tis extraordinary if you think about it. She lost her hearing as a result of her accident, but not her wits."

"It still doesn't explain why she perpetuated such a myth," Teague said.

Graeme related the story that Eveline had told him, of how she sought to protect herself from marriage to Ian McHugh only to find herself forced into marriage with Graeme.

Bowen and Teague both wore frowns when Graeme finished. Then Teague shook his head. "It was quite clever of the lass even if a little extreme."

"Not so extreme if it prevented her from falling into the hands of a man who'd sorely abuse her," Bowen murmured. "Think on it. The lass went to her father with her fears and he discounted them. Mayhap he wanted the alliance too much to put any credence into what she said. Or mayhap he just thought she was overly fearful and that once accustomed to the idea she'd come around. But 'tis clear she thought she had no choice."

Graeme nodded. "She didn't want to continue the deception, but she was fearful of my reaction. She thought that I was kind to her because I thought she was daft and that I would no longer look at her as someone to be pitied and that I'd despise her because of her heritage."

"And *were* you kind to her because you thought she was pitiable?" Bowen asked.

Graeme hesitated. "In the beginning, aye. I felt sympathy for her even as I felt frustration for being forced into marriage to a woman who could never be a wife to me. I was angry, but I also knew I could not be angry with her."

"But not now," Teague commented.

"Nay, not now. She's . . . special. I cannot explain it, but I do not regret our marriage."

Bowen blew out his breath. "You've a difficult path ahead, brother. It won't be a simple thing for her to win favor with our clan."

"Aye, I know it. But you and Teague will aid me in this, will you not?"

Teague and Bowen exchanged glances.

"Aye, we will," Teague said. "If the lass is what you want and you are content with her, then we trust your judgment and will do all we can to ease her way."

Graeme nodded. "My thanks. Rorie has accepted— nay, befriended—her already. 'Tis good for Rorie to have the companionship of other lasses. Rorie doesn't have much use for the women in our clan."

Teague chuckled. "That's because the lass is convinced she'd rather be a lad."

"The day will come when she will marry. I would have her prepared for that," Graeme said.

Bowen frowned. "We will not do as the Armstrongs were forced to do. We will not sacrifice her for alliances or favor with the crown. We have no need of either and I'll not have her marry someone who would treat her as Ian McHugh would have treated your Eveline."

His Eveline. Graeme liked the sound of it. She *was* his. Not fully, yet, but he'd remedy that soon enough.

"Rorie is happy here with us," Teague said with a scowl. "There's no reason for her to leave."

Graeme smiled. "I suggested no such thing. Rorie is young yet and she may change her mind. She may want to seek out a husband and settle down to have children of her own."

Bowen chuckled. "I wouldn't wager anything on that."

"My thanks again for your support of Eveline," Graeme said in a more serious tone. "It will mean much to her as well. Rorie has been the only friendly face she's seen since she arrived on our lands. I'm determined to change that."

"If you are content, then that is sufficient enough for me," Teague said.

"Do you want us to share all that you have told us?" Bowen asked.

"Most, yes," Graeme replied. "I want you to spread the word that Eveline is not daft, but that she is deaf and that she perpetuated the deception to escape marriage to Ian McHugh. We have no love for the Armstrongs, and I'm not above using our clan's dislike of them to rally support for Eveline. If 'tis believed that Eveline was a victim of the Armstrongs and the McHughs alike, then 'tis more likely she will find sympathy among our own kin."

"'Tis a dangerous game you play," Teague mused. "Eveline would not likely appreciate such things said about her family."

"'Tis true enough," Graeme said darkly. "Tavis Armstrong would have used his daughter for his own purposes despite her wishes. That they love and cherish her is not enough to satisfy my disgust over that fact."

Bowen nodded. "'Tis a good plan. Foster sympathy for Eveline by letting it be known that she is happier in our clan than she was in her own."

"Bowen and I will talk to the men," Teague said.

"Thank you. I will see the both of you in the hall for the evening meal."

Graeme turned and walked back toward the keep, suddenly anxious to see his wife again.

CHAPTER 24

Eveline dressed with care for the evening meal. She'd worn only simple dresses since her arrival. Plain, more suited to working within the keep or even outside the keep than anything that could be considered pretty or frivolous.

Tonight she dug out one of the silk underdresses that her mother had so carefully packed before Eveline had departed her father's lands.

It was lovely and Eveline adored the rich green color. It made her feel livelier. Appropriate for coming out of her self-imposed seclusion.

She wore a simple white overtunic that contrasted nicely against the vibrant green. The sleeves were long, nearly covering her hands.

Deciding that if she were going to wear something so grand, she may as well not hold back on the shoes, she dug out the jeweled slippers with sharp pointed toes and slipped them onto her feet.

At home she had a maid who'd arrange her hair, but here she hadn't been assigned any such person nor had she asked. With the women of the keep so ambivalent toward her, she hadn't wanted one to attend her.

She had pins and such, again thanks to her mother's

careful packing. Eveline would have likely left it all and gone to her new husband in bare feet and a much-worn linen dress.

After brushing and fussing with her hair, she gave up on pinning the heavy mass up and instead opted to pull some of it back away from her face, securing it at the back of her head.

The result was better than she'd anticipated. She even thought herself pretty. There hadn't been many occasions at home that had warranted her looking her absolute best. And those times her mother had always taken over and made sure Eveline was dressed appropriately.

It was perhaps too much for a simple evening meal with no guests in attendance, but for Eveline, this was an important evening. It was when Graeme would relate her secret—if he hadn't already. All eyes would be upon her. She wanted no one to be able to find fault with her—or at least her appearance.

She was nervous. Nay, she was terrified. It did no good to deny it.

She sank onto the edge of the bed and sat there a long moment investigating the looming shadows in the room. There were only two candles lit and the fire in the hearth had long since gone out.

A touch to her shoulder had her yanking her head up in surprise. Rorie stood beside her, an expression of concern on her face. Eveline hadn't noticed her coming into the chamber.

Rorie turned and picked up one of the candleholders and sat on the bed next to Eveline, so that Eveline would be able to see her face.

"I didn't mean to startle you," Rorie said. "Graeme sent me up to see if you were ready to come down to the hall for the evening meal."

Eveline smiled. "Thank you. I am."

Rorie's eyes widened. "You can speak."

Eveline nodded. "Has Graeme not told you all?"

"I heard. Talk, I mean. No one has said anything to me directly, but there are rumors now. That you cannot hear and aren't daft at all. Of course I knew you weren't daft, but I didn't know the rest. Why didn't you tell me?"

Eveline sighed. "I'll tell you the whole of it later. I do not want to leave Graeme waiting in the hall." She rose and then took a few steps back so Rorie could see her attire. "Do I look pleasing? Like a laird's wife even?"

Rorie also stood, bearing with her the candle. "You look beautiful, Eveline. Truly. I think Graeme will be more than pleased."

Rorie put the candle down and turned to leave the room, but Eveline put her hand out to catch Rorie's. Rorie turned back to Eveline, question in her eyes.

"Thank you," Eveline said.

Rorie cocked her head to the side. "For what?"

"For befriending me even when it was thought I was daft and when no one else in your clan was kind."

Rorie smiled, and then to Eveline's surprise leaned forward to catch Eveline in a fierce hug. Eveline returned the embrace, her heart gladdening at the acceptance of the younger girl.

When Rorie pulled away, she was still smiling. She kept hold of Eveline's hand and said, "Come now. Let's go down so that my clan can behold their new mistress in all her glory."

Graeme impatiently awaited Eveline's arrival. He'd sent Rorie up for her several minutes ago, and they'd yet to make an appearance.

His brothers were already seated and the other clansmen were filtering in and settling at the other tables. Any moment now the serving women would be in with the food, or at least he hoped Nora had found adequate replacements for the women he'd dismissed earlier in the day.

He was ready to go up to see if there was an issue when Eveline appeared at the end of the hall.

Graeme caught his breath. Indeed, the entire hall quieted. There wasn't a single murmur as all attention was directed at Eveline.

She was beautiful. Poised. Confident looking. Until his gaze reached her eyes and it was then he could see the fear and nervousness reflected in them.

He stood, without even processing his intention to do so. He stepped down from the dais and walked down the center between the tables lining the walls. When he reached her, he saw that Rorie was just behind her, watching, almost as if she was gauging whether she needed to intervene on Eveline's behalf.

He smiled at his sister, proud that Eveline had such a champion. Rorie smiled back.

Then he put his arm out to Eveline and turned his smile down to her. "You look beautiful, my lady."

The fear and nervousness fled her eyes as a smile took over her face. It was so brilliant that Graeme felt like someone had knocked the breath from him.

She slid her hand over his arm, her fingers just peeking from the sleeve of her overtunic. The cuffs were embroidered with dainty silver threads in a swirling feminine pattern that suited Eveline.

Turning, he paused a moment as they faced the hall. All eyes were on them as he began to lead her back down the center toward the head table where his brothers waited.

He noticed that his clansmen weren't attempting to say anything, even quietly at their tables. He had to hold back his smile. Since learning of Eveline's ability to see what one said without having to be in hearing distance, they'd likely all be more circumspect about saying anything around her.

When he helped Eveline up the step, his brothers rose and stood while he seated Eveline beside him. Rorie followed behind and slid into her place next to Bowen.

Eveline smiled warmly at Bowen and Teague and then settled gracefully onto the bench. Graeme sat at the head of the table and then offered his goblet to Eveline.

She took it with a murmured thank-you, too low for anyone to have heard. He barely caught it himself, but he wouldn't draw attention to her by telling her it was barely discernible. He didn't want to make her any more nervous than she already was.

Across the table, Teague motioned for Eveline's attention and when she turned her gaze his way, he said, "You look beautiful, Eveline."

She blushed to the roots of her hair, her cheeks a delightful shade of pink. This time when she said thank you, she said it loudly enough for those closest to her to hear.

Graeme reached underneath the table and squeezed her hand.

Just then, Nora came bustling into the hall followed by a procession of women whom Graeme noted had previously either worked in the fields or were assigned to washing of the clothes. A few looked nervous, having not served the laird directly, but the others dove into their new duty with confidence and began serving food and drink.

Graeme's table was served first and he made sure Eveline was given priority. By now, it was clear that he would tolerate no disrespect, so the women went out of their way to attend Eveline.

Satisfied that at least for this night there would be no upset for Eveline, Graeme settled back to eat his meal.

"Have you sent for Father Drummond?" Rorie asked.

Graeme sighed. "No, imp, I haven't."

She frowned at him, allowing him to see her displeasure over his response.

"You promised."

Eveline was glancing rapidly back and forth to follow the conversation so Graeme purposely slowed so she would be able to participate.

"Aye, I did at that. I've not had the time and to be honest, it hasn't been a priority with all else we have happening of late."

"But you promised, Graeme! You said if I was nice to Eveline, you'd send for the priest so I could learn to read and write."

As soon as the words were out of Rorie's mouth, she clamped her hand over her lips, an expression of horror etched on her face.

Eveline dropped her gaze, staring down at her food. But not before he saw the devastation in her eyes. It was instinctive for him to want to protect her. It made him furious that Rorie had been so careless.

"Damn it, Rorie," Graeme growled. "You go too far this time."

"I'm sorry!" Rorie cried. "Oh Graeme, it wasn't what I meant at all. You know it's not. I like Eveline."

Bowen sighed. "Your temper always makes trouble for you, Rorie. You have to learn to control your tongue."

Rorie looked near tears and her gaze was solidly fixed on Eveline, who still stared down at the bowl in front of her.

Graeme reached for Eveline's hand, but it was in her lap, her fingers balled into a fist. He touched her arm instead and she glanced up in question, as if all this time she'd been focused on eating and hadn't been privy to Rorie's outburst.

"She didn't mean it, Eveline," Graeme said.

Eveline's eyes widened in pretend confusion, and then she looked down again, but she never glanced in Rorie's direction. Her lips trembled, betraying her upset, and it was all Graeme could do not to carry her away from everyone. Take her up to their chamber and away from the world, where no one could hurt her again.

Rorie started to rise, but Graeme motioned her down. "Not now, Rorie. You've done enough."

"But I didn't *mean* it," Rorie said, distress obvious in her voice. "I can't allow her to think it a moment longer. What I said . . . What I said makes me no better than the women who maligned her. It makes me worse because she *trusted* me."

"She's right," Bowen said quietly. "Allow her to speak to Eveline, Graeme. If she doesn't, it will only hurt the both of them, and Eveline has already had an upsetting enough day."

Graeme reached for Eveline's hand, this time prying it from her lap and then gently uncurling her fingers. He raised it to his mouth and brushed a kiss over her palm. She looked shocked by the public display of affection. Her eyes were wide and her mouth open as she stared at him.

"Allow Rorie to state her case, Eveline. She didn't mean to hurt you. Look at her. See how upset she is."

Slowly Eveline turned, her gaze reluctantly going to Rorie, who by now was in tears, her nose red and eyes puffy. Eveline's lips turned down unhappily as if she couldn't bear the sight of Rorie's distress, even though Rorie had hurt her with her careless words.

Rorie shot up from her seat and hurried around, kneeling between Graeme and Eveline. She took Eveline's hand from Graeme and turned so she was facing Eveline directly.

"I did not mean it the way you heard—saw—it. When you first arrived, Graeme came to me—"

Rorie was talking so fast that Eveline was looking at her in complete bewilderment.

Graeme put his hand on his sister's shoulder. "Rorie, slow down. Start over. She cannot understand because you're speaking too fast."

Rorie took a deep breath and then began again, speaking more calmly.

"Graeme came to me because he wanted me to spend time with you, to make you more comfortable, and I bargained with him because I wanted him to send for Father Drummond so he could teach me to read and to write. I fully expected to hate you, or at the very least be only able to tolerate you, at best. Whatever my bargain with Graeme was, it had no bearing on our friendship, I vow it. You must believe me, Eveline. I do not want to lose your regard."

Eveline stared searchingly at her for a long moment and then finally allowed a small smile. Then she leaned down and kissed Rorie's cheek.

"I'll forgive you if I can sit in on your lessons with Father Drummond."

Rorie laughed and then launched herself at Eveline so hard, she nearly knocked them both from the bench. Bowen reacted quickly and caught Eveline before she fell backward.

Rorie hugged her tightly and then drew away so Eveline would see her mouth. "Of course you'll sit with me during the lessons. I'd be terribly bored without you."

Eveline squeezed her hand and then released it so Rorie could go back to her seat.

Graeme touched Eveline's arm in silent support. Then he mouthed the words so no one else would hear.

"You're very generous, Eveline. Thank you for that. Rorie would have been terribly upset over the thought of hurting you. She's young and until now has been very much alone, devoid of the company of other women even though she's surrounded by the women of our clan. She's attached herself to you. It will be good for her to spend time with another woman."

Eveline smiled slightly and then glanced back at Rorie, who was eating in silence. When she looked back at Graeme, she said in a very low voice, "I like her, too, and enjoy her company."

"Give the rest of the clan time," he said. "I've no doubt you'll win them over as well."

Eveline shrugged. Maybe she didn't believe him. He doubted it was that she didn't care. He'd seen how much it hurt her to field the attacks from the women. She had a tender heart and a gentle spirit. If anyone deserved kindness, it was she.

And he'd do everything necessary to ensure she received it. From him. From his clan.

If anyone had ever told him he'd feel so strongly about protecting someone named Armstrong, he would have laughed in their face. And yet here he sat with Tavis Armstrong's daughter, knowing that he'd do anything at all to ensure her happiness.

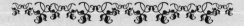

CHAPTER 25

After the meal, many of the clansmen gathered in the sitting area before the fire. Eveline watched from her seat at the table to see what it was they discussed. But all she could see was casual talk of the day, the training the men were undergoing. Two of the men engaged in a discussion of sheep and another joined after a moment when they began to talk horses.

From what she could glean, the first two took care of the clan's sheep while the other was in charge of the stables.

In her own home, she hadn't paid much heed to the day-to-day running of the keep. She wasn't completely ignorant of the workings in theory, but she lacked the practical knowledge. In keeping with her ruse, she hadn't been able to show any interest in the inner workings of her clan.

But now she considered that her life here would not only be dreadfully boring, but also extremely unproductive were she not to do anything more than trail around all day with Rorie or take an occasional swim in the river. It was a matter she'd have to take up with Graeme.

She needed a purpose. If she was going to gain her

new clan's acceptance, then it stood to reason she'd need to do something to earn it.

Her father had always said that respect was earned, not given. The Montgomerys weren't giving her anything. But there was nothing to say she could not secure it for herself.

Aye, she'd discuss it with Graeme. She would even approach Nora herself. She hadn't been one to malign Eveline, at least not to her face. She seemed kindly enough, even if she was a little wary around Eveline.

She blinked when she became aware of everyone standing around her. Graeme's brothers had risen and loomed over the table, making her feel very small and insignificant in comparison.

Graeme was every bit as large and fearsome as his brothers, but he didn't frighten or intimidate her. Bowen and Teague had been nice enough and even respectful, but she still wasn't sure where she stood with them.

After glancing warily in their direction, she also rose and moved instinctively toward Graeme. He tucked her in close to his side, putting his arm around her side. His hand rested possessively on her hip and she was shocked that he was holding her so in front of the entire clan.

As she glanced up, she saw him talking to his brothers.

". . . bid you a good night. Eveline and I are retiring."

She stopped breathing a moment as she processed what she'd seen on his lips. Her heart fluttered and dropped into her stomach as he urged her forward, still holding her against his side.

She offered Rorie a smile and only briefly made eye contact with Bowen and Teague. She was too embarrassed to look any longer because she had a firm idea that they knew why Graeme was taking her above stairs.

There was the fact that she didn't know for sure herself, however, he'd made himself perfectly clear earlier.

He'd left her with no doubt as to what his intentions were, and he didn't seem a patient sort of man.

He would take her to bed tonight and he'd make her his. Their marriage would be consummated, effectively sealing their union.

The kissing part she was more than ready for. The rest was what she wasn't overly certain of.

As soon as they left the hall, Graeme swept her into his arms and carried her up the stairs. Surprised by the sudden action, she looped her arms around his neck and hung on. His expression was intense. Focused.

He shouldered his way into the chamber and then walked to the bed and gently laid her down in the middle. Her dress spread out, the green and white vivid against the furs draped over the mattress.

He stood over her, merely staring down at her, his gaze taking in every inch of her.

She cocked her head to the side. "Why do you stare at me so?"

"Because you're the most beautiful woman I've ever had the pleasure of looking upon."

"Oh."

She was breathless. "Oh" was all she could muster. It didn't make for scintillating conversation, but what could she possibly say in response to words such as those?

"I do not even know what to do first, so tempted I am by you."

"Kiss me."

"Oh aye, I can do that," he said as he lowered himself over her.

His body pressed to hers, bore her farther into the mattress. His heat surrounded her, his scent. She inhaled as he kissed her. Deep. Searching. His tongue slid over hers, licking, advancing, and then retreating in slow, measured motions.

He pulled his head up and away from her and stared down, his eyes simmering in the low light. Leveraging his weight on one arm, he reached with his free hand and stroked through her hair, pushing it away from her face, touching her cheek, and then he caressed her jaw.

She'd thought that he wasn't a patient man, but now that they were here, he seemed only too willing to take his time, a fact she wasn't sure she liked or not.

Edgy impatience tugged at her. Deep inside, beneath her skin, it was as if something came alive and took over. She was restless, suddenly flushed with heat. The blood in her veins seemed ready to boil.

Her breasts were heavy, her nipples painfully erect. And lower, in her most private regions, need pooled, making it impossible for her to remain still.

Was this what desire felt like? Was this what it was like to want someone so badly that it hurt?

Each touch, each caress, she soaked up greedily, wanting and needing more. She craved his hands upon her. She wanted his tenderness and caring. She needed him to look upon her as he'd never looked upon another woman.

And then he pushed himself upward and moved back until he was off the bed, leaving her bereft of his warmth. She raised her head, ready to protest, but something in his eyes stopped her.

His gaze had darkened, sending shivers racing across her skin. There was something intensely predatory about his stare, and it awakened a keen sense of aching vulnerability within her.

He simply held out his hand and she didn't hesitate a moment reaching for it. His fingers closed around her palm and he pulled her upward until she sat on the edge of the bed.

Lowering his body, he knelt before her, palming her face so she had no choice but to see what it was he said.

"I'm going to light more candles. There's nothing I want more than to be able to look upon your beauty and miss nothing to the darkness. And then, when the room is sufficiently illuminated, I'm going to play lady's maid and undress you, piece by piece until you stand before me without the barrier of clothing."

She sucked in her breath and swallowed hard. Her pulse raced until she felt precariously light-headed.

He smiled and kissed her, moving those firm, warm lips over hers. When he drew away, he said, "Worry not, Eveline. I'll not do anything to harm or frighten you. 'Tis all night we have, and all night I plan to enjoy. There is no rush in our first time as man and wife. I would have you remember this occasion just as I will long commit it to memory."

With that, he stood once more and began lighting other candles, placing them strategically around the room until the entire chamber was aglow with warm candlelight. He took a moment to tend the fire, adding wood until the flames licked high.

Then he returned to the bed where she sat and once again offered his hand. He pulled her upward to stand beside him and he took her place, sitting on the edge of the bed with her standing before him.

With gentle hands, he began to peel away the overtunic, leaving her in the green underdress. She trembled, but she realized that it wasn't in fear. Nay, it was anticipation that had overtaken her and had left her shaking like a leaf in front of her husband.

He didn't just rip her clothing from her. He seemed quite content to slowly rid her of the dress she'd so painstakingly fretted over just hours before.

She sucked in a breath when he began to ease it down her body and then he let it go, allowing it to fall at her feet. In a few more moments, he'd divested her of her undergarments and she stood completely nude as he leaned back to gaze upon her body.

"Beautiful."

The one word said so much more. His gaze, the way he looked at her, the appreciation in his eyes and the way the muscles in his arms tightened. She was suddenly impatient to see him and to look upon him as he was looking upon her.

"Come to me."

She took a nervous step forward, and then his arms came around her, pulling her between his legs. He pressed his lips between the valley of her breasts and kissed right over her heart.

His hands smoothed down her bare back and down to her buttocks and then back up again. He turned his face up to capture her gaze, and then his hands tangled in her hair, pulling her down so she met his lips once more.

The kisses were less patient this time. Hot and demanding. Breathless. He was more forceful, his body tense against hers. She could feel the power emanating from him, knew that he could crush her with the slightest effort.

But he was exquisitely gentle with her. He treated her like she was a precious object he was afraid to break. She moaned softly into his mouth and relaxed against him, allowing some of the coiled tension to leave her body.

After a moment he broke from her mouth, but kept his lips on her flesh as he kissed a line down her neck and then to her breasts. When his mouth closed around one nipple, her knees buckled and he caught her to him to prevent her from falling.

It was like nothing she'd ever felt before. It was frightening for its sheer intensity. Streaks of pleasure bolted through her body. Her breasts throbbed and ached. Her groin ached.

A pulse began between her legs that was uncomfortable because she didn't know how to assuage it. She twisted restlessly, becoming more agitated by the moment.

He gave her other breast equal measure, lapping the tip with his rough tongue and then suckling it into his mouth. All the while, his hands roamed over her body, caressing, petting, becoming more intimate.

Palm down, he pressed his hand flat against her belly and then glided lower to her pelvis. Shocked at his daring, but eagerly anticipating the results of his bold touches, she held her breath when his fingers carefully delved into the nest of hair at her apex.

When his fingers stroked over the part of her that was throbbing, she flinched, not because he'd brought her displeasure, but because her reaction was uncontrollable.

He sucked strongly at her nipple as his fingers grew bolder, sliding deeper into sensitive flesh. She gasped as her sense of urgency mounted. Her body began to tighten unbearably. Pleasure built and built until she was baffled as to what she should do.

Her toes curled against the hard floor. Her hands flew to his shoulders, seeking purchase, something to hold on to before she lost all strength in her legs.

And then his finger slid inside her body, carefully probing as his thumb worked over the aching flesh above her entrance. It was too much for her to bear.

She closed her eyes as the chamber began to swirl around her. Spots flashed in her vision and she let out a cry that vibrated up her throat. She thought it must be loud because of the sensation it caused her.

The next thing she knew she was cuddled on Graeme's lap and he was stroking her body as he kissed her forehead. He was still fully clothed, which she thought was vastly unfair, and she was completely limp, no strength left in her shaking limbs.

She moved, tilting her head up so she could see his face. "What happened?"

He smiled and kissed the tip of her nose. "You found your woman's release."

It seemed such a nondescript term for what she'd experienced.

"It felt more like heaven," she breathed.

His smile broadened. Then she glanced down and frowned, her nose wrinkling. "You still have all your clothing on."

His eyebrows went up. "You object?"

"Aye, I do. I'd like to sit on the bed as you did and watch as you disrobe."

His eyes blazed and she found herself abruptly put aside as he stood. She stared up at him openmouthed as he loomed over the bed.

"Then, my lady, I'll certainly grant your wish."

CHAPTER 26

Graeme could barely contain his eagerness as he stood before Eveline, preparing to disrobe. God's teeth, but he didn't want to frighten the lass and it was taking all his restraint not to tear off his clothing and then slide between her legs.

His cock was nigh to bursting. Every ounce of his blood was pooled in his groin, engorging his manhood until he was grinding his teeth against the discomfort.

As he divested himself of his tunic and leggings, he was well aware of her curious gaze on his body. It only made him more desirous to take her long and hard. Those innocent eyes, so wide, as she took her first look at her husband without his clothing.

But then her gaze fell on his distended cock and they widened. She looked up to his face, then dropped her gaze back down and then back up again, almost as if she were asking him a thousand questions with that one look.

"Do you like what you see, wife?" he asked when her gaze returned to his face.

She licked her lips, the movement so sensuous and erotic that he groaned.

"Aye," she finally whispered. "'Tis a beautiful sight, your body."

Beautiful? It didn't seem appropriate that she used the same language to describe him as he'd used in describing her. He was nothing like her. He was hard where she was soft. Rough where she was smooth. Scarred where she had no marks to mar her lovely flesh.

He stalked forward and then tipped her back, tumbling her onto the bed as he loomed over her. He crawled between her splayed thighs and rubbed his body up hers until his lips hovered just over her mouth.

He rocked his body, mimicking the motions of being inside her though he rubbed over her soft, feminine flesh. He enjoyed the feel of her against his erection. He knew she wasn't yet prepared for him, not so soon after finding her own release. It would take time to make her ready, but he would enjoy every moment of it.

He dragged himself down and then back up her body, locking his mouth to hers. Their tongues clashed and tangled. Hot, breathless kisses. He swallowed her soft moans, knew she likely wasn't even aware of making the low sounds.

It had been a long while since he'd last given in to his baser urges. And yet he hadn't missed it. What he missed was what he'd never had. Intimacy. The feeling of closeness. The knowledge that he truly liked the woman he was coupling with.

He was well aware of the differences between him and other men, and even his own brothers. He'd never been one to throw his seed far and wide. Even as a youth, he hadn't been fast to lose his virginity. It had been even beyond when his younger brothers had enjoyed their first woman that Graeme had given in, and his first experience hadn't been particularly fantastic. In fact, it had been some time after that before he'd decided to indulge again.

But this? This was heaven. He knew without a doubt that there'd never be another woman who had such an effect on him, who could have him edgy with desire with a simple look.

She twisted his insides into knots he had no hope of loosening.

He kissed his way down her neck and to her collarbone, and then he licked the hollow of her throat, enjoying the way her pulse sped up.

He continued a path down to her breasts and rested his mouth in the valley between the two lush mounds. He wanted to stop and taste the delectable pink tips, but he had another destination in mind, one that had his heart pounding in anticipation.

Continuing his path downward, he grazed his lips over her soft belly and dipped his tongue into her navel. She shivered and twitched beneath him as he swirled his tongue, tasting every inch of her he could cover.

When he slid to the very edge of the bed so that his mouth hovered just over the soft blond curls between her legs, her head came up and her eyes were wide with shock. He saw the realization in her eyes, her knowledge of what he planned.

He smiled and then carefully ran his fingers over the velvety, plush lips of her womanhood. He'd never tasted a woman here, had never had the courage to perform such an act, though he'd heard other men speak of it.

He'd been told it was a task done to please a woman and the reactions differed. Some men enjoyed it and found it pleasurable, while others only did so in order for the woman to give them what they wanted. But all agreed that women enjoyed it immensely and he wanted to give Eveline such pleasure.

He touched his tongue to the nub of flesh just above her woman's opening. She came off the bed, her hips bucking upward. Her hoarse exclamation rang out and her fingers curled into the furs she lay on.

He grew bolder, lapping gently, absorbing her scent and her taste. It was a heady sensation, like drinking too much ale. There was a roar in his ears and the room seemed to dim around him as he continued his erotic exploration of her silken skin.

"Graeme," she said weakly. "'Tis happening again."

Her legs had begun to tremble. Her thighs shook and she was arching her pelvis upward to meet his mouth. He knew she was ready and that now was the best time, but he hated the idea of what had to come next.

No matter how prepared she was, no matter how much she might want fulfillment, what he would do would hurt her.

He drew away and then ran a finger around the mouth of her entrance, testing the smallness of the opening. She was tight around just his finger, and he knew she would tear when he thrust inside.

With a resigned sigh, he pushed himself upward and then crawled between her legs. He kissed her again and then drew away so she could see his mouth.

"It will be painful at first, Eveline. I'm sorry for that. I'll take care, I swear it."

Trust shone in her beautiful blue eyes. She reached for him, putting her hands on his face. They felt small and delicate against his jaw, so much like her.

"I think it will be wonderful," she whispered.

He didn't tell her that he disagreed, but he was happy she wasn't frightened. Carefully, he positioned himself at her entrance and pushed forward the tiniest bit, testing her resistance.

Her eyes widened and her hands fell to his shoulders, her nails digging into his flesh.

He pushed harder, her snugness enveloping him until sweat broke out on his forehead. It was instinctual to bury himself as deep and as hard as he could within her. It took everything he had to hold back and not to obey the overwhelming urges that bombarded him.

Her face puckered and doubt crept into her eyes when he persisted and she began to stretch around him. Then she winced and at that precise moment, he pushed through with one forceful stroke, seating himself inside her.

Her cry of pain was like a knife to his heart.

He went completely still, allowing her to adjust to his invasion. He kissed her face, her forehead, her eyes and nose, any part of her he could touch.

"Shhhh," he crooned, even knowing she probably wouldn't see what he said. "I'm sorry, so sorry. It will be over soon."

He rested his forehead against hers and sucked in deep, steadying breaths as his body raged at him to take her, to possess her, to make her irrevocably his in the most primitive fashion possible.

After a moment she stirred beneath him, moving restlessly as if trying to alleviate the pressure between her legs.

He reared back so he could gauge her expression.

Her brow was still wrinkled with strain and he touched his finger to one of the lines, smoothing his finger across her forehead in a gentle manner.

"'Tis all right if I move now?" he asked. "I won't move until you say me aye."

"Maybe just a little," she said hesitantly.

He smiled and then withdrew the barest of inches. It was the most exquisite torture imaginable. Buried inside her and yet unable to do more than move the tiniest amount.

"Did that hurt?"

She shook her head. "Nay."

He could tell she wasn't telling the truth, but she was

making such an effort to hide her discomfort that he didn't refute her denial.

"Move with me," he said as he slid forward once more. "Wrap your legs around me. Hold me close, Eveline."

It came out a hoarse plea that he knew she wouldn't pick up on. He sounded desperate, not at all like the solitary warrior he'd been for so long. In that moment he was glad she couldn't hear, because he didn't like the vulnerability in his own voice.

Tentatively she wrapped her legs around his hips. He closed his eyes and her hands slid warmly over his chest and to his shoulders. There was nothing more pleasurable than her touch. He needed it. Desired it more than anything.

He began to thrust, tightening his jaw to maintain control. After only a moment he was already in danger of spending himself and he'd barely begun.

Determined to make it as pleasurable as possible for the both of them, he forced himself to maintain a steady rhythm, but when she reached up to touch his face in a silent plea and he saw the need in her eyes, he was lost.

Over and over he plunged into her velvety heat. His muscles strained with effort. His entire body tightened unbearably until he was sure something would break.

"Eveline, Eveline," he whispered as he lost himself in the sweetness of her embrace.

Slowly he melted over her body, his flesh conforming to hers as they both struggled to catch their breath. She'd reached her woman's pleasure a second time, but he couldn't even say that had been his aim at the very end. He hadn't been able to register anything but the mind-numbing explosion that had wracked his body.

Now he collected her in his arms and rolled, holding her close. Their bodies were still connected and he was content to remain a part of her for as long as possible.

As she lay quietly beside him, nestled into his embrace, he stroked her back, caressing and soothing her trembling body.

So this was what it was like to be completely at peace, body and soul. To find solace with a woman who was more than just a warm, willing body to lie with.

He hadn't expected such a thing. Never would he have imagined feeling this way about the bride who had been forced upon him.

As he glanced down at her golden head, he couldn't imagine it any other way. He didn't *want* to imagine being without her.

CHAPTER 27

When Eveline awoke the next morning, sunlight was streaming through the window and right onto her face. She opened her eyes, then rapidly blinked and shut them again before turning her face away.

Who had pulled the furs aside?

She soon had her answer when the bed moved. Eveline's eyes popped open again to see Rorie sitting on the very end, her eyes brimming with impatience.

"There you are," she said. "You've been sleeping for ages. I didn't think you'd ever awaken."

Eveline blushed and made certain the furs stayed tightly arranged over her very naked body. The truth was she hadn't been sleeping for ages at all. Graeme had kept her awake most of the night with his hands and his mouth . . . She shivered in remembered delight.

The first rays of sunshine had begun to peek over the horizon by the time she'd drifted off to sleep. Graeme had kissed her and then had risen to dress. He hadn't bothered sleeping since he was due in the courtyard at dawn.

After the first time he'd made love to her, he'd insisted that she would be too sore for him to take her again, but that hadn't stopped him from pleasuring her the entire night.

She'd achieved release so many times that when he'd finally eased from bed, she'd been asleep before he'd fully left the chamber.

Yawning, she clutched the furs tighter around her and struggled to sit up.

"Why are you here?" Eveline asked Rorie.

Rorie bounced impatiently. "Graeme sent for Father Drummond this morning!"

Eveline smiled. "'Tis wonderful, Rorie. I know how badly you want to learn to read and write."

"You'll still study with me, won't you?"

Eveline nodded. "Since you're here, I'd like your help with something this morning as well."

Rorie cocked her head to the side. "You want my help? You aren't angry about last night? 'Tis part of the reason I came into your chamber. I wanted to again offer apology if I hurt you."

"'Tis forgotten," Eveline said. "And, aye, I need your help. I want to approach Nora. It's occurred to me that Graeme expects his clan to accept me even though I am from an enemy clan. But 'tis the truth, I've yet to *do* anything to gain their acceptance."

Rorie scowled. "It does not give them cause to abuse you as they have done."

"Nay, it doesn't. But I can't very well wander around the keep as I used to do in my own, acting the simpleton so no one ever expects anything from me. I'm the laird's wife and 'tis my duty to oversee the running of the keep."

A look of unease crossed Rorie's face. "Well, aye, 'tis true a laird's wife is usually tasked with the running of the keep, but my brothers share in the responsibility of ensuring the keep is well run. Perhaps 'tis best if you leave it to them."

"'Tis even more reason for me to step in," Eveline insisted. "Graeme should not be bothered with woman's work. Nor should Bowen and Teague. They have more important matters to attend to. Will you help me?"

Rorie hesitated and then said, "Aye, of course I'll help you. I'm uncertain as to what you want me to do, but I'll assist you in any way I can."

Eveline beamed over at her sister-in-law. "Wonderful. All I need is your support. 'Tis shameful of me to admit, but I'm a coward. It will ease me to have you at my side when I speak to Nora in the kitchens."

Rorie slid off the bed. "Well, then, you'd better rise and put some clothing on. You can't be running about the keep as you are."

Eveline blushed to her toes and groaned her embarrassment. Rorie sent her a cheeky grin and then went to one of Eveline's trunks to pull out suitable apparel. A moment later, she returned to the bed and held up the garb.

"Well, come on. I'll play lady's maid today. Graeme really must assign one of the women of the keep the duty. We can't have it said that the Montgomery lady has no maid."

Her nudity evidently didn't bother Rorie in the slightest so Eveline left the comfort and warmth of the furs and hurriedly pulled on the clothing Rorie offered. Afterward, Rorie helped her arrange her hair and then the two hastened down the stairs to the hall.

It was mostly empty and Eveline nearly lost her courage and opted to go outside with Rorie. Maybe go sit by the river and enjoy the day. But she knew she was being cowardly and it was time to stop hiding.

No one was going to give her a place in this clan. She was going to have to create one.

As it turned out, making a trip to the river was precisely what she and Rorie ended up doing. Nora was overseeing the washing of the clothing while a few of the other women washed their hair.

When Eveline was spotted approaching, work ceased and all eyes pointed in her direction. She stood a long moment before Rorie pushed her forward. She stumbled, righted herself, and then continued down to the bank, a bright smile on her face.

"Nora, is it?" she inquired of the older woman who was studying Eveline with a frown.

Nora's frown deepened as she nodded. "So 'tis true. You can speak. Is it also true you're not daft at all?"

Eveline's cheeks heated, but she shook her head slowly.

"Then what's wrong with you?" Nora demanded.

Eveline's hand automatically went to her ear and she fiddled with the lobe and the shell, fingering it absently.

"I cannot hear."

"What's that? Speak up, child. I cannot hear you."

Rorie pushed by her and angled herself so Eveline would be able to see.

"She cannot hear, Nora. So she doesn't always know how loudly she speaks. Sometimes 'tis hard to understand her, but all you need to do is ask that she speak up."

Nora's eyes narrowed. Behind her several of the women put their washing down completely and hovered in the background, watching and listening to the goings-on.

"What do you mean, she can't hear?" Nora said. "She understands what we say, that much is obvious."

"I can read the words that are formed on your lips," Eveline intervened. This time she made certain she spoke loudly enough. Perhaps it was too loud, because Nora took a step back, her eyes widening.

"How is that possible?" Nora asked suspiciously.

Eveline shrugged. "I have no desire to explain it. I can only say that I am able to understand when you speak as long as I'm looking directly at you."

"And why wouldn't you talk before now? Rumor is you haven't spoken in three long years."

There was a long pause as Eveline weighed just how honest she should be. There was little point in any further deception.

"Because I didn't feel safe," she said.

Nora looked taken aback. "Not safe? With your own clan?"

Behind her several of the other women were murmuring among themselves. Eveline's declaration had surprised them all. Some even looked at her with sympathy. Sympathy always made her cringe. It was something she'd had to live with for a very long time. But coming from these women, it didn't feel as smothering. They were horrified over the idea she wouldn't have felt safe among her own kin and she wasn't going to take the time to explain the entire story nor would she clarify the true reasons for her fear.

Another woman pushed in beside Nora, her brows drawn in question. "Yet you speak to us. Here, among the Montgomerys."

Eveline smiled and nodded.

"Why?" Nora asked, obviously perplexed.

"Because I feel safe."

Eyes widened all around at that.

Rorie, ever the impatient one, cut in. "Nora, Eveline wanted to ask your assistance in a matter."

Nora glanced back at Eveline. "Of course. What is it you wish to ask for?"

Eveline took in a deep breath. "Everyone has a duty here . . . save me. Rorie has told me that the laird and his brothers oversee the running of the keep. 'Tis my duty as wife of the laird and one I take seriously. But I need the assistance of someone who is well versed in the duties and has the knowledge to instruct me on the way of things."

Nora puffed up, her chin coming up a few inches. "Well, now, you've come to the right place, lass. Indeed, you have. You spend the day with me and I'll have you running the place in no time."

Eveline beamed back at her, excitement curling in her stomach. "Thank you!"

Rorie rolled her eyes. "I'll leave you two to your women's duties. I'm going to go straighten the accounting room for when Father Drummond arrives."

Eveline waved Rorie off, too excited by Nora's ready acceptance of Eveline's request for help to worry over the loss of Rorie's companionship.

It wasn't complete acceptance. Eveline still had a long way to go. But it was a step in the right direction. If the women saw that she was willing to throw herself into the Montgomery way of life, then perhaps they'd eventually soften toward her, forget that she was Eveline Armstrong and eventually think of her as Eveline Montgomery.

CHAPTER 28

Eveline didn't remember her mother ever scrubbing floors as part of her duties as a laird's wife, but it was also true, Eveline had spent little time inside the keep. And when she was indoors, she kept away from the main social areas.

During the long winter months and seemingly endless nights, she'd kept to her chamber in front of a roaring fire. Brodie and Aiden often came to visit her, and she enjoyed their company, even when they were saying nothing at all or merely conversing among themselves and not including her in the discussion.

Nora had insisted that true leaders led by example and if she wanted acceptance from her clansmen, she had to show them that she wasn't above a little dirt on her hands.

It all made sense when Nora explained it, but now, when Eveline was on her hands and knees, up to her elbows in soapy water, the idea didn't seem so sound any longer.

Still, she was too stubborn to cry off once she'd begun the task. She knew they watched her, and she wouldn't allow them to see her in a weak moment. She'd scrub the floor until it shone. Even if it killed her.

When she'd done the entire hall, she could barely stand. Her back protested loudly when she straightened, and she was fairly certain she'd groaned aloud.

Wiping the hair from her face, she lugged the pail of now dirty water to the back entrance and tossed it onto the ground. In the distance, she saw a group of women playing with the children, and her mouth drooped. It would have been fun to be outside on such a glorious day.

She trudged back indoors and went into the small room just off the kitchen where many of the utility items were stored. Nora met her as she came out, an approving smile on her face.

"'Tis a wonderful job you did on the floors, lass. I vow all the women will think so."

Somehow Eveline couldn't muster any enthusiasm over knowing they'd approve of the task she'd performed.

Thinking she'd love a brief respite and that she would investigate what the women and the children were doing on the hillside behind the keep, she made mention of doing just that to Nora, only for Nora to frown.

"Oh nay, lass. 'Tis too much to be done to be thinking about play. What would the others think if the laird's wife expected the women to work while she went off on a lark? Nay, 'tis not a good idea at all. Come and I'll show you where there's washing to be done. Mary has just finished preparing tonight's meal of oatcakes and fresh bread. There'll be a little stew leftover from last eve's meal, but I'm sure she'll have a pile of cooking pots and such just waiting to be cleaned."

Eveline's shoulder's slumped, but the last thing she wanted was to appear to be beneath such work to the other women of the keep. If they could perform such tasks on a daily basis, then she certainly could and would as well.

She followed Nora into the kitchens where Mary and one other woman, who spared Eveline only a quick glance—she didn't look very impressed with Eveline—were working and muttered an introduction in such a manner that Eveline couldn't read the name on her lips.

Not wanting to admit to such, she smiled brightly and then watched attentively as Nora instructed her on what she was to do. Oddly, though, as soon as Eveline began to scrub at the large pots used for cooking, the other women disappeared from the kitchen.

It was a long and arduous task, one that Eveline was certain she didn't do well. The pots were large and it was difficult to empty them of water once she'd added it to scrub the insides.

Even though the day was quite cool, and a steady breeze blew in from the window facing the back, sweat beaded Eveline's brow and at her nape, making her hair damp.

By the time she was finished, she no longer cared what the other women of the keep thought of her and she left the kitchens to head straight for her chamber, where she could at least wipe the sweat from her body. She would have gone for a swim in the river, but she was afraid she'd encounter Nora or one of the other women and immediately be tasked with something else to do.

She trudged up the stairs and into her chamber, her back aching and her bones weary. She grimaced when she looked down at her underdress. It was filthy and the smell made her nose wrinkle. She doubted even a good soaking in the river would save this one.

Peeling it away from her body, she stripped down until she was completely naked, and then she washed herself from head to toe. It wasn't a complete bath—she'd give anything for a good, long soak—but to do so would require having someone heat water and fill a tub and she wanted no comments from the other women, who no doubt did not take time out of their busy days to have an afternoon soak hours before it was time to sleep.

She settled for a good wipe down with some of the scented soaps from her clan. Afterward she changed into a fresh dress and plopped onto the bed. She would rest just for a moment. No one would even know.

She leaned over, burrowing her head into one of the pillows as she curled on top of the furs covering the bed. Just a moment. No more. Her eyes were closed before she was fully settled into a comfortable position.

Graeme entered the keep as the others began gathering for the evening meal. Truth be told, he was eager to see Eveline. He'd gone all day without seeing his wife even once. Throughout the day he'd tortured himself by reliving the prior night in vivid detail.

Though he hadn't managed any sleep, he'd never felt as refreshed and invigorated as he did today. It made him a complete pig, but he was tempted to take her again, even though she'd been a maiden just the night before and she'd be sore for days to come. She needed time to recover before she suffered his attentions again, but he had to remind himself of that hourly to combat the urge to go sate himself again and again.

His brothers would laugh if they knew how solidly his thoughts were occupied by coupling. They'd tease him and remark on how swiftly he'd gone from having the life of a monk to one more resembling a whore.

Ah well, 'twas what having a wife did to a man, or so he imagined.

He took quick stock of the hall and the area immediately surrounding the keep where other women were congregated, but not seeing Eveline, he mounted the stairs to see if she was in their chamber.

When he pushed the door open, he was surprised to

see her sprawled on the bed, fully dressed, and deeply asleep. He started to close the door quietly when he realized the absurdity of his actions.

Though he knew she was deaf, it was still hard to remember and he found himself acting on occasion as though she could hear. It didn't help that she was so adept at reading lips that it was easy to forget and turn his head as he spoke.

He went to the bedside and then gingerly settled down to perch on the edge. He touched her long blond hair and smoothed it away where it covered her face. She didn't even stir as he ran a hand down her side.

The lass was exhausted. Was it the long night before? But she'd slept well into the morning.

He considered whether he should awaken her to eat, but when he gently shook her shoulder, again, she didn't even twitch.

Deciding that she was in obvious need of rest, he withdrew and went back below stairs to search Rorie out. Perhaps she would know of Eveline's doings today and could offer more on why Eveline was so soundly asleep.

He caught Rorie as she was coming out of their father's accounting room and he motioned her away from the hall where she was about to enter.

Rorie frowned, her brow wrinkling in question as she let Graeme pull her to the side.

"Is something amiss?" she asked.

"Nay, I merely have a question about Eveline. She's above stairs sleeping the sleep of the dead and I wondered what occurred today that would exhaust her so. What did the two of you do?"

Rorie sighed and pressed her lips together, her eyes completely giving away the fact that something was up.

"Rorie," he said in a warning voice. "If you know something, you'd better speak up. You know I have no tolerance for such matters."

"She's resting because she's been working tirelessly with the other women."

Graeme frowned. "What?"

Rorie gave him an impatient look. "You cannot intervene, Graeme. 'Tis important to Eveline."

"What is important? I vow, Rorie, you make me want to tear my own hair out at times. Explain what is about before I throttle you."

"She asked me to take her to Nora so she could ask Nora to instruct her in the way of running the keep. She feels as though 'tis unfair of you to expect the clan to accept her when she's done nothing to gain that acceptance."

Graeme swore and shook his head. "She doesn't have to work herself into the ground to prove herself. 'Tis foolishness. She is their mistress. 'Tis she who should be directing their work, not the other way around."

Rorie nodded. "Aye, and 'tis the way it'll be, but first she must learn and who better to instruct her than Nora? I stood there myself, Graeme. Nora agreed. Eveline was all smiles and quite happy with the accomplishment. Once I was sure all was well, I took my leave and retreated to Da's chamber."

"I saw her above stairs. She was clearly exhausted," Graeme said in a grim voice. "I don't like it."

"She wants to fit in, Graeme," Rorie said softly. "She wants it so much that she'll do whatever it takes to achieve it. She wants a place in our clan, and this is how she feels she must accomplish it, whether you or I agree with her methods or not."

"She should not have to prove anything," Graeme said harshly.

"In that we are agreed. But Eveline does not feel that way. 'Tis important to her and so I'll not gainsay her, nor should you. Allow her this, Graeme. What does it hurt?"

She had him there. If Eveline was happy and content, then what was there for him to say on the matter? It didn't sit well with him that she felt she had to dirty her hands to gain the approval of the other women, but perhaps she was wiser than he.

He didn't try to understand the workings of a woman's mind. 'Twas a sure way for a man to remain permanently perplexed. And if Nora had indeed taken Eveline under her wing, it would bode well for her acceptance by the other women, because Nora was well thought of in the clan and her leadership role over the other women was well established.

"All right," he conceded. "I'll not step in or interfere in the matter. But I want you to watch closely, Rorie. If anything arises that I should know of, I expect you to bring it to my attention immediately."

Rorie nodded her agreement.

"See that she has something to eat when she awakens. I'll be taking a group of men hunting and won't return until late."

CHAPTER 29

Eveline was horrified when she awoke pressed soundly against Graeme's body. It was obvious it was long past the sleeping hour and that she'd slept right through the rest of the afternoon and beyond the evening meal.

Her husband was sound asleep in their bed and his arms were wrapped tightly around her so that her body was perfectly aligned with his.

For a moment she sighed and hovered in that delicious state between sleep and wakefulness. It was likely close to the hour when the keep would start to come awake and begin the new day, but she was loath to move from her warm spot in her husband's arms.

But she remembered Nora speaking the day before on when the women of the keep rose to make sure fires were set in the chambers and also the great hall, so that the chill would be taken from the rooms when the warriors began their day.

Regretfully, she eased from the warmth of her bed and quietly added wood to the hearth. There were no coals from the night before, so she had to use one of the half burned candles to add flame to wood.

Once a crackling blaze had begun and she was satisfied that her husband would wake to a fine fire, she smoothed the wrinkles from the dress she'd donned the evening before. Then she quickly pulled the rest of her hair around to braid it.

When she'd finished, she went below stairs in search of Nora or the other women. Stifling her yawn, she went into the kitchens to find Mary lighting a fire in the great hearth she used for cooking.

Eveline didn't miss the surprise in Mary's eyes when she looked up and saw Eveline. But it was quickly masked and she directed Eveline to set about the task of lighting a fire in the two hearths in the hall.

What she didn't bother telling Eveline was *how* she was to bring the wood in for such a task. The fireplaces were huge and the logs they used were much larger than in the smaller hearths in the chambers.

Not about to let an insignificant detail such as that prevent her from performing her task, she went outside, shivering as she glanced at the predawn sky that was just starting to lighten ever so slightly in the east.

Her breath came out in a visible puff and the air felt damp and cold on her face.

As suspected, she found a large woodpile where larger logs were stacked against the back wall of the keep, just outside the door that exited the kitchen.

She managed to wrest one of the logs from its perch, and it tumbled to the ground at her feet. She pushed it upright and after realizing there was no way she could lift it, she set about rolling it on its edge.

When she arrived at the stone steps leading back into the keep, she frowned and stared at the log she held upright.

One step at a time. She didn't have to lift it for long. Just enough to lug it up each step in turn until she reached the top.

Huffing from exertion, she strained to lift the log just enough that she could slide it onto the first step. For several moments she stood there huffing with exertion, and then she braced herself to pick it up to the next step. By the time she managed to make it to the top step, she'd been working for several minutes.

She propped it on the top step, leaning heavily on it as she eyed the stack of logs behind her. How would she ever manage to bring in enough to lay both fires in the hall by the time the men started trickling down to break their fast?

Well, she certainly wasn't going to manage the task standing here whimpering about it, that much was certain.

Determined not to be made a fool of, she rolled the log toward the hearth, eased it down to the floor, and then went back for another.

After four more trips, she had enough wood to start the first fire. She was so exhausted and weary that her hands shook as she went to maneuver the wood into the pit. She had the first situated and was about to duck back for the next when a hand tapped her on the shoulder.

Startled, she reared back and took in the horrified expression of one of the younger soldiers. He looked so appalled that she frowned, not understanding what it was she'd done wrong.

"My lady, 'tis my duty to set the logs each morn. 'Tis no job for a lass of your size. Please, allow me to finish. I would not displease the laird by having his wife do such an arduous task. Your hands, my lady. They're bleeding. Please go have one of the women tend to them."

She glanced down in bewilderment to see that her hands were torn and bleeding from her struggle with the wood. Perhaps she'd misunderstood Mary, or she'd simply read the wrong words from her lips. She'd thought that it was her task to set the fires, but she was fiercely glad that she wouldn't have to wrestle more wood into the hall. Her back ached horribly, and now that he'd drawn attention to her hands, they were starting to sting.

Graeme would be furious and the last thing she wanted was for the other members of her clan to see that she couldn't even handle the task of bringing in wood without it tearing up her tender, dainty hands.

Her overtunic had sleeves long enough that they'd hide her hands. She hadn't worn one over her underdress this morn, but she'd be certain to don it so that no one would see the damage she'd done to her palms and fingers.

For now, she had to find a place to wash in private. A glance outside told her the sun was already peeking over the horizon, which meant her husband would be making an appearance shortly.

She ducked out of the hall after thanking the young man who'd taken over the task of lighting the fires and then she headed toward the guard tower.

'Twas an inconvenience to have to go through a guard every time she wanted to walk down to the river, but she supposed she could appreciate Graeme's dedication to the safety of his people.

She called up to the guard, sure she was bellowing since she put all her strength behind the call. He stuck his head out, frowned as though she were completely daft, and then shook his head.

A moment later, a rider appeared, looking none too pleased that he was to accompany Eveline outside the gate. He likely had to miss breaking his fast.

"I'm only going to the river to wash my hands," she

said to the rider. "There's no reason for you to accompany me. The guard can see clear to the path I'm taking."

The rider didn't look impressed with her speech and he ignored her, riding forward and then looking at her expectantly.

Disgruntled with his rudeness, she took out, walking at a sedate pace across the dew dampened ground toward the river. There was a distinct chill to the air, but she enjoyed it, invigorated after the exhausting chore of wrestling with the logs for the fire.

Once she reached the bank where she'd taken her impromptu swim just days before, she knelt and stuck her hands into the chilly water.

Blood had already started to dry over the places where the skin was abraded and had broken. The water was a shock to the tender areas and she winced as she set about picking the splinters from the wounds.

It was then she noticed the blisters from the day before. Two had broken and weeped clear liquid, but there were still several tight pockets that hadn't yet burst. She sighed, knowing that she'd likely added several more this morning.

As she rose, her stomach growled and then clenched into a knot that had her wavering unsteadily. She hadn't supped the evening before and now she was late to break her fast. If she hurried, she might still be in time.

"Where the hell is my wife?" Graeme demanded, his voice booming over the hall.

One of his soldiers who was tending the fires looked uneasily in Graeme's direction and Graeme latched onto that expression and strode forward.

"Have you seen your mistress this morning?"

Anton swallowed nervously. "Aye, Laird. She was . . ." He winced and then continued on in a rush. "She was bringing in logs for the fires in the hall. I stopped her, of course, and told her it was my duty to attend the fires. She seemed relieved, but then she hurried out and I haven't seen her since."

"She was doing *what*?" Graeme roared.

Anton flinched. "I could not believe it either. The lass had no business trying to lug in the wood, but she had five logs lined up for the first fire before I came into the hall."

Graeme closed his eyes and shook his head. This was nonsense. Complete and utter nonsense and no matter what Rorie said or how valid her argument was, there was no way he was allowing this to continue.

He was prevented from demanding an accounting from every single woman in the keep when Eveline hurried in, her cheeks pale from the cold. Several tendrils of her hair had come loose from her braid and they framed her face. Despite her harried expression, she still managed to take Graeme's breath away.

"Oh, good morn, Graeme," she said breathlessly. She dipped a curtsy and then hurried on past him toward the table where food was already being served.

He blinked and swiveled so he could follow her progress across the room. She sat next to his chair and smiled at his brothers, who'd already taken their seats. Only Rorie was missing, but then the lass didn't always come to break her fast with the others.

Before he left to go sit with her and his brothers, he turned back to Anton with a quick frown. "Do not allow this to happen again. You make certain she doesn't try to carry wood inside this keep even if you have to stack it inside. She isn't to light these fires."

Anton nodded his agreement and Graeme left to go sit next to his wife.

She smiled brilliantly at him as he took his seat by her

side. Despite her seeming cheer, he could see the dark smudges underneath her eyes and it made him angry all over again that she was working so hard to find acceptance and his clan was being ridiculously thickheaded in their resistance.

Who could possibly resist a smile such as hers? Furthermore, how could anyone spend even a moment in Eveline's presence and think she was anything like her kin? The Armstrongs were a bloodthirsty, savage lot who thought nothing of killing others to suit their purposes. Eveline was a tenderhearted lass who didn't have a mean bone in her body.

Except that she had taken a sword to the women of his clan and had run them all out of the keep.

He frowned over that matter. The lass had been under duress and she could hardly be blamed for taking a stand in the face of such mean-spirited insults.

He fully intended to take up the matter of all this work she was performing over the morning meal, but she kept up a lively conversation with his brothers, though he had no idea of what the discussion was about, exactly. He wasn't sure his brothers had any more idea than he did, but they indulged her and responded in kind with a ready smile.

He appreciated their acceptance and their support, and he knew that in time it would bleed over into the rest of the clan. Perhaps Rorie was right and Eveline just needed some time to adjust and time to win over the women.

It seemed to him that she already had the support of his men. They didn't seem inclined to want her to suffer and thus far he'd heard of no man offering insult to her. The women, however, were another matter, but even then he couldn't exactly fault them for their loyalty to him and the Montgomery name.

He sighed. 'Twas a difficult matter to be certain. The

women had always been steadfast in support of the men of the clan. It was a matter that had always brought Graeme much pride. His own mother had been an important factor in bringing that kind of fierce, unbending loyalty to the women.

Before she'd died giving birth to Rorie, she'd often rallied the women around the men, preached the importance of having strong clan ties that extended to every single man, woman, and child. Graeme's father had oft chuckled and said it was a foolish man who tread in the path of his wife because she was fiercer than any warrior Robert Montgomery had ever trained.

His mother would have liked Eveline. Graeme didn't deceive himself by thinking that his mother's acceptance of Eveline would have been automatic. She would have greeted the marriage with every bit as much disdain as all the other members of the clan had. But given time, she would have been drawn to Eveline's charm and her resilience. She would have also heartily approved of Eveline being resourceful enough to have avoided marriage with a man who intended to sorely abuse her.

Graeme frowned when Eveline rose after having finished her meal. He'd fully intended to address the matter of her duties.

"A moment please, Eveline," he said when he was sure he had her attention.

"Oh, I'm sorry, Graeme. I don't have time right now. There are duties to attend and I'm sure you must be busy with the men. We'll discuss what it is you have on your mind at the evening meal."

With that she smiled and kissed him full on the lips in front of the entire hall. Then she patted his cheek and cheerfully went on by. She walked out of the hall at a fast clip, leaving Graeme completely befuddled.

It wasn't until a moment later that he realized he was

still frozen to his chair, the imprint of her mouth still tingling on his lips.

There were snickers and guffaws all around, but he paid them no heed. His gaze was riveted to the soft swing of his wife's bottom as she exited the hall.

CHAPTER 30

Father Drummond arrived the next day and Eveline was surprised to discover he was a young man, perhaps a few years younger than Teague.

He was cheerful looking, with a ready smile and an easy disposition. In a sea of warriors, he stood out because he was so different from the others. He was paler skinned, fair without a blemish that could be seen. He had blond hair, almost the same shade as Eveline's, and blue eyes that sparkled when he smiled.

Eveline thought they could be siblings because they resembled each other so closely.

It shamed her that she'd expected an older man, stern and forbidding, a harsh taskmaster who would be ruthless in his teachings.

It was obvious he was a friend to the Montgomery clan, because everyone greeted him warmly. He was treated to a series of slaps on the back that should have had him flat on the ground. Eveline winced every time a different warrior greeted him.

Rorie was practically dancing in delight, so excited was she by the priest's arrival. She could barely contain herself while she waited for Father Drummond's attention.

He greeted her warmly in turn, kissing her on either cheek when Graeme finally came around to the reason he'd sent for the father.

Father Drummond laughed when he was told of Rorie's intent to learn to read and write, but didn't seem surprised that he was to begin teaching her.

Then Graeme motioned for Eveline to come forward when he saw her standing on the periphery of the crowd assembled to greet Father Drummond.

"Father, this is Eveline, my wife," Graeme said, making certain he was turned so Eveline could see his mouth.

The priest smiled broadly and reached for both of Eveline's hands. "My lady, I've heard so much about you. You must tell me how you learned to read the words of others on their lips. 'Tis a most ingenious ability."

Eveline's cheeks heated under the praise and she smiled shyly back. She was careful to avoid allowing him to take her hands. She didn't want anyone to know of the blisters and broken skin. The roughness of her hands shamed her.

"It took some time and I'm still not adept at reading the words of everyone. Some people aren't as clear in their speech as others."

Graeme touched her gently on the arm. "A little louder, Eveline."

Embarassed, Eveline repeated herself again, making it a point to enunciate each of the words and speak in a louder volume. Graeme nodded slightly to let her know her tone was more audible this time.

"I'm fascinated by your ability to adapt to a hearing loss," the priest said. "'Tis a subject I very much want to discuss with you at a later time."

Eveline smiled, her heart warming at the father's easy acceptance. He didn't find her odd at all and, in fact, he seemed quite impressed with her ability. She hadn't realized just how stressful it had been to go so long without a kind word or a genuine smile. It made her heart ache for her own home, where her family loved her no matter if she were daft or completely normal. She was still loved and accepted.

For a moment grief was thick in her throat at the thought of a family she might well never see again. Graeme had been quite forceful on the matter of her kin ever setting foot on his lands, and her own father would not want to allow the Montgomerys on his lands, even if it meant not seeing his only daughter.

She excused herself from the company of her husband and Father Drummond and hurried away before her upset became evident.

She didn't even flinch when she came face-to-face with Nora, who had more tasks for Eveline to complete. Being busy would take her mind from her current sadness. She missed the hugs of her brothers and the company of her mother when they'd sit sewing in the evenings. She hadn't so much as picked up a needle since her arrival here, though she knew her mother had packed all her threads.

Ignoring the pain in her hands, she set about beating out the rugs that lined the hallways and corridors of the keep. She also made certain that the chamber the father would occupy was clean and aired out and a fresh fire lit to rid the room of its chill.

Graeme would be able to find no fault with her abilities to run the keep. She was ensuring their guest was taken care of and she'd already spoken to Mary about a special meal to welcome the priest.

But sadness plagued her the rest of the day and no matter how busy she kept herself, she wasn't able to shake the ache in her heart. With every skeptical glance thrown her way, she felt even more woefully inadequate and out of place.

By the time the call for the evening meal was made, Eveline was near to dropping. She was so tired that she could barely manage to trudge the distance to the hall. And she truly needed to climb the stairs to her chamber so she could freshen her appearance. Father Drummond would occupy a place of honor at Graeme's table this night and she was bedraggled, sweaty, and dirty.

With a groan, she mounted the steps and forced her way the remaining distance to her chamber.

Once there, she took special care to arrange her hair away from her face and to brush all the tangles from the tresses. She didn't want to wear the underdress and tunic she'd worn so recently, so she chose another of the dresses her mother had sewn.

It was a beautiful dark blue, similar to the dress she'd worn for her wedding, but not quite as grand. It was more suitable for an honored guest than the gown she'd worn for her marriage to Graeme.

There was a white overtunic, like the one she'd worn with the green underdress, only this one had an embroidered hem all the way around and the cuffs of the sleeve were also embroidered with a rich blue thread to match the underdress.

The sleeves covered much of her hands, a fact she was grateful for, because they were red and angry looking from the blisters and the places where she'd torn and scraped the skin. She looked at them with a grimace, thinking how horrified her mother would be over their appearance. They were not the hands of a gently bred lady.

Being a gently bred lady did nothing to gain her acceptance by Graeme's clan. Clearly they valued hard work over grace and elegance, and Eveline couldn't entirely blame them. A mistress of the keep who could work side by side with the other women was far preferable to a lady who could stitch a straight seam.

When she was satisfied that no fault could be found with her appearance, she braved the stairs again, groaning inwardly with every step down. Forcing a smile to her lips, she turned the corner to enter the hall and focused on the table where Graeme sat with his brothers.

Graeme looked her way and she could swear she saw relief and then pleasure in his eyes. It warmed her heart and alleviated some of the aching sadness that had been with her much of the day.

Her step became lighter and she was able to forget the pain and stiffness that accompanied her every movement.

As she drew near, Graeme rose and offered his hand to assist her onto the dais. Instead of taking his hand, she placed her fingertips on his arm, allowing him to aid her. She smiled at Bowen and Teague and then at Rorie, who beamed from ear to ear as she sat across from the priest. Then she gave another welcoming smile to Father Drummond and bade him welcome to their table.

Graeme surprised her by brushing a kiss over her forehead as he settled her down beside him. He started to take her hand, but she slipped it away, reaching for her goblet as if she hadn't noticed his gesture.

Rorie was animated through the meal, keeping up a lively stream of chatter that Eveline had to concentrate hard on to understand. She was sure she missed some of what was said, because she kept looking from person to person to see who responded and said what.

By the time most of the food had been consumed, Eveline was exhausted and her head ached from trying to keep up with the pace of the conversation.

All she wanted to do was go to bed and remain there for an entire sennight.

She sighed in relief when the meal was finished and Graeme suggested that the men retire to the fire at the other end of the hall to enjoy some of the clan's "finer" ale reserved for special occasions.

She was positively gleeful over the idea of being able to go up to bed until Graeme turned and extended his hand as the others stood. Confused and thinking he only meant to assist her down, she took his arm and allowed him to lead her away from the table.

When they reached the other end of the room, she smiled at the others and then tried to slip her hand from Graeme's arm so she could take her leave, but he tugged her back and she had to keep from wincing when his fingers pressed into one of the sore areas on her palm. Thankfully he didn't notice her grimace or the abrasions.

"Join us, Eveline," Graeme said. "I'd enjoy your company this eve."

Eveline blinked in surprise, but he took a seat in one of the grander chairs reserved for resting in front of the fire and then to her further befuddlement, he pulled her down to sit on his lap instead of offering her one of the nearby chairs.

But then by the time his brothers and Father Drummond took their seats and Rorie perched on another and a few of Graeme's senior men took their seats, all the chairs were filled.

She felt entirely too conspicuous sitting across Graeme's lap, even though there was nothing untoward or too intimate about his actions.

He rested his arm around her waist, holding her against his chest as the others conversed, drank ale, and laughed over jests and recounted tales of battle and training.

Graeme mostly remained quiet, though every once in a while, she could feel vibrations rumble from his chest and then the answering vibrations in her ears as his voice soothed her senses.

She loved listening to him, even if his words weren't discernible sounds.

Thankfully none of the conversation was directed at her, because she was simply too tired to keep up with what every person was saying. After a while, she relaxed fully into Graeme's embrace and enjoyed being held against his much larger body.

It was comfort at a time when she needed comforting the most. She was tired, heartsick, and lonely for her family. She was at a point when she feared never fitting in with her new clan, nor was she even sure she wanted to.

It was hard to be happy in a place where no one wanted her, no matter the effort she put into changing that fact.

Her head drooped more and more until finally Graeme tucked her underneath his chin and held her more firmly against him. She yawned broadly once and quickly clamped her mouth shut, determined not to show such rudeness in front of the others, but Graeme didn't seem to mind.

His hand soothed up and down her back and then slid back around to hold her once more. She sighed in utter contentment, wishing the moment could last forever.

Fatigue won the battle she'd fought all day and her eyes grew so heavy, she could no longer keep them open. She nuzzled her face into Graeme's neck and with one last sigh, she surrendered to the lure of sleep.

CHAPTER 31

Graeme stroked his fingers through Eveline's hair and listened as her soft breathing filled his ears. She was asleep, warm and contented in his arms. He'd known how exhausted she was and that she wanted to go up to bed, but he'd wanted her to remain below stairs with him.

Part of it was simple greed. If he could not go up to bed immediately with her, he wanted her with him so he could at least hold and touch her. He'd waited all day to be able to enjoy the simple joy of merely having his hands on her skin.

The other part was that he wanted to make it clear to his clan that he valued his wife and she had a permanent position in the clan. He'd use every opportunity to reinforce that idea. He wanted it well known that he fully supported his wife, Armstrong or not.

"Your wife has abandoned us," Bowen said in amusement.

"Aye," Graeme said. "She's sleeping soundly."

"Perhaps 'tis time you should retire," Teague offered. "The lass looks exhausted. I didn't think she'd be able to keep her head up during the meal."

So he wasn't the only one to note Eveline's fatigue. It

made Graeme angry that she was working so hard for acceptance when he'd already accepted her.

"Aye, I think it is time for me to take Eveline up to our chamber. If you'll excuse us."

He stood, bearing Eveline easily in his arms.

"Father," he said with a nod in the priest's direction. "We're glad to have you, and you may start on Rorie's instructions at your discretion."

"Eveline's too," Rorie piped up. "She wants to learn as well."

"Eveline, too, then," Graeme said in a soft voice.

Perhaps it would keep her too occupied to worry about doing hard labor in order to satisfy what she thought the women of the keep would respect. In truth, Eveline was far more worthy of their respect than they were worthy of hers.

"I look forward to instructing two such intelligent women," Father Drummond said, a broad smile on his face. "I have a feeling this will be one of the more entertaining tasks I've ever undertaken."

Graeme walked beyond the group of men and then glanced pointedly at Rorie to let her know she should take her leave as well. She reluctantly rose from her chair and bid the others good night.

When Graeme reached their chamber, he nudged the door closed behind him, and then he carefully set Eveline on the bed.

If he were a generous man, he'd simply divest her of her clothing and tuck her into bed. But he knew that was not what he wanted. He wanted to awaken her with kisses and caresses. He wanted to make her moan with pleasure, and then he wanted to possess her again.

Two days was all he could bear to wait for her to recover from their first union. He could be patient and tender with her. But what he couldn't do was wait another night to take her.

He'd thought of little else but how good she'd felt, how beautiful she was, and how . . . complete . . . she made him feel.

He leaned down to kiss her even as he began to ease her clothing from her body. The many layers confounded him and sorely tried his patience. He wanted nothing more than to just rend the material and bear her to his gaze as quickly as possible, but the gown she'd worn was obviously something of value and meticulously stitched.

He nibbled at her earlobe as he continued undressing her. She twisted and sighed, smiling in her sleep, which made him grin.

When she was completely naked on the bed, he lowered his mouth to gently suckle at her breast.

Her eyes flew open, still hazy with sleep, and she seemed disoriented for a moment. Then she seemed to realize where she was and what Graeme was doing. Her eyes widened and then darkened with answering desire.

She arched her body, stretching like a cat, clear invitation in her body language. It was all the encouragement Graeme needed.

He hurriedly stripped himself of clothing and found her propped on her elbow, watching as he returned to the bed. He reached for her, wanting nothing more than to feel her naked flesh against his.

When he was over her, propped on his elbows, his face just inches from hers, he said, "I've tried to give you time to recover, but God's teeth, Eveline, I want you so. I cannot wait any longer."

She smiled and lifted her chin so she could kiss him. "I've more than recovered. I want you, too, husband."

With a groan he crushed his mouth to hers, drinking deeply of her sweetness. His body was flush to hers and her softness beckoned, such a wondrous contradiction to the hard planes of his own body.

He rolled, taking her with him so they lay side by side and he simply stared into her eyes, absorbing the glaze in her expression. Desire was evident. It mirrored his own and he had to task himself with treating her gently, no matter that she said she was recovered.

His instinct was to roll back atop her and plunge as deeply into her welcoming body as he could. He wanted to remain inside her, simply feeling her around his cock. He would be content to spend the entire night surrounded by her warmth.

She stirred restlessly beside him, as if she, too, couldn't wait for him to possess her again. He ran a hand up her leg to her shapely hip and then up her side with a gentle caress until he reached the swell of her breast. There he cupped the soft mound and rubbed his thumb across her puckered crest until it hardened into a point. Then he angled his head down and drew the nipple into his mouth, sucking until she let out a moan and arched farther into him.

Pushing himself farther up so he was above her, he reached down, sliding his hand between her thighs, satisfied to find her hot and damp with desire.

He rubbed over the tiny nub hidden in her woman's flesh, eliciting another sigh of satisfaction from her. Then he pushed her gently onto her back so he had full access to her body, her breasts, everything he wanted to kiss and touch and caress.

He loved the contrast of the pale, plump mounds and the pink-tipped nipples. He could spend hours feasting on them, licking and sucking until he drove them both mad with lust.

Feeling particularly devilish, he licked over one and then followed it with little nips, his teeth grazing the points until they were hard and puckered. Then he licked the other, rubbing his tongue over and around, circling until she was writhing beneath him.

Then he pulled away, staring intently into her beautiful eyes. "Ah, lass, how you tempt me. I cannot spend another moment outside your sweetness."

He slid his fingers into her opening, wanting to ensure that she was prepared for him. They met with no resistance. She opened easily for him and then fit his fingers snugly as he moved them deeper.

It was enough to send him right over the edge.

He rotated his body over her, moving her thighs apart with his knee. Then he grasped his erection and worked it up and down, bathing himself in her moisture. Finally he positioned himself at her opening and pushed forward, entering her just enough that she fit snugly around the head of his cock.

She closed her eyes and her hands flew to his shoulders, her nails digging into his flesh. He pushed farther, gaining another inch. She trembled and then lifted her hips in silent plea for more.

He was more than happy to accommodate her. He surged forward, burying himself to the hilt. She cried out and he went completely still until he realized it wasn't a cry of pain but one of pleasure.

It was the most intense sensation he'd ever experienced. Never had he realized what it would feel like to be with the right woman. One he wasn't with for a quick rut and an even quicker release. This was right. So very right, and he knew he'd never feel such again. There would never be another woman for him.

She was his. His wife.

He loved her.

The realization was startling and it overwhelmed him. Love.

He loved Eveline Armstrong. How could it have happened so quickly? How could he love a woman whose clan had caused his family such grief? Logically he knew—and he'd already made it clear—that she could not be held accountable for the sins of her clan. He even knew that he felt a certain tenderness for her, and aye, a fierce protectiveness.

But love.

'Twas an extraordinary realization and one he hadn't been prepared for. It was like being hit by a mace.

"Graeme?"

Eveline's whisper reached his ears, and he realized he'd gone still and was hovering above her as he processed the magnitude of this moment.

"'Tis all right," he said, his voice breaking. And it was. Everything was perfect.

He was holding in his arms the woman meant for him. Nothing would ever feel this right if he lived to be a hundred.

He looked down at her, wanting to savor this moment, to commit to memory the moment he realized just how much Eveline Armstrong meant to him.

A tiny slip of a lass who'd snuck between his defenses. It was baffling even as it was satisfying.

He began to thrust again, this time with slow and measured movements meant to prolong their pleasure. He was besieged by tenderness, by the need to hold her and cherish her. How was he possibly to explain to her what she meant to him? How could he even find the words?

Aye, but he could show her. He could show her what he didn't yet have the words to describe. He might not be able to tell her what was in his heart, but he would show her in actions and deeds.

Gathering her in his arms, he slid into her deep and then retreated only to push back inside her.

Never had he felt so vulnerable, so completely unprotected, and yet it wasn't the terrible thing he would have imagined. He found he didn't mind trusting her with this softer side. Indeed, he wanted her to have it.

She wrapped her arms around his neck, pulling him closer. Her lips whispered over his jaw and then to his ear where she kissed and nibbled at the lobe, playful and yet sinfully sweet.

Her actions were unpracticed and yet he found it endearing that she sought to show him her affection and perhaps her love. He could only hope, for it was the worst sort of hell to imagine that she wouldn't return his feelings. She simply had to love him. He could entertain no alternative.

Closing his eyes, he buried his face in her hair, letting her surround him, hold him. He didn't trust this sudden overwhelming emotion. It was overpowering. Beyond simple lust. Beyond the pleasure of a beautiful woman's body. His heart was captured and it was a helpless, wondrous feeling.

"I love you," he whispered into her hair, knowing she wouldn't hear, but wanting to test the words on his lips. "I love you," he said again when he realized how easily they came.

He covered her completely, but it was she who held him in her tiny hands. She who possessed him, not the other way around.

His release was powerful, so much more intense than ever before. It came from a place much deeper inside him. His entire body drew up and he plunged deeper, harder until she tightened around him.

She went liquid around him, soft and satiny, and he thrust again, this time his satisfaction roaring through him like a storm. He held her so tightly, he feared he was hurting her and yet he couldn't let go.

He wanted to be inside her so deeply that they could never be separated, so that when they were apart, she would remember this moment when they were inseparable.

When they were one.

He relaxed onto her body, his loins still quivering with the last vestiges of his release. He rested there a moment, savoring the feel of her flesh imprinted on his. After a moment, he shifted to the side, bearing her with him, their legs tangled, their bodies still connected in the most intimate way possible.

She murmured something against his neck, but the roaring in his ears had yet to subside enough that he could make out what she said. He stroked her hair, down her back to cup her buttocks, holding her tightly against him so their link would not be severed.

It was a few moments later that he realized she was sound asleep, her head nestled underneath his chin, her mouth resting over his heartbeat. He smiled, more content than he'd ever been in his existence.

Her hand rested on her side and he reached to twine their fingers, fully intending to pull her arm over his side. When he touched her palm, he frowned and then lifted his head as he held up her hand in the dim light of the glowing candles.

Her palm and even the pads of her hand and fingers were ravaged. They were red, and there were still traces of dried blood where the skin had been broken. He turned it so he could better see and then swore when he saw the evidence of broken blisters.

Anger boiled through his veins, replacing his earlier contentment with rage. No more would he tolerate this, no matter Rorie's arguments. Eveline would come to no harm, his clan be damned. If they could not see the treasure that had been bestowed on their clan, then they were all fools and he would suffer no fools. No longer.

This matter would come to an end the very next day.

CHAPTER 32

Eveline woke with a start and for a moment was so disoriented, she couldn't gain her bearings. Then she smiled because she was snuggled tightly against her husband and his arm was thrown possessively over her body.

She closed her eyes and inhaled his scent. After the few days she'd had, she'd desperately needed what he'd given her the night before. Tenderness. Loving. His actions had shown her more than words ever could, that he valued her. That she meant something more than a wife he was forced into marriage with.

Perhaps one day . . . She sighed wistfully. Perhaps one day she would even gain his love. Oh to be able to hear those words. Really hear them. The idea sent an ache straight to her heart that nearly overpowered her.

She hadn't spent a lot of time dwelling on the fact that she'd lost her hearing. In the beginning, she'd done plenty of moping and had even wondered if it was God's punishment for her sins. But as time had gone on, she'd accepted that she'd never hear again. She'd never be normal and she'd never hear the things she'd taken for granted before. Music. Her mother's voice. Her brothers' teasing. And the rumble of her father's voice, full of patience for his free-spirited daughter.

But now she'd give anything to be able to hear words of love from her husband. If not love, affection. She wanted to be able to hear the things she saw in his eyes and felt when he touched her.

He might never grow to truly love her as her father loved her mother, but perhaps that kind of love didn't exist freely. She knew from hearing earlier accounts from her mother, that it hadn't always been so between her and Eveline's father. Theirs had been an arranged marriage, as so many were, and at first, neither had any liking for the suit.

But over time, they'd grown to love each other as fiercely as two people can love, and Eveline had grown up the beneficiary of that love and devotion. She wanted it for herself. She wanted it with a ferocity that she couldn't even articulate. It was why she'd been so adamant that she'd never marry Ian McHugh, because she'd known without a doubt that he was not a man who'd ever treat her well, much less regard her with any love or affection.

It was her mother's story of growing to love her father and his eventual love for her that gave Eveline hope that she too might find a love like theirs with her Montgomery warrior.

Fanciful, aye, she was that, but she'd set her mind to gaining acceptance from his clan. From him. And she wouldn't rest until she had it. If it took cleaning the keep from top to bottom and tearing her hands until they were rough and calloused, then she'd do it without regret.

It was that determination that drove her early from her warm bed next to her husband when she'd love nothing more than to wake him in a way he'd remember for days to come.

She rose, shivering, quickly dressed, and then set the

fire to blazing so Graeme would awaken in comfort. Then she went below stairs, prepared for another day of torment.

She wondered what today's tasks would bring. Maybe Nora would have her cleaning chamber pots. She shuddered at the thought, but didn't think it was out of the realm of possibility.

Nora looked surprised to see her and didn't quite cover her reaction. Eveline could swear she saw guilt in the older woman's eyes, but quickly set aside that ridiculous notion. Nora was a tough taskmaster and Eveline doubted she ever felt sorry for any of the women under her supervision.

"Good morn," Eveline sang out, determined to be cheerful despite the urge to run as fast as she could back up the stairs and dive underneath the warm blankets.

Nora sent her a disgruntled look and then motioned her over to where she stood with Mary and two other younger women Eveline didn't know by name.

"You can help finish up the preparations for the morning meal," Nora said. "'Tis simple enough fare. Oatcakes and bread with a bit of porridge for those who want it."

Eveline sighed in relief. It did sound simple enough, and it shouldn't be a threat to her aching hands.

After receiving instruction from Mary on how to fashion the oatcakes, she dove into the duty, determined not to show any reluctance whatsoever. She quickly discovered that preparing enough food for a hungry horde of warriors wasn't a simple matter at all.

Her attempts weren't as well shaped as Mary's had been, but they should suffice and it would taste the same. She couldn't imagine anyone quibbling over the appearance of something as unappetizing as an oatcake.

When she looked up after finishing as many as she had

mixture for, she discovered that the kitchen was empty and that the women had disappeared.

Frowning over that oddity, she wiped her hands on her skirts and glanced around to be certain she hadn't missed anything she was supposed to have prepared for the breaking of fast.

A moment later, Nora and Mary reappeared and hurried over to begin piling the oatcakes on serving trays while one of the other women took care of the bread.

Nora frowned over the misshapen oatcakes and then cast Eveline an impatient look. It was a look that said, "You're hopeless."

Disheartened, Eveline's shoulders sagged, but then she quickly squared them and held her hands out for one of the serving trays.

Mary readily handed over her tray and then shooed Eveline in the direction of the hall.

Suddenly nervous, Eveline hesitated at the doorway and peered into the hall. It was only half full, but the men were filtering in at a steady rate. Graeme and his brothers had yet to make an appearance, so Eveline started toward the first table to serve the warriors already seated.

She was greeted by looks of surprise and more than a few raised eyebrows. A few even scowled in the direction of the kitchen. Eveline had no idea what to make of that. Perhaps they preferred to be served by women of their own clan. Montgomery women. It only made her all the more determined to be the one to serve each and every one of them.

She was through the first table and was heading to the one opposite when all activity ceased. Several men at the table she was facing looked nervously behind her. One even dropped his goblet, spilling ale all over the table. Eveline winced, sure she'd somehow be blamed for the mishap.

She turned to see what all the fuss was about and met the gaze of her husband, and he looked furious. He stalked in her direction with such a black look that she hastily took two steps back, bumping into one of the seated warriors behind her.

"What the hell are you doing?"

She was sure he roared the question because the vibrations were strong in her ears.

Without waiting an answer, he yanked the tray from her hands, shoved it into the hands of a nearby serving woman and then took Eveline's arm to herd her toward the table where he always sat.

He sat her down and then immediately took her hands in his, turning them over so the blisters and raw skin on her palms were readily visible.

He waited until she lifted her gaze to him, and then he said so clearly that she couldn't possibly misinterpret his words, "Who did this to you?"

Her brow furrowed. "No one did this to me."

Graeme glanced up, and Eveline saw he was looking at Bowen and Teague, who'd arrived at the table. They must have asked him what was amiss because he held up her hands so they were visible to all, and his lips curled into a snarl.

"This is what is amiss. Look at her hands. Look at what they've done."

"But, Graeme, no one did this to me," she protested. "I scraped them when I was bringing wood into the hall yesterday morning and the blisters are from the washing and cleaning."

Bowen took the seat directly in front of her, his frown as fierce as Graeme's. She glanced nervously to where Teague had taken a seat next to Bowen. He didn't look pleased either. His mouth was set into a firm line.

"I don't understand," she said in bewilderment. She turned to Graeme. "Have I offended you in some way?"

Bowen's hand came down on the table, jerking her attention back to him. "What on earth were you doing trying to carry those logs in? Not even the lads can hoist those pieces of wood. 'Tis why we have one of the men do it, so none of the women incur injury trying to start the fires in the mornings."

Eveline's cheeks heated as realization struck her. The other women had well known that one of the men had the duty of carrying in the wood. Why then would they have wanted her to attempt it?

Her lips trembled, but she was determined that no one see her upset. She wouldn't give the women the satisfaction of knowing they'd made her feel foolish even for a moment.

Now she wondered just what else Nora had fabricated when she'd instructed Eveline on her duties. For the last couple of days, Eveline had worked harder than she'd ever worked in her life. She'd performed tasks that surely had to belong to the lowliest member of the clan. And yet she hadn't complained. She hadn't balked.

How they must have laughed behind her back as they watched her struggle to perform every single job that had been assigned to her. All that talk of leading by example. Eveline felt like the simpleton she'd been accused of being for so long.

She glanced down at her sore and torn hands and slipped the cuffs of her sleeves even farther over her palms.

Graeme touched her arm, but she refused to look up at him. She didn't want him to see the shame and humiliation in her eyes nor did she want to give in to the tears that threatened. Instead she stared down at the ill-formed oatcake in front of her and was tempted to hurl it across the room.

The table shook, and she glanced up in time to see

Graeme stalk away from the table. Those hated tears she fought so hard shimmered in her vision. How she hated them all right now. Everything had been so perfect between her and Graeme and now he was angry and she was miserable and so humiliated, she wanted to die from it.

She'd been a trusting idiot, so eager to please, so determined to win a place in the hearts of her new clan when such a thing was never going to be possible.

Bowen reached over the table to lay his hand on hers, and she turned her gaze to him, battling tears with everything she had inside her. Damned if she'd let them know how much they'd hurt her. Damn them all.

"Eveline, he is not angry with you," Bowen said, his expression gentle.

"They hate me," she whispered. "They all hate me and there is naught to do about it. Graeme can't make them accept me. I want to go home."

Teague abruptly stood and also turned and stalked from the table. Eveline closed her eyes at the rapidly forming nightmare that was her life. Her future. It had never looked so bleak as it did now.

"I'm not hungry," she announced. "I have a need for some fresh air."

Before Bowen could say anything more, she turned away from him so he was effectively silenced to her. She, too, left the table, but she retreated to the back entrance, the one that led to the back of the keep.

There was a gateway that led to the back meadow where the children often played. No one would be about this early, and she could walk beyond the bend in the river where it meandered through Montgomery land and slashed through the sloping hillside behind the keep.

A long walk was what she needed. Away from the others. Away from their scorn and ridicule and their childish games they played to make her feel stupid. She was finished being the object of their amusement. They could all go rot for all she cared. For the first time she understood her clan's hatred of the Montgomerys. A more horrid lot of people she'd never met.

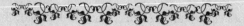

CHAPTER 33

Graeme was so furious that he had to step into the courtyard to collect himself or he feared harming someone in his rage. Never had he been so angry with members of his own clan. Never had he been in the grip of such a helpless rage. He wanted to strangle the lot of them.

The devastation and shame in Eveline's eyes had been his undoing. Seeing the damage wrought to her hands by the misdeeds of the women of his clan, not to mention the other abuses that had been heaped upon her, made him want to repay them in kind.

"Graeme, is ought amiss?"

He turned to see Father Drummond standing a few feet away, a concerned look on the young man's face.

"Aye," Graeme snapped, not volunteering more information.

"Is there something I can do?" the priest inquired softly. "I was on my way to the hall to break my fast and then to meet Rorie in the accounting room. The lass is determined to begin her lessons at once. I fear she'll keep me prisoner until she's mastered the art of reading and writing."

Father Drummond's attempt at levity fell flat as

Graeme continued to seethe. He tempered his words, though, because Father Drummond was a good man. A man of God and he deserved none of Graeme's ire.

"Go to Rorie," Graeme said. "'Tis best she is not present for what is to come."

Father Drummond cast him a worried look, but turned and went into the keep as Graeme had directed. Graeme then went in search of his most senior man. Douglas Montgomery had been a good and loyal man even before Graeme's father's death. He'd served faithfully under Robert Montgomery and had transferred that loyalty to Graeme when Graeme became laird.

He went to Douglas's cottage, one of the many that lined the hillside adjacent to the keep.

He knocked sharply, impatient as he waited for Douglas to appear. A moment later, the older man opened the door, his eyes darkening in concern when he saw Graeme standing there.

Without giving the other man the opportunity to speak, Graeme issued a terse order.

"Summon every last clansman and have them assemble in the courtyard. I want every man, woman, and child, and I want them there in five minutes. Anyone not present will be in defiance of my word and will be dealt with accordingly."

Douglas's eyebrows shot up, but he didn't question his laird's directive.

"I'll have them there at once, Laird."

Graeme nodded, then turned on his heel and stalked back to the courtyard to await the gathering. Bowen and Teague had both just stepped out of the keep when Graeme returned to the courtyard.

Soon the call could be heard, and it echoed over the keep and was relayed with urgency not used since the Montgomerys were last under siege.

"What do you plan?" Bowen asked with a frown as he approached Graeme.

"I know you are angry, brother, but think on your words before you act," Teague warned.

"Think?" Graeme snarled. "What I think is that I've never been more shamed by my clan as I am now. Never before have they given me cause to be shamed. But what they have done to an innocent woman brings disgrace to our entire clan."

Bowen sighed. "I know it, but do not react in anger. Give yourself a moment to calm before speaking to our kin."

"Did you *see* her hands?" Graeme demanded. "Did you see the humiliation and sadness in her eyes? As God is my witness, it sickens me that this has gone on behind the walls of this keep and it sickens me that I've allowed it. I am just as guilty as they are, for I stood by and let them treat her as they did."

"You did not sanction this," Teague bit out.

"Nay, but neither did I prevent it, and now I must live with the knowledge that I allowed my wife to be sorely abused by my kinsmen."

The courtyard began filling as his clansmen entered, their expressions apprehensive. There was tension in the air and murmurs spread until there was a buzz of quiet whispers in the still morning air.

After a few minutes, Douglas approached, his mouth set into a grim line. "They are all accounted for, Laird. I summoned even those patrolling our borders."

Graeme nodded. "Very good. Thank you, Douglas. You can stand down now."

Douglas stood back with the other senior men, but they all looked uncertain and wary. Rarely had Graeme ever displayed his temper. He'd firmly believed that as laird he must refrain from allowing his emotions to rule his actions. Today he had no such concern or thought of restraint.

He ascended the steps of the keep and then turned to survey his clan. Aye, they were all gathered, crowded into the courtyard until it looked nigh to bursting. He had to work to contain his rage, but he also wanted them all to see just how furious he was. It was time they felt the lash of his tongue and the heat of his anger.

"I made it clear when I took Eveline Armstrong to wife that she was to be accorded the respect and deference she deserved as my wife and mistress of this keep. To date she has been mocked, ridiculed, deceived, and betrayed by the clan she now calls her own. You are no better than the Armstrongs."

A series of gasps and murmurs of outrage rose from the assembled crowd. He ignored them all and plunged ahead, his stare taking in every last member of his clan.

"I will not tolerate the mistreatment that has been handed to my wife. I am done trying to coddle you and to understand your feelings of outrage and hatred over having to accept an Armstrong in our midst. She has acted with dignity and grace and has afforded you nothing but courtesy. She's had a smile for everyone who crosses her path. In return you've maligned her, made her feel miserable and unwelcome. You've manipulated her and used her eagerness to earn a place in our clan to further humiliate her."

He stopped and pinned the women of the clan with his fierce stare until they fidgeted and looked away. Nora had gone pale and Mary refused to even look up. The other women wore expressions of guilt and several had looks of dismay clearly written on their faces.

"Henceforth, any—and I mean *any*—infraction as deemed by me, will not go unpunished. You have a choice. You will either cease your despicable behavior or you will leave this clan and forever be outcast. You'll be stripped of the Montgomery name and the protection that goes with it."

"You cannot do that!" Macauley Montgomery exclaimed.

Graeme rounded on him, giving him a look that had him going pale. He took a hasty step backward until he stood next to his wife, one of the younger women who'd been party to Eveline's mistreatment.

"Is that a challenge?" Graeme asked in a deathly quiet tone. "Because know this: Any disagreement will be considered a direct challenge to my leadership and my position as laird. The fight will be to the death."

"N-nay," Macauley stammered. "You have my support, Laird."

"Do I?" Graeme demanded. He swung his gaze to encompass the entire courtyard. "Do I have your support? Or do you oppose my word on this?"

Several nays rose from the crowd.

"It is evident to me that I do *not* have your support," Graeme said in an icy tone. "Supporting me means you support my wife and your mistress. Nothing that any of you have done could be construed as support of Eveline. Best you keep in mind that any slight to her is a slight to me. Any abuse to her is abuse to me. Any insult to her is an insult to me."

Then he turned to Nora and singled her out in the crowd. "Henceforth you are relieved of duty. You will no longer oversee the women of the keep nor will you enjoy the privileges you've enjoyed till now. You may join the other women I removed from duty within the keep."

Nora gasped and promptly burst into tears. Her husband put an arm around her to comfort her and leveled a malevolent glare in Graeme's direction.

Teague drew his sword and was in front of Nora's husband before Graeme could even react to the blatant show of disrespect. He held the blade to the older man's throat, his teeth bared.

"You'll not show our laird such disrespect. Any man who goes against my brother will answer to me."

Bowen stepped forward, sword drawn. "And to me."

"And me," Douglas said quietly.

One by one his senior men-at-arms stepped forward to stand at Graeme's side.

"'Tis time you stop acting like children," Douglas said in a firm voice. "Robert Montgomery would be shamed by his clan's treatment of the laird's wife. He would never condone such hatred of a woman innocent of any wrongdoing save being born into an enemy clan. 'Tis Eveline's only sin. I've seen with my own eyes her effort to make the best of a distasteful situation. 'Tis time for the rest of you to open your eyes and your minds and rid yourself of such senseless hatred."

"You'll show her respect or suffer the consequences," Graeme vowed. "Now go about your duties and think on all I've said and make your choice. I will show no more leniency, as God is my witness."

His clansmen scattered as they hastened to go about their duties. Several of the women went away, their faces ravaged by tears. He had no sympathy, though. All he had to do was think on Eveline's ravaged hands and fury raged through him all over again.

"'Tis done," Bowen said quietly. "They'll not disobey you again. Not when you've made the consequences abundantly clear."

Graeme nodded. "Aye, 'tis done. I'll not go back on my word."

Teague nodded. "Aye, I know it."

Graeme stared over at his brother. "But you don't agree."

Teague slowly shook his head. "I saw what their actions have wrought. I'm as disgusted as you at their

258   Maya Banks

treatment of the lass. She does not deserve the treatment she has recevied. I fear they've crushed her spirit. I did not like what I saw in her eyes when she realized all that had been done."

Graeme's stomach knotted. He hadn't liked what he'd seen in Eveline's eyes either, and he only prayed that he'd not stepped in too late.

"She said she wanted to go home," Bowen said quietly. "'Twas the last thing she said before she left the table in the hall."

Graeme cursed and curled his fingers into a tight fist.

"Graeme!"

Graeme looked up to see Rorie pushing by several clansmen in her bid to leave the entrance to the keep. She hurried up, a frown marring her face.

"Where is Eveline? I went to summon her for our first lesson and I cannot find her anywhere."

Graeme frowned. "She was just in the hall not so long ago. Did you check her chamber?"

Rorie nodded. "Aye, of course I did. I even looked from the tower to the bend in the river. 'Tis one of her favorite places to visit. But I saw no sign of her."

"She left the keep from the back entrance," Bowen said. "She said she had need of fresh air. I assumed she'd walk where she so often walks when she leaves the keep."

"Return to your lesson, Rorie," Graeme ordered. "I'll go in search of Eveline."

"Do you want Teague and me to help you search?" Bowen asked.

Graeme paused a moment. "Nay, 'tis likely she's not far. I'll summon you if I need help. I need . . . I need to speak to her. She was upset by all that has occurred."

Teague and Bowen nodded their understanding.

"She's a good lass," Teague said gruffly. "Seeing her

hands . . . seeing the hurt in her eyes was more than I could bear."

Graeme's lips tightened. "Aye, 'tis more than I can bear either and I'll not allow her to be hurt this way again, even if it means punishing every single person who disobeys me."

CHAPTER 34

After a cursory search of the area immediately surrounding the keep, Graeme's stomach tightened into a knot and he went for his horse. Deciding they would cover more ground if his brothers did indeed aid him after all, he sent them to the north while he rode behind the keep in the direction of the river.

He nearly missed her as he topped a rise that overlooked the Armstrong border in the distance. She was hunched down in a patch of wildflowers, her knees hugged to her chest as she stared in the direction of her family's lands.

She presented a forlorn sight, her gaze distant as her hair lifted and blew in the breeze. She hadn't seen him and he didn't want to frighten her by approaching on horseback.

He rode as far as he dared and then quickly dismounted, leaving his horse to graze while he strode toward Eveline.

Her chin rested atop her knees and as he neared, he could see the tracks on her cheeks left by her tears. He let out a savage curse, anger billowing through him all ~~. again.

~~ moment he stood, watching her, suddenly unsure of himself. What could he say to her? How could he possibly make right all the wrongs that had been done to her?

He'd seen something in her eyes at the table when she'd realized that she never should have been tasked with bringing in heavy logs for the fires in the hall and that the women had been purposely giving her impossible tasks in their bid to make her feel foolish and unwanted. Something he'd never seen before in her expression.

He'd seen resignation.

She'd faced the situation she'd been forced into with resiliency that surprised Graeme and made him respect her all the more. It would have been a simple matter for her to be resentful, for her to have harbored as much hatred for him and his kin as they did of her.

But she'd done none of those things. She'd tried very hard to fit in with her new clan. And in return her effort had been thrown back in her face.

Seeing that look in her eyes, one that told him that she'd finally given up and that she was defeated . . . it scared him because he could literally feel her slipping away before he ever really had her.

As if sensing his presence, she turned her head and their gazes connected. There was sorrow in her eyes. Heavy sorrow that made his gut ache fiercely.

He walked forward, closing the distance between them. She didn't wait for him to say anything. As soon as he was within a goodly distance, he heard her soft, pained voice carry to him on the wind.

"I want to go home."

His first reaction was to shout, "Nay!" It took all his restraint not to shout the denial. A cold fist of dread clenched his throat and squeezed relentlessly. She wasn't happy. Even a fool could see that she was miserable.

He forced himself to remain calm as he came to stand

beside her. She was perched on a flat rock in the midst of the flowers. The grass was taller here in a small meadow where there was less slate and rock to prevent grass and flowers from growing.

He lowered himself to the ground next to her, but her attention was focused on a faraway point. She was staring toward her father's lands with a look of such longing that a lump formed in his throat.

"I know 'tis not possible," she said in a voice strained with tears. "But I do not want to be here any longer."

Tentatively he reached for her hand, but as soon as his fingers soothed over her palm, she yanked it away and clutched both hands together in her lap. She directed her gaze downward, refusing to look at Graeme, which effectively prevented him from speaking to her.

Impatience coupled with panic set in. He couldn't fight this, fight for her, if she refused to communicate with him. If she'd given up, truly given up, then what was there left for him to do?

He could not—would not—let her go. No matter what he had to do, she would stay by his side.

And yet the thought of her being so unhappy ripped his heart out. He wasn't selfless enough to grant her freedom. He wanted her wholly to himself. By his side. In his bed every night. In his arms. The very sight of her did odd things to his mood. Anyone who could look at Eveline and not smile was a harder man than he. She was . . . She was a ray of sunshine on the dreariest of days. She filled a hole he hadn't even thought occupied his heart.

He couldn't let her go.

He shifted closer to her and then reached to gently cup her chin so he could turn her face in his direction. Her ~~s~~ automatically lowered, but he waited, simply hold-
~~there~~ until finally, grudgingly, she looked up and

"Give me a chance to make you happy, Eveline."

Her eyes widened, and then her brow furrowed, as if she was trying to discern whether she'd correctly interpreted his words.

He released her chin and then brushed the backs of his fingers down the soft skin of her cheek.

"I know it has not been an easy transition for you."

She let out a snort, her lips twisting.

"Aye, I know, 'tis an understatement of the situation."

She nodded and it worried him that she'd resorted to not speaking, almost as if she'd withdrawn into the protective world she'd formed before.

He pushed himself to his feet and held down a hand for her. She glanced curiously up at him, but didn't put her hand into his.

"Walk with me, Eveline."

She hesitated a long moment and then slowly extended her hand so he could help her up. Relief overwhelmed him. She wasn't turning away from him. At least not yet.

He assisted her to her feet, glanced back to see where his horse was grazing, and then set off in the opposite direction, so the horse's presence wouldn't be unsettling to her.

Tucking her arm underneath his, he guided her through the meadow and up the incline where a bluff overlooked the boundary of Montgomery and Armstrong land. He didn't miss the wistful way in which she stared at the river that snaked through the small valley, marking the line between the two clans' holdings.

Then he turned so they were facing each other, but he kept her hands in his, not wanting separation between them.

Gently he turned her hands so they were palm up, the backs against his palms, exposing the raw and angry flesh. He lifted one and pressed his mouth to the abused skin and kissed every inch of flesh, soothed over every blistered and torn area.

Then he lifted her other hand and did the same.

When he was done, he rested her hands over his chest, cupped in his hold, his fingers circling her wrists. He made certain she was looking at him before he spoke.

"I understand why you want to go home. I don't even blame you. You've not been treated kindly by my clan."

Hurt flashed in her eyes and her bottom lip quivered, as if she was trying hard not to cry again.

"I allowed them to make a fool of me," she said, finally breaking her silence.

"Nay," he refuted forcefully. "You came to this clan willing to set aside your hatred or fear. You embraced a marriage that was forced on you and you've determined that you'll make the best of a very difficult situation. You were torn from the bosom of your family and everything that was familiar and dear to you. And yet you didn't allow that to cloud your judgment of your new clan. 'Tis more than I can say for any member of my clan and even myself. We were wrong, Eveline. We are wrong, and I want very much to have the opportunity to right this wrong against you."

"You cannot make them accept me," she said in a low voice that he had to strain to hear. "You cannot change what's in their hearts. I thought . . ." She sighed. "I thought I could if I just tried hard enough, if I made the effort. I was wrong."

The defeat in her words tore at him. He'd never felt so helpless and it wasn't a pleasant feeling. He was used to issuing an order and for that order to be followed, no question, no argument. He had been faulty in thinking it was as simple as ordering his people to accept his wife. He was used to being heeded, his word not being challenged. Now he faced the seemingly insurmountable task of changing the thinking of an entire clan and ridding them of hatred that had existed for countless years.

"Eveline," he began, his voice breaking as he tried to gain control of his emotions. "I was wrong in thinking that this would be a simple matter. I am to blame for not handling the situation with more thought and regard."

He took a deep breath and plunged forward, his heart beating against his chest like a drum.

"I want this marriage. I . . . value . . . this marriage. I value you. I was wrong to think the mindsets that are so deeply rooted could be changed in a matter of days. But I don't want you to give up, because I'm not giving up. We *will* make this work and I want you to believe in me if nothing else. Your place is here. With me, at my side. I need you to believe that in your heart, for it is what is in mine."

Eveline stared back at Graeme, her pulse racing. His gaze was completely earnest and in his eyes she saw something more, something she'd never imagined seeing in a warrior such as Graeme.

She saw pleading and vulnerability.

"I want to be here with you, too," she whispered, the words catching and scratching against her throat. "But they don't want me. They hate me. They'll always hate me for who I am and I cannot change the circumstances of my birth. I wouldn't even if I could. I love my family. I'm proud of my heritage. 'Tis nothing for me to feel shame over."

Graeme started to speak, but she extricated her hand from his hold and gently pressed a finger to his lips to silence him.

"I looked to this marriage with a mixture of emotions. I felt relief that I would be forever safe from an arrangement with Ian McHugh. I looked at you and saw someone I felt safe with, even though you were my clan's most hated enemy.

"But I was also fearful because I knew such a match was impossible. And I was right. Your clan will never accept me. You'll forever be at odds with them over me. A clan divided will fall on the battlefield. If you do not have their full support, how can you depend on them to do their duty when the time comes to protect your people?"

She sucked in a deep breath and plunged ahead while she still had the courage to say all that was in her heart.

"And yet I also was hopeful because I saw an opportunity to stop cowering behind a falsehood that had captured me in its grasp. One lie had led to another until it was impossible to escape the deception I had begun. Here, I'd hoped that I could be a normal lass with a husband who was kind and that eventually I could have children and forge a life beyond what was my reality in my own clan.

"But like you, I thought it would be a simple matter. I truly thought that once your clan saw that I was willing to set aside differences and that I was willing to work to gain their acceptance and regard, that past hatreds would be forgotten. It was a foolish thought. It's not possible any more than it would have been possible for my clan to accept a Montgomery in their midst."

Graeme framed her face in his hands, his expression fierce, his eyes blazing with determination.

"'Tis not impossible. Give me time, Eveline. I cannot let you go, and yet I do not want you to be unhappy. I vow that you will always have the unwavering support of me and my brothers. In time, the clan will move beyond their current mindset. 'Tis too soon to judge. We've both admitted that it takes time to change the minds and hearts of others. All I ask is that you trust me to protect you."

His grip tightened and he lowered his face until they were eye to eye and his gaze burned over her skin.

"Give me a chance, Eveline. 'Tis all I ask. Give me more time and if you still feel as you do come winter, then I'll return you to your family and ask no more of you. I'll take you to your father myself and I'll vow before God to uphold our treaty. I'll hold our marriage vows firm, but will allow you to live apart from me."

She swallowed, the ache in her heart growing. She wanted nothing more than to remain with Graeme. She thought she'd even grown to love him in the short time they'd been together, but was it enough? Could she ever hope to gain his love and would that love be enough to overshadow the rest of the clan's treatment of her?

But what then awaited her at home? She would be forced to explain all to her parents, to her brothers, and to her kin. They would be happy that she wasn't as affected by the accident as she'd led them to believe, but then would come the disappointment over her deception.

What was left for her in her own clan? She wanted a husband and children. She wanted to break free of the life she'd been forced to live due to her own fears and lies. If those were the things she most wanted, then she'd be forever denying herself the possibility of love, children, and having her own status in a clan were she to go back to the Armstrongs.

She broke free of Graeme's grasp and turned sideways to him, staring over the rolling terrain. For so long fear had ruled her existence. Fear, deception, lies. It was no way to live.

At least here, everything was honest. Nay, they didn't like her. They didn't accept her. But could she change that? Was she willing to travel a very difficult path if in the end her reward was the eventual acceptance of her new clan?

She wanted her mother, but she was no longer a young lass attached to her mother's skirts. Her mother was a very wise woman, and Eveline wanted her counsel now more than ever.

But it was time for her to stand on her own two feet, to stop hiding behind her clan and the protection they'd always offered. Nay, things wouldn't be easy here, but she wasn't willing to give up so easily just because she'd been made a fool of.

She was tired of running. Tired of hiding and of seeking the protection of others. Perhaps it was high time she took a stand, and not behind her husband, forcing him to go against his own kin in defense of her.

She turned, fully intending to tell Graeme of her decision when a flash of movement caught her eye. She frowned and stared beyond Graeme to see a man on horseback coming just over the rise. He wore a helmet that made seeing his face impossible.

To her utter horror, he raised a crossbow and urged his horse forward.

She screamed a warning to Graeme, but he'd already heard the hoofbeats and turned rapidly, drawing his sword.

He yelled something. She could not see his lips, but the vibrations buzzed through her ears. Then he shoved her so she fell forward to the ground.

Eveline scrambled up, fearing the worst, her heart in her throat. The horseman pulled up a distance away and sent an arrow flying in Graeme's direction.

"Nay!" she screamed.

Graeme flung himself to the side, sword still in hand, but the arrow caught him in the shoulder. He hit the ground with a thud and his head cracked against one of the jagged outcroppings that were scattered over the meadow.

She stood, terrified, staring at the horseman, knowing she could do nothing to prevent her own death. But her first instinct was to protect Graeme from further harm.

Screaming for help the entire way, she flew to Graeme, yanking at his heavy sword that now lay beside him. His eyes were closed and blood was smeared on the rock. The arrow protruded from his left shoulder and she knew it had nearly gone through because only a small part of the arrow remained outside his flesh.

Terror lending her strength, she pulled at the sword, managing to lift it high as she scrambled over his body to place herself between him and the intruder. The screams tore from her throat, painful and raw. One word over and over. "Help! Help!"

The horseman seemed spooked by her screams and he rapidly reined in his horse, turning him in the opposite direction, but not before Eveline saw the ornately decorated scabbard at his side.

It was unmistakable, the design that her father had commissioned for every senior Armstrong warrior. She went numb as realization barreled through her panicked senses. It was an Armstrong warrior who'd just attacked her husband, and he was even now riding as fast as his horse could run back toward Armstrong land.

CHAPTER 35

Eveline dropped the sword and turned to Graeme, who was still unconscious on the ground. She fell to her knees, hunched over him, unsure of what to do, whether she should touch him.

She put her hand to his head and gently turned it. All the breath left her body when she saw the gash where he'd hit the rock. Blood coated her fingers and she drew them away, staring in horror.

Oh God. Don't die.

She wasn't sure if she said the words or just thought them, but inside her head she was still screaming over and over.

What could she do? It was obvious no one had heard her cries for help. She looked back in the direction of the keep, but saw no one arriving to aid her. What if the archer came back? She couldn't leave Graeme and yet she couldn't lift him to get him back to the keep.

Her gaze lit on his horse, who'd evidently been spooked by what had occurred. He had run a short distance, but even now was making his way to his fallen master. His gait was agitated and he seemed nervous and wild-eyed.

The mere thought of trying to ride Graeme's horse

sent cold terror streaking through her veins, and yet she knew she had no other choice. It would take too long to run back to the keep. She couldn't leave Graeme unprotected for that long. She had to bring help or he'd die here in the meadow.

Summoning every ounce of her courage, she ran toward the horse. But he shied and scrambled back a few paces as she approached, forcing her to slow to a walk. She held out her hand, murmuring soothing nonsense in an attempt to calm him.

After a moment she was able to draw close enough to take the reins, but he immediately shied again, and she nearly lost her grip as the reins sawed across her torn hands. Sheer determination enabled her to hold on when every instinct screamed at her to drop the reins and move as far away from the horse as possible.

"I need your help," she said in a desperate voice. "Please, please let me mount."

She knew her obvious fear wasn't helping calm the horse any. Before he could bolt or she lost her courage, she grasped the saddle and swung herself up, her skirts tangling as she sought to right herself.

Grasping tight hold of the reins, she dug her heels into the horse's flanks and urged him forward. He rocketed forward, nearly unseating her, but she was determined to remain astride. Faster and faster she urged him, until they were streaking dangerously over the terrain and she was clinging to his back in a desperate bid not to fall off.

"Faster, please," she whispered, her heart nearly bursting from her chest.

Never before had she been so terrified. Flashes of her last ride blew through her memory. The reckless fall she'd taken in the storm. Her terror at the idea of dying and never being found or of her kin coming across her broken body at the bottom of the ravine.

But she swallowed back her fear and focused on her goal of summoning aid for Graeme.

As soon as she neared the keep, she began yelling for Bowen and Teague. They'd help her. They'd not turn a deaf ear to her screams.

The gate, which had remained open because Graeme had been out riding, loomed, and she lowered her head until she was hugging the horse's neck and urged him on faster, desperate cries tearing from her throat until each one sent agony through her vocal cords.

She thundered across the bridge and into the court-yard where Bowen, Teague, and dozens of other warriors had rushed upon hearing her cries for help. She knew not if the horse would even stop, and she realized that though she'd made it back to the keep, she could still die if the horse threw her.

The horse skidded to a sudden stop when Bowen and Teague ran forward. She closed her eyes and held on for dear life, but the sudden stop propelled her right over the horse's head.

She landed with a thump that shook her very bones. Pain screamed through her body, and she couldn't breathe. The air had been knocked solidly from her and she lay there, gasping and wheezing.

Bowen appeared over her followed by Teague. They were all talking at once and she couldn't even manage to focus on their lips to know what they said. The one thought that consumed her was that she had to go back to Graeme. She must bring help for him.

"Graeme!" she shouted, hoping to make herself heard above the din.

Bowen reached down, grasped her face, and forced her to look directly at him. His expression was terrible, his eyes so dark that it made her shiver.

"Eveline, tell me what has happened! Are you hurt? Where is Graeme?"

"Archer," she gasped out, still unable to draw a full breath. "Graeme was shot in the meadow. Hit his head when he fell. I had to leave him. I couldn't lift him. I had to leave him to summon aid!"

"Shhh," Bowen soothed. "You did right. Can you stand? Are you hurt anywhere?"

Ignoring the pain that wracked her bruised body, she struggled upward, already reaching for the reins of Graeme's horse, who stood to the side, his nostrils flaring as he huffed and snorted.

Teague made a grab for her. "Nay, Eveline! You'll stay here. Tell us where to find Graeme. We'll go for him."

Bowen was already shouting orders to the men and they scrambled to mount their horses. Eveline ignored Teague's order and shook off his restraining hand.

"I'll show you," she croaked out. "Please, you have to help him!"

She tried to remount the horse, but lacked the strength. Bowen caught her, and when she thought he'd physically restrain her and prevent her from mounting, he pushed upward, helping her gain her seat instead.

Without waiting, she urged the horse back through the gate and over the bridge. She raced across the meadow, uncaring of the pain or fear it caused her. Graeme needed her. He could be dying even now.

This time when she approached she was able to better control the horse and was able to slow him. Still, she was out of the saddle and stumbling to the ground before he'd come to a complete stop. She ran to Graeme's still body and hovered anxiously over him as she waited for the others to dismount.

Teague and Bowen pushed in, their expressions grim and worried as they examined Graeme. They looked at the wound on his head and then inspected the arrow deeply embedded in his flesh.

"He's not dead," Eveline said fiercely. She shook her head vigorously. "He's not dead!"

Teague lifted her and put his arm around her to support her. "Of course not, Eveline," he said. "We'll take him back to the keep. The healer has already been summoned and will be waiting to tend to his wounds when we return."

"But how?" she asked, peering anxiously around Teague to where the others gathered around Graeme.

Teague pulled her back and stared firmly into her eyes. "We'll fashion a litter and carry him back. You're not to worry. I don't want you riding his horse again. You could have killed yourself. You'll ride back with me because you're not fit to walk the distance."

She shook her head in vehement refusal. "I won't leave him."

Teague started to argue with her, but she looked away and then pushed around him so she wouldn't see what it was he said.

She hurried back to Graeme, who was being rolled onto a makeshift litter that the men would carry back to the keep. As soon as they hoisted him up, she fell into place beside him, reaching for his hand.

Bowen took up Teague's argument, insisting she ride back with one of them, but she was adamant about not leaving Graeme, not even for the time it took to return to the keep.

With a sigh, Bowen mounted his horse and then gathered the reins of Graeme's horse to lead him back. The men on horseback flanked the men carrying Graeme so he was protected on all sides. Eveline kept pace beside them, her hand tightly curled around Graeme's.

She didn't like the pallor of his face or that his head still bled from the wound. She shuddered every time she glanced at the shaft protruding from his shoulder. Even if the wound itself wasn't life-threatening, he could easily succumb to fever and die in the ensuing days.

The journey back seemed interminable, and by the time they walked into the courtyard, the entire clan was in a flurry of activity.

Rorie met them, her eyes red from crying. Father Drummond stood at her side, preventing her from running to the litter bearing Graeme.

Eveline hated to see her so upset, but she couldn't spare the time to go and comfort her sister-in-law. Her priority was Graeme and his well-being. Nothing was more important.

They bore Graeme up the stairs to his chamber and Eveline hurried in before them to pull back the furs on the bed.

Then she hastily built up the fire and lit as many candles as she could lay hands on, so the room would be well lighted for what was to come.

To her surprise, the healer wasn't a woman, but instead a young man named Nigel, about the age of Father Drummond. She frowned when he entered the chamber and began examining Graeme. She flew to Bowen's side to question him on the ability of the younger man to tend to Graeme's wounds.

Bowen assured her that all would be well and that the young warrior had much skill in healing. His mother had been the clan healer until her passing the winter before and she'd instructed him in the ways of healing.

But for Eveline, the final straw came when Nora and Mary pushed into the chamber, their intention to aid Nigel.

"Nay!" Eveline shrieked, flying forward to push them from the room. "Out! You'll not touch him. Begone, all of you. Leave my husband to his brothers and to me. No one will touch him without my by-your-leave. I swear by all that's holy I'll cut off the head of the person who defies me in this."

She was so distraught that in the end, Bowen and Teague firmly ordered the other women from Graeme's chambers. Eveline went to Graeme's bedside and looked earnestly at Nigel, who was cleaning the wound on Graeme's head.

"Why hasn't he awakened?" she asked anxiously. "Is it a serious injury? And what of the arrow?"

Nigel put his hand gently on Eveline's. "My lady, 'tis too soon to tell. I don't think the wound to his head is severe, but the longer he remains unconscious, the more it concerns me. I'll have to remove the arrow, though, so perhaps 'tis more merciful that he remains unconscious, at least until the arrow is out."

Eveline drew her hands away and then wrung them together fitfully. Bowen put his hand on Eveline's shoulder and squeezed comfortingly. She turned to look at him.

"It will be all right, Eveline. Graeme has suffered far worse than this before. He'll be just fine. You'll see."

The tears she'd been so valiantly trying to keep at bay flooded to the surface and a sob welled from her throat, painful from all the screaming she'd done.

"Come away," Bowen said, his touch still gentle on her shoulder. "Allow Nigel to do what he must. Go and sit by the fire where you'll be more comfortable. You suffered a terrible fall from the horse, and Nigel will need to look after you once he's finished with Graeme."

She rose shakily, reluctant to leave Graeme even for a moment. She hesitated, torn between the desire to warm herself by the fire and to remain with her husband.

Teague touched her arm and she slowly lifted her gaze to him.

"Eveline, come away. You've suffered a terrible shock. I don't want you near Graeme when Nigel removes the arrow. 'Tis possible he could become combative and harm you without even realizing it."

Numbly, she allowed Teague to guide her to the fire. He took one of the furs from the bed and draped it around her shoulders once she was settled on the bench.

"Would you like something to drink?" he asked.

It took a moment for her mind to process the words on his lips, and then she slowly shook her head.

She hunched next to the fire, her gaze never leaving her husband as Nigel set about removing the arrow. At some point, Graeme must have roused because she saw movement and then Bowen and Teague moved quickly to subdue him and hold him down.

Eveline clamped a hand to her mouth to stifle her cry. It was all she could do not to run to Graeme's side. She wanted him to know she was near. What if he thought she'd deserted him? Worse, what if he'd seen what she'd seen and thought she was behind the attack on him?

A moan tore from her throat, one that was audible because Teague and Bowen both yanked their heads around to look at her.

"He woke for a moment, Eveline," Bowen said. " 'Tis a good sign."

She latched onto the tiny beacon of hope and pulled the fur tighter around her as she watched Nigel cut off the fletching of the arrow, leaving the smooth shaft to punch through the other side of Graeme's shoulder. It would leave a gaping wound, but one much smaller than if they pulled it back the way it came.

Chills wracked her body as reaction set in. She shook uncontrollably and her teeth felt as though they would rattle right out of her head.

For how long she sat there, shivering and rocking back and forth, she wasn't sure. Nigel finally leaned back, his hands bloody, but clutching the arrow that had been lodged in Graeme's shoulder.

Then he began the slow process of cleaning the wounds and stitching them closed.

Bowen and Teague left Graeme's bedside and came to sit on either side of Eveline. They positioned themselves slightly in front of her so she could see each of their faces.

"Are you all right?" Teague asked, his brow creased with concern.

It took a long moment for the words to sink in. Bowen and Teague exchanged worried glances and finally Eveline nodded.

They spoke of other things, but Eveline was too numb to comprehend. She knew they had questions. Aye, they would want to know the whole of it and she lived in terror for what she must tell them.

She closed her eyes, only wanting to escape the nightmare that had been thrust on her. Graeme couldn't die. He couldn't.

Bowen touched her arm again, but she sat, her gaze locked on the bed where Graeme lay. Finally, Bowen and Teague rose and moved away. She let her gaze follow them for a moment, only to see that they were discussing immediate action and would ride out with the men to scour the area for the interloper.

A chill settled deep into her veins.

War would be inevitable once they learned the truth.

CHAPTER 36

Eveline refused to leave Graeme's side. She refused to sleep. She refused to eat. She remained steadfast at his bed as he drifted in and out of consciousness.

Bowen and Teague had given up trying to bully her into resting. She didn't even know how she was able to remain conscious herself. It was through sheer force of will that she was able to remain upright to tend to Graeme.

She even refused to have Nigel look her over after her fall from Graeme's horse. She could see for herself that she was bruised from head to toe. But nothing felt broken. She was stiff and sore, and if she moved too quickly, she wanted to scream in pain, but she kept mostly to Graeme's bedside and she could handle the discomfort caused by soreness just fine.

It was likely she was back to being considered completely mad by the people of Graeme's clan, but she cared not. She stoutly refused to allow anyone into his chamber save his brothers, Rorie, Father Drummond, or Nigel.

Graeme was . . . hers. The only person in his clan who'd made her welcome from the very start. He'd fought for her. He'd stood on the hillside and pleaded with her for a chance to make her happy. Perhaps if she hadn't been so rooted in her own misery, her husband wouldn't even now be lying in his bed with a stitched wound from an arrow.

She felt selfish and humbled and so very guilty. Someone from her own clan had tried to murder her husband. No one in the Montgomery clan had done something so dastardly. They may have mocked her, they may have worked her to the bone. But no one had ever actually tried to harm her. They may not have accepted her, but they'd never raised a hand to her.

And yet her own clan had done something so evil, she wanted to weep.

The sun hadn't yet risen on the second day after Graeme's injury and Eveline sat by his bed, cold and aching. She needed to tend the fire, but she'd been afraid of making the chamber overly warm if Graeme took a fever.

He'd awakened a moment during the night and he seemed to recognize her. He'd even spoken, but his lips had barely moved and she hadn't been able to read what he'd said. Frustrated with her inability to hear him, she'd leaned over and tried to prod him into speaking more clearly, but he'd slipped back into unconsciousness.

She touched his forehead and found it hot and dry to the touch. Icy dread filled her chest. She'd prayed ceaselessly that he wouldn't take a fever. She'd cleaned and rebandaged his wound many times in an effort to prevent swelling and redness.

Nigel had a deft hand and the stitches were tight and clean, effectively sealing the wound so the flesh would heal. The knock to Graeme's head hadn't opened the flesh enough that it required stitching, but there was a large bump that worried Eveline.

She knew well the damage an injury to the head could cause.

It took every bit of her strength and resolve to push herself up from the bed so she could hurry to dampen cloths for his forehead. She felt like a woman in the advanced stage of her life, gnarled and decrepit. She even moved like an old woman, hunched over, her muscles protesting every inch of the way.

Her fingers fumbled clumsily at the pitcher of water by the washbasin. She laid several strips of cloth in the bowl and lifted the pitcher to pour water to dampen them.

After wringing them out, she hurried back to the bed and laid one across Graeme's forehead and then set about wiping down his body with the rest of the cool cloths.

In her periphery she saw the door open and she swung her head up, prepared to defend her territory, but relaxed when she saw Bowen and Teague enter the chamber.

"How is he?" Bowen asked when he drew close enough to the bed for Eveline to see him.

"Fever," she croaked out.

She continued to swab the cloths over Graeme's chest, neck, and shoulders, but her own shoulders drooped with despair.

Teague touched her cheek, causing her to turn to him once more. "We must speak to you, Eveline. 'Tis very important we receive an accounting of what happened. We've been able to find no trace of the man you say shot Graeme."

Dread centered in her stomach, made worse by the fact she hadn't eaten in two days.

"Eveline?" Bowen frowned and knelt by the bed, his face level with hers. "You look fearful. You must know you're safe here. We won't allow any attack on the keep."

"'Tis what I must tell you that upsets me," she whispered.

Even as she spoke, she pulled away the cloth she'd been wiping over Graeme's flesh and balled it into her hand.

Bowen reached for her hand, rubbing it between his to infuse warmth into her icy fingers.

She swallowed hard, tears crowding her eyes because she knew that what she would say would only bring her heartbreak. The family she loved had tried to murder the husband she loved. There would be no peace, because Graeme's brothers would not allow such an attack to go unpunished. They would retaliate and there would be war.

Both clans would be branded outlaws and hunted to extinction.

It would be so easy to say nay, that she hadn't seen anything at all, but she refused to protect a clan that had acted without honor.

They'd made a vow before God and the king. They'd signed a blood treaty. And her family had broken that sacred vow.

Teague pulled a chair from across the room and placed it next to the bed so he was sitting next to Bowen in her line of vision. He wore a heavy frown and he stared intently at her.

"What is it?" Teague demanded. "What do you know of the attack?"

She took in a deep breath and then focused on both of the brothers, praying they wouldn't hate her for what she must confess.

"The man who shot Graeme was wearing a scabbard that my father had fashioned for his men. It's ornately designed and unmistakably a symbol of the Armstrong name."

Bowen reared back and she flinched, almost as if she expected him to lash out at her. Maybe she'd expected it. She turned her face away, determined to protect the one part of her that wasn't severely bruised.

She sat there shaking, eyes closed as she waited. Then a warm hand cupped her chin and turned her in a not-so-gentle fashion so she faced Bowen. Teague was clearly appalled and her gaze skittered quickly away from him to settle on Bowen as she awaited his reaction.

When she saw the fury on his face, she started to shut her eyes again, but he gave her a quick shake, forcing her to continue looking at him.

"My God, did you think I'd strike you?" Bowen asked, his face drawn in utter incredulity. "Did you think I would seek revenge upon you for what was done by your kin?"

Tears gathered in her eyes. They leaked down her cheeks and she raised a shaking hand to wipe them away, but Bowen was there first, moving his hand from her chin to gently wipe at the trail of dampness. She glanced back to Teague, realizing that he was appalled, not because of what she'd confessed, but because she'd feared reprisal. "I'm sorry," she said, the words difficult to say with her throat so raw.

Bowen's shoulders heaved as he took a deep breath. Then he glanced back at his brother and returned his gaze to Eveline.

"Are you certain it was one of your father's men?"

She nodded. "I could not see his face. He wore a battle helmet. But he came from the direction of the Armstrong border and he returned the same way when he fled. I do not know what he intended. He stopped when I began screaming and when I picked up Graeme's sword. Then he turned his horse and rode fast toward Armstrong land. But I saw the scabbard. 'Tis a mixture of metal and leather and only the more senior of his soldiers are given the honor of wearing them. They are reserved for those who've proven themselves in battle. 'Tis a costly thing to have fashioned, so they are coveted by our clan."

Teague swore, turning his face in midstream so Eveline could not see all of what he said.

"What will happen?" she choked out. " 'Tis an act of war they've performed. If you retaliate, it will break the treaty and both clans will be branded outlaws by the king."

Bowen cupped her cheek and then dropped his hand down to collect hers. He squeezed her fingers in a comforting gesture before he spoke.

"The most important matter here is for you not to fear me or Teague. We will not hurt you, Eveline. It took great courage for you to tell us the truth in this matter. Most would have pretended ignorance or simply said they saw naught. We've seen the loyalty you've given Graeme and to our clan. No one will blame you for what has been wrought by your father."

She pressed her lips together, anguish welling from deep within her chest.

"I do not understand why they have done this thing. I would never have believed that my father could act with such dishonor."

Teague frowned again and pursed his lips in thought. " 'Tis confusing to me why, if your father sought to murder Graeme, did he send a man who wore something that so clearly designated him as an Armstrong soldier. The manner in which the man attacked would lead one to believe that he wanted it done so no blame could be placed on the Armstrong clan, and yet the man wore the scabbard you described. If he cared not who knew of his intention, why not lead his entire army against our keep? Why launch such a cowardly attack? The warrior must have had to have lain in wait for days for the right opportunity to present itself."

Bowen's brow crinkled and he sat back, taking his hand from Eveline's. "Do you think it was only made to look as though the attack came from an Armstrong soldier?"

Eveline's eyes widened. "Who would do such a thing?"

"Anyone who is wary of the two most powerful clans in the highlands uniting," Teague said.

Hope flickered in Eveline's heart. "So you think it could have been someone posing as an Armstrong soldier?"

" 'Tis possible," Bowen conceded. "But how would he lay claim to a scabbard you say is only given to the most worthy Armstrong warriors?"

Eveline nibbled at her bottom lip, her face drawn into a tight frown. "I know not."

"It would appear that your father has some questions to answer," Teague said, his expression grim.

Eveline glanced nervously at Graeme, whose eyes were still closed. "What do we do, then?"

"We wait until Graeme has regained his senses and is well enough to decide the matter," Bowen said. "In the meantime, we'll add to our border patrol and send out a contingent of our best warriors to scour the countryside for a lone soldier wearing an Armstrong scabbard."

"Aye," Teague agreed. "When Graeme is well enough to hear an accounting, he will decide our course of action. A blood treaty is not to be taken lightly, and if your father did violate our peace agreement, it will mean war, no matter that the king forbids it. We'll not tolerate such an act of treachery against our laird."

Eveline lowered her gaze, but Bowen reached forward to touch her arm, directing her attention back to him.

"I know it hurts you, Eveline. 'Tis your clan, your beloved ones. 'Tis only because we have doubts that we do not ride even now on the Armstrong clan. But we'll further investigate the matter and await Graeme's word. He'll want to confront your father, regardless, to hear his word on the matter."

Eveline nodded. "'Tis fair. I do not want to believe this of my father. He should be given the opportunity to defend his name and his honor."

"You should rest now, Eveline," Teague said. "You're beyond your limits, 'tis plain enough for anyone to see."

She shook her head, adamant in her refusal. "I'll not leave him. He's taken a fever now and 'tis more important than ever that I not leave his side."

Bowen sighed, but he didn't argue further. He rose and Teague pushed the chair back into its place near the window.

"We must go now to see to this matter. If Graeme awakens for any length of time, send for us immediately."

Eveline nodded her agreement and then sagged in relief when the two brothers took their leave of the chamber.

She rose to redampen the cloths and returned to Graeme's bed to wipe his flesh down once more.

"Hurry and be well," she whispered. "I'm frightened, Graeme. I do not want war between our clans."

CHAPTER 37

It was two more days before Graeme's fever finally broke. Eveline remained holed up in their chamber, afraid more than ever to venture into the midst of the clan. By now they would have all heard that it was a possibility her father had planned the attack on Graeme. It would only give them more reason to hate her. Not that they seemed to need one.

She'd finally succumbed to utter exhaustion and had drifted into sleep, sitting up in bed beside Graeme an hour before dawn. He shifted against her, causing her to immediately come awake. The soft light of daybreak filtered through the furs that had partially been drawn aside.

She glanced down to see Graeme's eyes open and sweat beading his brow. He shoved at the furs and she could see that his entire body was bathed in sweat.

"Graeme! Oh, Graeme!" she exclaimed, not even sure she could be heard. Her throat was still sore and swollen even days after the attack, and it ached every time she tried to speak.

She leaned over him, touching him, feeling the clamminess of his skin, but he was no longer dry and hot!

His unfocused gaze rested on her for a long moment and then he frowned.

"What happened?"

"Do you not remember?" Eveline asked.

His brows drew together as if he was in deep thought. Then a rush of color entered his cheeks and his eyes sparked with rage. He grasped her shoulders, holding on tightly as he seemed to examine *her* for injury.

"Are you all right?" he demanded. "Did he hurt you? What happened after I took the arrow?"

"Graeme, you mustn't move your arm!" she scolded.

She took his left arm from her shoulder and eased it back down to the bed. A flash of pain registered in his eyes, and then he glanced impatiently at the bandages on his shoulder.

"Answer me, Eveline. Are you well?"

She touched his cheek, caressing the firm line of his jaw, relief so overwhelming that she felt weak with it.

"I'm perfectly fit," she said. "'Tis you who gave us all a fright."

His frown deepened. "How long have I been abed?"

"Four days. 'Tis truly a miracle that it's only been four days. You've had a fever and I expected it would last much longer than it has."

He immediately tried to rise, but she planted both hands on his chest and pushed him back down with a fierce scowl.

"You're not to move from this bed," she bellowed.

He flinched and his eyes widened at the volume of her demand. She knew it had been loud, but she wanted to be sure and make her point.

He settled back on the pillows and then studied her intently, his gaze going up and down her body.

"You look terrible, Eveline. Did you tell me an untruth? Were you harmed when I was attacked?"

It was simply too much. Everything hit her at once.

Relief. Exhaustion. Fear. So much relief. She burst into tears.

Through the sheen of moisture glazing her eyes, she saw Graeme try to sit up, and then he leaned his head back and bellowed something. A moment later, his brothers rushed in, and then Bowen was lifting her from the bed, his arm solidly around her.

But she couldn't stop crying. It was as if any and all strength she had left fled the moment she knew Graeme would be all right.

And then another arm slipped around her and she was guided to the bench by the fire.

To Eveline's shock, when she lifted her head, Nora was there, setting a fire. Nora tossed in several logs and set flame to wood. Then she turned and pinned Eveline with a determined look.

"Now, lass, I know you'll probably screech and try to drive me out of the laird's chamber, but you don't have the strength to do it and I'll not be budged this time. 'Tis time someone took care of you. You've been at the laird's bedside for days. You haven't eaten. You haven't slept. You're hurting from your own fall and begging your pardon, but you look terrible."

Fresh tears slipped down Eveline's cheeks. She was so exhausted that she couldn't summon the energy to do anything more than sit there and cry as the second person in as many minutes told her how awful she looked.

Nora stood, waiting, hands on her hips while Eveline wiped at her face. When she was sure Eveline was looking, she continued with her speech.

"I owe you an apology, lass. We all do. But there's no time for that right now. What's important is that you don't fall ill yourself and that the laird is taken care of."

Eveline started to protest, but Nora held up her hands.

"No one is saying you haven't done a fine job of tending the laird. I've never seen a fiercer champion. But he's recovering nicely and currently he's over in that bed demanding to know what's wrong with you."

Eveline tried to turn so she could reassure Graeme, but Nora caught her arm and held her firmly in place as she settled onto the bench next to her.

"Nay, you'll not spend another moment looking after the laird. He'll be just fine in no time. 'Tis you who needs looking after and I'm going to say my piece so he hears it all."

Eveline could do nothing but stare in shock at the other woman's vehemence.

"You can't keep up this pace any longer. You need food. You need rest. You need someone to look you over to make sure all is well with you. You can give in gracefully and allow me and the other women to help with the laird or I'll have the laird's brothers tie you to the bed, and I'll do it with the laird's blessing as soon as he's heard all you've done to yourself over the past days."

Eveline frowned. "Teague and Bowen wouldn't do such a thing."

Nora lifted one eyebrow. "'Twas their idea, my lady. We were on our way up to take matters into our own hands when we heard the laird bellow for us to come. They know you've had enough. We can all see it. I insisted on being the one to come to you. I owe you that much. We'll not let you or our laird down. I vow it."

"Why are you being nice to me now?" Eveline asked, rubbing her sore throat as she choked the words out.

Nora's gaze softened even as guilt flashed in her eyes. "'Tis my doing. 'Tis all our doing. This would not have happened if we hadn't driven you away. And even so, you fought fiercely for our laird. You didn't allow our actions to affect your loyalty to him. I'm deeply shamed. I was not the better person and you were. If you'll give me another chance to right the wrongs, I vow you'll not regret it."

Eveline stared at the older woman in bewilderment. She truly looked sincere. There was guilt and heavy regret in her eyes and the wrinkles and lines in her face seemed more pronounced.

"I *am* hungry," Eveline began.

Nora smiled. "Of course you are. You've not had a bite to eat in days. Now, what I want is for you to come below stairs with me. Mary is preparing a steaming bowl of venison stew as we speak. After you eat, the women are going to take you to the bathhouse so you can soak those sore muscles in a tub of hot water. Once we're finished, we're going to have Nigel give you a thorough examination to make sure all is well and that you suffer from nothing that a good rest won't right. After that you can rest with the laird, but be forewarned, if you do not sleep, I'll have you removed from the chamber and locked into another one. I'll pour a potion down your throat if I have to."

Eveline laughed at Nora's determined look and then grimaced at the pain it caused her throat.

"You poor lass," Nora said, sympathy brimming in her eyes. "You've hurt your throat with all the screaming you've done. We heard you all the way through the keep when you were riding in for help. 'Twas a brave thing you did, taking the laird's horse. He's a big brute and with you being so terrified of horses. The entire keep's talking about it. Everyone knows how fiercely you protected our laird. I think some are a little afraid of you now."

Eveline's lips twitched. It amused her to think anyone would fear her. She glanced back at Nora, studying the other woman intently.

This was her opportunity, one she'd waited for. She could hold on to her anger and refuse to grant forgiveness. Or she could rise above her anger and humiliation and start anew.

She reached for Nora's hand and squeezed. "I thank you. Venison stew and a hot bath sound next to heaven right now."

Nora helped her rise and Eveline nearly fell on her face. Her strength was gone. It was as if she'd remained stalwart until the moment she knew Graeme needed her no longer and now she was at her very end.

As they turned, she saw Graeme's fierce expression, the anger and the worry in his eyes. He was propped up in bed, pillows behind his back and surrounded by his two brothers. But his gaze never left her.

"Come here," he commanded.

With Nora's help, she managed to walk to the bed, but her knees were shaking so badly, she feared she wouldn't be able to remain standing.

He reached for her with his right arm and pulled her down to the bed until she was perched against his thigh. "You will listen to everything they tell you to do," he said. "You will do nothing but take care of yourself henceforth. Are we understood? Bowen has told me of your fall from my horse. God's teeth, lass, what were you thinking, mounting that beast when you're terrified of horses? He could have killed you."

He broke off, his chest heaving with exertion, but his eyes glittered with purpose.

"You will go down and eat and then you'll soak in hot water as Nora has directed. Then you are to return to this chamber and to me so that Nigel can properly examine you. Afterward you will rest until I grant permission for you to rise from this bed, and if you give any argument, I've given permission to Bowen and Teague to do whatever is necessary to ensure you follow my orders."

Eveline's eyes widened and then to her further befuddlement Graeme pulled her roughly to him and kissed her hard and deep. When he finally let her go, her thoughts were so muddled that she couldn't think straight.

"Now go," he said. "And hurry back to me so I can satisfy my concerns over your well-being."

CHAPTER 38

As soon as Eveline was gone from the chamber, Graeme turned to his brothers. "Tell me the truth. I want the whole of it. How is Eveline? Was she hurt?"

"I know not," Teague said honestly. "She's refused any sort of aid. She's been focused solely on you and your recovery. She took a terrible fall from your horse, but she stood back up, mounted him again, and led us back to you."

Graeme swore even as pain knifed through his shoulder. "You should not have allowed it. She should have been cared for first."

Bowen laughed. "You did not see your wee wife, brother. She had the entire keep terrified to cross her. She screamed like she was demented every time someone entered your chamber. She wouldn't allow anyone save me, Teague, Rorie, Father Drummond, and Nigel anywhere near you, and the father was only allowed if he didn't try to give you last rites. She wouldn't allow anyone to entertain, even for a moment, the idea that you wouldn't survive. She was a sight to behold."

"You frightened us all," Teague said gruffly.

"What happened?" Graeme asked. " 'Tis all a bit of a blur to me. I remember Eveline screaming at me and when I turned and drew my sword I saw a man on horseback approaching. The next thing I remember is throwing myself to the side to avoid the arrow and then I hit my head. I know nothing else."

"What happened is that Eveline frightened away your attacker by screaming like the hounds of hell were after you, then she took up your sword, prepared to do battle to protect you. The horseman fled and then Eveline threw herself on your horse and rode screaming the entire way back to the keep. She rode full speed into the courtyard and then your horse threw her over his head. She brought us back to you and we carried you on a litter. She refused to ride back with Bowen and walked beside you the entire way instead. She hasn't left your side since. She's refused food, care, and she hasn't slept."

"The little fool," Graeme bit out. "What would I do without her? I can't lose her."

It was said out loud before he could think better of blurting out his feelings for Eveline. He was furious over the risks she'd taken and he was shaking with fear, with the realization that he could have so easily lost her.

Bowen and Teague said nothing in response to his declaration, but he could see the knowledge in their eyes.

"Who did this? Did you track him down?" Graeme demanded.

His younger brothers exchanged uneasy glances.

"Tell me," he ground out.

"'Tis been more difficult for Eveline than you even know," Bowen said in a low voice.

Graeme froze, his veins turning to ice. "You said she wasn't hurt. Did he lay hands to her?"

Bowen shook his head. "Nay, 'tis just as we told you. Eveline . . . She saw the archer. She was able to give us identifying information."

"Possible identifying information," Teague cut in.

Bowen nodded. "Aye, we know not what to make of

it yet. We've sent out soldiers to search the area and we've added extra patrols to our border to ensure the safety of the clan, but we would not act on the information Eveline gave us until we spoke to you."

Graeme shook his head in confusion. "Eveline identified the man who shot me and you didn't act?"

Again, his brothers exchanged glances, and dread centered in Graeme's gut. He was weary and weak, and it made him furious that his wife was so badly in need of his support and all he could muster was the energy to lean against his pillows while his brothers spoke. He doubted he could even feed himself at this point.

"Eveline believes it was one of her clan," Teague said in a quiet voice.

Shock buzzed through Graeme's veins, momentarily giving him a surge of energy.

"She told you this?"

Bowen nodded. "She was devastated, but she did not withhold the truth. She fears what it will mean. We worried in the beginning that Eveline did not understand the circumstances of her marriage. She understands all too well. She knows a blood treaty was signed and that if we go to war, both clans will be branded outlaws and a bounty will be on our heads."

"And yet she told you the truth," Graeme said softly.

"Aye," Teague muttered. "I wouldn't have even blamed her if she'd withheld what she'd seen. I cannot say that I wouldn't have done so if I were in her position."

"She is an amazing lass," Graeme murmured.

"Aye, that she is," Bowen agreed. "And she's intensely loyal to you, Graeme."

Pride swelled in Graeme's chest. He remembered that just moments before he'd been struck by the arrow, he'd begged her to give him another chance. He'd begged her not to return to her clan. It appeared she'd made her choice. Savage satisfaction billowed through him, bolstering his flagging strength. She'd chosen him. Over her own clan. She hadn't lied to protect her kin. She'd done the just thing and told the truth.

Just as quickly as he reveled in that realization, the reality of the situation sunk in and his heart sank.

If Tavis Armstrong had ordered the murder of his daughter's husband, it would indeed mean war. Graeme would not stand back and allow the Armstrongs to threaten his clan. He'd bathe the earth in Armstrong blood and then take up the matter with his king.

But by doing so, he'd likely lose any love or regard Eveline held for him. How could she possibly love the man who destroyed her family?

It was a dilemma he thought never to face.

He could allow no threat to his kin, and yet how could he destroy Eveline's family? How could she ever forgive him?

He closed his eyes and leaned his head back against the pillow.

"It poses a problem, does it not?" Bowen said.

"Aye," Graeme muttered. "I don't want to lose her. I don't want her to look at me with hate in her eyes. It would be more than I could bear."

"Nor do I want her to look upon me with hatred," Teague admitted in a low voice. "I don't want to be the man who destroyed her family. I like her, Graeme. She's proven herself ten times over and has been humiliated, mocked, and worked to the bone, and yet she hasn't allowed that to turn her against us. She is loyal to us still."

"How many men can say they have a wife who would sacrifice so much for her husband?" Bowen asked.

"I can," Graeme said bluntly.

"I wanted to put to you the same question Teague brought up when he and I first spoke to Eveline about what she saw," Bowen said.

Graeme sent him a questioning look. "Go on."

"Do you not find it odd that if Tavis Armstrong wanted to secretly kill you that he'd send a man outfitted in distinctive Armstrong trappings?"

Teague nodded. "It could be that someone wanted it to look as if the Armstrongs made the attempt on your life, because even if the man did not succeed, it would certainly start a war between the two clans and accomplish the same thing. We would no longer be allies, grudging or not, and there are many whom I'm sure are uneasy over the two most powerful clans in the highlands joining forces."

"Aye, there are those who would prefer we remain bitter enemies and fight among ourselves. If we had a mind to, we could easily defeat any clan now that we have a larger combined army than even the king. That has to play heavily on their minds," Bowen added.

Graeme nodded. "What you say makes sense. Tavis Armstrong is not stupid. But he also may not care if he starts a war. 'Tis hard to know what is in his mind until we speak to him on the matter."

"What do we do?" Teague said. "You are in no shape to wage war."

Graeme simmered with impatience. He wanted to be out of bed now, readying his men for battle. But he knew he would be worthless as a leader and a warrior in his current state. As much as it aggrieved him to wait, he knew he must.

But it didn't mean he couldn't send word to Armstrong and demand a meeting in the coming days. He would take a few days to recover, and then he'd send a messenger, demanding a meeting on neutral ground. If he worded it just so, Tavis would be unable to refuse. He would want to know his daughter was well, and he'd also want to know what had driven Graeme to demand the meeting.

When he informed his brothers of his plan, they nodded their agreement, and relief was evident in their eyes. They had no desire for war any more than Graeme did himself. And yet, if Eveline's father had indeed instigated the threat against Graeme, battle was inevitable.

And he could lose Eveline.

He lifted his left arm, testing the weakness and the pain level of his shoulder. Fiery pain shot through his shoulder, nearly robbing him of breath. He let his arm drop, sucking in deep, steadying breaths.

"That was stupid," Teague growled. "You won't heal if you don't lay off that arm. You're of no use to us if you can't stand up in battle. You can't hurry this, Graeme. As much as it pains you to lie here and heal, 'tis what you must do."

"Aye, I know it," Graeme muttered. "And nay, I don't like it at all."

"Spend the time with Eveline. She needs much care right now," Bowen said. "She's not well, Graeme."

Graeme's lips formed a tight line. "She'll do nothing but rest. I'll make sure of it."

The door swung open and Nora bustled in, her gaze honing in immediately on Graeme.

"What is amiss?" he demanded, not liking the look in her eye.

"Now, Laird, remain calm. Nigel is carrying the lass up now."

He surged upward, and Teague and Bowen both leaped to push him back and they held him against the pillows.

"What happened?" he bellowed.

"She's given out," Nora said. "She ate, and then we put her to soaking in the bathhouse. The poor lass passed out or fell asleep, but either way, there was no waking her and so I wrapped her in a sheet and had Nigel carry her up the stairs. Ah, there he is now. In here, Nigel. Bring her to the laird. We'll put the poor lass to bed, and I'll look in on her later."

She gestured at the younger man, and he appeared in the chamber, holding Eveline's slight form in his arms. She looked small and delicate in his grasp. She looked *frail* and it sent a chill down Graeme's spine.

"Put her on my other side," he ordered, wanting her between the wall and himself so she would be protected.

Bowen and Teague stood and helped to carry Eveline over Graeme's body and settle her gently on his other side. She was completely wrapped in the bed linen and only her face was visible.

Nora shooed Nigel from the chamber and then turned to shoo Teague and Bowen out as well. Graeme saw purpose in Nora's eyes and realized that she wanted everyone out of the chamber because there was something she wanted to impart to him.

He waved his brothers away, promising he'd summon them in the next while. After they'd left, Nora closed the door and turned troubled eyes back to Graeme. She strode over to the bed and reached over to start loosening the sheet around Eveline's body.

"You need to see, Laird. The poor wee lass is bruised from head to toe. It nearly made me cry when we undressed her to put her to soak. I don't know how she's suffered the pain these last days and I know not how she didn't break something in her fall from the horse."

As the sheet loosened and fell open, baring Eveline's nude body to his gaze, his breath exploded from his lungs and he couldn't draw another.

Dear God. Deep, purple bruises were present over most of her body. Her knees and elbows were scraped and the flesh ragged. Her hip was nearly black. One of her shoulders was starting to turn an ugly greenish hue. There were several smaller bruises up and down her legs and multiple scrapes and cuts to her arms and lower legs.

"Sweet Jesu," he muttered.

"She cannot give any more to you, Laird," Nora said in a solemn voice.

"Don't you think I know that?" he snarled. "Do you think I would have approved of her sacrificing so much of herself for me? I would have bloody tied her to the damn bed and forced a potion down her throat myself."

"That's another thing," Nora said, not flinching away from his anger. "The lass screamed so much when she was calling for help and later when she screamed at anyone trying to enter your chamber, she injured her voice. She should use it as little as possible for the next few days. I'll bring hot cider from time to time. It will soothe the hurt in her throat."

Graeme nodded, impatient for her to be gone. He wanted Eveline to himself. He wanted to hold her. Feel her against him. Just have the comfort of her body so close to him. The pain was not so bad when she was near.

It was time for him to care for her. She'd given much of herself in the last few days. Far too much.

She'd sealed her fate when she stepped in like a lioness protecting her cubs and watched over him so faithfully. She may or may not have made her ultimate decision on that bluff where he'd begged her for time to make things right.

But now she was his. And nothing or no one would ever come between them. Not her family. Not his clan.

He wasn't ever going to give her up without one hell of a fight.

CHAPTER 39

Eveline slept the rest of the day, through the night, and well into the next morning. Graeme held her the entire time, anchoring her to him with his good arm. He'd slept off and on, remaining still and focusing on healing as rapidly as possible. Just having her there next to him, where he could feel her and smell her, gave him a sense of peace. She settled him. She made him content.

She hadn't so much as moved, and he was beginning to worry. When his brothers came through his chamber door, Graeme sent them to summon Nigel. But before they returned, he made certain she was completely covered by the sheet Nora had wrapped around her, and then he settled the furs over her so she wouldn't grow cold when he shifted away from her.

A moment later, Nigel appeared, and he went immediately to begin peeling back the bandage on Graeme's shoulder so he could check the wound. But Graeme waved him away.

"I didn't summon you for me. I'm worried about Eveline. She's not so much as stirred even once since you carried her to bed yesterday morn. Surely 'tis too long for her to sleep. The bruises she carries are severe. What if she was more seriously injured than we all thought?"

Nigel bent over Graeme and brushed his fingers underneath Eveline's nostrils. He put his hand to the furs, his intent to draw them away.

"With your permission, Laird," he said.

Graeme sent a fierce stare in his brothers' directions, causing them to turn around to face the other direction. Then Graeme nodded at Nigel.

Nigel carefully pulled the furs and then the sheet away and placed his hand over Eveline's chest. Nigel frowned when he saw plainly the bruises that marred Eveline's pale flesh.

"'Tis a miracle she didn't break her neck," Nigel muttered. "That horse could have killed her."

Graeme clenched his jaw tight, grinding his teeth together. He didn't like to be reminded how close his wife had come to death. It bothered him less that he'd taken an arrow to the shoulder than that Eveline had been injured, and the fact that she'd taken such a risk by mounting his horse. He couldn't even imagine the courage it must have taken to overcome her terror and panic at merely being near a horse, much less throwing herself upon him and riding recklessly back to the keep.

He would have a very long discussion with her over never taking such risks again in the future. Just as soon as she was well enough.

"I think she is well enough, Laird. Her breaths aren't labored. She appears to merely be deeply asleep. 'Tis likely she'll sleep through the night and into the morrow. She's gone days without rest and she sorely needs it. Try not to waken her and let her come around herself."

"Nay, I'll not do anything to wake her," Graeme vowed. "She'll sleep next to me as long as it takes for her to heal."

After arranging the covers back over Eveline, Nigel insisted on changing the dressing on Graeme's wound.

Nigel carefully washed it, inspected the stitches, and pressed a fresh cloth bandage over the wound, and wrapped the linen strips around and over his shoulder and underneath his arm to secure it back in place.

"Is it all right to look now?" Bowen said impatiently.

"Aye," Graeme called.

Nigel took his leave and Bowen and Teague pulled the chair and the bench to the side of Graeme's bed so they could sit and converse with their brother.

A knock sounded and Graeme bit out an impatient oath. But when the door opened and Rorie eased inside, a hesitant look on her face, Graeme softened and motioned her forward.

"Graeme?" she questioned, a slight quiver to her voice.

"Aye, sweeting. Come here."

Rorie walked to the side of the bed, her eyes troubled. She stared down at Eveline, tears filling her eyes.

"Will she be all right, Graeme? I saw the bruises when Nora and Mary put her to soak. I had no idea. She wouldn't allow anyone near her. She insisted that all attention be focused on you."

Graeme lifted his arm slowly and took her hand in his. "Aye, she'll be fine in no time. I vow it will take more than this to defeat that lass. She's a determined little thing when she's set her mind to something."

He kept his tone light so as not to worry his sister. She'd grown very attached to Eveline in the time Eveline had been here, and Graeme could see the worry in her eyes.

"Nigel just left here and he says she just needs to rest and gain back all that she has lost in the time she was caring for me. I'll not allow her out of bed until she's hale and hearty again."

Rorie nodded her approval, and then she went to her knees beside Graeme's bed, taking his hand with her.

"And you? Will you be all right as well? I've never been so frightened. I had no idea if you would live or die."

He squeezed her hand, and Bowen reached over to touch her hair in a gesture of comfort.

"'Tis naught but a scratch," Bowen said cheerfully. "I've seen far worse than his paltry wound."

Graeme glared at Bowen.

"How are your lessons going?" Teague asked, directing her attention to something she found more pleasing.

A smile bathed her face. Her eyes lit up and she all but bounced in her excitement. "I'm learning! Father Drummond says I'm a very apt student and that he's never taught someone who takes to it so quickly. He says I'll be reading and writing in no time."

Graeme smiled. "I suppose then you'll have to take over as the clan scribe."

She nodded vigorously.

"Ah, what will we ever do without you, Rorie?" Bowen teased. "One day you'll marry and move away and we'll be left with no one to educate our lowly minds."

She frowned and a shadow crossed her face. "I'm never leaving here. I've no wish to marry. I'm quite content to stay here with you. I won't have to leave, will I, Graeme?"

Graeme sent Bowen a look of admonishment, and then he said to Rorie in a gentle voice, "Of course not. You'll remain here as long as you like."

She practically wilted in relief, and then she pushed herself to her feet. "I must go. Father Drummond awaits me. I think he's tried to keep me as busy as possible so I would not worry over you and Eveline."

"'Tis a good practice," Graeme said. "There is naught for you to worry over. Eveline and I will both be fine."

Rorie leaned down to kiss Graeme's cheek, sent Eveline one last seeking look, and then turned to hurry out of the chamber.

"Two days," Graeme said when the chamber door had closed.

Teague's brow went up. "Two days for what?"

"Two days is all I'll wait before I send word to Tavis Armstrong."

Bowen shook his head. "You won't be healed by then."

Graeme shrugged. "The matter cannot wait. It will take a day or two, maybe longer to receive a response from Armstrong and then another few days to arrange the meeting. By then, I'll have had almost a fortnight to recover. Whether I am at full strength or not, we cannot wait to dig to the bottom of this matter."

Teague blew out his breath, but he nodded his acceptance.

"Have Father Drummond come to me so I can dictate the missive. Then choose an able warrior to ride under the banner of truce onto Armstrong land to deliver the message."

"I'll go myself," Bowen said in a terse voice.

"Not without me," Teague snapped.

"And I'll not allow either of you to leave, not when you're needed here at the keep. Our first priority is to protect our clan and guard our walls well. Find someone else to go."

Bowen didn't look happy with the directive, but neither did he argue.

Another knock sounded at the door, and this time it was Nora with food for Graeme.

"I brought enough for two," Nora said as she neared the bed with the tray. "But if the lass is still sleeping, 'tis best not to disturb her. I'll bring her something the moment she awakens."

"My thanks," Graeme said. "I find I'm hungry enough to eat both portions."

Nora beamed. "'Tis a good sign, Laird. A healthy appetite is a sign of a well and able body. You'll be up and back on your feet in no time at all."

Graeme froze when Eveline stirred beside him. It was the first time she'd moved at all since being placed in his bed. But all she did was make a slight humming sound, and then she rolled onto her belly, facing away from him, her eyes never opening.

The furs had slipped down her back, baring her shoulders, and Graeme quickly pulled at them, frustrated by the burst of pain that shot down his arm at so simple a task.

Teague and Bowen stood and hastily excused themselves, saying they'd be back later to further discuss the matter of the Armstrongs. Bowen said he'd send Father Drummond up after Graeme had time to eat his meal.

Nora fussed over Graeme for a moment until he was settled and his food in front of him, and then she sent a look of genuine concern in Eveline's direction before turning to leave the chamber.

But as she turned away, she paused and then looked back at Graeme, clear hesitation in her eyes.

"Say what's on your mind, Nora," Graeme said in resignation. At this point he just wanted to be left alone with Eveline so he could have some peace and mull over the matter before him.

"I offered the lass an apology," Nora said in a low voice. "But 'tis the truth I owe you one as well, Laird. I acted unforgivably and I wonder if you could find it in your heart to forgive an old woman for her bitterness. 'Tis a sad state of affairs when I encourage such spite against a wee lass who only has good in her heart."

Graeme smiled at Nora's description of Eveline because it was so true. It was also true that he held a lot of anger toward Nora and the other women, but Nora had done much to make amends.

"I am not happy with the way you and others acted toward my wife," Graeme said sternly. "You caused her endless grief and moreover, you made her so unhappy that she wanted to return to her own kin."

Nora gasped and put her hand to her mouth.

"I'm not prepared to let her go," Graeme said in a calm voice. "She means much to me and as such, she will remain a permanent fixture here, so see that your goodwill toward her continues and moreover, ensure that others regard her in the same manner as you now regard her. I'll not have any further patience or tolerance for any slight against her whatsoever."

Nora nodded and bobbed a curtsy. "Thank you, Laird. I'll not disappoint you or the lass."

Graeme waved her away and then glanced down at Eveline's tousled hair and the peaceful expression on her face. Her eyelashes rested delicately on her cheeks, and her lips were slightly parted as she breathed through her mouth.

He couldn't resist touching her. He reached down, angling his arm so his fingers brushed over the softness of her cheek. He pushed back the golden strands of hair behind her ear and softly stroked.

"I love you, Eveline," he whispered, though he knew she could not hear him. "Somehow, I'll make you hear me and you'll know that I love you as fiercely as it's possible for a man to love a woman."

CHAPTER 40

When Eveline awakened, she was completely confused. It took her several long moments to collect herself and realize that she was abed with Graeme. And she was starving.

She pushed upward, her entire body protesting the movement. She turned to squint toward the window as sunlight bathed her entire face. It had to be midday at the very least.

When she turned back to Graeme, intent on tending his wound, she found him awake and regarding her with a probing stare.

Her hand went to his shoulder, but he caught her palm and slid his fingers over hers, curling them around her hand. He moved it to his chest, holding it there for a long moment.

"Are you . . ." She cleared her throat, coughed, and then started again. Her throat wasn't as sore, but the words still felt blocked and rusty. "Are you well?" she asked. "Are you in pain? Should I fetch Nigel?"

Graeme pulled her to him so she was sprawled against his chest, her face just inches from his.

"The question is how are *you* feeling?" he said. "Do

you hurt still? Are you still fatigued? Perhaps you should rest awhile more."

She frowned and shook her head. "How long have I been sleeping?"

His lips quirked upward. "Two days."

"Two days!" she shrieked.

He winced, but nodded.

She yanked away from him and then wrung her hands in agitation. "Two days? 'Tis disgraceful. Who has tended to you for the last two days?"

He put his finger over her lips. "You were exhausted and hurting. I'm furious with you over the risks you took. You could have been killed or far more seriously injured. You needed to rest and you needed to eat."

"And you? Is your wound healing?" she asked anxiously. "Is your fever gone?"

"I'm in far better condition than you are," he said. "Now come here. I want to hold you."

Shocked by the sudden demonstration of affection, she didn't argue as he pulled her tightly into his arms. He tucked her beneath his uninjured shoulder and wrapped his arm around her until she could barely breathe.

He kissed her forehead and smoothed the hair from her brow. Calm descended. She sighed in contentment and burrowed into his big body. 'Twas nice to lie here in the middle of the day and rest in her husband's arms.

She had nearly drifted back into sleep when he lifted her away from him, but held her so that they were still close. He'd positioned her so she could see his mouth.

"There are things we must discuss, Eveline."

Her mouth turned down and she lowered her gaze. Bowen and Teague would have told him what she'd seen.

He nudged her chin upward with his fingers. "You know I must investigate whether this threat came from your clan."

She nodded reluctantly.

"Eveline, I will do all I can to avoid conflict with your family. But you have to understand that I cannot allow this to go unanswered."

"I know it," she whispered back, her heart aching at what must come.

"Come here and lie against me. For now, we'll not think on unpleasant things."

She snuggled back into his arms, closing her eyes in the sweetness of the moment. There were no guarantees of what tomorrow would bring, but today she would savor a brief respite in her husband's embrace and pretend that something so simple as love could bridge the gap made wider by decades of hatred.

After eating a light repast with Graeme in the comfort of their bed, Eveline was itching to rise. Her hunger sated, she was ready to turn her attention to other important matters such as a bath and walking enough to ease the stiffness and soreness from her muscles.

She was considering how to put the matter to her husband, who was insistent on her remaining abed, when she saw Graeme frown and then tell someone outside the door to remain so until Eveline was decent.

Her cheeks burned at the idea that whoever it was knew she hadn't a stitch on. Graeme patted her rump and then motioned her out of bed to dress.

She hurried from the warmth of his body and the furs and pulled on one of her simple day dresses. She took a brush to her hair to work the tangles and would have retreated to the far corner of the room, but she looked up and saw Bowen and Teague, accompanied by Father Drummond, enter the chamber. The priest had a scroll and quill and ink, and Eveline realized that Graeme meant to dictate the message to her father.

She went to Graeme's side and touched his arm. "I

would like to go below stairs and breathe a bit of fresh air. My muscles need stretching."

Graeme regarded her a long moment, and then his shoulders heaved in a sigh. Then he nodded. "Do not be gone overlong. I'll send a summons down when I've finished with my brothers and Father Drummond."

She nodded, her heart heavier with each breath. She didn't want to be about when he transcribed the message that might well send the two clans she called her own into battle against one another.

Graeme squeezed her hand, and then she eased away, setting the brush down before exiting the chamber.

It wasn't a total untruth she'd told Graeme. She was desperate to leave the suffocation of the chamber if only for a little while.

She stretched her arms and worked her shoulders as she descended the stairs to the hall. Despite having eaten a bit earlier, she went to the kitchens in search of a piece of bread or bit of cheese to nibble on. She was still hungry.

Mary was only too happy to accommodate her after demanding to know if her laird knew she was below stairs. Eveline gratefully took bread and cheese, and after conversing with Mary for several minutes, she exited the kitchens and stepped into the courtyard.

Dusk was rapidly falling, ushering in cooler breezes as the sun slid completely out of sight over the horizon. The entire land was bathed in purple and gray hues, and the air was still. Most of the clansmen had retired to their cottages and were preparing for the evening meal.

The torches that lit the guard tower threw shadows on the wall of the keep. Eveline closed her eyes and breathed deeply of the spring-scented air.

'Twas so peaceful. A time for gathering in the evening to tell stories, speak of the day's events, and share a good meal.

But she knew that the calm was deceptive because even now, the Montgomery soldiers were preparing for war.

The ground vibrated under her feet and she turned rapidly in time to see a Montgomery herald on horseback ride at a fast pace toward the gate. He wore a cloak bearing the Montgomery colors, but a white banner of truce was attached to the horse's mane.

A chill scuttled up her spine until she shivered. Dread centered in her belly, making her wish she hadn't eaten the bread and cheese Mary had offered.

A touch to her shoulder had her jumping in fright. She whirled around to see Kierstan standing in the fading light.

"My pardon for startling you, my lady."

Eveline took a step back, but focused on Kierstan's lips, not wanting to miss anything the other woman would say.

"I came in search of you when I heard you'd awakened. The hot soaking soothed your aches before and I thought to offer you my services to prepare another soak for you in the bathhouse."

Eveline's eyes widened at what seemed to be an offering of an olive branch from the woman who'd caused her no end of grief. Kierstan looked sincere. Moreover, she looked . . . contrite.

" 'Tis the least I can do," Kierstan said, her expression sad. "I've wronged you badly and I'd like to make amends."

Knowing this was yet another opportunity to mend some bridges, Eveline nodded and Kierstan smiled, seeming relieved by Eveline's agreement.

"Come this way. We'll walk around the keep. It will be shorter than navigating the hall. 'Tis filling up with those seeking the evening meal. I'll send someone to the laird's chamber to give him word of your whereabouts so he does not worry."

"Thank you," Eveline said with a smile. "A hot soak would be heavenly right now. I've been abed for far too long and my body aches."

Kierstan tucked Eveline's hand in hers and guided her through the now empty courtyard and around the side of the keep in the direction of the bathhouse. They were in the narrow passage between the stone skirt and the keep walls when someone stepped from the shadows.

Eveline started to scream a warning to Kierstan when a fist met with Eveline's jaw, sending her tumbling to the ground. So stunned was she that all she could do was lie there, holding her face in her palm.

The man bent down over her, his hand twisting in her hair. He yanked upward, forcing her to her feet, and before she could react, his fist flew at her temple. Pain exploded in her head, and then the world went black.

CHAPTER 41

Graeme frowned when several long minutes elapsed after he sent Bowen down to fetch Eveline. Growing restless, he pushed himself from his bed and stood, gingerly working his injured shoulder in a tight roll.

It still pained him greatly, but he could move it, and more important, the wound had sealed itself. The stitches could be taken out in a few more days.

His head still hurt if he moved too quickly, but the great knot that had risen had gradually gone down, and there was just a small scab over the wound to denote the injury.

He could use a bath himself. It was a wonder Eveline had been able to rest beside him. He probably smelled worse than a rotting carcass.

It was likely what Eveline was doing at any rate. She did enjoy a hot soak a few days ago, and she was likely still sore from all the bruising.

Deciding to give her a little more time before he started demanding to know her whereabouts, he set about washing himself with cloths and water from the basin. He even used a bit of Eveline's soap, deciding it certainly couldn't hurt to alleviate the stench of sweat and blood and illness.

Feeling refreshed after cleaning himself, he put on clean clothing and decided he'd go after his wife himself. All the better if he just happened to find her soaking naked in a tub of water.

Though he certainly wasn't up to loving and neither was his wee bruised wife, he certainly wasn't above enjoying the view.

With a grin, he started down the stairs, purposely putting the matter of the message he'd sent to Armstrong out of his mind. It did no good to dwell on it for now. Armstrong would either send a message back or he wouldn't. All Graeme could do was wait to see if Tavis Armstrong would be truthful or deceitful.

The hall was curiously devoid of people at a time when the evening meal should most certainly be served. He frowned when he realized that food was set out on the table and in some cases, even looked to be half eaten. It was as if the hall had emptied all of a sudden, right in the midst of the meal.

"Bowen! Teague!"

Receiving no answer, Graeme turned in the direction of the back entrance, his desire to ensure that Eveline was all right suddenly overwhelming him. He hurried out and broke into a run toward the bathhouse. He nearly ran into Teague as Teague came barreling out.

Graeme caught him by the shoulders, ignoring the pain in his shoulder at the sudden, forceful movement.

"What is amiss?" he demanded. "Where is Eveline?"

"I do not know," Teague said grimly. "We're searching for her now."

"What?" Graeme roared. "Why has no one summoned me? Why has no one told me of this?"

"We only just discovered that she was missing," Teague said. "I was on my way to summon you. Bowen and the others have spread out over the keep and the area surrounding the keep and are searching for her now."

"Tell me everything," Graeme ground out. "When was she last seen? Who saw her? And how long has she been missing?"

"She went into the kitchen and spoke with Mary a few moments. Mary gave her bread and cheese, and then Eveline left the kitchen. No one saw her after that. Rorie is searching the upstairs now. The women are looking close to the keep and the soldiers are searching the entire outer perimeter. We've sent word to the men patrolling the borders, asking if they've seen anything. We'll find her, Graeme. She can't have gone far."

"People don't just disappear," Graeme snarled. "I want to speak to every single member of this clan. Someone had to have seen her. Moreover, someone has to know what has happened to her."

Eveline came to gasping awareness in a nightmare she couldn't sort out. She was bouncing painfully up and down and the ground was weaving in and out of her line of vision.

It took several moments before she realized she was facedown over a horse, or at least the person she was draped across was astride a horse and she was flung over his lap like a sack of barley.

Nausea assailed her and she had to swallow back the bile working its way from her stomach and into her throat. The constant jostling was causing the reaction and there was little she could do about it.

Blessed darkness reclaimed her.

When she awakened a second time, she was in complete darkness. She had no understanding of how much time had passed or where she was. There was an overwhelming smell of dankness, of moldy, musty dampness. She could smell earth and dirt, but she couldn't see her hand in front of her face.

As she tried to raise her arm, she made the horrifying discovery that her hands were manacled to a damp, stone wall. Panicked, she tried to sit up only to find that like her wrists, her ankles were encased by thick, metal shackles.

Sweet Jesu, she was in a dungeon.

What could anyone want with her in a dungeon?

She thought hard on the events leading up to her capture. It was all a blur. She'd spoken to Mary and then stepped outside to eat her bread and cheese and enjoy a breath of fresh air. And then Kierstan . . .

Realization was sick and overwhelming. Kierstan had led her around the keep to the bathhouse. Kierstan was with her when the intruder had struck Eveline's jaw. Kierstan, who hadn't made a move to aid Eveline or to call for help.

Eveline drew up her arms as far as the chains would allow and tried to warm her cold fingertips. Then she yelled with all her might. She screamed as loudly as her throat would allow and she continued screaming until she was no longer certain she even had a voice.

In the distance she saw a flash of light. She leaned up, uncertain as to whether she imagined it. But nay, it was coming closer, and as it did, she could make out the silhouette of a man carrying the torch.

Her pulse thudded painfully against her chest and temples, making her head ache viciously from the two blows she'd taken earlier.

She drew her legs protectively against her body, determined to do whatever necessary to ensure she didn't incur further injury.

And then the torch was thrust forward, nearly blinding her. She flinched away from the sudden light, shielding her eyes with one hand.

The man yanked her hand down, twisting cruelly until she cried out in pain. Then he wrapped his hand in her hair, hauling upward so her face was forced closer to his. It was then she saw his features and knew who her captor was.

Fear rendered her immobile. Ian McHugh was a man she thought capable of all manner of evil. Over time his power had grown enormously in her mind until she imagined him some demon from hell.

But oddly, as he stood holding her at his mercy, he seemed much smaller than she'd remembered. He had a slight build, much smaller than the average warrior. How had he seemed so much larger than life just a few years before?

Had she made him more than he was because he talked so big and she feared him so deeply? Or maybe her panic was producing stupid thoughts, telling her that she could fight back, that she wouldn't let this evil idiot make her cower as he had when she was younger.

Perhaps the time with Graeme and his clan had given her a strength she lacked while in the protective bosom of her own clan. She'd had to fight for any respect she earned in the Montgomery clan. She was fiercely proud that no one had given her a thing.

"I've heard of your grand deception," Ian said, spittle rimming his lips. His face was red with rage that was only made more prominent by the flames from the torch.

He reached up to insert the torch into one of the sconces over Eveline's head, and then he yanked her upright until she was straining on tiptoe, his face just a breath from hers.

It was then she saw Ian's father, Patrick McHugh, standing off in the shadows. He looked uneasy, as if he wanted no part in the entire thing, and when he saw that Eveline was staring at him, he faded back so he was no longer in her line of sight.

Her heart sank. If Ian's father was an accomplice, what hope did she have? And he seemed frightened of Ian, which made no sense to her. Patrick was larger and stronger than Ian. He was a warrior. What warrior would allow his son to threaten him?

Her glance darted back to Ian when he shook her to gain her attention. Hatred shone like a beacon in his eyes. He was the mad one. He looked crazed.

"Played me for a fool. You act the simpleton to escape marriage and instead marry Montgomery. I cannot allow it. 'Twas supposed to be an alliance the McHughs forged with the Armstrongs. We would have been invincible! You'll pay for your deception, Eveline Armstrong. No one makes me look the fool and escapes retribution."

"Nay," she bit out, interrupting his tirade. "'Tis Eveline Montgomery now."

His eyes widened. "So the simpleton chooses to speak. Kierstan informed me that you found your tongue shortly after arriving at Montgomery Keep. I wondered if the lamb would find the courage to bite with the teeth of a lioness. I think I prefer the new and improved Eveline over the pale, skinny coward who went rigid with fright every time I came into contact with her. It will be a lot more entertaining to break the new Eveline."

"Why are you doing this?" she demanded as loudly as she could make her voice. "You have to know Graeme will kill you." Her glance darted to where she knew Patrick McHugh to be standing. "He'll kill all of you."

Ian smiled, and it sent a shiver down Eveline's spine.

"He'll never know where you are. And your father? Even now, he's likely riding on the Montgomerys, intent on war and revenge."

Fear rocketed through her chest, squeezing her, robbing her of air. "What have you done?"

"It doesn't look good that Graeme Montgomery's

new bride has gone missing. Nor does it sit well with the Montgomerys that a man bearing the dress of the Armstrong clan made an attempt on the Montgomery laird's life. What think you will happen when the two clans come head-to-head?"

"You were the one who shot Graeme with the arrow," Eveline breathed.

"Nay, not exactly. 'Twas not me, but a man under my command." He shrugged. "'Tis the same. The result is the same. There'll be no peace, no alliance between the Montgomerys and the Armstrongs. They'll be too busy fighting each other and will be branded outlaws by the king. They'll pose no threat to other clans. Instead, we'll take them down, one by one, and collect a rich purse as bounty. When I am done, the McHugh name will be the most highly revered in the highlands."

"You're mad," she said incredulously. "At least I only pretended madness. You are truly afflicted in the mind."

He backhanded her with his free hand, knocking her head back. But he held her in place with the hand he still had twisted in her hair so she had nowhere to go.

He turned her head forcefully back so she had to look him in the eye again. "And you, Eveline, will be thought dead when no one is able to discover your whereabouts. No one will hear your screams. No one will ever find you. You'll be mine to play with when I need amusement. In time you'll be grateful for any attention I bestow upon you."

"Never," she lashed out.

He forced her face even closer to his, and then he kissed her. It was a bruising, punishing force that so repulsed her, she gagged. She tried to insert her hands between them, but fell short when the chains prevented her from reaching that far.

When he deepened the kiss and she felt the brush of

his tongue over hers, she bit down, determined to put an end to the forced intimacy.

He thrust her away, rage in his eyes. He wiped at his mouth, and his hand came away stained with blood. This time when he struck her, he let her fall away, releasing her hair.

She fell to the floor, pain jolting through her limbs when the chains went taut, nearly yanking her arms from their sockets.

"Don't touch me again," she yelled with all the bravado she had left.

He stood over her, his mouth twisted into a sneer. "I'll do a whole lot more than touch, Eveline. You belong to me now. Be a good lass and I'll come visit you often. I'll even try to remember to bring you food and drink on occasion."

Then he reached over, took the torch from the sconce, and stalked away, taking the light with him.

Darkness settled over the small, airless room, and with it, despair so thick she choked. It overwhelmed her, seeping into her very soul.

Nay, she wouldn't allow herself to lose hope. Graeme would find her. She had every faith in her husband. She would remain strong until he came for her.

CHAPTER 42

Dawn crept over the horizon and Graeme stood before his assembled clan, fury, impatience, and worry vying for control. They'd searched the keep, the river, and the surrounding lands. They'd left no stone unturned and there was still no sign of Eveline.

He wouldn't accept that no one in his clan had seen Eveline or knew of what happened to her. There were no missing horses, and there was no way Eveline could have made it away on foot in her condition. Which meant that someone had to have taken her or aided her in some way.

He couldn't dwell on the latter thought, because then he'd have to accept that she'd gone willingly. She'd given him no cause to believe that she would have left so abruptly. After standing by his side and protecting him so fiercely, why would she have left him the moment he was recovering?

Nay, it didn't make sense, which meant that someone had her. Someone had taken her against her will and could be harming her even now. He had to push away the image of her frightened and hurt or he would lose all semblance of control.

"'Tis everyone, Graeme," Bowen said grimly. "Every last woman and child."

"Keep your eyes open," Graeme said in a low voice. "I cannot judge them all. Someone is telling an untruth. We must find out who before it's too late for Eveline."

Bowen's expression grew fiercer. He nodded and then motioned for Teague to go in one direction as he headed in the other, so they could better survey their gathered clansmen.

"Someone is not telling the truth," Graeme said loud enough that his voice carried over the quiet courtyard.

His soldiers, those he considered among his most trustworthy, were spread in a wide circle, their arms crossed menacingly over their chests. They watched just as Bowen and Teague watched, their gazes sweeping the crowd.

"Eveline was last seen by Mary in the kitchens last eve. Eveline disappeared just after and yet none of you witnessed anything."

"Maybe she went back to her own clan," someone called loudly from the midst of the assembled gathering.

"Hush your idiocy!" Nora yelled, her face mottled and red with anger. "The lass did not desert our laird. 'Tis disloyal of you to say such a thing."

"All I'm interested in hearing is who saw Eveline and if any of you have information on her current whereabouts. It will go far easier if you admit to such knowledge now. If 'tis found out later that you knew and something happens to Eveline as a result of your refusal to speak, the penalty will be death."

As Graeme said the last, his gaze drifted over the group of women who'd made things so difficult for Eveline. Most of them looked genuinely worried, but it was Kierstan's expression that drew further scrutiny.

She was pale, visibly nervous, and she kept glancing away and to the distance, as if she wanted to be as far from this place as possible. She wiped her hands down her skirts and tried to blend further into the crowd.

"And I promise, your death will not be quick," Graeme said, pointedly speaking toward Kierstan, hoping for a further reaction. "For every hurt heaped upon my wife, I'll exact equal measure from the person responsible. You'll pray for death before I am done."

Kierstan looked near to fainting. Desperation simmered in her eyes to the point Graeme was sure she must know more than she'd let on.

"You are dismissed," Graeme called out, surprising his brothers. "Think on all that I've said. I'll be willing to consider a more merciful punishment if you come to me now."

Bowen strode toward him, clear question in his eyes. "What are you doing, Graeme? You did not even press them."

Graeme held up his hand. "Bring Kierstan to me at once. Do not allow her out of the courtyard."

Bowen's eyes widened, and he glanced in the direction of the group of women who were moving with the crowd as they made to exit the courtyard. Without another word, he beckoned to Teague and they stalked quickly in Kierstan's direction.

A moment later, Bowen grasped Kierstan's arm, and she turned in alarm, fear radiating from her in waves. She didn't fight Bowen, however, and she allowed him to lead her over to where Graeme stood.

Bowen and Teague flanked her, looming over her, their scowls enough to frighten the toughest warrior.

"Y-you wanted to s-see me, Laird?" she stammered out.

"I'll only give you one opportunity to tell me the truth," Graeme bit out. "If you do not tell me what you know, your sentence will be death."

She went so white that Graeme feared she'd faint and be utterly useless.

"If I tell you what I know, do you vow to allow me to live?" she asked in a hoarse voice that cracked with fear.

"You do not bargain with me," Graeme roared. "I make you no promises, but you had better pray Eveline is returned safely to me or you'll sorely regret the mischief you've wrought."

"I already do," she said shakily.

She closed her eyes and swallowed deeply. When she opened them again, tears shone brightly.

"Ian McHugh has her."

"What?" Graeme bellowed. "What have you *done*?"

"Please," Kierstan begged. "I did not realize . . ."

"Do not lie," Teague spat. "You realized exactly what would happen to Eveline. You bargained with the devil. 'Tis time to pay the price. Tell him all or I swear I'll make you sorry."

She looked away, tears shining on her cheeks. "I had help from three Montgomery warriors. They were angry, as was I, that we were being forced to accept an Armstrong into our clan. One of them brought word of a bargain he'd struck with Ian McHugh. I met with Ian and told him that Eveline had played the simpleton to avoid marriage to him. He wanted to take her away so that you would be blamed by Eveline's kin. He intends to start war between you and the Armstrongs."

Fear and rage knotted Graeme's gut until he wanted to lay waste to an entire garrison of warriors. In that moment he had the strength and fury to be an unstoppable force.

Eveline, his precious, loving wife, was now in the hands of her worst tormentor. A man who'd described in exacting detail all that he'd make her suffer. His very blood froze in his veins, and suffocating dread made rational thought impossible for the space of several mo-

ments. All he could think was that he had to go to her.
He had to save her.

"Laird! Laird! The Armstrongs approach!"

Graeme swiveled and looked up to the guard tower
where his watchman was yelling out over the courtyard.

"They bear the entire might of their army!"

Graeme swore long and hard. Not now. Not when
Eveline needed his complete attention. He turned the entire force of his rage on Kierstan.

"See what you have wrought? You'll be the death of
us all."

Kierstan swayed unsteadily, her face completely devoid of blood.

"Don't you dare faint," Bowen hissed. "You'll tell us
what is left and I'll have the names of the warriors who
betrayed us."

"Ian took her," she blurted hastily. "I led her around
the side of the keep where Ian waited. Shamus, Gregory,
and Paul assisted Ian in leaving undetected."

Graeme swore. Gregory and Paul were two of the men
responsible for border patrol. It explained why Ian
McHugh could have come and gone on Montgomery
land without being apprehended.

"Have them imprisoned immediately," Graeme said
to Silas, who stood next to Graeme.

"'Tis my fault, Laird," Silas said, his head bowed. "I
should have known what was happening. They are
under my command."

"'Tis no one's fault save their own," Graeme snarled.
"Find them. Imprison them. And her," he said, gesturing
toward Kierstan.

"Nay!" she cried out. "I told you all!"

"And think you that speaking freely of your betrayal
pardons you from responsibility for your actions?
You've betrayed us all, Kierstan. Not just Eveline. Not
just me. You've betrayed all of your kin. If so much as

one man, woman, or child loses their life in battle with the Armstrongs, it will be a mark on your soul."

Kierstan burst into tears. "I did not know! I swear it, I did not know what would happen."

"Save the tears," Teague growled as he herded her toward one of the soldiers standing by Silas.

Graeme shouted up to the watchman. "How close?"

"They're coming over the rise!"

"Come," Graeme directed his brothers. "We'll ride out to meet them."

"Are you mad?" Bowen demanded. "We cannot ride alone to meet the might of their entire army."

"I cannot ride with the whole of *my* army," Graeme ground out. "It will be seen as an act of war. I can only hope I'm granted enough time to explain. Alert the others. Have them standing by to defend the keep. Let's hope that Armstrong is a reasonable man and will listen to all we have to say."

CHAPTER 43

Graeme rode out of the courtyard with his brothers at his sides and as directed, the gate was shut behind them while Silas rallied the men inside the keep. Tension was thick, and there was a sense of expectancy that permeated the air.

Everyone expected war. Most even wanted it. It was the chance to avenge the Montgomery losses to the Armstrong clan.

Graeme knew that if the slightest thing went wrong, his clan would swarm in like avenging angels and the entire valley would drip with blood.

He rode slightly ahead of his brothers, carrying a wide, white bedsheet as a sign of truce and that he planned no attack on the approaching army.

They swooped over the hill and down the other side to meet the Armstrong laird at the bottom.

Looking ahead, Graeme saw Tavis pause, then hold up his arm to halt the mass of soldiers behind him. 'Twas an impressive sight that forced Graeme to respect the might of the Armstrong fighting force.

Helmets and armor glistened in the sun. Shields reflected the light, sending blinding reflections from the well-honed metal. Crossbows and swords were held at the ready. It was an army that had come prepared to fight.

Tavis rode slightly ahead of his troops with his two sons at his sides. As he neared where Graeme and his brothers had stopped, he pulled away his helmet and pierced Graeme with the full weight of his stare.

"Where is my daughter?" he demanded.

"Ian McHugh has her," Graeme returned.

Tavis reared back in surprise and then frowned. Brodie and Aiden scowled, and then Brodie spit out, "Liar."

Graeme forced himself to keep his temper in check. It would be so easy to give the order to fight. His men were ready. They were itching to shed Armstrong blood. Everything Graeme had dreamed about was here, right in front of him. The chance to avenge his father's death and end the decades of strife caused by the blood feud between the two clans.

But Eveline was more important. For Eveline, he'd do whatever was necessary, even if meant crawling to her father on his hands and knees and humbling himself before the other chieftain.

"Why say you something so outlandish?" Tavis barked.

"We do not have time to stand here arguing," Graeme said in an even voice. "Eveline is what's important. If you love your daughter, have your men stand down so that we can talk over this matter between us and then form a plan to bring her back safely."

Tavis's eyes glittered with rage. "You dare question my affection for my daughter?"

"You're wasting time," Graeme pointed out. "Look at me, Armstrong. No army behind me. I rode here in good faith with only my brothers at my side. You could kill me now. I've raised no arms to you. I want my wife back and I'll have her if it's the last thing I do."

Tavis stared at Graeme for a long time, his brow furrowed in deep thought. "Speak your piece, Montgomery. I'll hear what you have to say and then render judgment on the matter."

"The man thinks he's God," Bowen muttered.

Graeme held up a hand to silence his brother.

"Did you know that Eveline is not daft at all? That she's a highly intelligent, cunning lass with a quick wit and a heart as big as the highlands?"

Tavis's jaw went slack, as though it were the very last thing he'd expected to hear Graeme say.

"She's deaf, Armstrong. Not simple. Not touched. Not mad. She merely cannot hear and yet she can read the lips of others and can understand what it is they say."

"How do you know all of this?" Armstrong asked hoarsely.

"She told me."

"You lie!" Aiden roared. "She cannot speak. She has not spoken since her accident."

Teague drew his sword in a flash. "You'll cease calling into question the honor of my brother. He speaks the truth. I've heard her myself."

Tavis bit out a rebuke to Aiden and ordered him to be silent. Then he turned back to Graeme. "She spoke to you? Is it true she cannot hear?"

Graeme nodded.

"Then *why*?"

The older man's hands shook and bewilderment was heavy in his eyes. He looked suddenly much older than his years. It was obvious what Graeme had said hurt him.

"Why would she perpetuate such a deception?" Tavis asked hoarsely.

"Because she feared she would be forced into marriage to Ian McHugh," Graeme said quietly. "She saw an opportunity to be able to cry off the marriage and so she allowed you and the rest of her clan to believe she was daft because it saved her from the one thing she feared the most. Ian terrorized her from the moment talks began of marriage. He spelled out in precise detail exactly how she'd suffer at his hands. She saw a way to escape and she seized it. Before long the lie took on a life of its own and she saw no way out."

Tavis whitened and then put a hand to his nape as he stared aghast at Graeme. "She told me . . . Sweet mother Mary, she came to me. She said . . . Oh God, I didn't believe her. I thought she was expressing normal maidenly fears. I had no idea. . . ."

"You left her no choice," Graeme bit out.

"And now? You say he has her? How did this happen? Did you not protect her as you should?" Tavis demanded.

"Nay, 'tis true enough that I did not do all I should do. 'Tis my fault she is even now in that bastard's hands."

"Nay!" Bowen cried out, his face red with anger. "I will not allow you to take blame for this. He was shot by an arrow less than a fortnight ago by a man wearing the scabbard that the Armstrong soldiers wear."

Tavis's head came up, his eyes sparking in anger. "I did not order an attack on my daughter's husband. I would have never endangered her in that manner. Furthermore, I would not dishonor a blood oath sworn before God and my king."

"I know you did not," Graeme said calmly. "I did not know it at the time, and it caused Eveline much grief, for she witnessed the entire thing, and it was she who told us of the scabbard and how they came to be made."

Tavis closed his eyes, his nostrils flaring. "My own daughter believes that I would betray her this way?"

"Eveline was betrayed by four members of my clan acting in conjunction with Ian McHugh. Last eve, Eveline was taken by McHugh and his escape was aided by men I trusted. I have no desire to engage you in battle, Armstrong. All I want is for my wife to be returned safely to my side."

Tavis stared at him for a long moment, his gaze burning into Graeme, peeling him back, layer by layer. Then his eyes widened in surprise.

"You care for my daughter."

"My love for her is stronger than my hatred of you. 'Tis why I'll not raise arms against you today. Instead I ask your aid in the battle against the McHughs."

Tavis, Brodie, and Aiden all stared at Graeme in astonishment. Then they looked at one another and then back to Graeme and his brothers.

Respect glimmered in Tavis's eyes as he met Graeme's gaze once more.

"Summon your men," Tavis said in a brisk tone. "The McHugh Keep is half a day's ride. We leave at once."

CHAPTER 44

" 'Tis as if they are not expecting battle," Bowen said as he stared down at the McHugh fortress.

Graeme frowned, though he was in agreement. There was little activity and indeed, it looked as though normal day-to-day operations were being carried out below.

They'd encountered no guards at the border. No one had given warning to the McHughs of the massive army approaching because there looked to be no readying of weapons or men.

Things were quiet. Too quiet. The sun was still well above the horizon and yet the entire keep looked to be readying for the day's end.

Such laziness and inattentiveness were unforgivable. Did McHugh care nothing for the protection of his clan? Or did he think the Armstrongs and Montgomerys were even now in battle and as such he had nothing to worry about?

Tavis leaned forward in the saddle and then centered his stare down the line at Graeme. "If this is a trick, Montgomery, I'll not rest until you and all of your kin are wiped from this earth."

In response, Graeme spurred his horse and began riding down the incline to the gate of the McHugh holding.

There was no way to be secretive with an army the size of the two combined clans. His hope was that in order to preserve the lives of his clansmen, the McHugh laird would give up supporting the madness wrought by his son and surrender Eveline into Graeme's hands.

If not, Graeme was prepared to slaughter every single McHugh.

As Graeme approached, and the hundreds of soldiers began appearing over the hillside, a cry of alarm went up inside the gates of the McHugh holding.

Panic sounded. Cries, shouts, the clank of metal. Screams from women and the sobs of children. Graeme refused to allow it to soften his mind. His wife was somewhere in there, terrified, and God only knew what she'd already been forced to endure.

Patrick McHugh appeared at the guard tower a moment later, fear in his eyes as he surveyed the threat before him.

"Tavis, what brings you here to my keep looking as though you are readying for battle?" he yelled.

"I've come for my wife," Graeme snarled before Tavis could respond.

Patrick looked pale and sweaty. "Your wife? Laird, I've not seen your wife. Why would you look for her here?"

Graeme only grew angrier. "You try my patience, McHugh. Present your sniffling, pitiful excuse for a son at once or I vow we'll kill every last one of your kin."

Patrick held up both hands. "Tavis, be reasonable. Please. Speak to Montgomery. You and I are friends. We are allies. I have not seen Eveline. You must believe me. I cannot fight the combined power of your two clans and hope to win. I'll not risk my people when we've done no wrong."

Tavis wavered, his gaze skirting to Graeme. For a moment, Graeme thought that Tavis would side with Patrick and question Graeme's account again. Graeme's blood surged with fury, but Tavis said in a low, urgent tone, "Is it possible Patrick could not know of what his son has done?"

Graeme's lip curled. "I find it hard to believe. However, if Patrick has done no wrong, then he should not object to producing his son to answer the charges against him, nor should he object to us searching the keep."

Tavis nodded his agreement.

"Produce your son," Graeme bellowed up. "If you claim you have done no wrong, then you'll let us question your son and you'll let us inside your gates to search the keep. Make no mistake, McHugh, this is not a request. We'll gain access one way or another. 'Tis up to you how it is done. Now do as I've said. I'll not wait a moment longer to be reunited with my wife."

"By all that's holy, I do not know of what you speak!"

Patrick's words were tinged with desperation. He was visibly shaken and it was obvious that he was seized with fear.

"Deliver your son," Graeme said in an icy tone. "'Tis all that will save you and your clan from annihilation."

"Give me but a moment. I beg you. I'll summon him. Do not harm him. He couldn't have done all you've accused him of."

"If he's innocent then you have nothing to fear," Tavis barked out. "Now stop wasting our time and present him forth. If my daughter has come to harm, 'tis not the Montgomerys you'll have to worry about."

Hearing the solidarity between the two rival clans, Patrick folded on the spot.

"Bring Ian to me," he barked back to one of his men. "And open the gates to admit the chieftains."

Tavis quickly turned and counted out a contingent of men to ride inside the gates with him and his sons. Graeme nodded to Bowen to direct him to do the same.

They'd not go in without enough men to successfully defend against an ambush. The rest would remain outside and on guard.

A moment later, the gate opened, and Graeme urged his horse forward. His pulse was pounding loudly in his ears, the taste of fear acid in his mouth. He feared he was too late. He feared that Ian would have already brutalized Eveline.

God, don't let him be too late.

Men and women alike scurried away as Graeme, his brothers, Tavis, and his sons were the first to ride into the courtyard. Behind them came forty other soldiers, all with weapons drawn, their gazes rapidly scanning for any threat.

Patrick rushed forward and a bare moment later, a sullen Ian was brought before Graeme by two of his father's men. Graeme's gaze honed in on the smaller man. He didn't seem remotely nervous or afraid. He stared boldly at the two chieftains still astride their horses and then sneered in their direction.

Graeme slid down, wanting to be face-to-face with Ian so he wouldn't have a false sense of safety. He wanted the younger man to know exactly what fate awaited him.

Behind him, his brothers also dismounted, and then Tavis and his sons came in close behind Graeme.

Ian's chin came up. The only evidence that his bravado was faltering was the hard swallow he took.

"Tell them," Patrick said. "Tell them you had nothing to do with Eveline's disappearance so they can be on their way."

"And you," Graeme said in a deadly quiet voice. "I hardly think your son acted alone, McHugh."

Patrick was openly sweating and his hands shook. "'Tis all ridiculous. I would never have done something so foolhardy, and neither would Ian."

"Of course I had nothing to do with her disappearance," Ian replied. "What would I want with the daft lass?"

Graeme took a menacing step forward, his hand reaching to grasp Ian's tunic. He yanked the much smaller man up until his toes were barely dragging the ground.

"If you've harmed a hair on her head, I'll quarter you and feed you to the buzzards," he hissed.

"Put him down, Montgomery," Patrick said angrily. "He's told you he had nothing to do with the lass's disappearance."

Still gripping Ian by the tunic, Graeme turned his cold stare on the older McHugh. "Then you'll not object to us searching the keep for her now, will you?"

Patrick's brows went up. "Of course not. She is not here. Don't you think I would know it if she were?"

The conviction on McHugh's face and in his speech bothered Graeme. It bothered him greatly. He knew *Ian* was lying, but Patrick seemed to be telling the truth. Either that or he was a better deceiver than his son.

Graeme tossed Ian in the direction of Silas. "Do not let him move." He gestured for his brothers and then stalked toward the keep entrance. He'd turn the entire place upside down if that was what it took.

Tavis and his sons followed quickly behind. A dozen of the Montgomery and Armstrong men filed in with Graeme and the others.

Graeme didn't bother issuing orders because he planned to cover every inch of the keep himself. He would not trust the well-being of his wife to anyone but himself.

He began in the first room he came to. Every corner, every space was invaded. He tossed furniture, tore back furs, upended beds, his fury growing with every room he found empty.

When he came out of the last chamber on the top level, a cloaked figure stood in the hallway, a hood drawn over his head so his face was not visible.

Upon taking a closer look, Graeme could see the figure was slight and small, obviously a lass or a very small lad. But when the person turned, a long lock of midnight black hair fell loose from the hood. A small hand came up to grip the hood so it remained covering the face and 'twas obvious it was a female's hand.

"Look below, Laird," she whispered. "In the dungeon."

Before Graeme could respond, the lass turned and fled down the passageway, disappearing into one of the far chambers.

Graeme barked an order for his brothers and then stalked down the stairs where he met Patrick McHugh at the bottom.

"Show me to your dungeon, McHugh. By all that's holy, if you've made my wife to suffer imprisonment in a dungeon, I'll kill you."

If possible, Patrick paled even more. "Of course, but it hasn't been used in well over two decades. There's not even a clear stairway into it anymore. Just a hole with a rope leading down."

"Show me," Graeme bit out.

His fury was growing with every minute that passed with no sign of Eveline. The idea of her being imprisoned in the dungeon had him shaking as they descended the stairs into darkness.

Patrick stopped to hand a torch to Graeme. He then lit two others and passed them to Tavis and Bowen so the way would be sufficiently lit.

At the bottom of the stairs, Patrick plucked a key from the wall and inserted it into an old, rusted lock. The clasp came away easily, despite the amount of rust and deterioration.

Graeme exchanged glances with Tavis to see if the older man had picked up on the lock. It should have creaked and groaned if it hadn't been in use for two decades. It never should have unlocked so easily.

Tavis realized it too, because his expression went from brooding to instant alertness. His entire stance stiffened and his face tightened in rage. He held up his hand to let Graeme know he understood and then put a finger to his lips to signal for complete quiet.

When all were through the iron barred door, Patrick led them to the middle of the decaying room and held up a torch to show them the rope leading down into the pit.

"Sweet Jesu," Bowen muttered. "Surely no one would put a wee lass down in this hole. It smells of death."

Graeme handed over his torch to one of his men and then ordered Teague to hold his torch so he could see his way down. Then he grasped the rope and quickly descended hand over hand into the darkness below.

When he hit the ground, he yelled up for Bowen to drop his torch. Not waiting for the others to climb down, Graeme immediately searched the surrounding area, going from one wall to the other and all points in between.

When the others dropped down, more light exploded into the chamber, enough to see that it was completely empty.

"See?" Patrick sputtered. "'Tis madness that you come bearing your army and accusing my son of such treachery."

"Come, Graeme, we've still to search the outlying cottages," Tavis said.

Graeme stared around the room, damning the fact that Eveline could not hear. He could not even call out to her and let her know that he was here, that she was safe and that all she had to do was call out to him.

He flashed the torch one last time and readied himself

to go back with the others, who were already climbing back up the rope, when his gaze fell on a disturbance in the dirt against the far wall.

He stalked forward, holding the torch in front of him as he drew near to the wall. There was a footprint, one that he and his men had not made, for it was not possible.

Half the print was visible. The other half seemed to disappear into the very wall.

"Bowen! Teague!" he barked. "Over here!"

A moment later, the others surrounded him and he pointed down.

"Where is she?" Brodie snarled, for the first time giving voice to the fact he believed all that Graeme had said.

"What is beyond this wall?" Graeme demanded.

Patrick shook his head, panic evident in his voice. "I have no idea. I swear it. I know not of anything beyond this wall."

Graeme dropped to his knees and began running his fingers along the seams of the stones. He pushed inward with his uninjured shoulder, but the wall would not budge.

Bowen dropped to his knees just a bit farther down the wall and began pushing on the various stones himself. When he was the length of six stones from Graeme, the wall suddenly pushed inward, sending Graeme tumbling forward.

Graeme scrambled to his feet, swinging the torch in all directions as he gained his bearings. 'Twas a small room. He swung around in a complete circle and nearly danced the torchlight right past her.

A gasp went up. He wasn't the only one to have seen the still body lying on the floor. He yanked the torch back and rushed forward, his heart screaming denial the entire way.

Behind him, there was a mad scramble and then more light. The entire chamber lit up and Graeme could see the chains and manacles that circled Eveline's wrists and ankles.

He let out an enraged howl that echoed and bounced off the stone walls. He tossed the torch back to one of his brothers and then dropped to his knees, gathering Eveline in his arms. He rocked back and forth, kissing her hair, her brow, her cheeks. Her skin was so very cold and she was so very still.

Her father knelt down beside Graeme, staring in horror at his daughter, so lifeless in Graeme's arms.

"I did not know!" Patrick babbled. "I swear it on my very life, I did not know!"

Enraged, Bowen slammed the older man against the wall. "Where are the keys to the manacles?"

But Graeme ignored them all. He pushed back Eveline's hair and with trembling fingers, felt for a pulse against the side of her neck.

"Is she . . ." Tavis broke off, unable to complete the sentence.

"She's alive!" Graeme said in a rush of relief. But even as he exclaimed it, he took in the bruises on her face, and rage blew through him like the fires of hell.

The chains were attached to the wall of the chamber with old hinges he doubted were that strong anymore. It would have been enough to restrain a lass, but not a warrior who was so filled with rage that he could have thrown a horse to free his wife.

He handed Eveline to her father. "Hold her and shield her."

Then he stood, reached for the chains, and with a bellow of rage, yanked the top hinge, which held the two chains attached to the manacles at her wrists, free from the wall. Before he could move to the one at her feet, Aiden gripped the chain and tore the hinge from the wall, freeing her so they could at least take her from the dungeon to remove the manacles.

Tavis was holding his daughter tightly to his chest and weeping softly into her hair. Graeme reached down for her, refusing to allow another to carry her from her prison. He would tend to her himself. No other would touch her.

Patrick was completely white with fear. He babbled a stream of nonsense and begging. His son was to blame. He had no knowledge of the plot.

Graeme shoved by him in disgust.

When Graeme reached the rope leading to the upper chamber, he stopped. He could not climb up while holding Eveline and neither could he make the climb with her over his shoulder.

Brodie pushed forward, Aiden on his heels.

"Give her to Father and you climb up," Brodie said to Graeme. "Aiden and I will form a human ladder and hand her up to you. 'Tis something we've done since we were lads. We'll not drop her, I swear it."

Graeme nodded, handing Eveline swiftly into her father's care. He shot up the rope, fear and anger lending him the strength of ten men. When he reached the top, he called down, and he saw Aiden climb atop Brodie's shoulders, balancing himself. Graeme stuck his head down through the opening, extending himself as far as he could without plummeting downward, but there was no way he'd be able to reach Eveline even if Aiden could bear her over his head.

"Bowen, climb up," Graeme ordered.

A moment later, his brother ascended the rope and Teague quickly scrambled up after him. Graeme lay down on his stomach and inched his way over the edge.

"Hold onto my legs," he directed. "You'll have to pull me and Eveline back up when I've gained hold of her."

Carefully, his brothers holding his ankles, Graeme

was lowered, and when he was almost able to touch Aiden's extended hands, Aiden called down for his father to lift Eveline up.

Helped by the other men, Tavis put Eveline into Aiden's arms, and then he raised her as high as he could while perched on Brodie's shoulders. Twice he nearly fell, but was able to successfully gain his balance without dropping her.

Finally, Graeme slipped his hands underneath Eveline's arms and then yelled back for his brothers to pull him up.

He scraped painfully over the rough floor and his injured shoulder protested the rough treatment, but he ignored all pain and discomfort. He had Eveline back in his arms. She was alive, though he didn't know the extent of her injuries or what had been done to her while she was in captivity.

He waited for the others to make the climb up only because he could not do what must be done while still holding Eveline.

They walked up the stairs to the first level of the keep in silence, Graeme holding Eveline tightly to his chest the entire way. When he reached the top, he turned, and when her father and her brothers cleared the top step, Graeme held Eveline out to Tavis.

"Guard her well," he said in a low voice. "And wait here until I've done what I must. I'll not have her exposed to him a moment longer. I would not want her to awaken and to see him in life or death."

Tavis nodded his understanding and took Eveline into his arms. Brodie and Aiden hovered close to their father, their eyes dark and worried.

Graeme turned to stalk away, leaving the others behind. He walked through the keep and back to the courtyard, his single-minded purpose to go back to where Silas was holding Ian.

The weak little bastard actually looked at Graeme in triumph when Graeme appeared in the courtyard without Eveline.

"See? I told you I had no use for the simpleton."

Graeme drew his sword in one smooth motion and before Ian could even process what was about to happen, Graeme thrust the sword through Ian's belly until the blade protruded out his back.

Ian stared up in shock, his eyes glazing over with death. Blood bubbled from his mouth and slid down his chin to drip on the ground.

"That was for my wife," Graeme snarled. "I hope you rot in hell."

CHAPTER 45

Ian dropped, folding like a ribbon in the wind. Graeme didn't even wait to see if he'd taken his last breath before he began searching his body for the keys to the manacles. He was the sort who would have carried them on his person, and Graeme was right. The key was in the pocket of Ian's tunic.

He sheathed his sword, not bothering to wipe Ian's blood from the blade. Then he hurried back to where Eveline was and carefully unlocked the manacles, prying them from her wrists and ankles.

When he stood back to toss aside the chains, he looked Eveline's father in the eye.

"I have no intention of breaking our treaty. I want only to return to my keep with Eveline."

He held out his arms for Eveline, but Tavis hesitated. His hold tightened around the precious bundle in his arms, and he looked at Graeme, his expression pleading.

"Our keep is closer. Let us go there so we can be sure all is well with Eveline. Do not deny me this, I beg you. Her mother will want to know all of what you've told me. She'll want to hold her daughter in her arms and know that she is safe and happy."

Graeme glanced at his brothers and then back to the Armstrong chieftain. It was no easy thing, what he requested. He was asking Graeme to lay aside the past, to walk onto Armstrong land as a . . . guest. And to remain there as . . . family.

He stared up again at his brothers and let his gaze linger, wanting their thoughts. Bowen and Teague exchanged looks and turned their heads slightly, taking in the expressions on the faces of Eveline's brothers and father, who still held Eveline tightly against his chest.

" 'Tis not a big thing they ask," Bowen said in a low voice. "A mother would want to know her only daughter is well after such an ordeal."

Graeme's heart lightened and relief crushed through his chest. For Eveline he could set aside years of hatred and the burning desire for revenge, but he could not expect his kin to feel the same.

"We should hasten, Graeme," Teague said. "The lass should awaken among those who love her and not here, where she has suffered abuse."

Graeme turned his gaze to Tavis. "If you'll have us, then we'll be grateful for your hospitality and for any care you can render to my wife."

Tavis took the three steps that separated him from Graeme and gently placed Eveline in Graeme's arms.

"Let's ride and allow Patrick to bury his dead. We can further settle the matter with the McHughs and conduct a full investigation once we are sure that Eveline will recover from her ordeal."

Graeme lowered his face to his wife's head and briefly closed his eyes in the sweet wonder of having her back, alive. Then he nodded his agreement to Tavis and turned to stalk back to where his horse was being kept by his men.

*   *   *

As soon as they approached Armstrong Keep, Robina Armstrong ran out to greet her husband, her expression frantic.

She stopped short when she took in the presence of the Montgomery soldiers. Her eyes widened as she stared in bewilderment at the impressive display of might. And then her gaze settled on Graeme, and her hand went to her mouth when she saw it was Eveline he held before him.

She ran, skirts flying, as fast as her feet would carry her until she was directly below Graeme. He had to hold his horse in place so she wouldn't be trampled.

"Damn it, Robina!" Tavis roared. "I told you to remain within the keep no matter what occurred!"

"What has happened to Eveline?" Robina asked, her distress evident in her choked words. She completely ignored the anger of her husband as she stared imploringly up at Graeme.

"I know not all of it," Graeme said in gentle tones. "Allow me passage so that Eveline may be tended to."

Robina stepped hastily to the side. "Of course."

Then she turned and ran as fast as she'd come back to the keep, leaving them to follow on horseback.

By the time they rode into the courtyard, Robina was waiting anxiously on the steps, her fingers laced together in a ball in front of her. Tears shone on her cheeks as she waited for the warriors to dismount.

Bowen circumvented Eveline's brothers when they would have reached up to lift Eveline down from Graeme's horse. In a clear message that he considered Eveline one of his own, Bowen reached for her, taking her from Graeme's arms and carefully lowering her.

He waited for Graeme to slide down and then handed her back into Graeme's care. Mindful not to jostle her, Graeme walked toward Robina, displaying no discomfort over the fact that he and his men were fully ensconced on Armstrong land and that they were, in effect, at the mercy of the Armstrong laird.

Robina urged him inside and then hurried ahead of him, directing him to follow her up the stairs. When she would have pushed into the chamber that Eveline had occupied before, Graeme halted.

"Will this chamber accommodate me too?" he demanded. "I'll not leave her."

Robina's eyes widened, and then she cleared her throat. "Perhaps it would be better then to put her in the chamber you rested in when you were here as a guest."

Graeme nodded and followed her farther down the hall until they came to the room where he and Eveline had had their first true conversation, even though Eveline hadn't spoken a word the entire time. How things had changed since then.

He lowered her to the bed and then sat on the edge and ran his hand over the dark bruise on her jaw. Another marred her entire temple. There were fingerprints on her cheek, as if Ian had grasped her harshly.

His fingers trembled and his nostrils flared. His emotions threatened to crumble as he stared down at his fragile, bruised wife. Oh God, he'd thought he'd never see her again. He'd never been so afraid in his life. Never had he cared so much for a woman that the mere idea of being without her had threatened to crush his entire world.

"You care for her," Robina Armstrong said in a shocked tone.

Graeme whipped his head around to pierce the other woman with his gaze. The others had gathered in the doorway. Some had already spilled into the room, their expressions worried. He cared not who heard his next words.

"My lady, I don't simply care for her. I *love* her. She is

my entire life. Without her, I am nothing. I *have* nothing."

Her eyes widened until they were enormous against her pale face. Tavis stepped in to take her by the shoulders, pulling her back against his chest.

"Let him be, love. His concern is foremost for Eveline. There is much we didn't know of her." He broke off, his voice thick with grief. "I made so many mistakes. It nearly cost us our daughter. It *could* have cost us our daughter."

"What do you speak of?" Robina demanded.

Tavis shook his head. "'Tis not the time. You will hear all when we are certain that Eveline is well and has recovered from her ordeal. For now, we will do all we can to make Graeme and his kin welcome in our home. He cares a great deal for Eveline and has set aside his thirst for revenge because he loves her more than he hates me."

Robina stared at Graeme in utter bewilderment. "'Tis true?"

Graeme issued a short nod and then turned his attention back to Eveline. Even though he knew she could not hear him, he was nearly compelled to speak to her. Instead, he contented himself with touching her, stroking his fingers over her face as he prayed for her to awaken.

Turning to the others, he issued a short command for them to leave the room so he could remove her damp clothing. Then he glanced at her father. "Will you have a serving woman build up the fire? I don't want Eveline to be cold."

"I'll fetch a warm sleeping gown for her to wear," Robina said, already hurrying for the door.

Tavis himself put wood in the bare fireplace and put flame to the logs. When Robina pushed back into the chamber, she shooed the others away, and then she came to stand beside Graeme.

"I'll tend to my daughter if you wish to step outside with the others."

"I'm not leaving her," Graeme said bluntly. "You can stay or go as you wish, but I am going to examine her myself so I can see what injuries she has sustained. Have you a healer you can summon if 'tis more serious than I fear?"

Robina nodded wordlessly, her expression still one of befuddlement over Graeme's fierceness when it came to Eveline. It was no matter. She'd learn soon enough that he had no intention of leaving Eveline's side.

Satisfied that she'd question him no further, he turned his attention to removing the tattered, dirty dress that clung damply to her skin.

Her mother gasped when the fading bruises that had already been present on Eveline came into view.

"Oh merciful heaven," Robina whispered.

"'Tis not what you think," Graeme said grimly. "She sustained these bruises not at the hands of Ian McHugh, but from a fall from a horse while she was still on Montgomery land."

"A horse?" Robina exclaimed. "Why on earth was she on a horse? Did you force her to ride?"

Graeme whipped his head around. "Of course I did not. She rode back to the keep to summon help for me when I was felled by an arrow."

Robina's eyes rounded once more in astonishment. It was an expression that seemed permanently imprinted on her face ever since Graeme's arrival. He supposed he understood her confusion. It would seem they'd known very little of their daughter, which was a shame, because Eveline was extremely special.

Graeme finished removing the gown, relieved when he saw no sign of further injury to her body. He could only pray that Ian had not raped her. The thought made his stomach clench and his heart ache.

With Robina's help, he gently bathed her skin, removing the dirt and grime from the dungeon, as well as the smell. He didn't want her to experience any discomfort. After she was clean, he attired her in a fresh woolen gown lined with fur that kept her warm and also prevented the wool from scratching her skin.

He gently pulled her hair away from her head and then meticulously ran his fingers over her scalp to check for any bumps or breaks in the skin.

"It would seem all he did was bruise her face," Graeme said in relief. He hoped with all his might that it was all. But what he feared the most was what the ordeal had done to her spirit.

"Tavis said you ran him through."

Graeme nodded, not turning away from Eveline.

"Good," Robina said fiercely.

Graeme leaned down and pressed his lips to Eveline's cool forehead. "Come back to me," he whispered. "I'm waiting, Eveline."

She stirred beneath his touch and his pulse rocketed up until it was hammering at his temples. He drew away, framing her face in his hands, cupping her cheeks, filling her with as much of his warmth as he could. He wanted her to awaken knowing she was safe.

As her eyelids fluttered and opened, he leaned even closer so his face would be the first she saw. She blinked several times as if trying to rid herself of her confusion, and then her eyes flooded with crushing relief.

She smiled, a more beautiful sight than Graeme had ever seen in his life.

"I knew you'd come," she whispered in a hoarse voice.

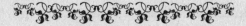

CHAPTER 46

It was more than Graeme could withstand. Tears burned his eyelids and his nostrils flared with the effort he exerted not to completely lose his composure.

Ignoring Robina's startled gasp over the fact Eveline had spoken, he focused solely on his beautiful wife and on reassuring her that she was safe and with those who loved her.

"Do not try to speak, my love," he said tenderly. "Your throat must pain you. You sound like a croaking frog."

Eveline grimaced and raised a hand to her throat. "I screamed, praying someone would hear. It was so dark." She broke off, tears swimming in her eyes as she sucked in deep breaths through her nostrils. "I was so afraid. He intended to keep me there."

Her voice completely trailed off even as her mouth still moved as she tried to speak. He put a finger to her lips, shushing her. Then he followed his finger with his own lips and kissed her, long and sweet, absorbing the sensation of being able to touch her and smell her and drink her in. To know that she was safe from harm. That she'd survived and he hadn't lost her.

He leaned his forehead against hers, and then he simply gathered her in his arms and held her close, rocking back and forth as he ran his hands up and down her back.

After a moment she went completely still. She put her hands on his arms and pushed away so that she could see his face. Her gaze went beyond him and scanned the room, and he knew she'd just realized that she was in her parents' home.

He glanced behind him, expecting to see Robina still standing there, but the chamber was empty. Robina had slipped away, giving the couple privacy after Eveline had awakened.

Eveline touched his cheek, her brow furrowed in confusion.

Graeme sighed. "Don't speak. Just listen to me. Your father came to Montgomery Keep with the might of his entire army. Ian must have sent him a message that he received just after I sent my own summons. I know not what the message said—I've yet to question your father—but it must have made him fearful for you, because the first thing he demanded was to know your whereabouts."

Eveline frowned.

"Prior to your father's arrival, Kierstan broke down and confessed that she conspired with Ian McHugh and that she led you around the side of the keep so that Ian could abduct you. He was aided by three of my men. Your father and his men rode with me and mine to the McHugh holding and I turned the keep upside down until I finally discovered you in a hidden room off the dungeon.

"After we took you out, I left you with your father long enough for me to kill Ian for his crime. I only wanted to return to our keep so that I could make sure that all was well with you, but your father asked that we come here since it was closer."

He paused a moment and then gathered Eveline's hands in his. "I told your father all. He knows that you allowed your clan to think you were affected by the accident and why. He was deeply distraught. I thought that if we visited here for a few days while you recovered, that it would give you time with your family to perhaps tell them all that you've wanted to tell them for so long."

Eveline's lips turned down into an expression of sorrow. She briefly closed her eyes, but Graeme touched her cheek until she looked back at him.

"Worry not, Eveline. I am with you. I'll always be with you. I'll stand by you when you speak to your parents for the first time. I'll not allow any upset."

She nodded, her shoulders heaving as she let out a long breath. "'Tis good they know. I hated deceiving them so."

"Aye, I know it," Graeme said gently.

He kissed her again, treasuring being able to do so when he had feared never seeing her again. Never holding her. Never having the chance to tell her all that was in his heart.

Now wasn't the time, but soon. He was near to bursting with all he wanted to say. But first he would care for her. Make sure she had food and rest.

"Would you like to see your mother and father now? I'll send down for food and hot water for a proper bath. You can see them now or after you've had time to eat and clean up."

"After," she croaked in a strained whisper.

He nodded and then rose to go tell her mother all Eveline needed.

* * *

Eveline submerged herself in the wooden tub until the steaming water lapped against her chin. She closed her eyes and allowed the warmth to seep into her bones, replacing the aching chill and soothing away the soreness of her muscles.

Graeme gathered her hair as it fell over the back and began brushing the tangles from the strands. She savored his touch, the comfort of having him so near. She feared nothing when he was with her.

When he was finished brushing her hair, he pulled it around one shoulder and let it drop into the water. Then he picked up a clay pitcher and knelt up so he could dip it in the water.

He turned her face so she could see his mouth and then instructed her to sit forward so he could wash her hair.

'Twas an exhilarating experience to have this hard warrior so tenderly wash and soothe away her aches and pains. She'd never felt so cherished. So . . . loved.

The thought sent a fierce ache into her very soul. What she wouldn't give to be able to hear those words from his lips. She'd give anything at all to have one day when she could hear. Just to rejoice in the sound of something so simple as a few spoken words from her husband's heart.

She closed her eyes and sat there limply while he finished soaping and rinsing her hair and then when he washed the rest of her body, even down to her toes.

As her foot slipped back down into the water, he leaned over the tub and captured her mouth in a deep, seeking kiss. It was a little less gentle than his kisses had been when she was still abed.

There was a desperation about him, almost as if he were still convincing himself that she was here and was safe. His palm cradled her jaw and held her as his kiss deepened and his tongue slid sensuously over hers.

I love you.

The words that she tried to say simply wouldn't come out. They died painfully in her throat, the strength to vocalize gone.

Graeme drew away, his gaze never leaving her as he reached for one of the drying linens. He took her hand, helped her to her feet, and assisted her in stepping over the rim and onto the chamber floor. Immediately he wrapped her from head to toe in the linen and ushered her toward the fire where a plate of bread and cheese, along with a bowl of steaming rabbit stew, awaited.

"I want you to eat every bite," he instructed.

She nodded, only too happy to comply with his dictate.

The fire warming her skin, she sucked the broth from her spoon and savored the trail of warmth down her throat. It soothed the rawness and moistened the ravaged flesh.

She ate until exhaustion claimed her and she could barely hold her head up any longer. Reaction set in and to her disgust she began to shake violently.

It was stupid. She was safe. She was miles away from Ian McHugh, and he was dead anyway. And yet she couldn't stop trembling. She couldn't stop the horrific realization that she could still be in that dark dungeon manacled to the wall.

Graeme swept her into his arms and carried her back to the bed. He tossed aside the linen he'd wrapped her in and pulled the wool gown back over her head. Taking only enough time to remove his boots, he tucked her beneath the furs and crawled in beside her, pulling her to his body so that his warmth seeped into hers.

He rubbed his hands up and down her back until finally some of her panic faded and she went limp against him. He kissed her temple, her still damp hair, and the shell of her ear. His breath blew warm over her cheek and she snuggled deeper into his embrace, her eyes closing.

She would face her family when she awakened. Maybe by then, her voice would have returned and she would be able to give them the words to explain what she'd done.

CHAPTER 47

Graeme sat propped in bed, Eveline perched on his lap, his arms wrapped around her in support as she faced her brothers and her parents with something she'd long withheld from them. The truth.

He sat quietly, merely holding her while she swallowed her courage and plunged ahead with the entire story, ending with her capture by Ian McHugh and the terror she felt that he'd follow through with all the promises he'd made when she was much younger.

Rage mottled the faces of Brodie and Aiden. Tears glistened in her father's eyes and he wouldn't even meet Eveline's gaze. Shame crowded his features and it hurt Eveline to see the pain on his face. Her mother was weeping softly, but there was also joy in her eyes, which heartened Eveline.

They weren't angry. Their emotions seemed to run from gladness to sorrow. And anger at Ian McHugh. But not at her.

She sagged against Graeme, taking comfort in his embrace. She'd gratefully seized on his strength, needing every ounce she could muster to brave her family.

"Why did you not tell *me*?" Brodie asked, sadness in

his gaze as he stared at Eveline. "You have to know I would have championed you."

"You could not have changed Papa's mind," she said.

"'Tis I who must shoulder the blame for all that you felt forced to do," her father said, his expression strained.

"Nay!" Eveline denied. "Please, I cannot bear to see you all so sad. It was a stupid thing to do. I accept that. I don't regret my actions, because perhaps things would not be as they are now. But it was not a good thing nor was it your fault. I lied. I deceived you. I became ensnared in a web I couldn't escape. I only wanted you to know the truth now and for you also to know that I do not blame you. I am not angry. I love you."

Her mother rose from her seat next to Eveline's father and came forward to where Eveline sat across Graeme's lap. She held out her arms and Eveline went willingly, hugging her mother as fiercely as her mother hugged her.

It had been so long since she'd had such contact with her mother and she savored the warmth and love of something as wondrous as a mother's hug. Even though she was no longer a child, she was not so old that she had no need of her mother's comfort. There was not a better feeling in the world.

Her mother drew away, framing Eveline's face. Tears slid down her mother's face, but then she smiled, her eyes shining with love and forgiveness.

"'Tis true then, you can read all that I say from merely watching my lips?"

Eveline nodded. "Aye."

"Clever lass," her mother said, patting her cheek.

Her father also rose and stood a short distance away, his eyes haunted. No longer able to bear the sadness on his face, Eveline pushed away from Graeme. Sensing her intention, Graeme helped her to her feet.

Eveline walked to where her father stood and wrapped

her arms around his waist, rested her cheek on his burly chest, and squeezed with all her strength.

His arms immediately came around her, holding her as tightly as she held him. His body shook against her and he kissed the top of her head.

When he pulled away, there were visible tear tracks on his cheeks and grief was heavy in his gaze.

"I'm sorry, my baby," he said.

She shook her head. "Nay, 'tis all forgiven. And 'twas I who should have begged your forgiveness. All is well now. 'Tis all that matters."

Her father nodded. "Aye, what's important is if you're happy and well cared for."

She smiled and then glanced back to where Graeme was now standing by the bed. His gaze never left her and she was struck by the depth of emotion in his eyes.

Without looking back at her father, she said, "Oh aye, I am well cared for, Papa."

Brodie and Aiden came to hug her. Brodie was fierce in his embrace, and he touched a gentle finger to the bruise so close to her mouth.

"I love you, little sister. Never forget your home here and the people who love you."

She smiled. "Nay, I'll not forget ever."

She returned to Graeme and he once more sat on the bed, pulling her into his lap. She felt safe and sheltered there, his warmth and strength aiding her own.

"There is more we must know, Eveline," Graeme said. "Ian McHugh took you, but when we rode to McHugh Keep, Patrick McHugh claimed he had no knowledge of his son's actions. We left the holding quickly because we feared that you were sorely injured. Can you tell us all that occurred, if 'tis not too painful for you to relate?"

Eveline stared at her husband in shock. "Not know of it? Graeme, he was there, in the dungeon when Ian struck me. I saw him and he backed into the shadows as if he didn't want me to see, but he was there. He knew of it all."

Graeme went rigid and he stared at the others in the room, his features locked in fury. She touched his cheek so he'd look at her once more.

"He acted *afraid* of his son. It made no sense to me. Ian was so much smaller than I remembered him to be. Much smaller than even his father. When I was younger, he seemed so huge, like a monster of myth. When I saw him again, I could scarcely believe that this was a man who'd fueled my nightmares for so long."

"He dies," Graeme said, his expression ice cold.

Eveline glanced worriedly at the others who wore similar expressions of fury. Her father's cheeks were red with rage.

Bowen stepped forward. "I know you are angry, Graeme. No one blames you. But Eveline needs you right now. You should not leave her side even to avenge her. You exacted punishment on the one who was most responsible for her torment. Let me take our men and ride to McHugh Keep to take care of the matter."

Graeme started to shake his head, but Eveline's father held up his hand. "Your brother is right, Graeme. 'Tis not a matter for you to take up. Your place is with your wife. I will lend troops. 'Tis likely they'll give up without a fight. They know they cannot win."

"I'll go with him," Aiden said, a scowl on his face.

"And I," Teague said.

Eveline's head swam from moving from face to face in order to see all that was said.

Tavis smiled as Brodie also took up the cause. Then he glanced at Graeme. "What say you, Graeme? Can two chieftains stand aside and allow their most loyal men to rid the highlands of a viper?"

"I lay claim to the holding," Graeme said. "It will be granted to Eveline and our daughter, no matter when she is born, be it first or last in line. Any son she bears me will eventually take over the role of chieftain to our clan. But I would have our daughter provided for so she never feels as Eveline did when she sought to escape marriage to a brutal monster."

Eveline's eyes filled with tears and she threw her arms around her husband's neck, holding him tightly as hot trails tracked down her cheeks.

When she finally pulled away, she kissed him full on the lips, uncaring of who witnessed the intimacy. He cradled her once more against him and she glanced at the assembled group of men who were steadily making plans for the Montgomerys and Armstrongs to go forth in their first joint task as newly formed allies.

Her brothers and Graeme's were already arguing over who was granted the task of executing Patrick McHugh for his lies and treachery. She forced her glance away, not wanting to dwell on death.

Graeme tipped her chin in his direction and stroked his hand over her cheek.

"Your mother wants to have some time with you. I'll go below stairs with the others while they discuss the planning. I'll come back up to check on you later."

He gently set her aside so she sat on the bed, and then he rose, gesturing to the others to exit the chamber.

When they were gone, Eveline turned her gaze to her mother, suddenly nervous now that they were alone.

Robina sat on the bed facing Eveline and took her hands in hers.

"You love him," her mother said, her expression soft.

"Oh aye," Eveline breathed. "So very much. He has been so wonderful to me."

Her mother smiled and squeezed her hands. She leaned forward and kissed Eveline's cheek and then pulled away, joy still shining on her face.

"'Tis obvious he loves you."

Eveline didn't immediately respond, but then she looked directly at her mother, her heart pounding all the while. "Aye, I believe he does. He has not said so, but I believe it to be with all my heart."

Her mother nodded. "Aye, I believe it too. He's so protective and tender with you, Eveline. 'Tis a glorious sight to behold."

Eveline sighed. "'Tis the one time I truly resent my inability to hear."

Her mother frowned. "Why so?"

"Because more than anything, I wish I could hear him say the words. 'Tis all I would ever ask again."

Graeme stood quietly outside the door, listening as the wistful tone came through in Eveline's words. It hurt him that she longed for the impossible, that she needed to hear those words so badly.

He considered the situation for a long moment as she and her mother continued to converse inside the chamber. Nay, she could not hear him through normal means. But somehow, he would find a way to make her hear him. He wanted there to be no doubt in her mind that he loved her more than it was possible to love any other.

He placed his hand on the closed chamber door and whispered softly, "I love you, Eveline. I'll make you hear me if 'tis the last thing I do."

CHAPTER 48

"I'd like this to be a new beginning between our clans," Tavis Armstrong said as goblets of ale were placed in front of Graeme, Bowen, and Teague as well as Brodie, Aiden, and Tavis.

"I'm listening," Graeme said.

His brothers exchanged glances, and then they both looked to Graeme. Graeme recognized the enormity of this moment. The unthinkable was occurring thanks to a blue-eyed, golden-haired lass who'd stormed into his life and made him think of other things than revenge and hatred.

She'd taught him to love.

"Together we are a force like no other," Tavis said.

Aiden nodded his agreement. Brodie was obviously in support of his father as well. He sat to the side without rancor or derision. He looked . . . eager . . . to make peace.

"No one, not even the crown, would have the power to defeat our combined forces," Tavis continued. "'Tis not that I'm suggesting any such insurrection. I'm merely pointing out the benefits of a *true* alliance between us. Not one forced upon us."

Graeme took in a deep breath, glanced toward his

brothers one last time. They met his gaze and nodded almost imperceptibly. Then Graeme looked back at the Armstrong chieftain.

"I'm willing."

There was such gladness and relief in Tavis's eyes that Graeme was taken aback.

"'Tis good that we can put decades of feuding behind us, not only for the sake of my daughter, but for your children and my sons' children. Instead, we can build an unbreakable alliance that will ensure the future of both of our clans."

Graeme nodded, peace settling deep into his heart. 'Twas the right decision. It was not one he could have made before Eveline. But he wanted his and Eveline's children to grow up surrounded by the protection of both clans. He never wanted the likes of Ian McHugh to threaten all he held dear.

Tavis held out his hand to Graeme. "A new oath, one that is not blood sworn, but instead is given freely and without coercion."

Graeme reached across the table to grasp the older man's hand. Tavis held on, surprising strength in his grip.

"I want to be a part of my daughter's life and to see the children of her womb. My grandchildren."

Graeme didn't misunderstand what Eveline's father was truly asking. He was asking that he be allowed on Montgomery land. Freely. At will. He was asking that Graeme open his gates to the Armstrongs and that goodwill be forged from this point forward.

He was asking that they act as a . . . family.

I'm sorry, Da. I cannot continue in the path I have followed for the last years. I love Eveline. She means everything to me. More than revenge. More than punishing those I hold accountable for your death. Forgive me, please.

He met Tavis's gaze. "You will always be welcome on Montgomery land. Eveline will be happy to see the family she loves, and 'tis my hope to provide the grandchildren you so hope to enjoy."

"You are a good man," Tavis said hoarsely. "I would have never imagined that we would be sitting here speaking of visitations and grandchildren. You've taught an old man much about being the better man. It would have been easy to resent and punish Eveline for a marriage forced upon you and alliance with a man you hate. And yet you treated her kindly."

Graeme withdrew his hand. Dread had left his heart. No longer did he feel the weight of hatred or the thirst for revenge. When he looked at Tavis Armstrong, he didn't see a man he'd hated for the better part of his life. He saw a man who loved his daughter and who wanted to forge a better future for her and her children.

"Tonight we celebrate the safe return of my daughter," Tavis announced. "We'll have a feast prepared and rejoice in a new alliance. 'Tis a new dawn in our clans' history. In the morning, my sons and your brothers will ride to avenge the wrong done to both our clans by the McHughs."

"Do you feel well enough to come down for the evening's celebration?" Robina Armstrong asked Eveline.

Eveline smiled and nodded. "Aye. I want to be with my husband and my family. 'Tis a joyous occasion. I'll not allow Ian McHugh to frighten me any longer."

Her mother smiled and hugged Eveline to her bosom. "Come, then, let's find you something stunning to wear. I have something that should suit you."

An hour later, Eveline's hair was partially upswept in a jeweled comb, while the rest was left to flow down her back. She wore a gown the colors of an autumn sunset. Russet, amber, and golden hues were woven into the fine material. Each stitch was intricately set. Eveline shone like a thousand suns. Not even the bruises on her face could disguise her beauty.

"The men await," Robina said. "Let us go before they grow impatient. They wait on us to begin the festivities."

Eveline descended the stairs behind her mother and when they entered the hall, she looked upon her husband standing by the hearth and was taken back to the time when she'd first laid eyes on Graeme Montgomery.

He'd been standing, just as he was standing now, and she'd felt the vibrations in her ears from his low, rumbling voice. She'd been fascinated by him from the very start.

He turned, his gaze settling on her as she stood across the room. There was deep satisfaction in his eyes, and then he started across the hall in her direction.

Her mother smiled and left her side to go to her husband. Graeme stopped a foot in front of her and held out his hand.

"You look beautiful, Eveline," Graeme said.

She slid her hand into his and let him lead her to stand before the fire while they waited for her father to begin the seating.

Teague and Bowen were a short distance away, conversing with Brodie and Aiden. When they saw her, however, they broke away and came to stand with her and Graeme.

Bowen leaned in and kissed her cheek. "'Tis wonderful to see you looking so lovely, little sister."

Eveline's face warmed and she returned his affectionate gesture with a kiss to his cheek. "Thank you."

Teague then leaned in and kissed her other cheek. "You're a fierce lass, Eveline. I'm glad you're on our side."

She laughed as joy and happiness filled her soul.

Graeme glanced around the rapidly filling room, and then he looked up at Tavis. Tavis made a nodding motion with his head and Graeme led Eveline to the raised high table. He seated her at the head of the table, where by all rights her father should have sat. She frowned when he turned her sideways in the chair so she faced the rest of the room.

Then to her utter amazement, he knelt before her, drawing her hands into his.

"Close your eyes, Eveline," he said, softness in his eyes.

She obeyed without question, closing her eyes and turning the room to darkness. It was an unsettling sensation, not being able to see or hear, but Graeme's hands were tightly around hers, and she knew she'd never come to harm when he was near.

Then she felt an intense vibration blow through her ears. She knew he'd spoken, nay—he must have *thundered* it for her to feel it so keenly.

He lifted her hands and pressed them to his chest and then the words rumbled out of his chest again, fluttering through her ears until it caused an itching sensation deep within. It was almost musical, though she hadn't heard him exactly. But it was soft and soothing, the closest she'd come to actually hearing in three long years.

And suddenly she knew what it was he said. Nay, she hadn't heard the words, but she'd *felt* them. In her heart. In her very soul.

Her eyes flew open and she saw the evidence in his eyes. There for the world to see. The entire hall was silent and gaping at the hulking warrior on his knees before her.

"You love me," she said in wonder.

He smiled. "Was there ever any doubt?"

She turned to her father who was standing a few feet away, his arm around her mother. "He loves me!"

Her father's shoulders shook with laughter. "Aye, I think the whole of Scotland now knows it, lass. Do you not have anything to say back to the lad?"

Eveline turned to her husband, her hands leaving his to frame his face. The stubble of his beard rasped over her palms, but she cradled his beloved face in her hands, her thumbs smoothing over the hard lines of his cheekbones.

"I LOVE YOU!" she roared, determined to yell it every bit as loudly as he had.

There were winces throughout the hall. Others openly laughed. Still others applauded. There were wide smiles, but none as wide as her husband's. He grinned so broadly that his cheeks looked ready to split. Overwhelming joy danced in his dark eyes. He reached up to touch her face, his fingers trailing down her jaw.

"Aye, I know it, wife. And the whole of Scotland likely knows it now, too."

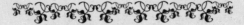

CHAPTER 49

Eveline rode before Graeme on his horse, turned sideways so she was nestled firmly against his chest. One arm was wrapped solidly about her body, while the other held the reins and guided the horse up the rise that overlooked the Montgomery holding below.

He pulled up, pausing as they stared down over Montgomery land. He turned to look at Eveline so she would see all he had to say.

"Can you be happy here, lass?"

She smiled and turned her gaze to the beautiful land covered in green and budding flowers. "I am happy wherever you are, husband."

He touched her cheek so she'd look at him once more. "Those who betrayed you will no longer threaten you."

Eveline's expression saddened, her heart growing heavy. "What will be done to them?"

"The men were executed. Kierstan has been banished from the clan."

Eveline winced even though she knew there had been no choice. They had brought great danger, not only to her, but to the entire Montgomery clan. Many lives could have been lost. Kierstan had also threatened the safety of Eveline's own kin, the Armstrongs.

"Where will she go?" Eveline asked softly.

"I care not. She was given provision enough to make her way. 'Tis more than should have been done, but I'd not turn a woman out of my clan to die a certain death. What she makes of her life from now on is solely up to her."

" 'Tis as we all will do," Eveline said.

Graeme smiled down at her. "Aye, lass, 'tis a true enough statement. From this day forward, our lives and a new beginning in our clans' history will be what we make it."

Eveline smiled back, and then her gaze sought the beautiful vista before her. The great expanse of Montgomery land her own children would one day roam and lay claim to as their own.

"I think what will be made is greatness never to be rivaled by another clan in all of Scotland."

"Bold words, befitting the mistress of the Montgomery clan," Graeme said in approval. "Come, wife. Let's go home. I have a need to show my lass just how much her laird loves her."

ACKNOWLEDGMENTS

Eveline's deafness is based on my husband's own hearing condition. No one ever knew how bad his hearing was until he was in his master's program in college. He'd taught himself to read lips and got through school by sitting close to the teachers so he could see their mouths. Like Eveline, he cannot hear higher pitches and only some lower tones. This book and the heroine is a nod to him and his perseverance.

*Look for the next book
in the Montgomerys and Armstrongs trilogy*

HIGHLANDER MOST WANTED

Coming in Spring 2013

Maya Banks brings to life a poignant, sensuous story of passion, as a reclusive woman content to live in the shadows shows a Highland warrior the true meaning of love.

Genevieve McInnes is locked behind the fortified walls of McHugh Keep, captive of a cruel laird who takes great pleasure in ruining her for any other man. Yet when Bowen Montgomery storms the gates on a mission of clan warfare, Genevieve finds that her spirit is bent but not broken. Still, her path toward freedom remains uncertain. Unable to bear the shame of returning to a family that believes her dead or to abandon others at the keep to an imposing new laird, Genevieve opts for the peaceful life of an abbess. But Bowen's rugged sensuality stirs something deep inside her that longs to be awakened by his patient, gentle caress—something warm, wicked, and tempting.

Bowen seizes his enemy's keep, unprepared for the brooding and reclusive woman who captures his heart. He's enchanted by her fierce determination, her unusual beauty, and her quiet, unfailing strength. But wooing her will take more than a seasoned seducer's skill. For loving Genevieve, he discovers, means giving her back the freedom that was stolen from her—even if it means losing her forever.

Read on for previews from the McCabe trilogy

IN BED
WITH A HIGHLANDER

Mairin Stuart knelt on the stone floor beside her pallet and bowed her head in her evening prayer. Her hand slipped to the small wooden cross hanging from a bit of leather around her neck, and her thumb rubbed a familiar path over the now smooth surface.

For several long minutes, she whispered the words she'd recited since she was a child, and then she ended it as she always did. *Please, God. Don't let them find me.*

She pushed herself from the floor, her knees scraping the uneven stones. The plain, brown garb she wore signaled her place along the other novices. Though she'd been here far longer than the others, she'd never taken the vows that would complete her spiritual journey. It was never her intention.

She went to the basin in the corner and poured from the pitcher of water. She smiled as she dampened her cloth, and Mother Serenity's words came floating to mind. *Cleanliness is next to Godliness.*

She wiped her face and started to remove her gown to extend her wash when she heard a terrible crash. Startled, she dropped the cloth and whirled around to stare at her closed door. Then galvanized to action, she ran and flung it open, racing into the hall.

Around her, the other nuns also filled the hall, their dismayed murmurs rising. A loud bellow echoed down the corridor from the abbey's front entrance. A cry of pain followed the bellow, and Mairin's heart froze. Mother Serenity.

Mairin and the rest of the sisters ran toward the sound,

some lagging back while others shoved determinedly ahead. When they reached the chapel, Mairin drew up short, paralyzed by the sight before her.

Warriors were everywhere. There were at least twenty, all dressed in battle gear, their faces unwashed, sweat drenching their hair and clothing. But no blood. They hadn't come for sanctuary or aid. The leader held Mother Serenity by the arm, and even from a distance, Mairin could see the abbess's face drawn in pain.

"Where is she?" the man demanded in a cold voice.

Mairin took a step back. He was a fierce-looking man. Evil. Rage coiled in his eyes like a snake waiting to strike. He shook Mother Serenity when she didn't respond, and she warbled in his grasp like a rag doll.

Mairin crossed herself and whispered an urgent prayer. The nuns around her gathered in a close ball and also offered their prayers.

"She is not here," Mother Serenity gasped out. "I've told you the woman you seek is not here."

"You lie!" he roared.

He looked toward the group of nuns, his gaze flickering coldly over them.

"Mairin Stuart. Tell me where she is."

Mairin went cold, fear rising to a boil in her stomach. How had he found her? After all this time. Her nightmare wasn't over. It was, indeed, just beginning.

Her hands shook so badly that she had to hide them in the folds of her dress. Sweat gathered on her brow, and her gut lurched. She swallowed, willing herself not to be sick.

When no answer was forthcoming, the man smiled, and it sent a chill straight down Mairin's spine. Still staring at them, he lifted Mother Serenity's arm so that it was in plain sight. Callously, he bent her index finger until Mairin heard the betraying pop of bone.

One of the nuns shrieked and ran forward only to be backhanded down by one of the soldiers. The rest of the nuns gasped at the bold outrage.

"This is God's house," Mother Serenity said in a reedy

voice. "You sin greatly by bringing violence onto holy ground."

"Shut up, old woman," the man snapped. "Tell me where Mairin Stuart is or I'll kill every last one of you."

Mairin sucked in her breath and curled her fingers into balls at her sides. She believed him. There was too much evil, too much desperation, in his eyes. He had been sent on a devil's errand, and he wouldn't be denied.

He grasped Mother Serenity's middle finger, and Mairin rushed forward.

"Charity, nay!" Mother Serenity cried.

Mairin ignored her. "I'm Mairin Stuart. Now let her go!"

The man dropped Mother Serenity's hand then shoved the woman back. He stared at Mairin with interest, then let his gaze wander suggestively down her body and back up again. Mairin's cheeks flamed at the blatant disrespect, but she gave no quarter, staring back at the man with as much defiance as she dared.

He snapped his fingers, and two men advanced on Mairin, grabbing her before she could think to run. They had her on the floor in a split second, their hands fumbling with the hem of her gown.

She kicked wildly, flailing her arms, but she was no match for their strength. Would they rape her here on the chapel floor? Tears gathered in her eyes as they shoved her clothing up over her hips.

They turned her to the right and fingers touched her hip, right where the mark rested.

Oh nay.

She bowed her head as tears of defeat slipped down her cheeks.

" 'Tis her!" one of them said excitedly.

He was instantly shoved aside as the leader bent over to examine the mark for himself.

He, too, touched it, outlining the royal crest of Alexander. Issuing a grunt of satisfaction, he curled his hand around her chin and yanked until she faced him.

His smile revolted her.

"We've been looking for you a long time, Mairin Stuart."

"Go to hell," she spat.

Instead of striking her, his grin broadened. "Tsk-tsk, such blasphemy in the house of God."

He stood rapidly, and before Mairin could blink, she was hauled over a man's shoulder, and the soldiers filed out of the abbey and into the cool night.

They wasted no time getting onto their horses. Mairin was gagged then trussed hand and foot and tossed over the saddle in front of one of the men. They were away, the thunder of hooves echoing across the still night, before she had time to react. They were as precise as they were ruthless.

The saddle dug into her belly, and she bounced up and down until she was sure she was going to throw up. She moaned, afraid she'd choke with the gag so securely around her mouth.

When they finally stopped, she was nearly unconscious. A hand gripped her nape, the fingers easily circling the slim column. She was hauled upward and dropped unceremoniously to the ground.

Around her, they made camp while she lay shivering in the damp air. Finally she heard one say, "You best be seeing to the lass, Finn. Laird Cameron won't be happy if she dies of exposure."

An irritated grunt followed, but a minute later, she was untied and the gag removed. Finn, the apparent leader of this abduction, leaned down over her, his eyes gleaming in the light of the fire.

"There's no one to hear you scream, and if you utter a sound, I'll rattle your jaw."

She nodded her understanding and crawled to an upright position. He nudged her backside with his boot and chuckled when she whirled around in outrage.

"There's a blanket by the fire. Get on it and get some sleep. We leave at first light."

She curled gratefully into the warmth of the blanket, uncaring that the stones and sticks on the ground dug into her skin. Laird Cameron. She'd heard talk of him from the soldiers who drifted in and out of the abbey. He was a ruthless man. Greedy and eager to add to his growing power. It was rumored that his army was one of the largest in all of Scotland and that David, the Scottish king, feared him.

Malcolm, bastard son of Alexander—and her half brother—had already led one revolt against David in a bid for the throne. Were Malcolm and Duncan Cameron to ally, they would be a near unstoppable force.

She swallowed and closed her eyes. The possession of Neamh Álainn would render Cameron invincible.

"Dear God, help me," she whispered.

She couldn't allow him to gain control of Neamh Álainn. It was *her* legacy, the only thing of her father's that she had.

It was impossible to sleep, and so she lay there huddled in the blanket, her hand curled around the wooden cross as she prayed for strength and guidance. Some of the soldiers slept while others kept careful watch. She wasn't fool enough to think she'd be given any opportunity to escape. Not when she was worth more than her weight in gold.

But they wouldn't kill her either, which granted her an advantage. She had nothing to fear by trying to escape and everything to gain.

An hour into her vigil of prayer, a commotion behind her had her sitting straight up and staring into the darkness. Around her, the sleeping soldiers stumbled upward, their hands on their swords when a child's cry rent the night.

One of the men hauled a kicking, wiggling child into the circle around the fire and dropped him on the ground. The child crouched and looked around wildly while the men laughed uproariously.

"What is this?" Finn demanded.

"Caught him trying to sneak one of the horses," the child's captor said.

Anger slanted Finn's features into those of the devil, made more demonic by the light of the fire. The boy, who couldn't be more than seven or eight years old, tilted his chin up defiantly as if daring the man to do his worst.

"Why you insolent little pup," Finn roared.

He raised his hand, and Mairin flew across the ground, throwing herself in front of the child as the fist swung and clipped her cheek.

She went reeling but recovered and quickly threw herself back over the child, gathering him close so she could cover as much of him as possible.

The boy struggled wildly under her, screeching obscenities in Gaelic. His head connected with her already aching jaw, and she saw stars.

"Hush now," she told him in his own language. "Be still. I won't let them hurt you."

"Get off him!" Finn roared.

She tightened around the little boy who finally stopped kicking and flailing. Finn reached down and curled his hand into her hair, yanking brutally upward, but she refused to let go of her charge.

"You'll have to kill me first," she said cooly when he forced her to look at him.

He dropped her hair with a curse then reared back and kicked her in the ribs. She hunched over in pain but was careful to keep the child shielded from the maniacal brute.

"Finn, enough," one man barked. "The laird wants her in one piece."

Muttering a curse, he backed away. "Let her keep the dirty beggar. She'll have to turn loose of him soon enough."

Mairin snapped her neck up to glare into Finn's eyes. "You touch this boy even once and I'll slit my own throat."

Finn's laughter cracked the night. "That's one crazy bluff, lass. If you're going to try to negotiate, you need to learn to be believable."

Slowly she rose until she stood a foot away from the much larger man. She stared up at him until his eyes flickered and he looked away.

"Bluff?" she said softly. "I don't think so. In fact, if I were you, I'd be guarding any and all sharp objects from me. Think you that I don't know what my fate is? To be bedded by that brute laird of yours until my belly swells with child and he can claim Neamh Álainn. I'd rather die."

Finn's eyes narrowed. "You're daft!"

"Aye, that might be so, and in that case I'd be worried one of those sharp objects might find its way between your ribs."

He waved his hand. "You keep the boy. The laird will deal with him and you. We don't take kindly to horse thieves."

Mairin ignored him and turned back to the boy who huddled on the ground, staring at her with a mixture of fear and worship.

"Come," she said gently. "If we snuggle up tight enough, there's plenty of blanket for the both of us."

He went eagerly to her, tucking his smaller body flush against hers.

"Where is your home?" she asked when he had settled against her.

"I don't know," he said mournfully. "It must be a ways from here. At least two days."

"Shh," she said soothingly. "How did you come to be here?"

"I got lost. My papa said I was never to leave the keep without his men, but I was tired of being treated like a baby. I'm not, you know."

She smiled. "Aye, I know. So you left the keep?"

He nodded. "I took a horse. I only meant to go meet Uncle Alaric. He was due back and I thought to wait near the border to greet him."

"Border?"

"Of our lands."

"And who is your papa, little one?"

"My name is Crispen, not 'little one.'" The distaste was evident in his voice, and she smiled again.

"Crispen is a fine name. Now continue with your story."

"What's your name?" he asked.

"Mairin," she answered softly.

"My papa is Laird Ewan McCabe."

Mairin struggled to place the name, but there were so many clans she had no knowledge of. Her home was in the highlands, but she hadn't seen God's country in ten long years.

"So you went to meet your uncle. Then what happened?"

"I got lost," he said mournfully. "Then a McDonald soldier found me and intended to take me to his laird to ransom, but I couldn't let that happen. It would dishonor my papa, and he can't afford to ransom me. It would cripple our clan."

Mairin stroked his hair as his warm breath blew over her breast. He sounded so much older than his tender years. And so proud.

"I escaped and hid in the cart of a traveling merchant. I rode for a day before he discovered me." He tilted his head up, bumping her sore jaw again. "Where are we, Mairin?" he whispered. "Are we very far from home?"

"I'm not sure where your home is," she said ruefully. "But we are in the lowlands, and I would wager we're at least a two days' ride from your keep."

"The lowlands," he spat. "Are you a lowlander?"

She smiled at his vehemence. "Nay, Crispen. I'm a highlander."

"Then what are you doing here?" he persisted. "Did they steal you from your home?"

She sighed. "'Tis a long story. One that began before you were born."

When he tensed for another question, she hushed him with a gentle squeeze. "Go to sleep now, Crispen. We must keep our strength up if we are to escape."

"We're going to escape?" he whispered.

"Aye, of course. That's what prisoners do," she said in a cheerful tone. The fear in his voice made her ache for him. How terrifying it must be for him to be so far from home and the ones who love him.

"Will you take me back home to my papa? I'll make him protect you from Laird Cameron."

She smiled at the fierceness in his voice. "Of course, I'll see to it that you get home."

"Promise?"

"I promise."

"Find my son!"

Ewan McCabe's roar could be heard over the entire courtyard. His men all stood at attention, their expressions solemn. Some were creased in sympathy. They believed Crispen to be dead, though no one dared to utter that possibility to Ewan.

It wasn't something Ewan hadn't contemplated himself, but he would not rest until his son was found—dead or alive.

Ewan turned to his brothers, Alaric and Caelen. "I cannot afford to send every man in search of Crispen," he said in a low voice. "To do so would leave us vulnerable. I trust you two with my life—with my son's life. I want you each to take a contingent of men and ride in different directions. Bring him home to me."

Alaric, the second oldest of the McCabe brothers, nodded. "You know we won't rest until he is found."

"Aye, I know," Ewan said.

Ewan watched as the two strode off, shouting orders to their men. He closed his eyes and curled his fingers into fists of rage. Who dared take his son? For three days he'd waited for a ransom demand, only none had been forthcoming. For three days he'd scoured every inch of McCabe land and beyond.

Was this a precursor to an attack? Were his enemies plotting to hit him when he was weak? When every available soldier would be involved in the search?

His jaw hardened as he gazed around his crumbling keep. For eight years he'd struggled to keep his clan alive and strong. The McCabe name had always been synonymous with power and pride. Eight years ago they'd withstood a crippling attack. Betrayed by the woman Caelen loved. Ewan's father and young wife had been killed, their child surviving only because he'd been hidden by one of the servants.

Almost nothing had been left when he and his brothers had returned. Just a hulking mass of ruins, his people scattered to the winds, his army nearly decimated.

There had been nothing for Ewan to take over when he became laird.

It had taken this long to rebuild. His soldiers were the best trained in the highlands. He and his brothers worked brutal hours to make sure there was food for the old, the sick, the women, and the children. Many times the men went without. And silently they grew, adding to their numbers until, finally, Ewan had begun to turn their struggling clan around.

Soon, his thoughts could turn to revenge. Nay, that wasn't accurate. Revenge had been all that sustained him for these past eight years. There wasn't a day he *hadn't* thought about it.

"Laird, I bring news of your son."

Ewan whipped around to see one of his soldiers hurrying up to him, his tunic dusty as though he'd just gotten off his horse.

"Speak," he commanded.

"One of the McDonalds came upon your son three days ago along the northern border of your land. He took him, intending to deliver him to their laird so he could ransom the boy. Only, the boy escaped. No one has seen him since."

Ewan trembled with rage. "Take eight soldiers and ride to McDonald. Deliver him this message. He will present the soldier who took my son to the entrance of my keep or he signs his own death warrant. If he doesn't comply, I will come for him myself. I will kill him. And it won't be quick. Do not leave a word out of my message."

The soldier bowed. "Aye, Laird."

He turned and hurried off, leaving Ewan with a mix of relief and rage. Crispen was alive, or at least he had been. McDonald was a fool for breaching their tacit peace agreement. Though the two clans could hardly be considered allies, McDonald wasn't stupid enough to incite the wrath of Ewan McCabe. His keep might be crumbling, and his people might not be the best-fed clan, but his might had been restored twofold.

His soldiers were a deadly fighting force to be reckoned with, and those close enough to Ewan's holdings realized it. But Ewan's sights weren't on his neighbors. They were on Duncan Cameron. Ewan wouldn't be happy until the whole of Scotland dripped with Cameron's blood.

SEDUCTION
OF A HIGHLAND LASS

Alaric McCabe looked out over the expanse of McCabe land and grappled with the indecision plaguing him. He breathed in the chilly air and looked skyward. It wouldn't snow this day. But soon. Autumn had settled over the highlands. Colder air and shorter days had pushed in.

After so many years of struggling to eke out an existence, to rebuild their clan, his brother Ewan had made great strides in restoring the McCabes to their former glory. This winter, their clan wouldn't go hungry. Their children wouldn't go without proper clothing.

Now it was time for Alaric to do his part for his clan. In a short time, he would travel to the McDonald holding where he would formally ask for Rionna McDonald's hand in marriage.

It was pure ceremony. The agreement had been struck weeks earlier. Now the aging laird wanted Alaric to spend time among the McDonalds, a clan that would one day become Alaric's when he married McDonald's daughter and only heir.

Even now the courtyard was alive with activity as a contingent of McCabe soldiers readied to make the journey with Alaric.

Ewan, Alaric's older brother and laird of the McCabe clan, had wanted to send his most trusted men to accompany Alaric on his journey, but Alaric refused. There was still danger to Ewan's wife, Mairin, who was heavily pregnant with Ewan's child.

As long as Duncan Cameron was alive, he posed a threat to the McCabes. He coveted what was Ewan's—Ewan's wife and Ewan's eventual control of Neamh Álainn, a legacy brought through his marriage to Mairin, the daughter of the former king of Scotland.

And now because of the tenuous peace in the highlands and the threat Duncan Cameron posed not only to the neighboring clans, but to King David's throne, Alaric agreed to the marriage that would cement an alliance between the McCabes and the only clan whose lands rested between Neamh Álainn and McCabe land.

It was a good match. Rionna McDonald was fair to look upon, even if she was an odd lass who preferred the dress and duties of a man over those of a woman. And Alaric would have what he'd never have if he remained under Ewan: his own clan to lead. His own lands. His heir inheriting the mantle of leadership.

So why wasn't he more eager to mount his horse and ride toward his destiny?

He turned when he heard a sound to his left. Mairin McCabe was hurrying up the hillside, or at least attempting to hurry, and Cormac, her assigned guard for the day looked exasperated as he followed in her wake. Her shawl was wrapped tightly around her, and her lips trembled with the cold.

Alaric held out his hand, and she gripped it, leaning toward him as she sought to catch her breath.

"You shouldn't be up here, lass," Alaric reproached. "You're going to freeze to death."

"Nay, she shouldn't," Cormac agreed. "If our laird finds out, he'll be angry."

Mairin rolled her eyes and then looked anxiously up at Alaric. "Do you have everything you require for your journey?"

Alaric smiled. "Aye, I do. Gertie has packed enough food for a journey twice as long."

She alternated squeezing and patting Alaric's hand, her eyes troubled as she rubbed her burgeoning belly with her other hand. He pulled her closer so she'd have the warmth of his body.

"Should you perchance wait another day? It's near to

noon already. Maybe you should wait and leave early on the morrow."

Alaric stifled his grin. Mairin wasn't happy with his leaving. She was quite used to having her clan right where she wanted them. On McCabe land. And now that Alaric was set to leave, she'd become increasingly more vocal in her worry and her dissatisfaction.

"I won't be gone overlong, Mairin," he said gently. "A few weeks at most. Then I'll return for a time before the marriage takes place and I reside permanently at McDonald keep."

Her lips turned down into an unhappy frown at the reminder that Alaric would leave the McCabes and, for all practical purposes, become a McDonald.

"Stop frowning, lass. It isn't good for the babe. Neither is you being out here in the cold."

She sighed and threw her arms around him. He took a step back and exchanged amused glances with Cormac over her head. The lass was even more emotional now that she was swollen with child, and the members of her clan were becoming increasingly more familiar with her spontaneous bursts of affection.

"I shall miss you, Alaric. I know Ewan will as well. He says nothing, but he's quieter now."

"I'll miss you, too," Alaric said solemnly. "Rest assured, I'll be here when you deliver the newest McCabe."

At that, her face lit up and she took a step back and reached up to pat him on the cheek.

"Be good to Rionna, Alaric. I know you and Ewan feel she needs a firmer hand, but in truth, I think what she most needs is love and acceptance."

Alaric fidgeted, appalled that she'd want to discuss matters of love with him. For God's sake.

She laughed. "All right. I can see I've made you uncomfortable. But heed my words."

"My lady, the laird has spotted you and he doesn't look pleased," Cormac said.

Alaric turned to see Ewan standing in the courtyard,

arms crossed over his chest and a scowl etched onto his face.

"Come along, Mairin," Alaric said as he tucked her hand underneath his arm. "I better return you to my brother before he comes after you."

Mairin grumbled under her breath, but she allowed Alaric to escort her down the hillside.

When they reached the courtyard, Ewan leveled a glare at his wife but turned his attention to Alaric. "Do you have all you need?"

Alaric nodded.

Caelen, the youngest McCabe brother, came to stand at Ewan's side. "Are you sure you don't want me to accompany you?"

"You're needed here," Alaric said. "More so as Mairin's time draws nigh. Winter snows will be upon us soon. It would be just like Duncan to mount an attack when he thinks we least expect it."

Mairin shivered at Alaric's side again, and he turned to her. "Give me a hug, sister, and then go back into the keep before you catch your death of cold. My men are ready, and I won't have you crying all over us as we try to leave."

As expected, Mairin scowled but once again threw her arms around Alaric and squeezed tight.

"God be with you," she whispered.

Alaric rubbed an affectionate hand over her hair and then pushed her in the direction of the keep. Ewan reinforced Alaric's dictate with a ferocious scowl of his own.

Mairin stuck her tongue out and then turned away, Cormac following her toward the steps of the keep.

"If you have need of me, send word," Ewan said. "I'll come immediately."

Alaric gripped Ewan's arm and the two brothers stared at each other for a long moment before Alaric released him. Caelen pounded Alaric on the back as Alaric went to mount his horse.

"This is a good thing for you," Caelen said sincerely once Alaric was astride his horse.

Alaric stared down at his brother and felt the first stirring of satisfaction. "Aye, it is."

He took a deep breath as his hands tightened on the reins. His lands. His clan. He'd be laird. Aye, this was a good thing.

Alaric and a dozen of the McCabe soldiers rode at a steady pace throughout the day. Since they'd gained a late start, what would normally be a day's ride would now require them to arrive on McDonald's land the next morning.

Knowing this, Alaric didn't press, and actually halted his men to make camp just after dusk. They built only one fire and kept the blaze low so it didn't illuminate a wide area.

After they'd eaten the food that Gertie had prepared for the journey, Alaric divided his men into two groups and told the first of the six men to take the first watch.

They stationed themselves around the encampment, providing protection for the remaining six to bed down for a few hours' rest.

Though Alaric was scheduled for the second watch, he couldn't sleep. He lay awake on the hard ground, staring up at the star-filled sky. It was a clear night and cold. The winds were picking up from the north, heralding a coming change in the weather.

Married. To Rionna McDonald. He tried hard but could barely conjure an image of the lass. All he could remember was her vibrant golden hair. She was quiet, which he supposed was a good trait for a woman to have, although Mairin was hardly a quiet or particularly obedient wife. And yet he found her endearing, and he knew that Ewan wouldn't change a single thing about her.

But then Mairin was all a woman should be. Soft and sweet, and Rionna was mannish in both dress and manner. She wasn't an unattractive lass, which made it puzzling that she would indulge in activities completely unsuitable for a lady.

It was something he'd have to address immediately.

A slight disturbance of the air was the only warning he

had before he lunged to the side. A sword caught his side, slicing through clothing and flesh.

Pain seared through his body, but he pushed it aside as he grabbed his sword and bolted to his feet. His men came alive and the night air swelled with the sounds of battle.

Alaric fought two men, the clang of swords blistering his ears. His hands vibrated from the repeated blows as he parried and thrust.

He was backed toward the perimeter set by his men and nearly tripped over one of the men he'd posted as guard. An arrow protruded from his chest, a testimony to how stealthily the ambush had been set.

They were sorely outnumbered, and although Alaric would pit the McCabe soldiers against anyone, anytime, and be assured of the outcome, his only choice was to call a retreat lest they all be slaughtered. There was simply no way to win against six-to-one odds.

He yelled for his men to get to their horses. Then he dispatched the man in front of him and struggled to reach his own mount. Blood poured from his side. The acrid scent rose in the chill and filled his nostrils. Already his vision had dimmed, and he knew if he didn't get himself on his horse, he was done for.

He whistled and his horse bolted forward just as another warrior made his charge at Alaric. Weakening fast from the loss of blood, he fought without the discipline Ewan had instilled in him. He took chances. He was reckless. He was fighting for his life.

With a roar, Alaric's opponent lunged forward. Gripping his sword in both hands, Alaric swung. He sliced through his attacker's neck and completely decapitated him.

Alaric didn't waste a single moment savoring the victory. There was another attacker bearing down on him. With the last of his strength, he threw himself on his horse and gave the command to run.

He could make out the outline of bodies as his horse thundered away, and with a sinking feeling, Alaric knew that they weren't the enemy. He'd lost most, if not all, of his soldiers in the attack.

"Home," he commanded hoarsely.

He gripped his side and tried valiantly to remain conscious, but with each jostle as the horse flew across the terrain, Alaric's vision dimmed.

His last conscious thought was that he had to get home to warn Ewan. He just hoped to hell there hadn't been an attack on the McCabe holding as well.

NEVER LOVE
A HIGHLANDER

The weather for her first wedding had been a splendor of nature. An unseasonably warm day in January. Quite balmy with nary a breeze to ruffle her carefully arranged hair. It was as if the world stood still to witness the joining of two souls.

A snort rippled from Rionna McDonald's throat, eliciting a raised eyebrow from her soon-to-be husband.

The weather for her second wedding? Gloomy and dank with a winter storm pushing in from the west. Already a brisk chill had set in and the wind blew in fierce, relentless sheets. As if the world knew just how uncertain she was about the man who stood beside her, ready to recite the vows that would bind him to her forever.

A shiver skirted up her spine despite the fact that they stood in front of the huge fire in the great hall.

Caelen frowned and stepped closer to Rionna as if to shield her from the draft blowing through the furs at the window. She took a hasty step back before thinking better of it. The man made her nervous, and not many people intimidated her.

He frowned harder, then turned his attention back to the priest.

Rionna cast a quick glance around, hoping no one had witnessed that particular exchange. It wouldn't do for people to think she was afraid of her new husband. Even if she was.

Ewan McCabe, the oldest McCabe brother and the first man she was supposed to have married, stood by his brother's side, his arms crossed over his broad chest. He looked anxious to be done with the whole thing.

Alaric McCabe, the man she'd very nearly wed after Ewan got himself married to Mairin Stuart, also looked impatient and kept glancing toward the stairs as if he might run out at any moment. Rionna couldn't blame him, though. His new wife, Keeley, was above stairs recovering from a wound that had nearly ended her life.

Third time was a charm, right?

King David wasn't standing for the occasion. He sat regally by the fire, looking on with approval as the priest droned on. Around him, also sitting, were the many lairds from neighboring lands. All waiting for the alliance between the McDonalds and the McCabes. An alliance that would be sealed upon her marriage to Caelen McCabe, the youngest—and last—McCabe brother.

It was important to denote last because if anything went amiss with this wedding, there were no more McCabes for her to marry, and at this point, her pride couldn't withstand another rejection.

Her gaze skittered from the king and assembled lairds to her dour-faced father who sat away from the assembled warriors, an unmanly, sullen pout twisting his features.

For a moment their stares locked and then his lip turned up into a snarl. She hadn't supported him in his bid to keep his position of laird. It was probably disloyal of her. She wasn't sure that Caelen McCabe would be a better laird, but surely he was a better man.

She became aware that all eyes were on her. She glanced nervously toward the priest and realized that she'd missed her cue to recite her vows. Even more embarrassing, she had no idea what the man had said.

"This is where you promise to obey me, cleave only unto me, and remain faithful all your days," Caelen drawled.

His words stiffened her spine and she couldn't call back the glare as she speared him with her gaze.

"And what exactly are you promising me?"

His pale green eyes stroked coolly over her, assessing and then lifting as if he found nothing of import. She didn't like that look. He'd all but dismissed her.

"You'll gain my protection and the respect due a lady of your station."

"That's all?"

She whispered the words, and she'd have given anything not to have let them slip. It was no wonder she'd been left wanting, though. Ewan McCabe clearly adored his wife, Mairin, and Alaric had just defied king and country to be with the woman he loved—effectively casting Rionna aside in the process.

Not that she was angry. She dearly loved Keeley, and Keeley deserved happiness. That a man as strong and handsome as Alaric had publicly proclaimed his love for Keeley gladdened Rionna's heart.

But it also brought home how sterile her own marriage would be.

Caelen made a sound of exasperation. "Exactly what is it that you want, lass?"

She raised her chin and stared back at him every bit as cool. "Nothing. 'Tis enough. I'll have your respect and your regard. I won't be needing your protection, though."

His eyebrow rose. "Is that so?"

"Aye. I can see to my own protection."

Caelen chuckled and more laughter rose from the assembled men. "Say your vows, lass. We don't have all day. The men are hungry. They've been waiting a feast for nearly a fortnight now."

Agreement rumbled through the room and her cheeks burned. This was her wedding day and she wouldn't be rushed. Who cared about the food and the men's stomachs?

As if sensing that she was working herself into a righteous fury, Caelen reached over, snagged her hand, and pulled her up next to his side until his thigh burned into hers through the material of her dress.

"Father," Caelen said respectfully, "if you'll tell the lass what she needs to say again."

Rionna fumed the entire way through the recitation. Tears pricked her eyelids but she couldn't even say why. It wasn't as if she and Alaric had been a love match any more than she and Caelen were. The entire idea of wedding one of the McCabe brothers had been hatched by her father and embraced by the McCabes and the king himself.

She was but a pawn to be used and discarded.

She sighed and then shook her head. It was ridiculous to be this maudlin. There were worse things. She should be happy. She'd rediscovered the sister of her heart in Keeley, who was now happily married even if she faced a long recovery in the days ahead. And Rionna's father would no longer be laird of their clan.

She chanced another look only to see her father throw back yet another goblet of ale. She supposed she couldn't entirely blame him for being so deep into his cups. His entire way of life was gone in a moment's time. But she couldn't muster any regret.

Her clan could be great—*would* be great—under the right leadership. It had never been her father. He'd weakened the McDonald name until they'd been reduced to begging for the aid and alliance of a stronger clan.

Her free hand curled into a tight fist at her side. It had been her dream to restore their glory. To shape the soldiers into a formidable fighting force. Now it would be Caelen's task and she would be relegated to a position of observation rather than the participation she craved.

She gasped in surprise when Caelen suddenly leaned in and brushed his lips across hers. He was gone almost before she registered what he'd done and she stood there staring wide-eyed as she raised a trembling hand to her mouth.

The ceremony was done. Even now the serving women were flooding into the hall, bearing a veritable bounty of food, much of which came from her own stores after her father's foolish wager several months ago.

Caelen watched her a moment and then gestured for her to walk ahead of him toward the high table. Rionna was gratified to see Mairin join her husband. In a sea of gruff, indistinguishable faces, Mairin McCabe was a ray of sunshine. Tired sunshine, but warm nonetheless.

Mairin hurried forward with a bright smile. "Rionna,

you look so beautiful. There isn't a woman here who can hold a candle to you today."

Rionna's cheeks warmed under Mairin's praise. 'Twas the truth Rionna was a little ashamed to be wearing the same dress she'd worn when she nearly married Alaric. She felt wrinkled, rumpled, and worn through. But the sincerity in Mairin's smile bolstered Rionna's flagging spirits.

Mairin gathered Rionna's hands in hers as if to offer further encouragement.

"Oh, your hands are like ice!" Mairin exclaimed. "I did so want to be present for your joining. I hope you'll accept my regrets."

"Of course," Rionna said with a genuine smile. "How is Keeley fairing this day?"

Some of the worry lifted from Mairin's gaze. "Come, sit so we may be served. And then I'll tell you of Keeley."

It irked Rionna that she first looked to her new husband only to catch his nod of permission. She gritted her teeth and moved to the table to sit beside Mairin. Already she was acting like a docile nitwit and she hadn't been married five minutes.

But in truth, Caelen frightened her. Alaric hadn't. Even Ewan didn't intimidate her. Caelen scared her witless.

Rionna slid into the chair beside Mairin, hoping for a brief reprieve before Caelen joined her. She wasn't so fortunate. Her husband pulled out the chair next to her and scooted to the table, his leg so close to hers that it pressed to the whole of her thigh.

Deciding it would be rude—and obvious—were she to slide toward Mairin, she decided instead to ignore him. She couldn't forget that it was acceptable for him to be so familiar now. They were wed.

She sucked in her breath as the realization hit her that he would of course exert his marital rights. Indeed, there was the whole wedding night, virginal deflowering. All the things women tittered about behind their hands when the men weren't around.

The problem was that Rionna was always with the men and she'd never tittered in her life. Keeley had been separated from her at a young age, long before Rionna had grown curious over such matters.

With a lecher for a father and Rionna's constant fear for Keeley, the mere thought of coupling nauseated her. Now she had a husband who'd expect . . . Well, he'd expect certain things, and God help her, she had no idea what.

Humiliation tightened her cheeks. She could ask Mairin. Or one of the McCabe women. They were all generous to a fault and they'd all been kind to Rionna. But the idea of having to admit to them all just how ignorant she was of such matters made her want to hide under the table.

She could wield a sword better than most men. She could fight. And she was fast. She could be ruthless when provoked. She didn't suffer a gentle constitution nor did she faint at the sight of blood.

But she didn't know the way of kissing.

"Are you going to eat?" Caelen asked.

She looked up to see that the places had been set and the food was on the table. Caelen had thoughtfully cut a choice piece of meat and placed it on her plate.

"Aye," she whispered.

'Twas the truth, she was fair to starving.

"Would you like water or ale?"

'Twas also true she never partook of spirits, but somehow today ale seemed to be the wise choice.

"Ale," she said, and waited as Caelen poured a gobletful. She reached for it but to her surprise, he put it to his mouth and first sniffed and then drank a small portion of the ale.

"'Tis not poisoned," he said as he slid it toward her place.

She gaped at him, not comprehending what he'd just done.

"But what if it *had* been poisoned?"

He touched her cheek. Just once. It was the only affectionate gesture he'd offered her and it might not even be construed as affectionate, but it was soft and a little comforting.

"Then you wouldn't have partaken of the poison, nor

would you have died. We already nearly lost one McCabe to such cowardice. I'll not risk another."

Her mouth fell open. "That's ridiculous! Think you that *you* dying somehow makes it all better?"

"Rionna, I just took sacred vows to protect you. That means I'd lay down my life for you and for any future children we have. We've already a snake in our midst trying to poison Ewan. Now that you and I are wed, what better way to prevent the alliance between our clans than to kill you?"

"Or you," she felt compelled to point out.

"Aye, 'tis a possibility. But if McDonald's only heir is dead then his clan effectively crumbles, which makes it easy pickings for Duncan Cameron. You are the heart of this alliance, Rionna. Whether you wish to believe it or not. Much rides on your shoulders. I guarantee you it won't be easy for you."

"Nay, I never imagined differently."

"Smart lass."

He piddled with the goblet before sliding it toward her. Then he solicitously lifted it and held it to her mouth, just as a new husband would do for his bride during the wedding feast.

"Drink, Rionna. You look exhausted. You're on edge. You're so stiff that it can't be comfortable. Take a drink and try to relax. We've a long afternoon to endure."

He hadn't lied.

Rionna sat wearily at the table as toast after toast was given. There were toasts to the McCabes. Toasts to the new McCabe heir. Ewan and Mairin were the proud parents of a newborn lass, who also happened to be the heir to one of the largest and choicest holdings in all of Scotland.

Then there were toasts to Alaric and Keeley. To Keeley's health. Then the toasts to her marriage to Caelen began.

At one point they degenerated into lewd toasts to Caelen's prowess, and two lairds even began a wager as to how fast Rionna would find herself with child.

Rionna's eyes were glazing over and she wasn't entirely sure it was due to the lengthy accolades being tossed about.

Her goblet had been refilled more times than she remembered but she drank on, ignoring the way it swirled around in her belly and made her head swim.

Laird McCabe had decreed that despite the many issues that bore discussion and the decisions that must be made, today would be spent in celebration of his brother's marriage.

Rionna suspected that Mairin had everything to do with that decree. She needn't have bothered, though. There was little cause for celebration in Rionna's mind.

She glanced sideways to see Caelen sitting back in his chair, lazily surveying the occupants of the table. He tossed back an insult when one was flung his way by one of the McCabe men. Something to do with his manhood. Rionna shuddered and purposely blanked her mind to the innuendo.

She gulped down another mouthful of the ale and put the goblet back down on the table with a bang that made her wince. No one seemed to notice, but then it *was* unbearably loud.

The food before her swam in her vision, and the idea of putting it to her mouth, despite Caelen having cut the meat into bite-sized morsels, turned her stomach.

"Rionna, is anything amiss?"

Mairin's soft inquiry jolted Rionna from her semidaze. She glanced guiltily up at the other woman and then blinked when Mairin suddenly became two people.

"I should like to see Keeley," she blurted.

If the laird's wife thought it odd that Rionna would wish to visit with Keeley on Rionna's wedding day, she didn't react.

"I'll go up with you if you like."

Rionna sighed in relief then started to rise from her seat. Caelen's hand snapped around her wrist and he tugged her back down, a frown marring his features.

"I wish to see Keeley since she wasn't able to attend my wedding," Rionna said. "With your permission, of course."

She nearly choked on the words.

He studied her for a brief moment then relaxed his grip on her wrist. "You may go."

It sounded so imperious. So . . . husbandlike.

Her stomach heaved as she excused herself to the laird. Married. Jesus wept, but she was married. She was expected to submit to her husband. To obey him.

Her hands shook as she followed Mairin toward the stairs. They walked quietly up, one of Ewan's men tagging along behind, but then Mairin went nowhere without an escort.

Merciful heaven, would she be expected to be led about by the reins now that she was married to Caelen? The idea of being unable to go anywhere or do anything without someone breathing down her neck suffocated her.

At Keeley's door, Mairin knocked softly. Alaric answered, and Mairin spoke in low tones with her brother by marriage.

Alaric nodded and stepped out but then said, "Try not to be overlong. She tires easily."

Rionna glanced at the man who would have been her husband and couldn't help a silent comparison between him and his younger brother. The man she now found herself wed to.

There was no doubt both were fierce warriors, but she still couldn't help but feel she would have preferred marriage to Alaric. He didn't seem as . . . cold . . . as Caelen. Or indifferent. Or . . . something.

She couldn't quite put her finger on it, but there was something in Caelen's eyes that unsettled her, that made her wary, like prey poised to flee a predator. He made her feel tiny, defenseless. *Feminine*.

"Rionna," Alaric said with a nod. "Congratulations on your marriage."

There was still a hint of guilt in his eyes, and truly, she wasn't resentful. Not of why he hadn't married her. His falling in love with Keeley hadn't quite managed to banish her humiliation of being jilted, though. She was working on it.

"Thank you," she murmured.

She waited until Alaric passed her and then she entered Keeley's chamber.

Keeley lay propped on an abundance of pillows. She was pale and lines of fatigue etched grooves on her forehead. Still, she smiled weakly when her gaze met Rionna's.

"So sorry I missed your wedding," Keeley said.

Rionna smiled and went to her bed. She perched on the edge so she wouldn't cause Keeley pain and then gingerly reached for her hand.

"'Twas not of import. I barely remember it myself."

Keeley snorted and a spasm of pain crossed her face.

"I had to see you," Rionna whispered. "There was something . . . I wanted to seek your counsel on something."

Keeley's eyes widened in surprise and then she glanced beyond Rionna to Mairin. "Of course. Is it all right if Mairin stays? She's completely trustworthy."

Rionna cast a hesitant glance in Mairin's direction.

"Perhaps I should go down and fetch us some ale," Mairin suggested. "'Twill give you time to speak freely."

Rionna sighed. "Nay, I'll wait. 'Tis the truth I could use the counsel of more than one woman. Keeley is newly married after all."

A soft blush suffused Keeley's cheeks and Mairin chuckled. "I'll send for the ale then, and we'll talk. You have my word, naught will pass the doors of this chamber."

Rionna looked gratefully at Mairin, and then Mairin went to the door and conversed with Gannon, the warrior who'd accompanied them up the stairs.

"How easily is sound carried through the doors?" Rionna whispered to Keeley.

"I can assure you that nothing can be heard from the halls," Keeley said, a twinkle in her eyes. "Now what matter would you like to discuss?"

Rionna dutifully waited until Mairin returned to Keeley's bedside and then she licked her lips, feeling the worst sort of fool for exposing her ignorance.

"'Tis about the marriage bed."

"Ah," Mairin said knowingly.

"Ah, indeed," Keeley said with a nod.

Rionna blew out her breath in frustration. "What am I to do? What am I supposed to do? I know nothing of kissing and coupling or . . . anything. 'Tis a sword and fighting I have knowledge of."

Mairin's expression softened and the amusement fled from her eyes. She covered Rionna's hand with her own and squeezed. "'Tis the truth that not too long ago, I was in your same position. I sought out the counsel of some older ladies of the clan. 'Twas an eye-opening experience to be sure."

"Aye, as did I," Keeley admitted. "It isn't as though we're born with such knowledge, and none of us had mothers to guide us through such things." She cast an apologetic look to Rionna. "At least I assume your mother never discussed such delicate issues with you."

Rionna snorted. "She despaired of me from the time I grew breasts."

Keeley's eyebrows rose. "You grew breasts?"

Rionna flushed and glanced down at her bosom. Her flat bosom. If Keeley—or anyone—actually knew what lay beneath the wrappings . . . Her husband would know soon enough, unless Rionna figured out a way to consummate a marriage fully clothed.

Mairin smiled. "'Tis not so difficult, Rionna. The men do most of the work, as they should in the beginning. Once you learn your way around, well, then you can certainly do all manner of things."

"Alaric is wonderful at loving," Keeley said with a sigh.

Mairin colored and cleared her throat. "'Tis the truth I didn't think Ewan overly skilled at first. Our wedding night was hastened by the fact that Duncan Cameron's army bore down on us. 'Twas an insult Ewan took exception to and made great effort to remedy. With very satisfying results, I might add."

Rionna's cheeks warmed as she glanced between the two women. Their eyes became all dreamy and soft as they spoke of their husbands. Rionna couldn't imagine ever having such a reaction to Caelen. He was simply too . . . forbidding. Aye, that was an apt description.

A knock at the door interrupted the discussion and the women went silent. Mairin issued a summons, and Gannon stepped inside, a disapproving look on his face.

"Thank you, Gannon," Mairin said, as he set the flagon and the goblets on the small table beside Keeley's bed. "You may go now."

He scowled but backed out of the room. Rionna glanced up at Mairin, curious as to why she accepted such insolence from her husband's man. Mairin simply smiled smugly as she poured the ale into the goblets.

"He knows we're up to mischief and it's killing him to say nothing."

She handed Rionna a goblet and then carefully placed one into Keeley's hand.

"'Tis the truth it will dull the pain," Keeley said.

"I'm sorry, Keeley. Would you like me to go? I have no wish to cause you further distress," Rionna said.

Keeley sipped at the ale and then leaned back against her pillows with a sigh. "Nay. I'm about to go mad being sequestered in my chamber. I welcome the company. Besides, we must ease your fears about your wedding night."

Rionna gulped at her ale and then extended the goblet to Mairin for it to be refilled. She had a feeling she wasn't going to like this conversation.

"'Tis no reason to fear," Mairin soothed. "I've no doubt Caelen will take care with you." Then she wrinkled her nose. "Give thanks you don't have an army bearing down on you. 'Tis the truth I had no liking for my wedding night."

Rionna felt the blood drain from her face.

"Hush, Mairin. You aren't helping," Keeley chided.

Mairin patted Rionna's hand. "All will be well. You'll see."

"But what do I *do*?"

"Exactly what is it that you know?" Keeley asked. "Let's start there."

Rionna closed her eyes in misery and then downed the entire contents of her goblet. "Nothing."

"Oh dear," Mairin said. "'Tis the truth I was ignorant,

but the nuns at the abbey did see fit to provide me cursory information."

"I think you should be honest with Caelen about your fears," Keeley suggested. "He'd be a brute to ignore a maiden's worry. If he has half of Alaric's skill, you'll not be left wanting."

Mairin giggled at the boast, and Rionna held out her goblet for another round of ale.

The very *last* thing she wanted was to talk to Caelen about her maidenly fears. The man would probably laugh at her. Or worse, give her that cool, indifferent gaze that made her feel so . . . insignificant.

"Will it hurt?" she strangled out.

Mairin's lips pursed in thought. Keeley's brow wrinkled a moment.

"'Tis the truth it's not overly pleasant. At first. But the pain passes quickly and if the man is skilled, it's quite wonderful in the end."

Mairin snorted. "Again, as long as there isn't an army bearing down on you."

"Enough with the army," Keeley said in exasperation. "There is no army."

Then the two women looked at each other and laughed until Keeley groaned and went limp against her pillows.

Rionna just stared at them, never more certain that she had no desire to indulge in this marriage bed business. She yawned broadly and the room spun in curious little circles. Her head felt as though it weighed as much as a boulder, and it was harder and harder for her to hold it up.

She stood from her perch on the edge of Keeley's bed and started for the door, disgusted with her cowardice. She was acting . . . Well, she was acting just like a woman.

To her utter dismay, she ended up at the window and she blinked in confusion as a blast of cold air hit her in the face and the corner of the furs blew up.

"Careful, there," Mairin said in her ear.

She guided Rionna to a chair in the corner of the room and eased her down.

"Perhaps 'tis best if you sit here awhile. It wouldn't do

for you to navigate those stairs, and we don't want the men to know what we've been about."

Rionna nodded. She did feel a bit peculiar. Aye, it would be best if she sat awhile until the room stopped spinning in such spectacular fashion.

Caelen looked toward the stairs for what seemed like the hundredth time, and Ewan looked impatient as well. Rionna and Mairin had been gone for some time. It was late into the night and Caelen was ready to have done with the entire wedding celebration.

Some celebration. His bride had been stiff and distant throughout the entire ceremony, and afterward she'd sat silent while the room celebrated around her.

If her demeanor was anything to go by, she was even less thrilled than he with the match. It mattered naught. They were both bound by duty. And right now his duty was to consummate his marriage.

His loins tightened, and the surge of lust took him by surprise. It had been a long while since he'd had such a strong reaction to a woman. But it had been thus since the day he'd laid eyes on Rionna.

He'd been shamed by his reaction to his brother's betrothed. It was disloyal and disrespectful to feel such a keen burning in his gut.

But no matter that he damned himself, it didn't change the fact that she had only to walk in the room and his body leapt to life.

And now she was his.

He searched the entrance to the stairs one more time and then sent a pointed stare toward Ewan. It was time to collect his wife and take her to bed.

Ewan nodded then stood. It didn't seem to matter that the king was still heartily enjoying himself. Ewan merely announced that the festivities were at their end and that everyone should seek their beds.

Everyone would reconvene in the morning and talks would begin. Ewan had a legacy to claim on behalf of his daughter and there was a war to wage against Duncan Cameron.

Caelen followed Ewan up the stairs where they were met by Gannon.

"Lady McCabe took to her chamber an hour ago when the babe awoke for feeding," Gannon said to Ewan.

"And my wife?" Caelen drawled.

"Still within Keeley's chamber. Alaric is in Keeley's old chamber, but he's losing patience and fair itching to get back to Keeley."

"You may tell him Rionna will be gone within the minute," Caelen said as he strode toward the door.

He knocked, only because 'twas Keeley's chamber and he had no wish to alarm her by barging in. 'Twas an insult for Rionna to have spent so much time above stairs, missing most of their wedding celebration.

Upon hearing Keeley's soft summons, he opened the door and entered.

His expression eased when he saw Keeley propped haphazardly on her pillows. She looked as though she was about to slide off the bed, and he hurried to prop her up. Exhaustion ringed her eyes and she grunted as he positioned her better.

"Sorry," he muttered.

"'Tis all right," she said with a small smile.

"I've come for Rionna." He frowned when he realized she wasn't present.

Keeley nodded toward the far corner. "She's there."

Caelen turned and, to his surprise, saw her propped in a chair against the wall, sound asleep, her mouth open and her head tilted back. Then as he took a closer look around the room, he saw the tankard of ale and the empty goblets.

With a suspicious frown, he peered into the tankard only to find it empty. He glanced back at Keeley, whose eyes looked precariously close to rolling back in her head, and then back to Rionna, who hadn't stirred a wit. He remembered all the ale she'd consumed at the table below stairs and how little she'd eaten.

"You're soused!"

"Maybe," Keeley mumbled. "All right, probably."

Caelen shook his head. Foolheaded females.

He started toward Rionna when Keeley's soft entreaty stopped him.

"Be gentle with her, Caelen. She's afraid."

He stopped, stared down at the passed out woman in the chair, and then slowly turned to look back at Keeley. "Is that what this is about? She got herself soused because she's afraid of me?"

Keeley's brow wrinkled. "Not of you particularly. Well, I suppose that could be part of it. But, Caelen, she's frightfully . . . ignorant of . . ."

She broke off and blushed to the roots of her hair.

"I understand your meaning," Caelen said gruffly. "No offense, Keeley, but 'tis a matter between me and my wife. I'll be taking her now. You should be resting, not consuming ridiculous amounts of ale."

"Has anyone ever told you that you're too rigid?" Keeley groused.

Caelen leaned down and slid his arms underneath Rionna's slight body and lifted her. She weighed next to nothing, and to his surprise, he liked the feel of her in his arms. It was . . . nice.

He strode toward the door, barked an order to Gannon whom he knew to be standing on the other side, and the door quickly opened. In the hall Caelen met Alaric, who raised his eyebrow inquiringly.

"See to your own wife," Caelen said rudely. "She's probably unconscious by now."

"What?" Alaric demanded.

But Caelen ignored him and continued on to his chamber. He shouldered his way in and then gently laid Rionna down on his bed. With a sigh, he stepped back to stare down at her.

So the little warrior was frightened. And to escape him, she'd drank herself into oblivion. Hardly complimentary to Caelen, but then he supposed he couldn't blame her. He hadn't been . . . Well, he hadn't been a lot of things.

With a shake of his head, he began peeling away her

clothing until she was down to her underclothes. His hands shook as he smoothed the thin linen garment over her body.

He could see nothing of her breasts. She was a slight woman and she didn't have much in the way of a bosom. Her body was lean and toned, unlike any other woman he'd ever encountered.

He ached to lift the hem of her underdress and pull it away from her body until she was naked to his gaze. It was his right. She was his wife.

But he couldn't bring himself to do it.

He could wake her now and assert his husbandly rights, but he had a sudden desire to see her eyes flame with the same want he felt. He wanted to hear her soft cries of pleasure. He didn't want her to be afraid.

He smiled and shook his head. When she woke in the morning, she'd likely have a raging headache, and she'd wonder what the hell happened the night before.

He might have a conscience about taking what was rightfully his until she was prepared to surrender herself body and soul, but that didn't mean she had to know it right away.

He slid into bed beside her and pulled the heavy fur over the both of them. The scent of her hair curled through his nose, and the warmth from her body beckoned to him.

With a muttered curse, he turned over until he faced away.

To his utter dismay, she murmured in her sleep and then snuggled up against his back, her warm, lush body molded so tightly to his that he hadn't a prayer of sleeping this night.

She looked angelic. Impossibly beautiful. He'd never seen anything her equal. It wasn't that she was the most beautifully fashioned woman he'd ever seen, but she was easily the most . . .

He frowned. The most what?

There was something quite irresistible about her and he couldn't even put his finger on it. She lacked the practiced graces of older, more mature women. But neither did she look like a maiden too young for a man to even look at.

She was . . . just right.

God's teeth, was he lusting over his bride? Self-loathing filled him. He should be treating her gently and kindly. It was obvious there was something off about the lass, even if he didn't know the extent, and here he was looking at her as a prospective wife with all the benefits entailed.

No matter that she was an Armstrong. It was clear she couldn't be punished for or defined by the actions of her family when it was likely she was unaware of most things around her.

As much as he didn't want to label any Armstrong a victim, he had enough intelligence to know she didn't deserve this union any more than he deserved to be forced into it.

She would be taken from her home—the only safe haven she had. From everyone who protected and loved her—and it was obvious she was well loved by her family. She would be thrust into a hostile environment. Could any Armstrong ever find a place in the Montgomery clan? It was going to be a difficult matter, no matter how it was handled, and it was she who stood to lose the most, while all he gained was an unwanted wife and a grudging truce with the Armstrongs.